CLEEK OF SCOTLAND YARD

"My only kingdom is here . . . in this dear woman's arms. Walk
with me, Ailsa . . . as my queen *and* my wife"

THE INTERNATIONAL ADVENTURE LIBRARY

THREE OWLS EDITION

CLEEK OF SCOTLAND YARD

Detective Stories

BY

T. P. HANSHEW

Author of "Cleek the Master Detective",
"Cleek's Government Cases" etc.

W. R. CALDWELL & CO.
NEW YORK

Cleek of Scotland Yard

PROLOGUE

The Affair of the Man Who Vanished

MR. MAVERICK NARKOM, Superintendent at Scotland Yard, flung aside the paper he was reading and wheeled round in his revolving desk-chair, all alert on the instant, like a terrier that scents a rat.

He knew well what the coming of the footsteps toward his private office portended; his messenger was returning at last.

Good! Now he would get at the facts of the matter, and be relieved from the sneers of carping critics and the pin pricks of overzealous reporters, who seemed to think that the Yard was to blame, and all the forces connected with it to be screamed at as incompetents if every evildoer in London was not instantly brought to book and his craftiest secrets promptly revealed.

Gad! Let them take on his job, then, if they thought the thing so easy! Let them have a go at this business of stopping at one's post until two o'clock in the morning trying to patch up the jumbled fragments of a puzzle of this sort, if they regarded it as such child's play — finding an assassin whom nobody had seen and who struck with a method which neither medical science nor legal acumen could trace or name. *Then*, by James . . .

The door opened and closed, and Detective Sergeant Petrie stepped into the room, removing his hat and standing at attention.

"Well?" rapped out the superintendent, in the sharp staccato of nervous impatience. "Speak up! It was a false alarm, was it not?"

"No, sir. It's even worse than reported. Quicker and sharper than any of the others. He's gone, sir."

"Gone? Good God! you don't mean *dead?*"

"Yes, sir. Dead as Julius Cæsar. Total collapse about twenty minutes after my arrival and went off like that" — snapping his fingers and giving his hand an outward fling. "Same way as the others, only, as I say, quicker, sir; and with no more trace of what caused it than the doctors were able to discover in the beginning. That makes five in the same mysterious way, Superintendent, and not a ghost of a clue yet. The papers will be ringing with it to-morrow."

"Ringing with it? Can they 'ring' any more than they are doing already?" Narkom threw up both arms and laughed the thin, mirthless laughter of utter despair. "Can they say anything worse than they have said? Blame any more unreasonably than they have blamed? 'It is small solace for the overburdened taxpayer to reflect that he may be done to death at any hour of the night, and that the heads of the institution he has so long and so consistently supported are capable of giving his stricken family nothing more in return than the "Dear me! dear me!" of utter bewilderment; and to prove anew that the efficiency of our boasted police-detective system may be classed under the head of "Brilliant Fiction."' That sort of thing, day after day — as if I had done nothing but pile up failures of this kind since I came into office. No heed of the past six years' brilliant success. No thought for the manner in which the police departments of other countries were made to sit up and to marvel at our methods. Two months' failure and *that* doesn't count! By the Lord Harry! I'd give my head to make those newspaper fellows eat their words — gad, yes!"

"Why don't you, then, sir?" Petrie dropped his voice a
tone or two and looked round over the angle of his shoulder
as he spoke; then, recollecting the time and the improba-
bility of anybody being within earshot, took heart of grace
and spoke up bolder. "There's no use blinking the fact,
Mr. Narkom; it was none of us — none of the regular force,
I mean — that made the record of those years what it was.
That chap Cleek was the man that did it, sir. You know
that as well as I. I don't know whether you've fallen out
with him or not; or if he's off on some secret mission that
keeps him from handling Yard matters these days. But if
he isn't, take my advice, sir, and put him on this case at
once."

"Don't talk such rot!" flung out Narkom, impatiently.
"Do you think I'd have waited until now to do it if it could
be done? Put him on the case, indeed! How the devil
am I to do it when I don't know where on earth to find him?
He cleared out directly after that Panther's Paw case six
months ago. Gave up his lodgings, sacked his housekeeper,
laid off his assistant, Dollops, and went the Lord knows
where and why."

"My hat! Then that's the reason we never hear any
more of him in Yard matters, is it? I wondered! Disappeared, eh? Well, well! You don't think he can have
gone back to his old lay — back to the wrong 'uns and his
old 'Vanishing Cracksman's' tricks, do you, sir?"

"No, I don't. No backslider about that chap, by James!
He's not built that way. Last time I saw him he was out
shopping with Miss Ailsa Lorne — the girl who redeemed
him — and judging from their manner toward each other, I
rather fancied — well, never mind! That's got nothing
to do with you. Besides, I feel sure that if they had, Mrs.
Narkom and I would have been invited. All he said was
that he was going to take a holiday. He didn't say why, and
he didn't say where. I wish to heaven I'd asked him. I

could have kicked myself for not having done so when that she-devil of a Frenchwoman managed to slip the leash and get off scot free."

"Mean that party we nabbed in the house at Roehampton along with the Mauravanian baron who got up that Silver Snare fake, don't you, sir? Margot, the Queen of the Apaches. Or, at least, that's who you declared she was, I recollect."

"And that's who I still declare she was!" rapped in Narkom, testily, "and what I'll continue to say while there's a breath left in me. I never actually saw the woman until that night, it is true, but Cleek told me she was Margot; and who should know better than he, when he was once her pal and partner? But it's one of the infernal drawbacks of British justice that a crook's word's as good as an officer's if it's not refuted by actual proof. The woman brought a dozen witnesses to prove that she was a respectable Austrian lady on a visit to her son in England; that the motor in which she was riding broke down before that Roehampton house about an hour before our descent upon it, and that she had merely been invited to step in and wait while the repairs were being attended to by her chauffeur. Of course such a chauffeur was forthcoming when she was brought up before the magistrate; and a garage-keeper was produced to back up his statement; so that when the Mauravanian prisoner 'confessed' from the dock that what the lady said was true, that settled it. *I* couldn't swear to her identity, and Cleek, who could, was gone — the Lord knows where; upon which the magistrate admitted the woman to bail and delivered her over to the custody of her solicitors pending my efforts to get somebody over from Paris to identify her. And no sooner is the vixen set at large than — presto! — away she goes, bag and baggage, out of the country, and not a man in England has seen hide nor hair of her since. Gad! if I could but have got word to Cleek at that time —

just to put him on his guard against her. But I couldn't.
I've no more idea than a child where the man went — not
one."

"It's pretty safe odds to lay one's head against a brass
farthing as to where the woman went, though, I reckon,"
said Petrie, stroking his chin. "Bunked it back to Paris,
I expect, sir, and made for her hole like any other fox. I
hear them French 'tecs are as keen to get hold of her as we
were, but she slips 'em like an eel. Can't lay hands on her,
and couldn't swear to her identity if they did. Not one
in a hundred of 'em's ever seen her to be sure of her, I'm
told."

"No, not one. Even Cleek himself knows nothing of
who and what she really is. He confessed that to me.
Their knowledge of each other began when they threw in
their lot together for the first time, and ceased when they
parted. Yes, I suppose she did go back to Paris, Petrie —
it would be her safest place; and there'd be rich pickings
there for her and her crew just now. The city is *en fête*,
you know."

"Yes, sir. King Ulric of Mauravania is there as the
guest of the Republic. Funny time for a king to go visiting another nation, sir, isn't it, when there's a revolution threatening in his own? Dunno much about the ways
of kings, Superintendent, but if there was a row coming up
in *my* house, you can bet all you're worth I'd be mighty
sure to stop at home."

"Diplomacy, Petrie, diplomacy! he may be safer where
he is. Rumours are afloat that Prince What's-his-name,
son and heir of the late Queen Karma, is not only still
living, but has, during the present year, secretly visited
Mauravania in person. I see by the papers that that ripping old royalist, Count Irma, is implicated in the revolu-
tionary movement and that, by the king's orders, he has
been arrested and imprisoned in the Fort of Sulberga on a

charge of sedition. Grand old johnny, that — I hope no harm comes to him. He was in England not so long ago. Came to consult Cleek about some business regarding a lost pearl, and I took no end of a fancy to him. Hope he pulls out all right; but if he doesn't — oh, well, we can't bother over other people's troubles — we've got enough of our own just now with these mysterious murders going on, and the newspapers hammering the Yard day in and day out. Gad! how I wish I knew how to get hold of Cleek — how I wish I did!"

"Can't you find somebody to put you on the lay, sir? some friend of his — somebody that's seen him, or maybe heard from him since you have?"

"Oh, don't talk rubbish!" snapped Narkom, with a short, derisive laugh. "Friends, indeed! What friends has he outside of myself? Who knows him any better than I know him — and what do I know of him, at that? Nothing — not where he comes from; not what his real name may be; not a living thing but that he chooses to call himself Hamilton Cleek and to fight in the interest of the law as strenuously as he once fought against it. And where will I find a man who has 'seen' him, as you suggest — or would know if he had seen him — when he has that amazing birth gift to fall back upon? *You* never saw his real face — never in all your life. *I* never saw it but twice, and even I — why, he might pass me in the street a dozen times a day and I'd never know him if I looked straight into his eyes. He'd come like a shot if he knew I wanted him — gad, yes! But he doesn't; and there you are."

Imagination was never one of Petrie's strong points. His mind moved always along well-prepared grooves to time-honoured ends. It found one of those grooves and moved along it now.

"Why don't you advertise for him, then?" he suggested. "Put a Personal in the morning papers, sir. Chap like that's sure to read the news every day; and it's bound to come to his notice sooner or later. Or if it doesn't, why, people will get to knowing that the Yard's lost him and get to talking about it and maybe he'll learn of it that way."

Narkom looked at him. The suggestion was so bald, so painfully ordinary and commonplace, that, heretofore, it had never occurred to him. To associate Cleek's name with the banalities of the everyday Agony Column; to connect *him* with the appeals of the scullery and the methods of the raw amateur! The very outrageousness of the thing was its best passport to success.

"By James, I believe there's something in that!" he said, abruptly. "If you get people to talking. . . . Well, it doesn't matter, so that he *hears* — so that he finds out I want him. You ring up the *Daily Mail* while I'm scratching off an ad. Tell 'em it's simply got to go in the morning's issue. I'll give it to them over the line myself in a minute."

He lurched over to his desk, drove a pen into the ink pot, and made such good haste in marshalling his straggling thoughts that he had the thing finished before Petrie had got farther than "Yes; Scotland Yard. Hold the line, please; Superintendent Narkom wants to speak to you."

The Yard's requests are at all times treated with respect and courtesy by the controlling forces of the daily press, so it fell out that, late as the hour was, "space" was accorded, and, in the morning, half a dozen papers bore this notice prominently displayed:

"CLEEK — Where are you? Urgently needed. Communicate at once. — *Maverick Narkom*."

The expected came to pass; and the unexpected followed close upon its heels. The daily press, publishing the full account of the latest addition to the already long list of mysterious murders which, for a fortnight past, had been adding nervous terrors to the public mind, screamed afresh — as Narkom knew that it would — and went into paroxysms of the Reporters' Disease until the very paper was yellow with the froth of it. The afternoon editions were still worse — for, between breakfast and lunch time, yet another man had fallen victim to the mysterious assassin — and sheets pink and sheets green, sheets gray and sheets yellow were scattering panic from one end of London to the other. The police-detective system of the country was rotten! The Government should interfere — must interfere! It was a national disgrace that the foremost city of the civilized world should be terrorized in this appalling fashion and the author of the outrages remain undetected! Could anything be more appalling?

It could, and — it was! When night came and the evening papers were supplanting the afternoon ones, that something "more appalling" — known hours before to the Yard itself — was glaring out on every bulletin and every front page in words like these:

LONDON'S REIGN OF TERROR
APPALLING ATROCITY IN
CLARGES STREET
SHOCKING DYNAMITE
OUTRAGE

Clarges Street! The old "magic" street of those "magic" old times of Cleek, and the Red Limousine, and the Riddles that were unriddled for the asking! Narkom grabbed the report the instant he heard that name and began to read it breathlessly.

It was the usual station advice ticked through to headquarters and deciphered by the operator there, and it ran tersely, thus:

"4:28 P. M. Attempt made by unknown parties to blow up house in Clarges Street, Piccadilly. Partially successful. Three persons injured and two killed. No clue to motive. Occupants, family from Essex. Only moved in two days ago. House been vacant for months previously. Formerly occupied by retired seafaring man named Capt. Horatio Burbage, who ——"

Narkom read no farther. He flung the paper aside with a sort of mingled laugh and blub and collapsed into his chair with his eyes hidden in the crook of an upthrown arm, and the muscles of his mouth twitching.

"Now I know why he cleared out! Good old Cleek! Bully old Cleek!" he said to himself; and stopped suddenly, as though something had got into his throat and half choked him. But after a moment or two he jumped to his feet and began walking up and down the room, his face fairly glowing; and if he had put his thoughts into words they would have run like this:

"Margot's crew, of course. And he must have guessed that something of the sort would happen *some* time if he stopped there after that Silver Snare business at Roehampton — either from her lot or from the followers of that Mauravanian johnnie who was at the back of it. They were after him even in that little game, those two. I wonder why? What the dickens, when one comes to think of it, could have made the Prime Minister of Mauravania interest himself in an Apache trick to 'do in' an ex-cracksman? Gad! she flies high, sometimes, that Margot! Prime Minister of Mauravania! And the fool faced fifteen years hard to do the thing and let her get off scot free! Faced it and — took it; and is taking it still, for the sake of helping her to wipe off an old score against a reformed criminal. Wonder if Cleek ever crossed *him* in something? Wonder if he, too, was on the 'crooked side' once, and wanted to make sure of its never being shown up? Oh, well, he got his medicine. And so, too, will this unknown murderer who's doing the secret killing in London, now that this Clarges Street affair is over. Bully old Cleek! Slipped 'em again! Had their second shot and missed you! Now you'll come out of hiding, old chap, and we shall have the good old times once more."

His eye fell upon the ever-ready telephone. He stopped short in his purposeless walking and nodded and smiled to it.

"We'll have you singing your old tune before long, my friend," he said, optimistically. "I know my man — gad, yes! He'll let no grass grow under *his* feet now that this thing's over. I shall hear soon — yes, by James! I shall."

His optimism was splendidly rewarded. Not, however, from the quarter nor in the manner he expected. It had but just gone half-past seven when a tap sounded, the door of his office swung inward, and the porter stepped into the room.

"Person wanting to speak with you, sir, in private," he announced. "Says it's about some Personal in the morning paper."

"Send him in — send him in at once!" rapped out Narkom excitedly. "Move sharp; and don't let anybody else in until I give the word."

Then, as soon as the porter had disappeared, he crossed the room, twitched the thick curtains over the window, switched on the electric light, wheeled another big chair up beside his desk and, with face aglow, jerked open a drawer and got out a cigarette box which had not seen the light for weeks.

Quick as he was, the door opened and shut again before the lid of the box could be thrown back, and into the room stepped Cleek's henchman — Dollops.

"Hullo! You, is it, you blessed young monkey?" said Narkom gayly, as he looked up and saw the boy. "Knew

I'd hear to-day — knew it, by James! Sent you for me, has he, eh? Is he coming himself or does he want me to go to him? Speak up, and — Good Lord! what's the matter with you? What's up? Anything wrong?"

Dollops had turned the colour of an under-baked biscuit and was looking at him with eyes of absolute despair.

"Sir," he said, moving quickly forward and speaking in the breathless manner of a spent runner — "Sir, I was a-hopin' it was a fake, and to hear you speak like that — Gawd's truth, guv'ner, you don't mean as it's real, sir, do you? That *you* don't know either?"

"Know? Know what?"

"Where he is — wot's become of him? Mr. Cleek, the guv'ner, sir. I made sure that you'd know if anybody would. That's wot made me come, sir. I'd 'a' gone off me bloomin' dot if I hadn't — after you a-puttin' in that Personal and him never a-turnin' up like he'd ort. Sir, do you mean to say as you don't know *where* he is, and haven't seen him even yet?"

"No, I've not. Good Lord! haven't you?"

"No, sir. I aren't clapped eyes on him since he sent me off to the bloomin' seaside six months ago. All he told me when we come to part was that Miss Lorne was goin' out to India on a short visit to Cap'n and Mrs. 'Awksley — Lady Chepstow as was, sir — and that directly she was gone he'd be knockin' about for a time on his own, and I wasn't to worry over him. I haven't seen hide nor hair of him, sir, since that hour."

"Nor heard from him?" Narkom's voice was thick and the hand he laid on the chair-back hard shut.

"Oh, yes, sir, I've heard — I'd have gone off my bloomin' dot if I hadn't done *that*. Heard from him twice. Once when he wrote and gimme my orders about the new place he's took up the river — four weeks ago. The second time, last Friday, sir, when he wrote me the thing that's fetched

me here — that's been tearin' the heart out of me ever since
I heard at Charing Cross about wot's happened at Clarges
Street, sir."

"And what was that?"

"Why, sir, he wrote that he'd jist remembered about some
papers as he'd left behind the wainscot in his old den, and
that he'd get the key and drop in at the old Clarges Street
house on the way 'ome. Said he'd arrive in England either
yesterday afternoon or this one, sir; but whichever it was,
he'd wire me from Dover before he took the train. And he
never done it, sir — my Gawd! he never done it in this
world!"

"Good God!" Narkom flung out the words in a sort of
panic, his lips twitching, his whole body shaking, his face
like the face of a dead man.

"He never done it, I tell you!" pursued Dollops in an
absolute tremble of fright. "I haven't never had a blessed
line; and now this here awful thing has happened. And
if he done what he said he was a-goin' to do — if he come to
town and went to that house ——"

If he said more, the clanging of a bell drowned it completely. Narkom had turned to his desk and was hammering furiously upon the call gong. A scurry of flying
feet came up the outer passage, the door opened in a flash,
and the porter was there. And behind him Lennard, the
chauffeur, who guessed from that excited summons that
there would be a call for *him*.

"The limousine — as quick as you can get her round!"
said Narkom in the sharp staccato of excitement. "To the
scene of the explosion in Clarges Street first, and if the bodies
of the victims have been removed, then to the mortuary
without an instant's delay."

He dashed into the inner room, grabbed his hat and coat
down from the hook where they were hanging, and dashed
back again like a man in a panic.

"Come on!" he said, beckoning to Dollops as he flung open the door and ran out into the passage. "If they've 'done him in' — *him!* — if they've 'got him' after all —— Come on! come on!"

Dollops "came on" with a rush; and two minutes later the red limousine swung out into the roadway and took the distance between Scotland Yard and Clarges Street at a mile-a-minute clip.

Arrival at the scene of the disaster elicited the fact that the remains — literally "remains," since they had been well-nigh blown to fragments — had, indeed, been removed to the mortuary; so thither Narkom and Dollops followed them, their fears being in no wise lightened by learning that the bodies were undeniably those of men. As the features of both victims were beyond any possibility of recognition, identification could, of course, be arrived at only through bodily marks; and Dollops's close association with Cleek rendered him particularly capable of speaking with authority regarding those of his master. It was, therefore, a source of unspeakable delight to both Narkom and himself, when, after close and minute examination of the remains, he was able to say, positively, "Sir, whatever's become of him, praise God, neither of these here two dead men is him, bless his heart!"

"So they didn't get him after all!" supplemented Narkom, laughing for the first time in hours. "Still, it cannot be doubted that whoever committed this outrage was after him, since the people who have suffered are complete strangers to the locality and had only just moved into the house. No doubt the person or persons who threw the bomb knew of Cleek's having at one time lived there as 'Captain Burbage' — Margot did, for one — and finding the house still occupied, and not knowing of his removal — why, there you are."

"Margot!" The name brought back all Dollops' banished fears. He switched round on the superintendent and laid a nervous clutch on his sleeve. "And Margot's 'lay' is Paris. Sir, I didn't tell you, did I, that it was from there the guv'ner wrote those two letters to me?"

"Cinnamon! From Paris?"

"Yes, sir. He didn't say from wot part of the city nor wot he was a-doin' there, anyways, but — my hat! listen here, sir. *They're* there — them Mauravanian johnnies — and the Apaches and Margot there, too, and you know how both lots has their knife into him. I dunno wot the Mauravanians is got against him, sir (he never tells nothin' to nobody, he don't), but most like it's summink he done to some of 'em that time he went out there about the lost pearl; but *they're* after him, and the Apaches is after him, and between the two! . . . Guv'ner!" — his voice rose thin and shrill — "guv'ner, if one lot don't get him, the other may; and — sir — there's Apaches in London this very night. I know! I've seen 'em."

"Seen them? When? Where?"

"At Charing Cross station, sir, jist before I went to the Yard to see you. As I hadn't had no telegram from the guv'ner, like I was promised, I went there on the off chance, hopin' to meet him when the boat train come in. And there I see 'em, sir, a-loungin' round the platform where the Dover train goes out at nine to catch the night boat back to Calais, sir. I spotted 'em on the instant — from their walk, their way of carryin' of theirselves, their manner of wearin' of their bloomin' hair. Laughin' among themselves they was and lookin' round at the entrance every now and then like as they was expectin' some one to come and join 'em; and I see, too, as they was a-goin' back to where they come from, 'cause they'd the return halves of their tickets in their hatbands. One of 'em, he buys a paper at the bookstall and sees summink in it as tickled him wonderful, for I see nim go up to the others and point it out to 'em, and then the whole lot begins to larf like blessed hyenas. I spotted wot the paper was and the place on the page the blighter was a-pointin' at, so I went and bought one myself to see wot it was. Sir, it was that there Personal of yours. The minnit I read that, I makes a dash for a taxi, to go to you at once, sir, and jist as I does so, a newsboy runs by me with a bill on his chest tellin' about the explosion; and then, sir, I fair went off me dot."

They were back on the pavement, within sight of the limousine, when the boy said this. Narkom brought the car to his side with one excited word, and fairly wrenched open the door.

"To Charing Cross station — as fast as you can streak it!" he said, excitedly. "The last train for the night boat leaves at nine sharp. Catch it, if you rack the motor to pieces."

"Crumbs! A minute and a half!" commented Lennard, as he consulted the clock dial beside him; then, just waiting for Narkom and Dollops to jump into the vehicle, he brought her head round with a swing, threw back the clutch, and let her go full tilt.

But even the best of motors cannot accomplish the impossible. The gates were closed, the signal down, the last train already outside the station when they reached it, and not even the mandate of the law might hope to stay it or to call it back.

"Plenty of petrol?" Narkom faced round as he spoke and looked at Lennard.

"Plenty, sir."

"All right — *beat it!* The boat sails from Dover at eleven. I've got to catch it. Understand?"

"Yes, sir. But you could wire down and have her held over till we get there, Superintendent."

"Not for the world! She must sail on time; I must get

aboard without being noticed — without some persons I'm following having the least cause for suspicion. Beat that train — do you hear me? — *beat* it! I want to get there and get aboard that boat before the others arrive. Do you want any further incentive than that? If so, here it is for you: Mr. Cleek's in Paris! Mr. Cleek's in danger!".

"Mr. Cleek? God's truth! Hop in sir, hop in! I'll have you there ahead of that train if I dash down the Admiralty Pier in flames from front to rear. Just let me get to the open road, sir, and I'll show you something to make you sit up."

He did. Once out of the track of all traffic, and with the lights of the city well at his back, he strapped his goggles tight, jerked his cap down to his eyebrows, and leaned over the wheel.

"For Mr. Cleek — do you hear?" he said, addressing the car as if it were a human being. "Now, then, show what you're made of! There! Take your head! Now *go*, you vixen! GO!"

There was a sudden roar, a sudden leap; then the car shot forward as though all the gales of all the universe were sweeping it on, and the wild race to the coast began.

Narkom jerked down the blinds, turned on the light, and flung open the locker, as they pounded on.

"Dip in. Get something that can be made to fit you," he said to Dollops. "We can't risk any of those fellows identifying you as the chap who was hanging round the station to-night. Toss me over that wig — the gray one— in the far corner there. God knows what we're on the track of, but if it leads to Cleek I'll follow it to the end of time!" Then, lifting his voice until it sounded above the motor's roar, "Faster, Lennard, faster!" he called. "Give it to her! give it to her! We've got to beat that train if it kills us!"

They did beat it. The engine's light was not even in

sight when the bright glare of the moon on the Channel's waters flashed up out of the darkness before them; nor was the sound of the train's coming even faintly audible as yet, when, a few minutes later, the limousine swung down the incline and came to a standstill within a stone's throw of the entrance to the pier, at whose extreme end the packet lay, with gangways down and fires up and her huge bulk rising and falling with the movements of the waves.

"Beat her, you see, sir," said Lennard, chuckling as he got down and opened the door for the superintendent to alight. "Better not go any nearer, sir, with the car. There's a chap down there standing by the gangplank and he seems interested in us from the way he's watching. Jumped up like a shot and came down the gangplank the instant he heard us coming. Better do the rest of the journey afoot, sir, and make a pretence of paying me — as if I was a public taxi. What'll I do? Stop here until morning?"

"Yes. Put up at a garage; and if I don't return by the first boat, get back to town. Meantime, cut off somewhere and ring up the Yard. Tell 'em where I've gone. Now then, Dollops, come on!"

A moment later the limousine had swung off into the darkness and disappeared, and what might properly have been taken for a couple of English curates on their way to a Continental holiday moved down the long pier between the glimmering and inadequate lamps to the waiting boat. But long before they reached it the figure at the gangplank — the tall, erect figure of a man whom the most casual observer must have recognized as one who had known military training — had changed its alert attitude and was sauntering up and down as if, when they came nearer and the light allowed him to see what they were, he had lost all interest in them and their doings. Narkom gave the man a glance from the tail of his eye as they went up the gangplank and boarded the boat, and brief as that glance was, it was sufficient to assure him of two things: First, that the man was not only strikingly handsome but bore himself with an air which spoke of culture, birth, position; second, that he was a foreigner, with the fair hair and the slightly hooked nose which was so characteristic of the Mauravanians.

With Dollops at his side, Narkom slunk aft, where the lights were less brilliant and the stern of the boat hung over the dark, still waters, and pausing there, turned and looked back at the waiting man.

A French sailor was moving past in the darkness. He stopped the man and spoke to him.

"Tell me," he said, slipping a shilling into the fellow's hand, "do you happen to know who that gentleman is, standing on the pier there?"

"Yes, m'sieur. He is equerry to his Majesty King Ulric of Mauravania. He has crossed with us frequently during his Majesty's sojourn in Paris."

"Gawd's truth, sir," whispered Dollops, plucking nervously at the superintendent's sleeve as the sailor, after touching his cap with his forefinger, passed on. "Apaches at one end and them Mauravanian johnnies at the other! I tell you they're a-workin' hand in hand for some reason — workin' against *him!*"

Narkom lifted a silencing hand and turned to move away where there would be less likelihood of anything they might say being overheard; for at that moment a voice had sounded and from a most unusual quarter. Unnoticed until now, a fisher's boat, which for some time had been nearing the shore, swept under the packet's stern and grazed along the stone front of the pier.

"Voila, m'sieur," said, in French, the man who sailed it. "Have I not kept my word and brought your excellency across in safety and with speed?"

"Yes," replied the passenger whom the fisher addressed.

He spoke in perfect French, and with the smoothness of a man of the better class. "You have done well indeed. Also it was better than waiting about at Calais for the morning boat. I can now catch the very first train to London. Fast is she? There is your money. Adieu!"

Then came the sound of some one leaving the boat and scrambling up the water stairs, and hard on the heels of it the first whistle of the coming train. Narkom, glancing round, saw a slouching, ill-clad fellow whose appearance was in distinct contrast with his voice and manner of speaking, come into view upon the summit of the pier. His complexion was sallow, his matted hair seemed to have gone for years uncombed; a Turkish fez, dirty and discoloured, was on his head, and over his arm hung several bits of tapestry and shining stuff which betokened his calling as that of a seller of Oriental draperies.

This much Narkom saw and would have gone on his way, giving the fellow no second thought, but that a curious thing happened. Moving away toward the footpath which led from the pier to the town, the pedler caught sight suddenly of the man standing at the gangplank; he halted abruptly, looked round to make sure that no one was watching, then, without more ado, turned round suddenly on his heel, walked straightway to the gangplank and boarded the boat. The Mauravanian took not the slightest heed of him, nor he of the Mauravanian. Afterward, when the train had arrived, Narkom thought he knew why. For the present he was merely puzzled to understand why this dirty, greasy Oriental pedler who had been at the pains to cross the Channel in a fisher's boat should do so for the apparent purpose of merely going back on the packet to Calais.

By this time the train had arrived, the pier was alive with people, porters were running back and forth with luggage, and there was bustle and confusion everywhere. Narkom looked along the length of the vessel to the teeming gangway. The Mauravanian was still there, alert as before, his fixed eyes keenly watching.

A crowd came stringing along, bags and bundles done up in gaudy handkerchiefs in their hands, laughing, jostling, jabbering together in low-class French.

"Here they are, guv'ner — the Apaches!" said Dollops in a whisper. "That's the lot, sir. Keep your eye on them as they come aboard, and if they are with him — Crumbs! Not a sign; not a blessed one!" For the Apaches, stringing up the gangplank by twos and threes and coming within brushing distance of the waiting man, passed on as the Oriental pedler had passed on, taking no notice of him, nor he of them, nor yet of how, as they advanced, the pedler slouched forward and slipped into the thick of them.

"By James! one of them — that's what the fellow is!" said Narkom, as he observed this. "If during the voyage the Mauravanian speaks to one man of the lot ——"

He stopped and sucked in his breath and let the rest of the sentence go by default. For of a sudden there had come into sight upon the pier a dapper little French dandy, fuzzy of moustache, mincing of gait, with a flower in his buttonhole and a shining "topper" on his beautifully pomaded head; and it came upon Narkom with a shock of remembrance that he had seen this selfsame living fashion plate pass by Scotland Yard twice that very day!

Onward he came, this pretty monsieur, with his jaunty air and his lovely "wine-glass waist," onward, and up the gangway and aboard the packet; and there the Mauravanian still stood, looking out over the crowd and taking no more heed of him than he had taken of anybody else. But with the vanishing of this exquisite, to whom he had paid no heed, his alertness and his interest seemed somehow to evaporate; for he turned now and again to watch the sailors and the longshoremen at their several duties, and strolled leisurely aboard and stood lounging against the rail of the lower deck when the call of "All ashore that's going!" rang through the vessel's length, and was still lounging there when the packet cast off her mooring, and swinging her bows round in the direction of France, creamed her way out into the Channel and headed for Calais.

A wind, unnoticed in the safe shelter of the harbour, played boisterously across the chopping waves as the vessel forged outward, sending clouds of spray sweeping over the bows and along the decks, and such passengers as refrained from seeking the shelter of the saloon and smoke-room sought refuge by crowding aft.

"Come!" whispered Narkom, tapping Dollops' arm. "We can neither talk nor watch here with safety in this crowd. Let us go 'forrard.' Better a drenching in loneliness than shelter with a crowd like this. Come along!"

The boy obeyed without a murmur, following the larger and heavier built "curate" along the wet decks to the deserted bows, and finding safe retreat with him there in the dark shadow cast by a tarpaulin-covered lifeboat. From this safe shelter they could, by craning their necks, get a half view of the interior of the smoke-room through its hooked-back door; and their first glance in that direction pinned their interest, for the pretty "Monsieur" was there, smoking a cigarette and sipping now and again at a glass of absinthe which stood on a little round table at his elbow. But of the Mauravanian or the Apaches or of the Oriental pedler, there was neither sight nor sound, nor had there been since the vessel started.

"What do you make of it?" queried Narkom, when at the end of an hour the dim outlines of the French coast blurred the clear silver of the moonlit sky. "Have we come on a wild goose chase, do you think? What do you suppose has become of the Apaches and of the pedler chap?"

"Travellin' second class," said Dollops, after stealing out and making a round of the vessel and creeping back into the shadow of the lifeboat unseen. "Pallin' with 'em, he is, sir. Makin' a play of sellin' 'em things for their donahs — for the sake of appearances. One of 'em, he is; and if either that Frenchy or that Mauravanian johnny is mixed up with them — lay low! Smeller to the ground, sir, and eyes and ears wide open! We'll know wot's wot now!"

For of a sudden the Mauravanian had come into view far down the wet and glistening promenade deck and was whistling a curious, lilting air as he strolled along past the open door of the smoke-room.

Just the mere twitch of "Monsieur's" head told when he heard that tune. He finished his absinthe, flung aside his cigarette, and strolled leisurely out upon the deck. The Mauravanian was at the after end of the promenade — a glance told him that. He set his face resolutely in the direction of the bows and sauntered leisurely along. He moved on quietly, until he came to the very end of the covered promenade where the curving front of the deck-house looked out upon the spray-washed forward deck, then stopped and planted his back against it and stood silently waiting, not ten feet distant from where Narkom and Dollops crouched.

A minute later the Mauravanian, continuing what was to all appearances a lonely and aimless promenade round the vessel, came abreast of that spot and of him.

And then, the deluge!

"Monsieur" spoke out — guardedly, but in a clear, crisp tone that left no room for doubt upon *one* point, at least.

"Mon ami, it is done — it is accomplished," that crisp voice said. "You shall report that to his Majesty's ministers. Voila, it is done!"

"It is not done!" replied the Mauravanian, in a swift, biting, emphatic whisper. "You jump to conclusions too quickly. Here! take this. It is an evening paper. The thing was useless — he was not there!"

"Not there!   Grande Dieu!"

"Sh-h!   Take it — read it.   I will see you when we land. Not here — it is too dangerous.   Au revoir!"

Then he passed on and round the curve of the deckhouse to the promenade on the other side; and "Monsieur," with the paper hard shut in the grip of a tense hand, moved fleetly back toward the smoke-room.

But not unknown any longer.

"Gawd's truth — a woman!" gulped Dollops in a shaking voice.

"No, not a woman — a devil!" said Narkom through his teeth.   "Margot, by James!   Margot, herself!   And what is he — what is Cleek — that a king should enter into compact with a woman to kill him?   Margot, dash her!   Well, I'll have you now, my lady — yes, by James, I will!"

"Guv'ner!   Gawd's truth, sir, where are you going?"

"To the operator in charge of the wireless — to send a message to the chief of the Calais police to meet me on arrival!" said Narkom in reply.   "Stop where you are.   Lay low!   Wait for me.   We'll land in a dozen minutes' time. I'll have that Jezebel and her confederates and I'll rout out Cleek and get him beyond the clutches of them if I tear up all France to do it."

"Gawd bless you, sir, Gawd bless you and forgive me!" said Dollops with a lump in his throat and a mist in his eyes.   "I said often you was a sosidge and a muff, sir, but you aren't — you're a man!"

Narkom did not hear.   He was gone already — down the deck to the cabin of the wireless operator.   In another moment he had passed in, shut the door behind him, and the Law at sea was talking to the Law ashore through the blue ether and across the moonlit waves.

It was ten minutes later.   The message had gone its way and Narkom was back in the lifeboat's shadow again, and close on the bows the lamps of Calais pier shone yellow in the blue-and-silver darkness. On the deck below people were bustling about and making for the place where the gangplank was to be thrust out presently, and link boat and shore together. On the quay, customs officials were making ready for the coming inspection, porters were scuttling about in their blue smocks and peaked caps, and, back of all, the outlines of Calais Town loomed, shadowy and grim through the crowding gloom.

The loneliness of the upper deck offered its attractions to the Mauravanian and to Margot, and in the emptiness of it they met again — within earshot of the lifeboat where Narkom and the boy lay hidden — for one brief word before they went ashore.

"So, you have read: you understand how useless it was?" the Mauravanian said, joining her again at the deckhouse, where she stood with the crumpled newspaper in her hand. "His Majesty's purse cannot be lightened of all that promised sum for any such bungle as this. Speak quickly; where may we go to talk in safety? I cannot risk it here — I will not risk it in the train. Must we wait until we reach Paris, mademoiselle? Or have you a lair of your own here?"

"I have 'lairs,' as you term them, in half the cities of France, Monsieur le Comte," she answered with a vicious little note of resentment in her voice. "And I do not work for nothing — no, not I! I paid for my adherence to his Majesty's Prime Minister and I intend to be paid for my services to his Majesty's self, even though I have this once failed. It must be settled, that question, at once and for all — now — to-night."

"I guessed it would be like that," he answered, with a jerk of his shoulders. "Where shall it be, then? Speak quickly. They are making the landing and I must not be seen talking with you after we go ashore. Where, then?"

"At the Inn of the Seven Sinners — on the Quai d'Lorme — a gunshot distant. Any cocher will take you there."

"Is it safe?"

"All my 'lairs' are safe, monsieur. It overhangs the water. And if strangers come, there is a trap with a bolt on the under side. One way: to the town and the sewers and forty other inns. The other: to a motor boat, always in readiness for instant use. You could choose for yourself should occasion come. You will not find the place shut — my 'lairs' never are. A password? No, there is none — for any but the Brotherhood. Nor will you need one. You remember old Marise of the 'Twisted Arm' in Paris? Well, she serves at the Seven Sinners now. I have promoted Madame Serpice to the 'Twisted Arm'. She will know you, will Marise. Say to her I am coming shortly. She and her mates will raise the roof with joy, and — la! la! The gangway is out. They are calling all ashore. Look for me and my lads close on your heels when you arrive. Au revoir."

"Au revoir," he repeated, and slipping by went below and made his way ashore.

She waited that he might get well on his way — that none might by any possibility associate them — then turning, went down after him and out to the pier, where her crew were already forgathering; and when or how she passed the word to them that it was not Paris to-night but the Inn of the Seven Sinners, neither Narkom nor Dollops could decide, close as they came on after her, for she seemed to speak to no one.

"No Inn of the Seven Sinners for you to-night, my lady, if my friend M. Ducroix has attended to that wireless message properly," muttered Narkom as he followed her. "Look sharp, Dollops, and if you see a Sergeant de Ville let me know. They've no luggage, that lot, and, besides, they are natives, so they will pass the customs in a jiffy.

Hullo! there goes that pedler chap — and without his fez or his draperies, b'gad! Through the customs like a flash, the bounder! And there go the others, too. And she after them — she, by James! God! Where are Ducroix and his men? Why aren't they here?" — looking vainly about for some sign of the Chief of Police. "I can't do anything without *him* — here, on foreign soil. Why in heaven's name doesn't the man come?"

"Maybe he hasn't had time, guv'ner — maybe he wasn't on hand when the message arrived," hazarded Dollops. "It's not fifteen minutes all told since it was dispatched. So if ——"

"There she goes! there she goes! Passed, and through the customs in a wink, the Jezebel!" interposed Narkom, in a fever of excitement, as he saw Margot go by the inspector at the door and walk out into the streets of the city. "Lord! if she slips me now ——"

"She shan't!" cut in Dollops, jerking down his hat brim and turning up his collar. "Wait here till the cops come. I'll nip out after her and see where she goes. Like as not the cops'll know the place when you mention it; but if they don't — watch out for me; I'll come back and lead 'em."

Then he moved hurriedly forward, passed the inspector, and was gone in a twinkling.

For ten wretched minutes after he, too, had passed the customs and was at liberty to leave, Narkom paced up and down and fretted and fumed before a sound of clanking sabres caught his ear and, looking round, he saw M. Ducroix enter the place at the head of a detachment of police. He hurried to him and in a word made himself known.

"Ten million pardons, m'sieur; but I was absent when the message he shall be deliver," exclaimed Ducroix in broken English. "I shall come and shall bring my men as soon as he shall be receive. M'sieur, who shall it be this great criminal you demand of me to arrest? Is he here?"

"No, no. A moment, Ducroix. Do you know a place called the Inn of the Seven Sinners?"

"Perfectly. It is but a stone's throw distant — on the Quai d'Lorme."

"Come with me to it, then. I'll make you the most envied man in France, Ducroix: I'll deliver into your hands that witch of the underworld, Margot, the Queen of the Apaches!"

Ducroix's face lit up like a face transfigured.

"M'sieur!" he cried. "That woman? You can give me that woman? You know her? You can recognize her? But, yes, I remember! You shall have her in your hands once in your own country, but she shall slip you, as she shall slip everybody!"

" She won't slip *you*, then, I promise you that!" said Narkom. "Reward and glory, both shall be yours. I have followed her across the channel, Ducroix. I know where she is to be found for a certainty. She is at the Inn of the Seven Sinners. Just take me there and I'll turn the Jezebel over to you."

Ducroix needed no urging. The prospect of such a capture made him fairly beside himself with delight. In twenty swift words he translated this glorious news to his men — setting them as wild with excitement as he was himself — then with a sharp, "Come, m'sieur!" he turned on his heel and led the breathless race for the goal.

Halfway down the narrow, ink-black street that led to the inn they encountered Dollops pelting back at full speed.

"Come on, guv'ner, come on, all of you!" he broke out as he came abreast of them. " She's there — they're all there — kickin' up Meg's diversions, sir, and singin' and dancin' like mad. And, sir, he's there, too — the pedler chap! I see him come up and sneak in with the rest. Come on! This way, all of you."

If they had merely run before, they all but flew now; for

this second assurance that Margot, the great and long-sought-for Margot, was actually within their reach served to spur every man to outdo himself; so that it was but a minute or two later when they came in sight of the inn and bore down upon it in a solid phalanx. And then — just then — when another minute would have settled everything — the demon of mischance chose to play them a scurvy trick.

All they knew of it was that an Apache coming out of the building for some purpose of his own looked up and saw them, then faced round and bent back in the doorway; that of a sudden a very tornado of music and laughter and singing and dancing rolled out into the night, and that when they came pounding up to the doorway, the fellow was lounging there serenely smoking; and, inside, his colleagues were holding a revel wild enough to wake the dead.

In the winking of an eye he was carried off his feet and swept on by this sudden inrush of the law; the door clashed open, the little slatted barrier beyond was knocked aside, and the police were pouring into the room and running head-long into a spinning mass of wild dancers.

The band ceased suddenly as they appeared, the dancers cried out as if in a panic of alarm, and at Ducroix's commanding " Surrender in the name of the Law!" a fat woman behind the bar flung up her arms and voiced a despairing shriek.

"Soul of misfortune! for what, m'sieur — for what?" she cried. "It is no sin to laugh and dance. We break no law, my customers and I. What is it you want that you come in upon us like this?"

Ah, what indeed? Not anything that could be seen. A glance round the room showed nothing and no one but these suddenly disturbed dancers, and of Margot and the Mauravanian never a sign.

"M'sieur!" began Ducroix, turning to Narkom, whose

despair was only too evident, and who, in company with Dollops, was rushing about the place pushing people here and there, looking behind them, looking in all the corners, and generally deporting themselves after the manner of a couple of hounds endeavouring to pick up a lost scent. M'sieur, shall it be an error, then?"

Narkom did not answer. Of a sudden, however, he remembered what had been said of the trap and, pushing aside a group of girls standing over it, found it in the middle of the floor.

"Here it is — this is the way she got out!" he shouted. "Bolted, by James! bolted on the under side! Up with it, up with it — the Jezebel got out this way." But though Ducroix and Dollops aided him, and they pulled and tugged and tugged and pulled, they could not budge it one inch.

"M'sieur, no — what madness! He is not a trap — no, he is not a trap at all!" protested old Marise. "It is but a square where the floor broke and was mended! Mother of misfortune, it is nothing but that."

What response Narkom might have made was checked by a sudden discovery. Huddling in a corner, feigning a drunken sleep, he saw a man lying with his face hidden in his folded arms. It was the pedler. He pounced on the man and jerked up his head before the fellow could prevent it or could dream of what was about to happen.

"Here's one of them at least!" he cried, and fell to shaking him with all his force. "Here's one of Margot's pals, Ducroix. You shan't go empty-handed after all."

A cry of consternation fluttered through the gathering as he brought the man's face into view. Evidently they were past masters of the art of acting, these Apaches, for one might have sworn that every man and every woman of them was taken aback by the fellow's presence.

"Mother of Miracles! who shall the man be?" exclaimed Marise. "Messieurs, I know him not. I have not seen

him in all my life before. Cochon, speak up! Who are
you, that you come in like this and get a respectable widow
in trouble, dog? Eh?"

The man made a motion first to his ears, then to his
mouth, then fell to making movements in the sign language, but spoke never a word.

"La, la! he is a deaf mute, m'sieur," said Ducroix. "He
hears not and speaks not, poor unfortunate."

"Oh, doesn't he?" said Narkom with an ugly laugh.
"He spoke well enough a couple of hours back, I promise
you. My young friend here and I heard him when he paid
off the fisherman who had carried him over to Dover just
before he sneaked aboard the packet to come back with
Margot and the Mauravanian."

The eyes of the Apaches flew to the man's face with a
sudden keen interest which only they might understand;
but he still stood, wagging his great head either drunkenly
or idiotically, and pointing to ears and mouth.

"Lay hold of him — run him in!" said Narkom, whirling him across into the arms of a couple of stalwart Ser-
geants de Ville. "I'll go before the magistrate and lay a
charge against him in the morning that will open your eyes
when you hear it. One of a bloodthirsty, dynamiting crew,
the dog! Lay fast hold of him! don't let him get away on
your lives! God! to have lost that woman! to have lost
her after all!"

It was a sore blow, certainly, but there was nothing to do
but to grin and bear it; for to seek Margot at any of the
inns which might communicate with the sewer trap, or to
hunt for her and a motor boat on the dark water's surface,
was in very truth like looking for a needle in a haystack,
and quite as hopeless. He therefore, decided to go, for the
rest of the night, to the nearest hotel; and waiting only to
see the pedler carried away in safe custody, and promising
to be on hand when he was brought up before the local

magistrate in the morning, took Dollops by the arm and dejectedly went his way.

The morning saw him living up to his promise; and long before the arrival of the magistrate or, indeed, before the night's harvest of prisoners was brought over from the lockup and thrust into the three little "detention rooms" below the court, he was there with Dollops and Ducroix, observing with wonder that groups of evil-looking fellows of the Apache breed were hanging round the building as he approached, and that later on others of the same kidney slipped in and took seats in the little courtroom and kept constantly whispering one to the other while they waited for the morning session to begin.

"Gawd's truth, guv'ner, look at 'em — the 'ole blessed place is alive with the bounders," whispered Dollops. "Wot do you think they are up to, sir? Makin' a rush and settin' the pedler free when he comes up before the Beak? There's twenty of 'em waitin' round the door if there's one."

Narkom made no reply. The arrival of the magistrate focussed all eyes on the bench and riveted his attention with the rest.

The proceedings opened with all the trivial cases first — the night's sweep of the dragnet: drunks and disorderlies, vagrants and pariahs. One by one these were brought in and paid their fines and went their way, unheeded; for this part of the morning's proceedings interested nobody, not even the Apaches. The list was dragged through monotonously; the last blear-eyed sot — a hideous, cadaverous, monkey-faced wretch whose brutal countenance sickened Narkom when he shambled up in his filthy rags — had paid his fine, and gone his way, and there remained now but a case of attempted suicide to be disposed of before the serious cases began. This latter occupied the magistrate's time and attention for perhaps twenty minutes or so, then that,

too, was disposed of; and then a voice was heard calling out
for the unknown man arrested last night at the Inn of the
Seven Sinners to be brought forward.

In an instant a ripple of excitement ran through the little
court. The Apache fraternity sat up within and passed the
word to the Apache fraternity without, and these stood at
attention — close-lipped, dark-browed, eager, like human
tigers waiting for the word to spring. Every eye was fixed
on the door through which that pretended mute should be
led in; but although others had come at the first call, he
came not even at the second, and the magistrate had just
issued an impatient command for the case to be called yet
a third time, when there was a clatter of hasty footsteps and
the keeper of the detention rooms burst into the court pale
as a dead man and shaking in every nerve.

"M'sieur le Juge!" he cried out, extending his two arms.
"Soul of Misfortunes, how shall I tell? He is not there—
he is gone — he is escape, that unknown one. When I
shall unlock the room and call for Jean Lamareau, the
drunkard, at the case before the last, there shall come out of
the dimness to me what I shall think is he and I shall bring
him here and he shall be fine and dismissed. But, m'sieur,
he shall not be Jean Lamareau after all! I shall go now and
call for the unknown and I shall get no answer; I shall go
in and make of the place light, and there he shall be, that
real Jean Lamareau — stripped of his clothes, choked to
unconsciousness, alone on the floor, and the other shall
have paid his fine and gone!"

A great cry went up, a wild confusion filled the court.
The Apaches within rose and ran with the news to the
Apaches without; and these, joining forces, scattered and
ran through the streets in the direction the escaped prisoner
had been seen to take.

But through it all Narkom sat there squeezing his hands
together and laughing in little shaking gusts that had a

heart throb wavering through them; for to him this could mean but one thing.

"Cleek!" he said, leaning down and shrilling a joyous whisper into Dollops' ear. "But one man in all the world could have done that thing — but one man in all the world would have dared. It was he — it was Cleek! God bless his bully soul!"

"Amen, sir," said Dollops, swallowing something; then he rose at Narkom's bidding and followed him outside.

A minute later a gamin brushing against them put out a grimy hand and said whiningly.

"Boulogne, messieurs. Quai des Anges. Third house back from the waterside; in time for the noon boat across to Folkestone. Give me two francs, please. The monsieur said you would if I said that to you when you came out."

The two francs were in his hand almost as he ceased speaking, and in less than a minute later a fiacre was whirling Narkom and Dollops off to the railway station and the next outgoing train to Boulogne. It was still short of midday when they arrived at the Quai des Anges and made their way to the third house back from the waterside — a little tavern with a toy garden in front and a sort of bowered arcade behind — and there under an almond tree, with a cigarette between his fingers and a bunch of flowers in his buttonhole, they came upon *him* at last.

"Guv'ner! Oh, Gawd bless you, guv'ner, is it really you again?" said Dollops, rushing up to him like a girl to a lover.

"Yes, it is really I," he answered with one of his easy laughs. Then he rose and held out his hand as Narkom advanced; and for a moment or two they stood there palm in palm, saying not one word, making not one sound.

"Nearly did for me, my overzealous friend," said Cleek, after a time. "I could have kicked you when you turned up with that lot at the Seven Sinners. Another ten minutes and I'd have had that in my hands which would have compelled his Majesty of Mauravania to give Irma his liberty and to abdicate in his consort's favour. But you came, you dear old blunderer; and when I looked up and recognized you — well, let it pass! I was on my way back to London when I chanced to see Count Waldemar on watch beside the gangway of the Calais packet — he had slipped me, the hound, slipped me in Paris — and I saw my chance to run him down. Gad! it was a close squeak that, when you let those Apaches know that I had just crossed over from this side and had gone aboard the packet because I saw Waldemar. They guessed then. I couldn't speak there, and I dared not speak in the court. They were there, on every hand — inside the building and out — waiting to knife me the instant they were sure. I had to get out — I had to get past them, and — voila."

He turned and laid an affectionate hand on Dollops' shoulder and laughed softly and pleasantly.

"New place all right, old chap? Garden doing well, and all my traps in shipshape order, eh?"

"Yes, sir, Gawd bless you, sir. Everything, sir, everything."

"Good lad! Then we'll be off to them. My holiday is over, Mr. Narkom, and I'm going back into harness again. You want me, I see, and I said I'd come if you did. Give me a few days' rest in old England, dear friend, and then — out with your riddles and I'm your man again."

CHAPTER I

"THIS will be it, I think, sir," said Lennard, bringing the limousine to a halt at the head of a branching lane, thick set with lime and chestnut trees between whose double wall of green one could catch a distant glimpse of the river, shining golden in the five o'clock light.

"Look! see! There's the sign post — 'To the Sleeping Mermaid' — over to the left there."

"Anything pinned to it or hanging on it?" Mr. Narkom spoke from the interior of the vehicle without making even the slightest movement toward alighting, merely glancing at a few memoranda scribbled on the back of a card whose reverse bore the words "Taverne Maladosie Quai des Anges, Boulogne," printed upon it in rather ornate script.

"A bit of rag, a scrap of newspaper, a fowl's feather — anything? Look sharp!"

"No, sir, not a thing of any sort that I can see from here. Shall I nip over and make sure?"

"Yes. Only don't give away the fact that you are examining it in case there should be anybody on the lookout. If you find the smallest thing — even a carpet tack — attached to the post, get back into your seat at once and cut off townward as fast as you can make the car travel."

"Right you are, sir," said Lennard, and forthwith did as he had been bidden. In less than ninety seconds, however, he was back with word that the post's surface was as smooth as your hand and not a thing of any sort attached to it from top to bottom.

Narkom fetched a deep breath of relief at this news, tucked the card into his pocket, and got out immediately.

"Hang round the neighbourhood somewhere and keep your ears open in case I should have to give the signal sooner than I anticipate," he said; then twisted round on his heel, turned into the tree-bordered lane, and bore down in the direction of the river.

When still short, by thirty yards or so, of its flowered and willow-fringed brim, he came upon a quaint little diamond-paned, red-roofed, low-eaved house set far back from the shore, with a garden full of violets and primroses and flaunting crocuses in front of it, and a tangle of blossoming things crowding what once had been a bower-bordered bowling green in the rear.

"Queen Anne, for a ducat!" he commented as he looked at the place and took in every detail from the magpie in the old pointed-topped wicker cage hanging from a nail beside the doorway to the rudely carved figure of a mermaid over the jutting, flower-filled diamond-paned window of the bar parlour with its swinging sashes and its oak-beam sill, shoulder high from the green, sweet-smelling earth.

"How the dickens does he ferret out these places, I wonder? And what fool has put his money into a show like this in these days of advancement and enterprise? Buried away from the line of traffic ashore and shut in by trees from the river. Gad! they can't do a pound's worth of business in a month at an out-of-the-way roost like this!"

Certainly, they were not doing much of it that day; for, as he passed through the taproom, he caught a glimpse of the landlady dozing in a deep chair by the window, and of the back of a by-no-means-smartly-dressed barmaid — who might have been stone deaf for all notice she took of his entrance — standing on a stool behind the bar dusting and polishing the woodwork of the shelves. The door of the bar parlour was open, and through it Narkom caught a glimpse of a bent-kneed, stoop-shouldered, doddering old man shuffling about, filling match-boxes, wiping ash trays, and carefully refolding the rumpled newspapers that lay on the centre table. That he was not the proprietor, merely a waiter, the towel over his arm, the shabby old dress coat, the baggy-kneed trousers would have been evidence enough without that added by the humble tasks he was performing.

"Poor devil! And at his age!" said Narkom to himself, as he noted the pale, hopeless-looking, time-worn face and the shuffling, time-bent body; then, moved by a sense of keen pity, he walked into the room and spoke gently to him.

"Tea for two, uncle — at a quarter-past five to the tick if you can manage it," he said, tossing the old man a shilling. "And say to the landlady that I'd like to have exclusive use of this room for an hour or two, so she can charge the loss to my account if she has to turn any other customers away."

"Thanky, sir. I'll attend to it at once, sir," replied the old fellow, pocketing the coin, and moving briskly away to give the order. In another minute he was back again, laying the cloth and setting out the dishes, while Narkom improved the time of waiting by straying round the room and looking at the old prints and cases of stuffed fishes that hung on the oak-panelled walls.

It still wanted a minute or so of being a quarter-past five when the old man bore in the tea tray itself and set it upon the waiting table; and, little custom though the place enjoyed, Narkom could not but compliment it upon its promptness and the inviting quality of the viands served.

"You may go," he said to the waiter, when the man at length bowed low and announced that all was ready; then, after a moment, turning round and finding him still shuffling about, "I say you may go!" he reiterated, a trifle sharply. "No, don't take the cosy off the teapot — leave it as it is. The gentleman I am expecting has not arrived yet, and — look here! will you have the goodness to let that cosy alone and to clear out when I tell you? By James! if you don't —— Hullo! What the dickens was that?"

"That" was undoubtedly the tingle of a handful of gravel against the panes of the window.

"A sign that the coast is quite clear and that you have not been followed, dear friend," said a voice — Cleek's voice — in reply. "Shall we not sit down? I'm famishing." And as Narkom turned round on his heel — with the certainty that no one had entered the room since the door was closed and he himself before it — the tea cosy was whipped off by a hand that no longer shook, the waiter's bent figure straightened, his pale, drawn features writhed, blent, settled into placid calmness and — the thing was done!

"By all that's wonderful — Cleek!" blurted out Narkom, delightedly, and lurched toward him.

"Sh-h-h! Gently, gently, my friend," he interposed, putting up a warning hand. "It is true Dollops has signalled that there is no one in the vicinity likely to hear, but although the maid is both deaf and dumb, recollect that Mrs. Condiment is neither; and I have no more wish for her to discover my real calling than I ever had."

"Mrs. Condiment?" repeated Narkom, sinking his voice, and speaking in a tone of agitation and amazement. "You don't mean to tell me that the old woman you employed as housekeeper when you lived in Clarges Street is here?"

"Certainly; she is the landlady. Her assistant is that same deaf and dumb maid-of-all-work who worked with her at the old house, and is sharing with her a sort of 'retirement' here. 'Captain Burbage' set the pair of them up in business here two days after his departure from Clarges Street and pays them a monthly wage sufficient to make up for any lack of 'custom.' All that they are bound to do is to allow a pensioner of the captain's — a poor old half-witted ex-waiter called Joseph — to come and go as he will and to gratify a whim for waiting upon people if he chooses to do so. What's that? No, the 'captain' does not live here. He and his henchman, Dollops, are supposed to be out of the country. Mrs. Condiment does not know *where* he lives — nor will she ever be permitted to do so. You may, some day, perhaps —— that is for the future to decide; but not at present, my dear friend; it is too risky."

"Why risky, old chap? Surely I can come and go in disguise as I did in the old days, Cleek? We managed secret visits all right then, remember."

"Yes — I know. But things have changed, Mr. Narkom. You may disguise yourself as cleverly as you please, but you can't disguise the red limousine. It is known and it will be followed; so, until you can get another of a totally different colour and appearance I'll ring you up each morning at the Yard and we can make our appointments over your private wire. For the present we must take no great risks. In the days that lie behind, dear friend, I had no 'tracker' to guard against but Margot, no enemies but her paltry crew to reckon with and to outwit. In these, I have many. They have brains, these new foes; they are rich, they are desperate, they are powerful; and behind them is the implacable hate and the malignant hand of —— No matter! You wouldn't understand."

"I can make a devilish good guess, then," rapped in Narkom, a trifle testily, his vanity a little hurt by that final suggestion, and his mind harking back to the brief enlightening conversation between Margot and Count Waldemar that night on the spray-swept deck of the Channel packet. "Behind them is 'the implacable hate and the malignant hand' of the King of Mauravania!"

"What utter rubbish!" Cleek's jeering laughter fairly stung, it was so full of pitying derision. "My friend, have you taken to reading penny novelettes of late? A thief-

taker and a monarch! An ex-criminal and a king! I should
have given you credit for more common sense."

"It was the King of Mauravania's equerry who directed
that attempt to kill you by blowing up the house in Clarges
Street."

"Very possibly. But that does not incriminate his royal
master. Count Waldemar is not only equerry to King
Ulric of Mauravania, but is also nephew to its ex-Prime
Minister — the gentleman who is doing fifteen years' energetic labour for the British Government as a result of that
attempt to trap me with his witless 'Silver Snare.' "

"Oh!" said Narkom, considerably crestfallen; then
grasped at yet another straw with sudden, breathless eager-
ness. "But even then the head of the Mauravanian Government must have had some reason for wishing to 'wipe you
out,' " he added, earnestly. "There could be no question
of avenging an uncle's overthrow at that time. Cleek!" —
his voice running thin and eager, his hand shutting suddenly
upon his famous ally's arm — "Cleek, trust me! Won't
you? Can't you? As God hears me, old chap, I'll respect it. Who are you? What are you, man?"

"Cleek," he made answer, calmly drawing out a chair
and taking his seat at the table. "Cleek of Scotland Yard;
Cleek of the Forty Faces—which you will. Who should
know that better than you whose helping hand has made
me what I am?"

"Yes, but before, Cleek? What were you, who were you,
in the days before?"

"The Vanishing Cracksman — a dog who would have
gone on, no doubt, to a dog's end but for your kind hand
and the dear eyes of Ailsa Lorne. Now give me my tea —
I'm famishing — and after that we'll talk of this new riddle
that needs unriddling for the honour of the Yard. Yes,
thanks, two lumps, and just a mere dash of milk. Gad!
It's good to be back in England, dear friend; it's good, it's
good!"

CHAPTER II

"FIVE men, eh?" said Cleek, glancing up at Mr. Narkom, who for two or three minutes past had been giving him a sketchy outline of the case in hand. "A goodish many that. And all inside of the past six weeks, you say? No wonder the papers have been hammering the Yard, if, as you suggest, they were not accidental deaths. Sure they are not?"

"As sure as I am that I'm speaking to you at this minute. I had my doubts in the beginning — there seemed so little to connect the separate tragedies — but when case after case followed with exactly, or nearly exactly, the same details in every instance, one simply *had* to suspect foul play."

"Naturally. Even a donkey must know that there's food about if he smells thistles. Begin at the beginning, please. How did the affair start? When and where?"

"In the neighbourhood of Hampstead Heath at two o'clock in the morning. The constable on duty in the district came upon a man clad only in pajamas lying face downward under the wall surrounding a corner house — still warm but as dead as Queen Anne."

"In his pajamas, eh?" said Cleek, reaching for a fresh slice of toast. "Pretty clear evidence that that poor beggar's trouble, whatever it was, must have overtaken him in bed and that that bed was either in the vicinity of the spot where he was found, or else the man had been carried in a closed vehicle to the place where the constable discovered him. A chap can't walk far in that kind of a get-up with-

out attracting attention. And the body was warm, you
say, when found. Hum-m! Any vehicle seen or heard in
the vicinity of the spot just previously?"

"Not the ghost of one. The night was very still, and the
constable must have heard if either cab, auto, carriage, or
dray had passed in any direction whatsoever. He is positive that none did. Naturally, he thought, as you suggested just now, that the man must have come from
some house in the neighbourhood. Investigation, however,
proved that he did not — in short, that nobody could be
found who had ever seen him before. Indeed, it is hardly
likely that he could have been sleeping in any of the surrounding houses, for the neighbourhood is a very good one,
and the man had the appearance of being a person of the
labouring class."

"Any marks on the clothing or body?"

"Not one — beyond a tattooed heart on the left fore-
arm, which caused the coroner to come to the conclusion
later that the man had at some time been either a soldier
or a sailor."

"Why?"

"The tattooing was evidently of foreign origin, he said,
from the skilful manner in which it had been performed and
the brilliant colour of the pigments used. Beyond that,
the body bore no blemish. The man had not been stabbed,
he had not been shot, and a post-mortem examination of the
viscera proved conclusively that he had not been poisoned.
Neither had he been strangled, etherized, drowned, or bludgeoned, for the brain was in no way injured and the lungs were
in a healthy condition. It was noticed, however, that the
passages of the throat and nose were unduly red, and that
there was a slightly distended condition of the bowels.
This latter, however, was set down by the physicians as
the natural condition following enteric, from which it was
positive that the man had recently suffered. They at-

tributed the slightly inflamed condition of the nasal passage and throat to his having either swallowed or snuffed up
something — camphor or something of that sort — to
allay the progress of the enteric, although even by analysis
they were unable to discover a trace of camphor or indeed
of any foreign substance whatsoever. The body was held
in the public mortuary for several days awaiting identification, but nobody came forward to claim it; so it was eventually buried in the usual way and a verdict of 'Found
Dead' entered in the archives against the number given to
it. The matter had excited but little comment on the part
of the public or the newspapers, and would never have been
recalled but for the astonishing fact that just two nights
after the burial a second man was found under precisely
similar circumstances — only that this second man was
clad in boots, undervest, and trousers. He was found in
a sort of gulley (down which, from the marks on the side, he
had evidently fallen), behind some furze bushes at a far
and little frequented part of the heath. An autopsy
established the fact that this man had died in a precisely
similar manner to the first, but, what was more startling,
that he had evidently pre-deceased that first victim by
several days; for, when found, decomposition had already
set in."

"Hum-m-m! I see!" said Cleek, arching his brows and
stirring his tea rather slowly. "A clear case of what Paddy
would term 'the second fellow being the first one.' Go on,
please. What next?"

"Oh, a perfect fever of excitement, of course; for it now
became evident that a crime had been committed in both
instances; and the Press made a great to-do over it. Within the course of the next fortnight it was positively frothing, throwing panic into the public mind by the wholesale,
and whipping up people's fears like a madman stirring a
salad; for, by that time a third body had been found —

under some furze bushes, upward of half a mile distant from where the second had been discovered. Like the first body, this one was wearing night clothes; but it was in an even more advanced state of decomposition than the second, showing that the man must have died long before either of them!"

"Oho!" said Cleek, with a strong rising inflection. "What a blundering idiot! Our assassin is evidently a raw hand at the game, Mr. Narkom, and not, as I had begun to fancy, either a professional or the appointed agent of some secret society following a process of extermination against certain marked men. Neither the secret agent nor the professional bandit would be guilty of the extreme folly of operating several times in the same locality, be assured; and here is this muddling amateur letting himself be lulled into a feeling of security by the failure of anybody to discover the bodies of the first victims, and then going at it again in the same place and the same way. For it is fair to assume, I daresay, that the fourth man was discovered under precisely similar circumstances to the first."

"Not exactly — very like them, but not exactly like them, Cleek. As a matter of fact, he was alive when found. I didn't credit the report when I first heard it (a newspaper man brought it to me), and sent Petrie to investigate the truth of it."

"Why didn't you believe the report?"

"Because it seemed so wildly improbable. And, besides, they had hatched up so many yarns, those newspaper reporters, since the affair began. According to this fellow, a tramp, crossing the heath in quest of a place to sleep, had been frightened half out of his wits by hearing a voice which *he* described as being like the voice of some one strangling, calling out in the darkness, 'Sapphires! Sapphires!' and a few moments later, when, as the reporter said, the tramp told him, he was scuttling away in a panic, he came suddenly upon the figure of a man who was dancing round and round like a whirling dervish, with his mouth wide open, his tongue hanging out, and the forefinger of each hand stuck in his nostril as if —— ”

“What’s that? What’s that?” Cleek’s voice flicked in like the crack of a whip. “Good God! Dancing round in circles? His mouth open? His tongue hanging out? His fingers thrust into his nostrils? Was that what you said?”

“Yes. Why? Do you see anything promising in that fact, Cleek? It seems to excite you.”

“Never mind about that. Stick to the subject. Was that report found to be correct, then?”

“In a measure, yes. Only, of course, one had to take the tramp’s assertion that the man had been calling out ‘Sapphires’ upon faith, for when discovered and conveyed to the hospital, he was in a comatose condition and beyond making any sound at all. He died, without recovering consciousness, about twenty minutes after Petrie’s arrival; and, although the doctors performed a post-mortem immediately after the breath had left his body, there was not a trace of anything to be found that differed in the slightest from the other cases. Heart, brain, liver, lungs — all were in a healthy condition, and beyond the reddened throat and the signs of recent enteric there was nothing abnormal.”

“But his lips — his lips, Mr. Narkom? Was there a smear of earth upon them? Was he lying on his face when found? Were his fingers clenched in the grass? Did it look as if he had been biting the soil?”

“Yes,” replied Narkom. “As a matter of fact there was both earth and grass in the mouth. The doctors removed it carefully, examined it under the microscope, even subjected it to chemical test in the hope of discovering some foreign substance mixed with the mass, but failed utterly to discover a single trace.”

"Of course, of course! It would be gone like a breath, gone like a passing cloud if it were that."

"If it were what? Cleek, my dear fellow! Good Lord! you don't mean to tell me you've got a clue?"

"Perhaps — perhaps — don't worry me!" he made answer testily; then rose and walked over to the window and stood there alone, pinching his chin between his thumb and forefinger and staring fixedly at things beyond. After a time, however:

"Yes, it could be that — assuredly it could be that," he said in a low-sunk voice, as if answering a query. "But in England — in this far land. In Malay, yes; in Ceylon, certainly. And sapphires, too — sapphires! Hum-m-m! They mine them there. One man had travelled in foreign parts and been tattooed by natives. So that the selfsame country —— Just so! Of course! Of course! But who? But how? And in England?"

His voice dropped off. He stood for a minute or so in absolute silence, drumming noiselessly with his finger tips upon the window-sill, then turned abruptly and spoke to Mr. Narkom.

"Go on with the story, please," he said. "There was a fifth man, I believe. When and how did his end come?"

"Like the others, for the most part, but with one startling difference: instead of being undressed, nothing had been removed but his collar and boots. He was killed on the night I started with Dollops for the Continent in quest of you; and his was the second body that was not actually found *on* the heath. Like the first man, he was found under the wall which surrounds Lemmingham House."

"Lemmingham House? What's that — a hotel or a private residence?"

"A private residence, owned and occupied by Mr. James Barrington-Edwards."

"Any relation to that Captain Barrington-Edwards who

was cashiered from the army some twenty years ago for 'conduct unbecoming an officer and a gentleman'?"

"The same man!"

"Oho! the same man, eh?" Cleek's tone was full of sudden interest. "Stop a bit! Let me put my thinking box into operation. Captain Barrington-Edwards — humm-m! That little military unpleasantness happened out in Ceylon, did it not? The gentleman had a fancy for conjuring tricks, I believe; even went so far as to study them first hand under the tutelage of native fakirs, and was subsequently caught cheating at cards. That's the man, isn't it?"

"Yes," said Narkom, "that's the man. I'll have something startling to tell you in connection with him presently, but not in connection with that card-cheating scandal. He always swore that he was innocent of that. In fact, that it was a put-up job by one of the other officers for the sake of ruining him."

"Yes, I know — they all say that. It's the only thing they can say."

"Still, I always believed him, Cleek. He's been a pretty straightforward man in all my dealings with him, and I've had several. Besides which, he is highly respected these days. Then, too, there's the fact that the fellow he said put up the job against him for the sake of blackening him in the eyes of his sweetheart, eventually married the girl, so it does look rather fishy. However, although it ruined Barrington-Edwards for the time being, and embittered him so that he never married, he certainly had the satisfaction of knowing that the fellow who had caused this trouble turned out an absolute rotter, spent all his wife's money and brought her down to absolute beggary, whereas, if she'd stuck to Barrington-Edwards she'd have been a wealthy woman indeed, to-day. He's worth half a million at the least calculation."

"How's that? Somebody die and leave him a fortune?"

"No. He had a little of his own. Speculated, while he was in the East, in precious stones and land which he had reason to believe likely to produce them; succeeded beyond his wildest hopes, and is to-day head of the firm of Barrington-Edwards, Morpeth & Firmin, the biggest dealers in precious stones that Hatton Garden can boast of."

"Oho!" said Cleek. "I see! I see!" and screwed round on his heel and looked out of the window again. Then, after a moment: "And Mr. Barrington-Edwards lives in the neighbourhood of Hampstead Heath, does he?" he asked quite calmly. "Alone?"

"No. With his nephew and heir, young Mr. Archer Blaine, a dead sister's only child. As a matter of fact, it was Mr. Archer Blaine himself who discovered the body of the fifth victim. Coming home at a quarter to one from a visit to an old college friend, he found the man lying stone dead in the shadow of the wall surrounding Lemmingham House, and, of course, lost no time in dashing indoors for a police whistle and summoning the constable on point duty in the district. The body was at once given in charge of a hastily summoned detachment from the Yard and conveyed to the Hampstead mortuary, where it still lies awaiting identification."

"Been photographed?"

"Not as yet. Of course it will be — as were the other four — prior to the time of burial should nobody turn up to claim it. But in this instance we have great hopes that identification *will* take place on the strength of a marked peculiarity. The man is web-footed and —— "

"The man is *what?*" rapped in Cleek excitedly.

"Web-footed," repeated Narkom. "The several toes are attached one to the other by a thin membrane, after the manner of a duck's feet; and on the left foot there is a peculiar horny protuberance like —— "

"Like a rudimentary sixth toe!" interrupted Cleek, fairly flinging the eager query at him. "It is, eh? Well, by the Eternal! I once knew a fellow — years ago, in the Far East — whose feet were malformed like that; and if by any possibility —— Stop a bit! A word more. Is that man a big fellow — broad shouldered muscular, and about forty or forty-five years of age?"

"You've described him to a T, dear chap. There is, however, a certain other peculiarity which you have not mentioned, though that, of course, may be a recent acquirement. The palm of the right hand —— "

"Wait a bit! Wait a bit!" interposed Cleek, a trifle irritably. He had swung away from the window and was now walking up and down the room with short nervous steps, his chin pinched up between his thumb and forefinger, his brows knotted, and his eyes fixed upon the floor.

"Saffragam — Jaffna — Trincomalee! In all three of them — in all three!" he said, putting his running thoughts into muttered words. "And now a dead man sticks his fingers in his nostrils and talks of sapphires. Sapphires, eh? And the Saffragam district stuck thick with them as spangles on a Nautch girl's veil. The Bareva for a ducat! The Bareva Reef or I'm a Dutchman! And Barrington-Edwards was in that with the rest. So was Peabody; so was Miles; and so, too, were Lieutenant Edgburn and the Spaniard, Juan Alvarez. Eight of them, b'gad — eight! And I was ass enough to forget, idiot enough not to catch the connection until I heard again of Jim Peabody's web foot! But wait! Stop — there should be another marked foot if this is indeed a clue to the riddle, and so —— "

He stopped short in his restless pacing and faced round on Mr. Narkom.

"Tell me something," he said in a sharp staccato. "The four other dead men — did any among them have an injured foot — the left or the right, I forget which — from

which all toes but the big one had been torn off by a croco-
dile's bite, so that in life the fellow must have limped a
little when he walked? Did any of the dead men bear a
mark like that?"

"No," said Narkom. "The feet of all the others were
normal in every particular."

"Hum-m-m! That's a bit of a setback. And I am
either on the wrong track or Alvarez is still alive. What's
that? Oh, it doesn't matter; a mere fancy of mine, that's
all. Now let us get back to our mutton, please. You were
going to tell me something about the right hand of the man
with the web foot. What was it?"

"The palm bore certain curious hieroglyphics traced upon
it in bright purple."

"Hieroglyphics, eh? That doesn't look quite so promising," said Cleek in a disappointed tone. "It is quite possible that there may be more than one web-footed man in
the world, so of course —— Hum-m-m! What were these
hieroglyphics, Mr. Narkom? Can you describe them?"

"I can do better, my dear chap," replied the superintendent, dipping into an inner pocket and bringing forth
a brown leather case. "I took an accurate tracing of them
from the dead hand this morning, and — there you are.
That's what's on his palm, Cleek, close to the base of the
forefinger running diagonally across it."

Cleek took the slip of tracing paper and carried it to the
window, for the twilight was deepening and the room was
filling with shadows. In the middle of the thin, transpar-
ent sheet was traced this:

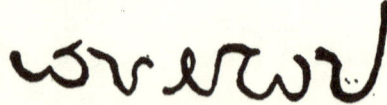

He turned it up and down, he held it to the light and
studied it for a moment or two in perplexed silence, then

of a sudden he faced round, and Narkom could see that his eyes were shining and that the curious one-sided smile, peculiar unto him, was looping up his cheek.

"My friend," he said, answering the eager query in the superintendent's look, "this is yet another vindication of Poe's theory that things least hidden are best hidden, and that the most complex mysteries are those which are based on the simplest principles. With your permission, I'll keep this" — tucking the tracing into his pocket — "and afterward I will go to the mortuary and inspect the original. Meantime, I will go so far as to tell you that I know the motive for these murders, I know the means, and if you will give me forty-eight hours to solve the riddle, at the end of that time I'll know the man. I will even go farther and tell you the names of the victims; and all on the evidence of your neat little tracing. The web-footed man was one, James Peabody, a farrier, at one time attached to the Blue Cavalry at Trincomalee, Ceylon. Another was Joseph Miles, an Irishman, bitten early with the 'wanderlust" which takes men everywhere, and in making rolling stones of them, suffers them to gather no moss. Still another — and probably, from the tattoo mark on his arm, the first victim found — was Thomas Hart, ablebodied seaman, formerly in service on the P & O line; the remaining two were Alexander McCurdy, a Scotchman, and T. Jenkins Quegg, a Yankee. The latter, however, was a naturalized Englishman, and both were privates in her late Majesty's army and honourably discharged."

"Cleek, my dear fellow, are you a magician?" said Narkom, sinking into a chair, overcome.

"Oh, no, my friend, merely a man with a memory, that's all; and I happen to remember a curious little 'pool' that was made up of eight men. Five of them are dead. The other three are Juan Alvarez, a Spaniard, that Lieutenant Edgburn who married and beggared the girl Captain Barrington-Edwards lost when he was disgraced, and last of all the ex-Captain Barrington-Edwards himself. Gently, gently, my friend. Don't excite yourself. All these murders have been committed with a definite purpose in view, with a devil's instrument, and for the devil's own stake — riches. Those riches, Mr. Narkom, were to come in the shape of precious stones, the glorious sapphires of Ceylon. And five of the eight men who were to reap the harvest of them died mysteriously in the vicinity of Lemmingham House."

"Cleek! My hat!" Narkom sprang up as he spoke, and then sat down again in a sort of panic. "And he — Barrington-Edwards, the man that lives there — *deals* in precious stones. Then that man —— "

"Gently, my friend, gently — don't bang away at the first rabbit that bolts out of the hole — it may be a wee one and you'll lose the buck that follows. *Two* men live in that house, remember; Mr. Archer Blaine is Mr. Barrington-Edwards' heir as well as his nephew and — who knows?"

CHAPTER III

"CINNAMON! what a corroboration — what a horrible corroboration! Cleek, you knock the last prop from under me; you make certain a thing that I thought was only a woman's wild imaginings," said Narkom, getting up suddenly, all a-tremble with excitement. "Good heavens! to have Miss Valmond's story corroborated in this dreadful way."

"Miss Valmond? Who's she? Any relation to that Miss Rose Valmond whose name one sees in the papers so frequently in connection with gifts to Catholic Orphanages and Foundling Homes?"

"The same lady," replied Narkom. "Her charities are numberless, her life a psalm. I think she has done more good in her simple, undemonstrative way than half the guilds and missions in London. She has an independent fortune, and lives, in company with an invalid and almost imbecile mother, and a brother who is, I am told, studying for the priesthood, in a beautiful home surrounded by splendid grounds, the walls of which separate her garden from that of Lemmingham House."

"Ah, I see. Then she is a neighbour of Barrington-Edwards?"

"Yes. From the back windows of her residence one can look into the grounds of his. That is how — Cleek!" Mr. Narkom's voice shook with agitation — "You will remember I said, a little time back, that I would have something startling to tell you in connection with Barrington-Edwards —something that was not connected with that old army scandal? If it had not been for the high character of my informant; if it had been any other woman in all England I should have thought she was suffering from nerves — fancying things as the result of an overwrought mind sent into a state of hysteria through all those abominable crimes in the neighbourhood; but when it was she, when it was Miss Valmond ——"

"Oho!" said Cleek, screwing round suddenly. "Then Miss Valmond told you something with regard to Barrington-Edwards?"

"Yes — a horrible something. She came to me this morning looking as I hope I shall never see a good woman look again — as if she had been tortured to the last limit of human endurance. She had been fighting a silent battle for weeks and weeks she said, but her conscience would not let her keep the appalling secret any longer, neither would her duty to Heaven. Wakened in the dead of night by a sense of oppression, she had gone to her window to open it for air, and, looking down by chance into the garden of Lemmingham House, she had seen a man come rushing out of the rear door of Barrington-Edwards' place in his pajamas, closely followed by another, whom she believed to be Barrington-Edwards himself, and she had seen that man unlock the door in the side wall and push the poor wretch out into the road where he was afterward found by the constable."

"By Jupiter!"

"Ah, you may be moved when you connect that circumstance with what you have yourself unearthed. But there is worse to come. Unable to overcome a frightful fascination which drew her night after night to that window, she saw that same thing happen again to the fourth, and finally, the fifth man — the web-footed one — and that last time she saw the face of the pursuer quite plainly. It *was* Barrington-Edwards!"

"Sure of that, was she?"

"Absolutely. It was the positive certainty it was he that drove her at last to speak!"

Cleek made no reply, no comment; merely screwed round on his heel and took to pacing the floor again. After a minute however:

"Mr. Narkom," he said halting abruptly. "I suppose all my old duds are still in the locker of the limousine, aren't they? Good! I thought so. Give Lennard the signal, will you? I must risk the old car in an emergency like this. Take me first to the cable office, please; then to the mortuary, and afterward to Miss Valmond's home. I hate to torture her further, poor girl, but I must get all the facts of this, first hand."

He did. The limousine was summoned at once, and inside of an hour it set him down (looking the very picture of a solicitor's clerk) at the cable office, then picked up and set him down at the Hampstead mortuary, this time, making so good a counterpart of Petrie that even Hammond, who was on guard beside the dead man, said "Hullo, Pete, that you? Thought you was off duty to-day," as he came in with the superintendent.

"Jim Peabody fast enough, Mr. Narkom," commented Cleek, when they were left together beside the dead man. "Changed, of course, in all the years, but still poor old Jim. Good-hearted, honest, but illiterate. Could barely more than write his name, and even that without a capital, poor chap. Let me look at the hand. A violet smudge on the top of the thumb as well as those marks on the palm, I see. Hum-m-m! Any letters or writing of any sort in the pockets when found? None, eh? That old bone-handled pocket knife there his? Yes, I'd like to look at it. Open it, please. Thanks. I thought so, I thought so. Those the socks he had on? Poor wretch! Down to that at last, eh? — down to that! Let me have one of them for a day or so, will you? and — yes — the photographs of the other four. please. Thanks very much. No, that's all. Now then, to call on Miss Valmond, if you don't mind. Right you are. Let her go, Lennard. Down with the blinds and open with the locker again, Mr. Narkom, and we'll 'dig' Mr. George Headland' out of his two-months' old grave." And at exactly ten minutes after eight o'clock, Mr. George Headland *was* 'dug up' and was standing with Mr. Narkom in Rose Valmond's house listening to Rose Valmond's story from her own lips, and saying to himself, the while, that here surely was that often talked-of, seldom-seen creature, a woman with an angel's face.

How it distressed her, to tell again this story which might take away a human life, was manifest from the trembling of her sweet voice, the painful twitching of her tender mouth, and the tears that rose so readily to her soft eyes.

"Oh, Mr. Headland, I can hardly reconcile myself to having done it even yet," she said pathetically. "I do not know this Mr. Barrington-Edwards but by sight, and it seems such a horrible thing to rise up against a stranger like that. But I couldn't keep it any longer; I felt that to do so would be equivalent to sharing his guilt, and the thought that if I kept silent I might possibly be paving the way to the sacrifice of other innocent lives almost drove me out of my mind."

"I can quite understand your feelings, Miss Valmond," said Cleek, touched to the very heart by the deep distress of her. "But may I say I think you have done right? I never yet knew Heaven to be anything but tender to those who do their duty, and you certainly have done yours — to yourself, to your fellow creatures, and to God!"

Before she could make any response to this, footsteps sounded from the outer passage, and a deep, rich, masculine voice said, "Rose, Rose dear, I am ready now," and almost in the same moment a tall, well-set-up man in priestly clothing crossed the threshold and entered the room. He stopped short as he saw the others and made a hasty apology.

"Oh, pardon me," he said. "I did not know that you had visitors, dear; otherwise —— Eh, what? Mr. Narkom, is it not?"

"Yes, Mr. Valmond," replied the superintendent, hold-ing out a welcoming hand. "It is I, and this is my friend and assistant, Mr. George Headland. We have just been talking with your sister over her trying experience."

"Terrible — terrible is the proper word, Mr. Narkom. Like you, I never heard of it until to-day. It shocked me to the very soul, you may believe. Delighted to meet you, Mr. Headland. A new disciple, eh, Mr. Narkom? Another follower in the footsteps of the great Cleek? By the way, I see you have lost touch with that amazing man. I saw your advertisement in the paper the other day. Any clue to his whereabouts as yet?"

"Not the slightest!"

"Ah, that's too bad. From what I have heard of him he would have made short work of this present case had he been available. But pray pardon me if I rush off, my time is very limited. Rose, dear, I am going to visit Father Burns this evening and shall stop at the orphanage on the way, so if you have the customary parcel for the chil-dren ——"

"It is upstairs, in my oratory, dear," she interposed. "Come with me — if the gentlemen will excuse us for a moment — and I will get it for you."

"May we not all go up, Miss Valmond?" interposed Cleek. "I should like, if you do not mind, to get a view of the garden of Lemmingham House from the window where you were standing that night, and to have you explain the positions of the two men if you will."

"Yes, certainly — come, by all means," she replied, and led the way forthwith. They had scarcely gone halfway down the passage to the staircase, however, when they came abreast of the open doorway of a room, dimly lit by a shaded lamp, wherein an elderly woman sat huddled up in a deep chair, with her shaking head bowed over hands that moved restlessly and aimlessly — after the uneasy manner of an idiot's — and the shape of whose face could be but faintly seen through the veil of white hair that fell loosely over it.

Cleek had barely time to recall Narkom's statement regarding the semi-imbecile mother, when Miss Valmond gave a little cry of wonder and ran into the room.

"Why, mother!" she said in her gentle way, "whatever are you doing down here, dearest? I thought you were still asleep in the oratory. When did you come down?"

The imbecile merely mumbled and muttered, and shook her nodding head, neither answering nor taking any notice whatsoever.

"It is one of her bad nights," explained Miss Valmond, as she came out and rejoined them. "We can do nothing with her when she is like this. Horace, you will have to come home earlier than usual to-night and help me to get her to bed." Then she went on, leading the way upstairs, until they came at length to a sort of sanctuary where Madonna faces looked down from sombre niches, and wax lights burnt with a scented flame on a draped and cushioned prie dieu. Here Miss Valmond, who was in the lead, went in, and, taking a paper-wrapped parcel from beside the little altar, came back and put it in her brother's hand and sent him on his way.

"Was it from there you saw the occurrence, Miss Valmond?" asked Cleek, looking past her into "the dim religious light" of the sanctuary.

"Oh, no," she made reply. "From the window of my bedroom, just on the other side of the wall. In here, look, see!" And she opened a door to the right and led them in, touching a key that flashed an electric lamp into radiance and illuminated the entire room.

It was a large room furnished in dull oak and dark green after the stately, sombre style of a Gothic chapel, and at one end there was a curtained recess leading to a large bow window. At the other there was a sort of altar banked high with white flowers, and at the side there was a huge canopied bed over the head of which hung an immense crucifix fastened to the wall that backed upon the oratory. It was a majestic thing, that crucifix, richly carved and exquisitely designed. Cleek went nearer and looked at it, his artistic eye captured by the beauty of it; and Miss Valmond, noting his interest, smiled.

"My brother brought me that from Rome," she said. "Is it not divine, Mr. Headland?"

"Yes," he said. "But you must be more careful of it, I fear, Miss Valmond. Is it not chipping? Look! Isn't this a piece of it?" He bent and picked a tiny curled sliver of wood from the narrow space between the two down-filled pillows of the bed, holding it out to her upon his palm. But, of a sudden, he smiled, lifted the sliver to his nose, smelt it, and cast it away. "The laugh is on me, I fear — it's only a cedar paring from a lead pencil. And now, please, I'd like to investigate the window."

She led him to it at once, explaining where she stood on the eventful night; where she had seen the two figures pass, and where was the wall door through which the dying man had been thrust.

"I wish I might see that door clearer," said Cleek; for night had fallen and the moon was not yet up. "Don't happen to have such a thing as a telescope or an opera glass, do you, Miss Valmond?"

"My brother has a pair of field glasses downstairs in his room. Shall I run and fetch them for you?"

"I'd be very grateful if you would," said Cleek; and a

moment after she had gone. "Run down and get my sketching materials out of the locker, will you, Mr. Narkom?" he added. "I want to make a diagram of that house and garden." Then he sat down on the window-seat and for five whole minutes was alone.

The field glasses and the sketching materials were brought, the garden door examined and the diagram made, Miss Valmond and Narkom standing by and watching eagerly the whole proceeding.

"That's all!" said Cleek, after a time, brushing the charcoal dust from his fingers, and snapping the elastic band over the sketch book. "I know my man at last, Mr. Narkom. Give me until ten o'clock to-morrow night, and then, if Miss Valmond will let us in here again, I'll capture Barrington-Edwards red-handed."

"You are sure of him, then?"

"As sure as I am that I'm alive. I'll lay a trap that will catch him. I promise you that. So if Miss Valmond will let us in here again ——"

"Yes, Mr. Headland, I will."

"Good! Then let us say at ten o'clock to-morrow night — here in this room; you, I, your brother, Mr. Narkom — all concerned!" said Cleek. "At ten to the tick, remember. Now come along, Mr. Narkom, and let me be about weaving the snare that shall pull this Mr. Barrington-Edwards to the scaffold." Speaking, he bowed to Miss Valmond, and taking Mr. Narkom's arm, passed out and went down the stairs to prepare for the last great act of tragedy.

"Got you, Miss Rosie Edgburn! Got you, Señor Juan Alvarez," rapped Cleek. . . .
'' Stop him. nab him. Mr. Narkom'

CHAPTER IV

A T TEN to the tick on the following night, he had
said, and at ten to the tick he was there — the old
red limousine whirling him up to the door in company with
Mr. Narkom, there to be admitted by Miss Valmond's
brother.

"My dear Mr. Headland, I have been on thorns ever
since I heard," said he. "I hope and pray it is right,
this assistance we are giving. But tell me, please — have
you succeeded in your plans? Are you sure they will not
fail?"

"To both questions, yes, Mr. Valmond. We'll have our
man to-night. Now, if you please, where is your sister?"

"Upstairs — in her own room — with my mother. We
tried to get the mater to bed, but she is very fractious to-
night and will not let Rose out of her sight for a single
instant. But she will not hamper your plans, I'm sure.
Come quickly, please — this way." Here he led them on
and up until they stood in Miss Valmond's bedroom and in
Miss Valmond's presence again. She was there by the
window, her imbecile mother sitting at her feet with her
face in her daughter's lap, that daughter's solicitous hand
gently stroking her tumbled hair, and no light but that of
the moon through the broad window illuminating the hushed
and stately room.

"I keep my word, you see, Miss Valmond," said Cleek,
as he entered. "And in five minutes' time if you watch
from that window you all shall see a thing that will amaze
you."

"You have run the wretched man down, then, Mr. Headland?"

"Yes — to the last ditch, to the wall itself," he answered, making room for her brother to get by him and make a place for himself at the window. "Oh, it's a pretty little game he's been playing, that gentleman, and it dates back twenty years ago when he was kicked out of his regiment in Ceylon."

"In Ceylon! I — er — God bless my soul, was he ever in Ceylon, Mr. Headland?"

"Yes, Mr. Valmond, he was. It was at a time when there was what you might call a sapphire fever raging there, and precious stones were being unearthed in every unheard-of quarter. He got the fever with the rest, but he hadn't much money, so when he fell in with a lot of fellows who had heard of a Cingalese, one Bareva Singh, who had a reef to sell in the Saffragam district, they made a pool between them and bought the blessed thing, calling it after the man they had purchased it from, the Bareva Reef, setting out like a party of donkeys to mine it for themselves, and expecting to pull out sapphires by the bucketful."

"Dear me, dear me, how very extraordinary! Of course they didn't? Or — did they?"

"No, they didn't. A month's work convinced them that the ground was as empty of treasure as an eggshell, so they abandoned it, separated, and went their several ways. A few months ago, however, it was discovered that if they had had the implements to mine deeper, their dream would have been realized, for the reef was a perfect bed of sapphires — and eight men held an equal share in it. The scheme, then, was to get rid of these men, secretly, one by one; for one — perhaps two men — to get the deeds held by the others; to pretend that they had been purchased from the original owners, and to prevent by murder those original owners from —— "

He stopped suddenly and switched round. Miss Valmond had risen and so had her mother. He was on the pair of them like a leaping cat; there was a sharp click-click, a snarl, and a scream, and one end of a handcuff was on the wrist of each.

"Got you, Miss Rosie Edgburn! Got you, Senor Juan Alvarez!" he rapped out sharply; then in a louder tone, as the Reverend Horace made a bolt for the door: "Stop him, nab him, Mr. Narkom! Quick! Played sir, played. Come in, Petrie; come in, Hammond. Gentlemen, here they are, all three of them: Lieutenant Eric Edgburn, his daughter Rose, and Senor Juan Alvarez, the three brute beasts who sent five men to their death for the sake of a lode of sapphires and the devil's lust for gain!"

"It's a lie!" flung out the girl who had been known as Rose Valmond.

"Oh, no, it's not, you vixen! You loathsome creature that prostituted holy things and made a shield of religion to carry on a vampire's deeds. Look here, you beast of blasphemy: I know the secret of this," he said, and walked over and laid his hand on the crucifix at the head of the bed. "Petrie! round into the oratory with you. There's a nob at the side of the prayer desk — press it when I shout. Oh, no, Miss Edgburn; no, I shan't dance circles nor put my fingers into my nose, nor bite the dust and die. Look how I dare it all. Now Petrie, *now!*"

And lo! as he spoke, out of the nostrils of the figure on the cross there rushed downward two streams of white vapour which beat upon the pillows and upon him, smothering both in white dust.

"Face powder, Miss Edgburn, only face powder from your own little case over there," he said. "I removed the devil's dust last night when I was in this room alone."

She made him no reply — only, like a cornered wretch, screamed out and fainted.

"Mr. Narkom, you have seen the method of administering the thing which caused the death of those five men; it is now only fair that you should know what that thing was," he said, turning to the superintendent. "It is known by two names — Devil's Dust and Dust of Death, and both suit it well. It is the fine, feathery powder that grows on the young shoots of the bamboo tree — a favourite method of secret killing with the natives of the Malay Peninsula and those of Madagascar, the Philippines and Ceylon. When blown into the nostrils of a living creature it produces first an awful agony of suffocation, a feeling as though the brain is coming down and exuding from the nostrils, then delirium, during which the victim invariably falls on his face and bites the earth; then comes death. Death without a trace, my friend, for the hellish dust all but evaporates, and the slight sediment that remains is carried out of the system by the spasm of enteric it produces.[1] That is the riddle's solution. As for the rest, those men were lured here by letters — from Alvarez — telling them of the reef's great fortune, of the necessity for coming at once and bringing their deeds with them, and impressing upon them the possibility of being defrauded if they breathed one word to a mortal soul about their leaving or why. They came, they were invited to spend the night and to sleep upon that accursed bed, and — the devil's dust did the rest. I traced that out through poor Jim Peabody's sock. It was one of the blue yarn kind that are given to the inmates of workhouses. I traced him through that; and the others through the photographs. Each had been known to have received a letter from London, and each had in turn vanished without a word. Poor chaps! poor unhappy chaps! Let us hope, dear friend, that they have found 'the Place of Sapphires' after all."

CHAPTER V

"HOW did I come to suspect the girl?" said Cleek, answering Narkom's query, as they swung off through the darkness in the red limousine, leaving Edgburn and his confederates in the hands of the police. "Well, as a matter of fact, I did not suspect her at all, in the beginning — her saintly reputation saved her from any such thing as that. It was only when her father came in that I knew. And later, I knew even better — when I saw that pretended imbecile sitting there in that room; for the blundering fool had been ass enough to kick off his slippers and sit there in his stocking feet, and I spotted the Alvarez foot on the instant. Still, I didn't know but what the girl herself might be an innocent victim — a sort of dove in a vulture's nest — and it was not until I found that scrap of wood from a sharpened lead pencil that I began to doubt her. It was only when I promised that Barrington-Edwards should be trapped, that I actually knew. The light that flamed in her eyes in spite of her at that would have made an idiot understand. What's that? What should I suspect from the finding of that scrap of pencil? My dear Mr. Narkom, carry your mind back to that moment when I found the stain on poor Jim Peabody's thumb, and then examined the blade of his pocket knife. The marks on the latter showed clearly that the man had sharpened a pencil with it — and, of course, with the point of that pencil against the top of his thumb. By the peculiar bronze-like shine of the streaks, and the small particles of dust adhering to the knife blade, I felt persuaded that the pencil was an indelible one — in short, one of those which write a faint, blackish-lilac hue which, on the application of moisture, turns to a vivid and indelible purple. The moisture induced by the act of thrusting his forefingers up his nostrils to allay the horrible sensation of the brain descending, which that hellish powder produces, together with the perspiration which comes with intense· agony, had made such a change in the smears his thumb and forefinger bore, and left no room for doubt that at the time he was smitten he had either just begun or just concluded writing something with an indelible pencil which he had but recently sharpened. Poor wretch! he of all the lot had some one belonging to him that was still living — his poor old mother. It is very fair to suppose that, finding the Alvarez place so lavishly furnished, and having hopes that great riches were yet to be his, he sat down on that bed and began to write a few lines in his illiterate way to that mother before wholly undressing and getting between the sheets. The mark on his palm is a clear proof that when the powder suddenly descended upon him he involuntarily closed his hand on that letter and the perspiration transferred to his flesh the shape of the scrawl upon which it rested. Pardon? How did I know through that scrawl that I was really on the track, and that it was the Bareva Reef that was at the bottom of the whole game? My dear Mr. Narkom, I won't insult your intelligence by explaining that. All you have to do is to turn that tracing upside down and look *through* it — or at it in a mirror — and you'll have the answer for yourself. What's that? The parcel the girl gave Edgburn to carry out on the pretext of taking it to an orphanage? Oh, that was how they were slowly getting rid of the victims' clothes. Cutting them up into little pieces and throwing them into the river, I suppose, or if not ——"

He stopped suddenly, his ear caught by a warning sound; then turned in his seat and glanced through the little window at the back of the limousine.

"I thought as much," he said, half aloud; then leaned for‹
ward, caught up the pipe of the speaking tube, and signalled
Lennard. "Look sharp — taxi following us!" he said.
"Put on a sudden spurt — that chap will increase speed to
keep pace with us — then pull up sharp and let the other
fellow's impetus carry him by before he can help himself.
Out with the light, Mr. Narkom — out with it quick!"

Both Lennard and his master followed instructions. Of
a sudden the lights flicked out, the car leapt forward with
a bound, then pulled up with a jerk that shook it from end
to end. In that moment the taxi in the rear whizzed by
them, and Narkom, leaning forward to look as it flashed
past, saw seated within it the figure of Count Waldemar of
Mauravania.

"By James! Did you see that, Cleek?" he cried, and
switched round and made a grab for Cleek's arm.

But Cleek was not there. His seat was empty, and the
door beside it was swinging ajar.

"Well, I'll be jiggered!" exclaimed the superintendent,
fairly carried out of himself — for, even in his old Vanish‑
ing Cracksman's days, when he had slipped the leash and
eluded the police so often, the man had not made a more
adroit, more silent, more successful getaway than this.
"Of all the astonishing ——! Gad, an eel's a fool to him
for slipping out of tight places. When did he go, I wonder,
and where?"

Never very strong on matters of detail, here curiosity
tricked him into absolute indiscretion. Sliding along the
seat to the swinging door he thrust it open and leaned out
into the darkness, for a purpose so evident that he who ran
might read. That one who ran *did*, he had good reason to
understand in the next instant, for, of a sudden, the taxi in
advance checked its wild flight, swung round with a noisy
scroo-op, and pelted back until the two vehicles stood cheek
by jowl, so to speak, and the glare of its headlights was

pouring full force upon Mr. Narkom and into the interior of the red limousine.

"Here! Dash your infernal impudence," began he, blinking up at the driver through a glare which prevented him seeing that the taxicab's leather blinds had been discreetly pulled down, and its interior rendered quite invisible; but before he could add so much as another word to his protest the chauffeur's voice broke in with a blandness and an accent which told its own story.

"Dix mille pardons, m'sieur," it commenced, then pulled itself up as if the owner of it had suddenly recollected himself — and added abruptly in a farcical attempt to imitate the jargon of the fast-disappearing London cabby. "Keep of the 'air on, ole coq! Only wantin' to arsk of the question civile. Lost my bloomin' way. Put a cove on to the short cut to the 'Igh Street will yer, like a blessed Christian? I dunno where I are."

Mr. Narkom was not suffered to make reply. Before he had more than grasped the fact that the speaker was undeniably a Frenchman, Lennard — out of the range of that dazzling light — had made the discovery that he was yet more undeniably a Frenchman of that class from which the Apaches are recruited, and stepped into the breach with astonishing adroitness.

"Oh, that's the trouble, is it?" he interposed. "My hat! Why, of course we'll put you on the way. Wot's more, we'll take you along and show you — won't we, guv'ner, eh? — so as you won't go astray till you gets there. 'Eads in and door shut, Superintendent," bringing the limousine around until it pointed in the same direction as the taxicab. "Now then, straight ahead, and foller yer nose, Jules; we'll be rubbin' shoulders with you the whole blessed way. And as the Dook of Wellington said to Napoleon Bonaparte, 'None of your larks, you blighter — you're a-comin' along with me!'"

That he was, was a condition of affairs so inevitable that the chauffeur made no attempt to evade it; merely put on speed and headed straight for the distant High Street for the purpose of getting rid of his escort as soon as possible; and Lennard, putting on speed, likewise, and keeping pace with him, ran him neck and neck, until the heath was left far and away behind, the darkness gave place to a glitter of street lamps, the lonely roads to populous thoroughfares, and the way was left clear for Cleek to get off unfollowed and unmolested.

CHAPTER VI

SCREENED by that darkness, and close sheltered by the matted gorse which fringed and dotted the expanse of the nearby heath, he had been an interested witness to the entire proceeding.

"Played, my lad, played!" he commented, putting his thoughts into mumbled words of laughing approval, as Lennard, taking the taxicab under guard, escorted it and its occupants out of the immediate neighbourhood; then, excessive caution prompting him to quell even this little ebullition, he shut up like an oyster and neither spoke, nor moved, nor made any sound until the two vehicles were represented by nothing but a purring noise dwindling away into the distance.

When that time came, however, he rose, and facing the heath, forged out across its mist-wrapped breadth with that long, swinging, soldierly stride peculiar unto him, his forehead puckered with troubled thought, his jaw clamped, and his lips compressed until his mouth seemed nothing more than a bleak slit gashed in a gray, unpleasant-looking mask.

But after a while the night and the time and the place worked their own spell, and the troubled look dropped away; the dull eyes lighted, the grim features softened, and the curious crooked smile that was Nature's birth-gift to him broke down the rigid lines of the "bleak slit" and looped up one corner of his mouth.

It was magic ground, this heath — a place thick set as the Caves of Manheur with the Sapphires of Memory — and to a nature such as his these things could not but appeal.

Here Dollops had come into his life — a starvelling, an outcast; derelict even in the very morning time of youth — a bit of human wreckage that another ten minutes would have seen stranded forever upon the reefs of crime.

Here, too — on that selfsame night, when the devil had been cheated, and the boy had gone, and they two stood alone together in the mist and darkness — he had first laid aside the mask of respectability and told Ailsa Lorne the truth about himself! Of his Apache times — of his Vanishing Cracksman's days — and, in the telling, had watched the light die out of her dear eyes and dread of him darken them, when she knew.

But not for always, thank God! For, in later days — when Time had lessened the shock, when she came to know him better, when the threads of their two lives had become more closely woven, and the hope had grown to be something more than a mere possibility . . .

He laughed aloud, remembering, and with a sudden rush of animal spirits twitched off his hat, flung it up and caught it as it fell, after the manner of a happy boy.

God, what a world — what a glorious, glorious world! All things were possible in it if a man but walked straight and knew how to wait.

Well, please God, a part, at least, of *his* long waiting would be over in another month. *She* would be back in England then — her long visit to the Hawksleys ended and nothing before her now but the pleasant excitement of trousseau days. For the coming autumn would see the final act of restitution made, the last Vanishing Cracksman debt paid, to the uttermost farthing; and when that time came . . . He flung up his hat again and shouted from sheer excess of joy, and forged on through the mist and darkness whistling.

His way lay across the great common to the Vale of Health district, and thence down a slanting road and a slop-

ing street to the Hampstead Heath Station of the Tube
Railway, and he covered the distance to such good effect
that half-past eleven found him "down under," swaying to
the rhythmic movement of an electric train and arrowing
through the earth at a lively clip.

Ten minutes later he changed over to yet another underground system, swung on for half an hour or so through
gloom and bad air and the musty smell of a damp tunnel
before the drop of the land and the rise of the roadbed carried the train out into the open and the air came fresh and
sweet and pure, as God made it, over field and flood and
dewy garden spaces; and away to the west a prickle of lights
on a quiet river told where the stars mirrored themselves in
the glass of Father Thames.

At a toy station in the hush and loneliness of the pleasant
country ways his long ride came to an end at last, and he
swung off into the balm and fragrance of the night to face
a two-mile walk along quiet, shadow-filled lanes and over
wet wastes of young bracken to a wee little house in the
heart of a green wilderness, with a high-walled, old-world
garden surrounding it, and, in the far background, a gloom
of woodland smeared in darker purple against the purple
darkness of the sky.

No light shone out from the house to greet him — no light
could come from behind that screening wall, unless it were
one set in an upper window — yet he was certain the place
was not deserted; for, as he came up out of the darkness,
catlike of tread and catlike of ear, he was willing to swear
that he could catch the sound of some one moving about
restlessly in the shadow of that high, brick wall — and the
experiences of the night made him cautious of things that
moved in darkness.

He stopped short, and remained absolutely still for half a
minute, then, stooping, swished his hand through the
bracken in excellent imitation of a small animal running,

and shrilled out a note that was uncannily like the death squeal of a stoat-caught rabbit.

"Gawd's truth, guv'ner, is it you at last, sir? And me never seein' nor hearin' a blessed thing!" spoke a voice in answer, from the wall's foot; then a latch clicked and, as Cleek rose to his feet, a garden door swung inward, a rectangle of light shone in the darkness, and silhouetted against it stood Dollops.

"What are you doing out here at this time of night, you young monkey? Don't you know it's almost one o'clock?" said Cleek, as he went forward and joined the boy.

"Don't I know it, says you? Don't I *just!*" he gave back. "There aren't a minute since the night come on that I haven't counted, sir — not a bloomin' one; and if you hadn't turned up just as you did —— Well, let that pass, as the Suffragette said when she heaved 'arf a brick through the shop window. Gawd's truth, guv'ner, do you realise that you've been gone since yesterday afternoon and I haven't heard a word from you in all that time?"

"Well, what of that? It's not the first time by dozens that I've done the same thing. Why should it worry you at this late day? Look here, my young man, you're not developing 'nerves' are you? Because, if you are —— Turn round and let's have a look at you! Why, you are as pale as a ghost, you young beggar, and shaking like a leaf. Anything wrong with you, old chap?"

"Not as I knows of," returned Dollops, making a brave attempt to smile and be his old happy-go-lucky, whimsical self, albeit he wasn't carrying it off quite successfully, for there was a droop to his smile and a sort of whimper underlying his voice, and Cleek's keen eyes saw that his hand groped about blindly in its effort to find the fastenings of the garden door.

"Leastwise, nothing as matters now that you are here, sir. And I *am* glad yer back, guv'ner — Lawd, yuss!

'Nothin' like company to buck you up,' as the bull said when he tossed the tinker; so of course ——"

"Here! You let those fastenings alone. I'll attend to them!" rapped in Cleek's voice with a curious note of alarm in it, as he moved briskly forward and barred and locked the wall door. "If I didn't know that eating, not drinking, was your particular failing ——"

Here he stopped, his half-uttered comment cut into by a bleating cry, and he screwed round to face a startling situation. For there was Dollops, leaning heavily against a flowering almond tree, his face like a dead face for colour, and his fingers clawing frantically at the lower part of his waistcoat, doubling and twisting in the throes of an internal convulsion.

The gravelled pathway gave forth two sharp scrunches, and Cleek was just in time to catch him as he lurched forward and sprawled heavily against him. The man's arms closed instinctively about the twisting, sweat-drenched, helpless shape, and with great haste and infinite tenderness gathered it up and carried it into the house; but he had scarcely more than laid the boy upon a sofa and lit the lamp of the small apartment which served them as a general living-room, when all the agony of uncertainty which beset his mind regarding the genesis of this terrifying attack vanished in a sudden rush of enlightenment.

All that was left of a bounteous and strikingly diversified afternoon tea still littered the small round dining table, and there, on one plate, lay the shells of two crabs, on another, the remains of a large rhubarb tart, on a third, the skins of five bananas leaning coquettishly up against the lid of an open pickle jar, and hard by there was a pint tumbler with the white blur of milk dimming it.

"Good Lord! The young anaconda!" blurted out Cleek, as he stood and stared at this appalling array. "No wonder, no wonder!" Then he turned round on his heel, looked at the writhing and moaning boy, and in a sudden fever of doing, peeled off his coat, rolled up his sleeves, and made a bolt for the kitchen stove, the hot-water kettle, and the medicine chest.

The result of Master Dollops' little gastronomic experiment scarcely needs to be recorded. It is sufficient to say that he had the time of his life that night; that he kept Cleek busy every minute for the next twenty-four hours wringing out flannels in hot water and dosing him with homely remedies, and that when he finally came through the siege was as limp as a wet newspaper and as feeble as a good many dry ones.

"What you need to pull yourself together is a change, you reckless young ostrich — a week's roughing it in the open country by field and stream, and as many miles as possible from so much as the odour of a pastry cook's shop," said Cleek, patting him gently upon the shoulder. "A nice sort of assistant you are — keeping a man out of his bed for twenty-four hours, with his heart in his mouth and his hair on end, you young beggar. Now, now, now! None of your blubbing! Sit tight while I run down and make some gruel for you. After that I'll nip out and 'phone through to the Yard and tell Mr. Narkom to have somebody look up a caravan that can be hired, and we'll be off for a week's 'gypsying' in Yorkshire, old chap."

He did — coming back later with a piece of surprising news. For it just so happened that the idea of a week's holiday-making, a week's rambling about the green lanes, the broad moors, and through the wild gorges of the West Riding, and living the simple life in a caravan, appealed to Mr. Maverick Narkom as being the most desirable thing in the world at that moment, and he made haste to ask Cleek's permission to share the holiday with him. As nothing could have been more to his great ally's liking, the matter was settled forthwith. A caravan was hired by telegram to Sheffield, and at ten the next morning the little party turned its back upon London and fared forth to the pleasant country lands, the charm of laughing waters, and the magic that hides in trees.

For five days they led an absolutely idyllic life; loafing in green wildernesses and sleeping in the shadow of whispering woods; and this getting back to nature proved as much of a tonic to the two men as to the boy himself — refreshing both mind and body, putting red blood into their veins, and breathing the breath of God into their nostrils.

Having amply provisioned the caravan before starting, they went no nearer to any human habitation than they were obliged to do in passing from one district to another; and one day was so exact a pattern of the next that its history might have stood for them all: up with the dawn and the birds and into woodland pool or tree-shaded river; then gathering fuel and making a fire and cooking breakfast; then washing the utensils, harnessing the horses, and moving on again — sometimes Cleek driving, sometimes Narkom, sometimes the boy — stopping when they were hungry to prepare lunch just as they had prepared breakfast, then forging on again until they found some tree-hedged dell or bosky wood where they might spend the night, crooned to sleep by the wind in the leaves, and watched over by the sentinel stars.

So they had spent the major part of the week, and so they might have spent it all, but that chance chose to thrust them suddenly out of idleness into activity, and to bring them — here, in this Arcadia — face to face again with the evils of mankind and the harsh duty of the law.

It had gone nine o'clock on that fifth night when a curious thing happened: they had halted for the night by the banks of a shallow, chattering stream which flowed through a wayside spinney, beyond whose clustering treetops they had seen, before the light failed, the castellated top of a distant tower and, farther afield, the weathercock on an up-lifting church spire; they had supped and were enjoying their ease — the two men sprawling at full length on the ground enjoying a comfortable smoke, while Dollops, with a mouth harmonica, was doing "Knocked 'Em in the Old Kent Road," his back against a tree, his eyes upturned in ecstasy, his long legs stretched out upon the turf, and his feet crossed one over the other — and all about them was peace; all the sordid, money-grubbing, crime-stained world seemed millions of miles away, when, of a sudden, there came a swift rush of bodies — trampling on dead leaves and brushing against live ones — then a voice cried out com-mandingly, "Surrender yourselves in the name of the king!" and scrambling to a sitting position, they looked up to find themselves confronted by a constable, a gamekeeper, and two farm labourers — the one with drawn truncheon and the other three with cocked guns.

CHAPTER VII

"HULLO, I say!" began Mr. Narkom, in amazement. "Why, what the dickens —— " But he was suffered to get no farther.

"You mind your P's and Q's! I warn you that anything you say will be used against you!" interjected sharply and authoritatively the voice of the constable. "Hawkins, you and Marlow keep close guard over these chaps while me and Mr. Simpkins looks round for the animal. I said it would be the work of gypsies, didn't I now, Mr. Simpkins?" addressing the gamekeeper. "Come on and let's have a look for the beast. Keep eyes peeled and gun at full cock, Mr. Simpkins, and give un both barrels if un makes to spring at us. This be a sharp capture, Mr. Simpkins — what?"

"Aye, but un seems to take it uncommon cool, Mr. Nippers — one on 'em's larfiin' fit to bust hisself!" replied the gamekeeper as Cleek slapped both thighs, and throwing back his head, voiced an appreciative guffaw. "Un doan't look much loike gypsies either from t' little as Ah can see of 'em in this tomfool loight. Wait a bit till Ah scoop up an armful o' leaves and throw 'em on the embers o' fire yon."

He did so forthwith; and the moment the dry leaves fell on the remnants of the fire which the caravanners had used to cook their evening meal there was a gush of aromatic smoke, a sudden puff, and then a broad ribbon of light rushed upward and dispelled every trace of darkness. And by the aid of that ribbon of light Mr. Nippers saw something which made him almost collapse with astonishment and chagrin.

The great of the world may, and often do, forget their meetings with the small fry, but the small fry never cease to remember their meetings with the great, or to treasure a vivid remembrance of that immortal day when they were privileged to rub elbows with the elect.

Five years had passed since Mrs. Maverick Narkom, seeking a place wherein to spend the summer holidays with the little Narkoms and their nurses, had let her choice fall upon Winton-Old-Bridges and had dwelt there for two whole months. Three times during her sojourn her liege lord had come down for a week-end with his wife and children, and during one of these brief visits, meeting Mr. Ephraim Nippers, the village constable in the public highway, he had deigned to stop and speak to the man and to present him with a sixpenny cigar.

Times had changed since then; Mr. Nippers was now head constable for the district, but he still kept that cigar under a glass shade on the drawing-room whatnot, and he still treasured a vivid recollection of the great man who had given it to him and whom he now saw sitting on the ground with his coat off and his waistcoat unbuttoned, his moustache uncurled, wisps of dried grass clinging to his tousled hair, and all the dignity of office conspicuous by its absence.

"Oh, lummy!" said Mr. Nippers with a gulp. "Put down the hammers of them guns, you two — put 'em down quick! It's Mr. Narkom — Mr. Maverick Narkom, superintendent at Scotland Yard!"

"Hullo!" exclaimed Mr. Narkom, shading his eyes from the firelight and leaning forward to get a clearer view of the speaker. "How the dickens do you know that, my man? And who the dickens are you, anyway? Can't say that I remember ever seeing your face before."

Mr. Nippers hastened to explain that little experience of

five years ago; but the circumstance which had impressed itself so deeply upon his memory had passed entirely out of the superintendent's.

"Oh, that's it, is it?" said he. "Can't say that I recall the occasion; but Mrs. Narkom certainly did stop at Winton-Old-Bridges some four or five summers ago, so of course it's possible. By the way, my man, what caused you to make this sudden descent upon us? And what are these chaps who are with you bearing arms for? Anything up?"

"Oh, lummy, sir, yes! A murder's just been committed — leastwise it's only just been discovered; but it can't have been long since it *was* committed, Mr. Narkom, for Miss Renfrew, who found him, sir, and give the alarm, she says as the poor dear gentleman was alive at a quarter to eight, 'cause she looked into the room at that time to ask him if there was anything he wanted, and he spoke up and told her no, and went on with his figgerin' just the same as usual."

"As usual?" said Cleek. "Why do you say 'as usual,' my friend? Was the man an accountant of some sort?"

"Lummy! no, sir. A great inventor is what he is — or was, poor gentleman. Reckon you must 'a' heard of un some time or another — most everybody has. Nosworth is the name, sir — Mr. Septimus Nosworth of the Round House. You could see the tower of it over yon if you was to step out into the road and get clear of these trees."

Cleek was on his feet like a flash.

"Not the great Septimus Nosworth?" he questioned eagerly. "Not the man who invented Lithamite? — the greatest authority on high explosives in England? Not that Septimus Nosworth, surely?"

"Aye — him's the one, poor gentleman. I thought it like as the name would be familiar, sir. A goodish few have heard of un, one way and another."

"Yes," acquiesced Cleek. "Lithamite carried his name from one end of the globe to the other; and his family

affairs came into unusual prominence in consequence.
Widower, wasn't he? — hard as nails and bitter as gall. Had
an only son, hadn't he? — a wild young blade who went the
pace: took up with chorus girls, music hall ladies, and persons of that stripe, and got kicked out from under the par-
ental roof in consequence."

"Lummy, now! think of you a-knowin' about all that!"
said Mr. Nippers, in amazement. "But then, your bein'
with Mr. Narkom and him bein' what he is — why, of
course! Scotland Yard it do know everything, I'm told,
sir."

"Yes — it reads the papers occasionally, Mr. Nippers,"
said Cleek. "I may take it from your reply, may I not,
that I am correct regarding Mr. Septimus Nosworth's son?"

"Indeed, yes, sir — right as rain. Leastwise, from what
I've heard. I never see the young gentleman, myself.
Them things you mention happened before Mr. Nosworth
come to live in these parts — a matter of some four years
or more ago. Alwuss had his laboratory here, sir — built
it on the land he leased from Sir Ralph Droger's father in the
early sixties — and used to come over frequent and shut
hisself in the Round House for days on end; but never come
here to live until after that flare-up with Master Harry.
Come then and built livin' quarters beside the Round House
and, after a piece, fetched Miss Renfrew and old Patty Dax
over to live with un."

"Miss Renfrew and old Patty Dax? Who are they?"

"Miss Renfrew is his niece, sir — darter of a dead sister.
Old Patty Dax, she war the cook. I dunno what her be
now, though — her died six months ago and un hired Mistress Armroyd in her place. French piece, her am, though
bein' widder of a Lancashire man, and though I doan't
much fancy foreigners nor their ways, this I will say: her
keeps the house like a pin and her cookin's amazin' tasty
— indeed, yes."

"You are an occasional caller in the servants' hall, I see,
Mr. Nippers," said Cleek, serenely, as he took up his coat
and shook it, preparatory to putting it on. "I think, Mr.
Narkom, that in the interests of the public at large it will
be well for some one a little more efficient than the local constabulary to look into this case, so, if you don't mind making yourself a trifle more presentable, it will be as well for
us to get Mr. Nippers to show us the way to the scene of
the tragedy. While you are doing it I will put a few 'Headland' questions to our friend here if you don't mind assur-
ing him that I am competent to advise."

"Right you are, old chap," said Narkom, taking his cue.
"Nippers, this is Mr. George Headland, one of the best of
my Yard detectives. He'll very likely give you a tip or two in
the matter of detecting crimes, if you pay attention to what
he says."

Nippers "paid attention" forthwith. The idea of being
in consultation with any one connected with Scotland Yard
tickled his very soul; and, in fancy, he already saw his name
getting into the newspapers of London, and his fame spread-
ing far beyond his native weald.

"I won't trouble you for the full details of the murder,
Mr. Nippers," said Cleek. "Those, I fancy, this Miss Renfrew will be able to supply when I see her. For the present, tell me: how many other occupants does the house hold
beyond these two of whom you have spoken — Miss Renfrew and the cook, Mrs. Armroyd?"

"None, sir, but the scullery maid, Emily, and the parlour maid, Clark. But both of them is out to-night, sir —
havin' went to a concert over at Beattie Corners. A friend
of Mistress Armroyd's sent her two tickets, and her not
bein' able to go herself, her thought it a pity for 'em to be
wasted, so her give 'em to the maids."

"I see, no male servants at all, then?"

"No, sir; not one. There's Jones — the handy man — as

comes in mornin's to do the rough work and the haulin'
and carryin' and things like that; and there's the gardener
and Mr. Kemper — him as is Mr. Nosworth's assistant
in the laboratory, sir — but none of 'em is ever in the house
after five o'clock. Set against havin' men sleep in the house
was Mr. Nosworth — swore as never another should after
him and Master Harry had their fallin' out. Why, sir, he
was that bitter he'd never even allow Mr. Charles to set
foot in the place, just because him and Master Harry used
to be friends — which makes it precious hard on Miss Renfrew, I can tell you."

"As how? Is this 'Mr. Charles' connected with Miss
Renfrew in any way?"

"Lummy! yes, sir — he's her young man. Been sweet on
each other ever since they was in pinafores; but never had
no chance to marry because Mr. Charles — Mr. Charles
Drummond is his full name, sir — he hasn't one shillin'
to rub against another, and Miss Renfrew she's a little
worse off than him. Never gets nothin', I'm told, for
keepin' house for her uncle — just her food and lodgin' and
clothes — and her slavin' like a nigger for him the whole
blessed time. Keeps his books and superintends the runnin'
of the house, she do, but never gets a brass farthin' for it,
poor girl. I don't like to speak ill of the dead, Mr. Headland, sir, but this I must say: A rare old skinflint was Mr.
Septimus Nosworth — wouldn't part with a groat unless
un was forced to. But praise be, her'll get her dues now;
fegs, yes! unless old skinflint went and changed his will
without her knowin'."

"Oho!" said Cleek, with a strong rising inflection. "His
will was made in Miss Renfrew's favour, was it?"

"Aye. That's why her come and put up with un and all
his hardheartedness — denyin' her the pleasure o' ever
seein' her young man just because him and Master Harry
had been friends and playmates when t' pair of un was just

boys in knickers and broad collars. There be a stone heart for you."

"Rather. Now one more question: I think you said it was Miss Renfrew who gave the alarm when the murder was discovered, Mr. Nippers. How did she give it and to whom?"

"Eh, now! to me and Mistress Armroyd, of course. Me and her war sittin' in the kitchen havin' a bite o' supper at the time. Gorham, he war there, too, in the beginnin'; but un didn't stop, of course — 'twouldn't 'a' done for the pair of us to be off duty together."

"Oh! is Gorham a constable, then?"

"Aye — under constable: second to me. Got un appointed six months ago. Him had just gone a bit of a time when Miss Renfrew come rushin' in and shrieked out about the murder; but he heard the rumpus and came poundin' back, of course. I dunno what I'd 'a' done if un hadn't, for Miss Renfrew her went from one faintin' fit to another — 'twas just orful. Gorham helped Ah to carry her up to the sittin'-room, wheer Mistress Armroyd burnt feathers under her nose, and when we'd got her round a bit we all three went outside and round to the laboratory. That's when we first see the prints of the animal's feet. Mistress Armroyd spied 'em first — all over the flower bed just under the laboratory window."

"Oho! then that is what you meant when you alluded to an 'animal' when you pounced down upon us, was it? I see. One word more: what kind of an animal was it? Or couldn't you tell from the marks?"

"No, sir, I couldn't — nobody could unless it might be Sir Ralph Droger. He'll be like to, if anybody. Keeps all sorts of animals and birds and things in great cages in Droger Park, does Sir Ralph. One thing I can swear to, though, sir: they warn't like the footprints of any animal as I ever see. Theer be a picture o' St. Jarge and the Dragon

on the walls o' Town Hall at Birchampton, Mr. Headland, sir, and them footprints is more like the paws of that
dragon than anything else I can call to mind. Scaly and
clawed they is — like the thing as made 'em was part bird
and part beast — and they're a good twelve inches long,
every one of 'em."

"Hum-m-m! That's extraordinary. Deeply imprinted,
are they?"

"Lummy! yes, sir. The animal as made 'em must have
weighed ten or twelve stone at least. Soon as I see them,
sir, I knowed I had my work cut out, so I left Gorham in
charge of the house, rattled up these two men and Mr. Simpkins, here — which all three is employed at Droger Park,
sir — and set out hot foot to look for gypsies."

"Why?"

"'Cause Mistress Armroyd she says as she see a gypsy
lurkin' round the place just before dark, sir; and he had a
queer thing like a bear's muzzle in his hand."

"Ah, I see!" said Cleek; and gave one of his odd smiles
as he turned round and looked at the superintendent. "All
ready, Mr. Narkom? Good! Let us go over to the Round
House and investigate this interesting case. Dollops, stop
where you are and look after the caravan. If we are away
more than a couple of hours, tumble into bed and go to
sleep. We may be a short time or we may be a long one.
In affairs like this one never knows."

"Any ideas, old chap?" queried Narkom in a whisper as
they forged along together in the wake of Nippers and his
three companions.

"Yes — a great many," answered Cleek. "I am particularly anxious, Mr. Narkom, to have a look at those footprints and an interview with Miss Renfrew. I want to
meet that young lady very much indeed."

CHAPTER VIII

TWENTY minutes later his desires in that respect were granted; and, having been introduced by Mr. Nippers to the little gathering in the sitting-room of the house of disaster as "a friend of mine from Scotland Yard, miss," he found himself in the presence of one of those meek-faced, dove-eyed, "mousy" little bodies who seem born to be "patient Griseldas"; and in looking at her he was minded of the description of "Lady Jane" in the poem:

> "Her pulse was slow, milk white her skin —
> She had not blood enough to sin."

Years of repression had told upon her, and she looked older than she really was — so old and so dragged out, in fact, that Mrs. Armroyd, the cook, appeared youthful and attractive in contrast. Indeed, it was no wonder that Mr. Ephraim Nippers had been attracted by that good soul; for, although her hair was streaked with gray, and her figure was of the "sack of flour" order, and her eyes were assisted in their offices by a pair of steel-bowed spectacles, her face was still youthful in contour, and Mr. Narkom, looking at her, concluded that at twenty-four or twenty-five she must have been a remarkably pretty and remarkably fascinating woman. What Cleek's thoughts were upon that subject it is impossible to record; for he merely gave her one look on coming into the room, and then took no further notice of her whatsoever.

"Indeed, Mr. Headland, I am glad — I am very, very

glad — that fortune has sent you into this neighbourhood at this terrible time," said Miss Renfrew when Cleek was introduced. "I do not wish to say anything disparaging of Mr. Nippers, but you can see for yourself how unfitted such men as he and his assistant are to handle an affair of this importance. Indeed, I cannot rid my mind of the thought that if more competent police were on duty here the murder would not have happened. In short, that the assassin, whoever he may be, counted upon the blundering methods of these men as his passport to safety."

"My own thought precisely," said Cleek. "Mr. Nippers has given me a brief outline of the affair — would you mind giving me the full details, Miss Renfrew? At what hour did Mr. Nosworth go into his laboratory? Or don't you know, exactly?"

"Yes, I know to the fraction of a moment, Mr. Headland. I was looking at my watch at the time. It was exactly eight minutes past seven. We had been going over the monthly accounts together, when he suddenly got up, and without a word walked through that door over there. It leads to a covered passage connecting the house proper with the laboratory. That, as you may have heard, is a circular building with a castellated top. It was built wholly and solely for the carrying on of his experiments. There is but one floor and one window — a very small one about six feet from the ground, and on the side of the Round House which looks away from this building. Nothing but the door to that is on this side, light being supplied to the interior by a roof made entirely of heavy corrugated glass."

"I see. Then the place is like a huge tube."

"Exactly — and lined entirely with chilled steel. Such few wooden appliances as are necessary for the equipment of the place are thickly coated with asbestos. I made no comment when my uncle rose and walked in there without a word. I never did. For the past six or seven months he had been absorbed in working out the details of a new invention; and I had become used to his jumping up like that and leaving me. We never have supper in this house — my uncle always called it a useless extravagance. Instead, we defer tea until six o'clock and make that the final meal of the day. It was exactly five minutes to seven when I finished my accounts, and as I had had a hard day of it, I decided to go to bed early, after having first taken a walk as far as the old bridge where I hoped that somebody would be waiting for me."

"I know," said Cleek, gently. "I have heard the story. It would be Mr. Charles Drummond, would it not?"

"Yes. He was not there, however. Something must have prevented his coming."

"Hum-m-m! Go on, please."

"Before leaving the house, it occurred to me that I ought to look into the laboratory and see if there was anything my uncle would be likely to need for the night, as I intended to go straightway to bed on my return. I did so. He was sitting at his desk, immediately under the one window of which I have spoken, and with his back to me, when I looked in. He answered my inquiry with a curt 'No — nothing. Get out and don't worry me!' I immediately shut the door and left him, returning here by way of the covered passage and going upstairs to make some necessary changes in my dress for the walk to the old bridge. When I came down, ready for my journey, I looked at the clock on the mantel over there. It was exactly seventeen minutes to eight o'clock. I had been a little longer in dressing than I had anticipated being; so, in order to save time in getting to the trysting place, I concluded to make a short cut by going out of the rear door and crossing diagonally through our grounds instead of going by the public highway as usual. I had scarcely more than crossed the threshold when I ran plump into Constable Gorham. As he is rather a favourite with good Mrs. Armroyd here, I fancied that he had been paying her a visit, and was just coming away from the kitchen. Instead, he rather startled me by stating that he had seen something which he thought best to come round and investigate. In short, that, as he was patrolling the highway, he had seen a man vault over the wall of our grounds and, bending down, dart out of sight like a hare. He was almost positive that that man was Sir Ralph Droger Of course that frightened me almost out of my wits."

"Why?"

"There was bad blood between my uncle and Sir Ralph Droger — bitter, bad blood. As you perhaps know, my uncle held this ground on a life lease from the Droger estate. That is to say, so long as he lived or refused to vacate that lease, no Droger could oust him nor yet lift one spadeful of earth from the property."

"Does Sir Ralph desire to do either?"

"He desires to do both. Borings secretly made have manifested the fact that both Barnsley thick-coal and iron ore underlie the place. Sir Ralph wishes to tear down the Round House and this building and to begin mining operations. My uncle, who has been offered the full value of every stick and stone, has always obstinately refused to budge one inch or to lessen the lease by one half hour. 'It is for the term of my life,' he has always said, 'and for the term of my life I'll hold it!'"

"Oho!" said Cleek; and then puckered up his lips as if about to whistle.

"Under such circumstances," went on Miss Renfrew, "it was only natural that I should be horribly frightened, and only too willing to act upon the constable's suggestion that we at once look into the Round House and see if everything was right with my uncle."

"Why should the constable suggest that?"

"Everybody in the neighbourhood knows of the bitter

ill feeling existing between the two men; so, of course, it was only natural."

"Hum-m-m! Yes! Just so. Did you act on Constable Gorham's suggestion, then?"

"Yes. I led the way in here and then up the covered passage to the laboratory and opened the door. My uncle was sitting exactly as he had been when I looked in before — his back to me and his face to the window — but although he did not turn, it was evident that he was annoyed by my disturbing him, for he growled angrily, 'What the devil are you coming in here and disturbing me like this for, Jane? Get out and leave me alone.'"

"Hum-m-m!" said Cleek, drawing down his brows and pinching his chin. "Any mirrors in the Round House?"

"Mirrors? No, certainly not, Mr. Headland. Why?"

"Nothing — only that I was wondering, if as you say, he never turned and you never spoke, how in the world he knew that it really *was* you, that's all."

"Oh, I see what you mean," said Miss Renfrew, knotting up her brows. "It does seem a little peculiar when one looks at it in that way. I never thought of it before. Neither can I explain it, Mr. Headland, any more than to say that I suppose he took it for granted. And, as it happened, he was right. Besides, as you will remember, I had intruded upon him only a short time before."

"Quite so," said Cleek. "That's what makes it appear stranger than ever. Under the circumstances one might have expected him to say *not* 'What are you coming in here for,' but, 'What are you coming in for *again*.' Still, of course, there's no accounting for little lapses like that. Go on, please — what next?"

"Why, of course I immediately explained what Constable Gorham had said, and why I had looked in. To which he replied, 'The man's an ass. Get out!' Upon which I closed the door, and the constable and I went away at once."

"Constable there with you during it all, then?"

"Yes, certainly — in the covered passage, just behind me. He saw and heard everything; though, of course, neither of us actually entered the laboratory itself. There was really no necessity when we knew that my uncle was safe and sound, you see."

"Quite so," agreed Cleek. "So you shut the door and went away — and then what?"

"Constable Gorham went back to his beat, and I flew as fast as I could to meet Mr. Drummond. It is only a short way to the old bridge at best, and by taking that short cut through the grounds, I was there in less than ten minutes. And by half-past eight I was back here in a greater state of terror than before."

"And why? Were you so much alarmed that Mr. Drummond did not keep the appointment?"

"No. That did not worry me at all. He is often unable to keep his appointments with me. He is filling the post of private secretary to a large company promoter, and his time is not his own. What terrified me was that, after waiting a few minutes for him, I heard somebody running along the road, and a few moments later Sir Ralph Droger flew by me as if he were being pursued. Under ordinary circumstances I should have thought that he was getting into training for the autumn sports (he is, you may know, very keen on athletics, and holds the County Club's cup for running and jumping), but when I remembered what Constable Gorham had said, and saw that Sir Ralph was coming from the direction of this house, all my wits flew; I got into a sort of panic and almost collapsed with fright."

"And all because the man was coming from the direction of this house?"

"Not that alone," she answered with a shudder. "I have said that I should under ordinary circumstances have thought he was merely training for the autumn sports —

for, you see, he was in a running costume of white cotton
stuff and his legs were bare from the knee down — but as
he shot past me in the moonlight I caught sight of something
like a huge splash of blood on his clothes, and coupling that
with the rest I nearly went out of my senses. It wasn't
until long afterward I recollected that the badge of the
County Club is the winged foot of Mercury wrought in
brilliant scarlet embroidery. To me, just then, that thing
of red was blood — my uncle's blood — and I ran and ran
and ran until I got back here to the house and flew up the
covered passage and burst into the Round House. He was
sitting there still — just as he had been sitting before. But
he didn't call out to me this time; he didn't reprove me for
disturbing him; didn't make one single movement, utter
one single sound. And when I went to him I knew why.
He was dead — stone dead! The face and throat of him
were torn and rent as if some furious animal had mauled
him, and there were curious yellow stains upon his clothes.
That's all, Mr. Headland. I don't know what I did nor
where I went from the moment I rushed shrieking from that
room until I came to my senses and found myself in this
one with dear, kind Mrs. Armroyd here bending over me and
doing all in her power to soothe and to comfort me."

"There, there, cherie, you shall not more distress yourself. It is of a hardness too great for the poor mind to
bear," put in Mrs. Armroyd herself at this, bending over
the sofa as she spoke and softly smoothing the girl's hair.
"It is better she should be at peace for a little, is it not,
monsieur?"

"Very much better, madame," replied Cleek, noting how
softly her hand fell, and how gracefully it moved over the
soft hair and across the white forehead. "No doubt the
major part of what still remains to be told, you in the goodness of your heart, will supply ——"

"Of a certainty, monsieur, of a certainty."

"— But for the present," continued Cleek, finishing the interrupted sentence, "there still remains a question or two which must be asked, and which only Miss Renfrew herself can answer. As those are of a private and purely personal nature, madame, would it be asking too much ——" He gave his shoulders an eloquent Frenchified shrug, looked up at her after the manner of her own countrymen, and let the rest of the sentence go by default.

"Madame" looked at him and gave her little hands an airy and a graceful flirt.

"Of a certainty, monsieur," she said, with charming grace. "*Cela m'est egal*," and walked away with a step remarkably light and remarkably graceful for one of such weight and generous dimensions.

"Miss Renfrew," said Cleek, sinking his voice and look-ing her straight in the eyes, as soon as Mrs. Armroyd had left them, "Miss Renfrew, tell me something please: Have you any suspicion regarding the identity or the purpose of the person who murdered your uncle?"

"Not in the slightest, Mr. Headland. Of course, in the beginning, my thoughts flew at once to Sir Ralph Droger, but I now see how absurd it is to think that such as he ——"

"I am not even hinting at Sir Ralph Droger," interposed Cleek. "Two other people in the world have a 'motive' quite as strong as any that might be assigned to him. You, of course, feel every confidence in the honour and integrity of Mr. Charles Drummond?"

"Mr. Headland!"

"Gently, gently, please! I merely wished to know if in your heart you had any secret doubt; and your flaring up like that has answered me. You see, one has to remember that the late Mr. Nosworth is said to have made a will in your favour. The statement is correct, is it not?"

"To the best of my belief — yes."

"Filed it with his solicitors, did he?"

"That I can't say. I think not, however. He was always sufficient unto himself, and had a rooted objection to trusting anything of value to the care of any man living. Even his most important documents — plans and formulas of his various inventions, even the very lease of this property — have always been kept in the desk in the laboratory."

"Hum-m-m!" said Cleek, and pinched his chin hard. Then, after a moment. "One last question," he went on suddenly. "What do you know, Miss Renfrew, of the recent movements of Mr. Harry Nosworth — the son who was kicked out?"

"Nothing, absolutely nothing!" she answered, with a look of something akin to horror. "I know what you are thinking of, but although he is as bad as man can be, it is abominable to suppose that he would lift his hand against his own father."

"Hum-m-m! Yes, of course! But still, it has been known to happen; and, as you say, he was a bad lot. I ran foul of the young gentleman once when —— No matter; it doesn't signify. So you don't know anything about him, eh?"

"Nothing, thank God. The last I did hear, he had gone on the stage and taken up with some horrible creature, and the pair of them were subsequently sent to prison for enticing people to dreadful places and then drugging and robbing them. But even that I heard from an outside source; for my uncle never so much as mentioned him. No, I know nothing of him — nothing at all. In fact, I've never seen him since he was a boy. He never lived here, you know; and until I came here, I knew next to nothing of my uncle himself. We were poor and lived in a quite different town, my mother and I. Uncle Septimus never came to see us while my mother lived. He came for the first time when she was dead and his son had gone away: and I was so poor and so friendless I was glad to accept the home he offered. No, Mr. Headland, I know nothing of Harry Nosworth. I hope, for his own sake, he is dead."

Cleek made no reply. He sat for a minute pinching his chin and staring at the carpet, then he got up suddenly and faced round in the direction of the little group at the far end of the room.

"That's all for the present," he said. "Mr. Narkom, Mr. Nippers — get a light of some sort, please, and let's go out and have a look at those footprints."

CHAPTER IX

THE suggestion was acted upon immediately — even Mrs. Armroyd joining in the descent upon the portable lamps and filing out with the rest into the gloom and loneliness of the grounds; and Miss Renfrew, finding that she was likely to be left alone in this house of horrors, rose quickly and hurried out with them.

One step beyond the threshold brought them within sight of the famous Round House. Bulked against the pale silver of the moonlit sky, there it stood — a grim, unlovely thing of stone and steel with a trampled flower bed encircling the base of it, and a man on guard — Constable Gorham.

"Lummy! I'd clean forgot *him!*" exclaimed Mr. Nippers as he caught sight of him. "And theer un be keepin' guard, like I told un, out here in the grounds whiles weem ben talkin' comfortable inside. 'E do be a chap for doin' as heem tole, that Gorham —indeed, yes!"

Nobody replied to him. All were busily engaged in following the lead of Scotland Yard, as represented by Cleek and Superintendent Narkom, and bearing down on that huge stone tube within whose circular walls a dead man sat alone.

"Dreary post this, Constable," said Cleek, coming abreast of the silent guard.

"Yes, sir, very. But dooty's dooty—and there you be!" replied Gorham, touching his helmet with his finger; then, as the light from the lamps fell full upon Cleek's face and let him see that it was no face he had ever seen in this district before, his eyes widened with a puzzled stare which never quite left them even when the entire group had passed on and turned the curve of the Round House wall.

And beyond that curve Cleek came to a sudden halt. Here, a curtainless window cut a square of light in the wall's dark face and struck a glare on the trunk and the boughs of a lime tree directly opposite, and under that window a trampled flower bed lay, with curious marks deep sunk in the soft, moist surface of it.

Cleek took the lamp from Mrs. Armroyd's hand, and, bending, looked at them closely. Mr. Nippers had not exaggerated when he said that they were all of twelve inches in length. Nor was he far out when he declared that they looked like the footprints of some creature that was part animal and part bird; for there they were, with three huge-clawlike projections in front and a solitary one behind, and so like to the mark which a gigantic bird could have made that one might have said such a creature *had* made them, only that it was impossible for anything to fly that was possessed of weight sufficient to drive those huge footprints so deeply into the earth as they had been driven, by the mere walking of the Thing. Claws and the marks of scales, Mr. Nippers had asserted; and claws and the marks of scales the prints in the soft earth showed.

"La! la! the horror of them," exclaimed Mrs. Armroyd, putting up her little hands and averting her face. "It could kill and kill and kill — horses, oxen, anything — an abominable creature like that! What do you figure it to have been, monsieur? — souls of the saints, *what?*"

"Blest if I know," said Cleek. "Only, of course, it couldn't possibly be anything human; so we may put the idea of the old chap having been killed by anything of his kind out of our minds altogether. It is perfectly clear that the creature, whatever it might be, got in through the window there (you see it is open) and killed him before he could call out for help or strike a blow in his own defence."

"Eh, but window's six foot up, Mr. Headland, sir," put in Nippers excitedly; "and howm a thing the weight o' that goin' to fly in?"

"Didn't fly in, my friend," replied Cleek with an air of lofty superiority. "Use your wits, man. It *jumped* in — from the tree there. Look here — see!" going to it and tapping certain abrasions upon the trunk. "Here's where it peeled off the bark in climbing up. Lord, man! why, it's plain as the nose on your face. Ten to one we shall find the same sort of footprints when we go into the laboratory — damp ones, you know, from the moisture of the earth; and to make sure, in case we do find 'em let's take the length of the things and see. Got a tape measure with you? No? Oh, well, lend me your handcuffs, if you've got a pair with you, and we can manage a measurement with those. Thanks very much. Now, then, let's see. One, two, three, by Jupiter — three fingers longer than these things, chain and all. That'll do. Now, then, let's go in and see about the others. Lead the way, Miss Renfrew, if you will."

She would, and did. Leading the way back to the covered passage, she opened a door in the side of it — a door designed to let the inventor out into the grounds without going through the house, if he so desired — and conducted them to the laboratory, leaving Constable Gorham to continue his dreary sentry duty outside.

At any time the interior of that huge, stone-walled, steel-lined tube must have been unlovely and depressing to all but the man who laboured in it. But to-night, with that man sitting dead in it, with his face to the open window, a lamp beside him, and stiff hands resting on the pages of a book that lay open on the desk's flat top, it was doubly so; for, added to its other unpleasant qualities, there was now a disagreeable odour and a curious, eye-smarting, throat-roughening heaviness in the atmosphere which was like to nothing so much as the fumes thrown off by burnt chemicals.

Cleek gave one or two sniffs at the air as he entered, glanced at Mr. Narkom, then walked straightway to the desk and looked into the dead man's face. Under the marks of the scratches and cuts upon it — marks which would seem to carry out the idea of an animal's attack — the features were distorted and discoloured, and the hair of beard and moustache was curiously crinkled and discoloured.

Cleek stopped dead short as he saw that face, and his swaggering, flippant, cocksure air of a minute before dropped from him like a discarded mantle.

"Hullo! this doesn't look quite so promising for the animal theory as it did!" he flung out sharply. "This man has been shot — shot with a shell filled with his own soundless and annihilating devil's invention, lithamite — and bomb throwing is *not* a trick of beasts of a lower order than the animal tribe! Look here, Mr. Narkom — see! The lock of the desk has been broken. Shut the door there, Nippers. Let nobody leave the room. There has been murder and robbery here; and the thing that climbed that tree was not an animal nor yet a bird. It was a cutthroat and a thief!"

Naturally enough, this statement produced something in the nature of a panic; Miss Renfrew, indeed, appearing to be on the verge of fainting, and it is not at all unlikely that she would have slipped to the floor but for the close proximity of Mrs. Armroyd.

"That's right, madame. Get a chair; put her into it. She will need all her strength presently, I promise you. Wait a bit! Better have a doctor, I fancy, and an inquiry into the whereabouts of Mr. Charles Drummond. Mr. Narkom, cut out, will you, and wire this message to that young man's employer."

Pens and papers were on the dead man's desk. Cleek bent over, scratched off some hurried lines, and passed them to the superintendent.

"Sharp's the word, please; we've got ugly business on hand and we must know about that Drummond chap without delay. Miss Renfrew has not been telling the truth to-night! Look at this man. *Rigor mortis* pronounced. Feel him — muscles like iron, flesh like ice! *She* says that he spoke to her at a quarter to eight o'clock. *I* tell you that at a quarter to eight this man had been dead upward of an hour!"

"Good God!" exclaimed Mr. Narkom; but his cry was cut into by a wilder one from Miss Renfrew.

"Oh, no! Oh, no!" she protested, starting up from her seat, only to drop back into it, strengthless, shaking, ghastly pale. "It could not be — it could not. I have told the truth — nothing but the truth. He did speak to me at a quarter to eight — he did, he did! Constable Gorham was there — he heard him; he will tell you the same."

"Yes, yes, I know you said so, but — will he? He looks a sturdy, straightgoing, honest sort of chap who couldn't be coaxed or bribed into backing up a lie; so send him in as you go out, Mr. Narkom; we'll see what he has to say."

What he had to say when he came in a few moments later was what Miss Renfrew had declared — an exact corroboration of her statement. He *had* seen a man whom he fancied was Sir Ralph Droger run out of the grounds, and he had suggested to Miss Renfrew that they had better look into the Round House and see if all was right with Mr. Nosworth. They had looked in as she had said; and Mr. Nosworth had called out and asked her what the devil she was coming in and disturbing him for, and it was a quarter to eight o'clock exactly.

"Sure about that, are you?" questioned Cleek.

"Yes, sir, sure as that I'm telling you so this minute."

"How do you fix the exact time?"

"As we came out of the covered passage Miss Renfrew looked at her wrist-watch and says, impatient like, 'There, I've lost another two minutes and am that much later for nothing. See! It's a quarter to eight. Good night.' Then she cut off over the grounds and leaves me."

"La! la!" exclaimed Mrs. Armroyd approvingly. "There's the brave heart, to come to mademoiselle's rescue so gallantly. But, yes, I make you the cake of plums for that, *mon cher*. Monsieur of the yard of Scotland, he can no more torture the poor stricken child after that—not he."

But Cleek appeared to be less easy to convince that she had hoped, for he pursued the subject still; questioning Gorham to needless length it seemed; trying his best to trip him up, to shake his statement, but always failing; and, indeed, going over the same ground to such length that one might have thought he was endeavouring to gain time. If he was, he certainly succeeded; for it was quite fifteen minutes later when Mr. Narkom returned to the Round House, and he was at it still. Indeed, he did not conclude to give it up as a bad job until the superintendent came.

"Get it off all right, did you, Mr. Narkom?" he asked, glancing round as he heard him enter.

"Quite all right, old chap. Right as rain — in every particular."

"Thanks very much. I'm having rather a difficult task of it, for our friend the constable here corroborates Miss Renfrew's statement to the hair; and yet I am absolutely positive that there is a mistake."

"There is no mistake — no, not one! The wicked one to say it still!"

"Oh, that's all very well, madame, but I know what I know; and when you tell me that a dead man can ask questions — Pah! The fact of the matter is the constable merely fancies he heard Mr. Nosworth speak. That's

where the mistake comes in. Now, look here! I once knew
of an exactly similar case and I'll tell you just how it happened. Let us suppose" — strolling leisurely forward —
"let us suppose that this space here is the covered passage,
and you, madame — step here a moment, please. Thanks
very much — and you are Miss Renfrew, and Gorham here
is himself, and standing beside her as he did then."

"Wasn't beside her, sir — at least not just exactly. A
bit behind her — like this."

"Oh, very well, then, that will do. Now, then. Here's
the passage and here are you, and I'll just show you how a
mistake could occur, and how it did occur, under precisely
similar circumstances. Once upon a time when I was in
Paris ———"

"In Paris, monsieur?"

"Yes, madame — this little thing I'm going to tell you
about happened there. You may or may not have heard
that a certain Frenchy dramatist wrote a play called *Chanticler* — or maybe you never heard of it? Didn't, eh?
Well, it's a play where all the characters are barnyard
creatures — dogs, poultry, birds and the like — and the
odd fancy of men and women dressing up like fowls took
such a hold on the public that before long there were Chanticler dances and Chanticler parties in all the houses, and
Chanticler 'turns' on at all the music halls, until wherever
one went for an evening's amusement one was pretty sure
to see somebody or another dressed up like a cock or a hen,
and running the thing to death. But that's another story,
and we'll pass over it. Now, it just so happened that one
night — when the craze for the thing was dying out and
barnyard dresses could be bought for a song — I strolled
into a little fourth-rate café at Montmarte and there saw
the only Chanticler dancer that I ever thought was worth
a sou. She was a pretty, dainty little thing — light as a
feather and graceful as a fairy. Alone, I think she might

have made her mark; but she was one of what in music-halldom they call 'a team.' Her partner was a man — bad dancer, an indifferent singer, but a really passable ventriloquist."

"A ventriloquist, monsieur — er — er!"

"Cleek, madame — name's Cleek, if you don't mind."

"Cleek! Oh, Lummy!" blurted out Mr. Nippers. But neither "madame" nor Constable Gorham said anything. They merely swung round and made a sudden bolt; and Cleek, making a bolt, too, pounced down on them like a leaping cat, and the sharp click-click of the handcuffs he had borrowed from Mr. Nippers told just when he linked their two wrists together.

"Game's up, Madame Fifine, otherwise Madame Nosworth, the worthless wife of a worthless husband!" he rapped out sharply. "Game's up, Mr. Henry Nosworth, bandit, pickpocket, and murderer! There's a hot corner in hell waiting for the brute-beast that could kill his own father, and would, for the simple sake of money. Get at him, quick, Mr. Narkom. He's got one free hand! Nip the paper out of his pocket before the brute destroys it! Played, sir, played! Buck up, Miss Renfrew, buck up, little girl — you'll get your 'Boy' and you'll get Mr. Septimus Nosworth's promised fortune after all! 'God's in his heaven, and all's right with the world.'"

CHAPTER X

"YES, a very, very clever scheme indeed, Miss Renfrew," agreed Cleek. "Laid with great cunning and carried out with extreme carefulness — as witness the man's coming here and getting appointed constable and biding his time, and the woman serving as cook for six months to get the entrée to the house and to be ready to assist when the time of action came round. I don't think I had the least inkling of the truth until I entered this house and saw that woman. She had done her best to pad herself to an unwieldy size and to blanch portions of her hair, but she couldn't quite make her face appear old without betraying the fact that it was painted — and hers is one of those peculiarly pretty faces that one never forgets when one has ever seen it. I knew her the instant I entered the house; and, remembering the Chanticler dress with its fowl's-foot boots, I guessed at once what those marks would prove to be when I came to investigate them. She must have stamped on the ground with all her might, to sink the marks in so deeply — but she meant to make sure of the claws and the exaggerated scales on the toes leaving their imprint. I was certain we should find that dress and those boots among her effects; and — Mr. Narkom did. What I wrote on that pretended telegram was for him to slip away into the house proper and search every trunk and cupboard for them. Pardon? No, I don't think they really had any idea of incriminating Sir Ralph Droger. That thought came into the fellow's mind when you stepped out and caught him stealing away after the murder had been committed. No doubt he, like you, had seen Sir Ralph practising for the sports, and he simply made capital of it. The main idea was to kill his father and to destroy the will; and of course, when it became apparent that the old gentleman had died intestate, even a discarded son must inherit. Where he made his blunder, however, was in his haste to practise his ventriloquial accomplishment to prevent your going into the Round House and discovering that his father was already dead. He ought to have waited until you had spoken, so that it would appear natural for the old man to know, without turning, who it was that had opened the door. That is what put me on the track of him. Until that moment I hadn't the slightest suspicion where he was nor under what guise he was hiding. Of course I had a vague suspicion, even before I came and saw her, that 'the cook' was in it. Her readiness in inventing a fictitious gypsy with a bear's muzzle, coupled with what Nippers had told me of the animal marks she had pointed out, looked a bit fishy; but until I actually met her nothing really tangible began to take shape in my thoughts. That's all, I think. And now, good-night and good luck to you, Miss Renfrew. The riddle is solved; and Mr. Narkom and I must be getting back to the wilderness and to our ground-floor beds in the hotel of the beautiful stars!"

Here, as if some spirit of nervous unrest had suddenly beset him, he turned round on his heel, motioned the superintendent to follow, and brushing by the awed and staring Mr. Ephraim Nippers, whisked open the door and passed briskly out into the hush and darkness of the night.

The footpath which led through the grounds to the gate and thence to the long lonely way back to Dollops and the caravan lay before him. He swung into it with a curious sort of energy and forged away from the house at such speed that Narkom's short, fat legs were hard put to it to catch up with him before he came to the path's end.

"My dear chap, are you going into training for a match with that Sir Ralph What's-his-name of whom Miss Renfrew spoke?" he wheezed when he finally overtook him. "You long, lean beggars are the very old boy for covering the ground. But wait until you get to be *my* age, by James!"

"Perhaps I shan't. Perhaps they won't let me!" threw back Cleek, in a voice curiously blurred, as if he spoke with his teeth hard shut. "Donkeys do die, you know — that little bit of tommyrot about the absence of their dead bodies to the contrary."

"Meaning what, old chap?"

"That I've been as big an ass as any of the thistle-eating kind that ever walked. Gad! such an indiscretion! Such an example of pure brainlessness! And the worst of it is that it's all due to my own wretched vanity — my own miserable weakness for the theatrical and the spectacular! It came to me suddenly — while I was standing there explaining things to Miss Renfrew — and I could have kicked myself for my folly."

"Folly? What folly?"

" 'What folly?' What? Good heavens, man, use your wits! Isn't it enough for me to be a blockhead without you entering the lists along with me?" said Cleek, irritably. "Or, no! Forgive that, dear friend. My nerves were speaking, not my heart. But in moments like this — when we had built a safe bridge, and my own stupidity has hacked it down — Faugh! I tell you I could kick myself. Didn't you hear? Didn't you see?"

"I saw that for some special reason you were suddenly obsessed with a desire to get out of the house in the midst of your talking with Miss Renfrew, if that's what you refer to — is it?"

"Not altogether. It's part of it, however. But not the worst part, unfortunately. It was at that moment then the recollection of my indiscretion came to me and I realized what a dolt I had been — how completely I had destroyed our splendid security, wrecked what little still remains of this glorious holiday — when I couldn't let 'George Headland' have the centre of the stage, but needs must come in like the hero of a melodrama and announce myself as Cleek. To Nosworth and his wife! To Nippers! To all that gaping crowd! You remember that incident, surely?"

"Yes. Of course I do. But what of it?"

"What of it? Man alive, with a chap like that Nippers, how long do you suppose it will remain a secret that Cleek is in Yorkshire? In the West Riding of it? In this particular locality? Travelling about with Mr. Maverick Narkom in a caravan — a *caravan* that can't cover five miles of country in the time a train or a motor car is able to get over fifty!"

"Good lud! I never thought of that. But wait a bit. There's a way to overcome that difficulty, of course. Stop here a minute or two and I'll run back and pledge that Nippers fool to keep his mouth shut about it. He'll give me his promise, *I* know."

"To be sure he will. But how long do you suppose he will keep it? How long do you suppose that an empty-headed, gabbling old fool like that fellow will refrain from increasing his own importance in the neighbourhood by swaggering about and boasting of his intimacy with the powers at Scotland Yard and — the rest of it? And even if he shouldn't, what about the others? The gathering of rustics that heard what he heard? The gamekeepers from the Droger estate? The Nosworths, as well as they? Can their mouths, too, be shut? They will not love me for this night's business, be sure. Then, too, they have lived in Paris. The woman is French by birth. Of Montmartre — of the Apache class, the Apache kind — and she will know of the 'Cracksman,' be assured. So will her husband.

And they won't take their medicine lying down, believe me.
An accused man has the right to communicate with coun-
sel, remember; and a wire up to London will cost less than
a shilling. So, as between Margot's crew and our friend
Count Waldemar — *la, la!* There you are."

Mr. Narkom screwed up his face and said something
under his breath. He could not but follow this line of reasoning when the thing was put before him so plainly.

"And we had been so free from all worry over the beggars
up to this!" he said, savagely. "But to get a hint — to
pick up the scent — out here — in a wild bit of country like
this! Cinnamon, it makes me sweat! What do you pro-
pose to do?"

"The only thing that's left us to do," gave back Cleek.
"Get out of it as quickly as possible and draw a red herring
over the scent. In other words, put back to Dollops, aban-
don the caravan, make our way to some place where it is
possible to telephone for the chap we hired it from to send
out and get it; then, to make tracks for home."

"Yes, but why bother about telephoning, old chap? Why
can't we drop in ourselves and tell the man when we get
back to Sheffield on our way to London?"

"Because we are not going back to Sheffield, my friend —
not going in for anything so silly as twice travelling over
the same ground, if it's all the same to you," replied Cleek,
as he swung off from the highway on to the dark, still moor
and struck out for the place where they had left Dollops
and the caravan. "At best, we can't be more than thirty
miles from the boundary line of Cumberland. A night's
walking will cover that. There we can rest a while —
at some little out-of-the-way hostelry — then take a train
over the Scottish border and make for Dumfries. From
that point on, the game is easy. There are six trains a
day leaving for St. Pancras and eight for Euston. We can
choose which we like, and a seven hours' ride will land us in

London without having once 'doubled on our tracks' or crossed the route by which we came out of it."

"By James! what a ripping idea," said Mr. Narkom approvingly. "Come along then, old chap — let's get back to the boy and be about it as soon as possible." Then he threw open his coat and waistcoat to get the full benefit of the air before facing the ordeal, and, falling into step with Cleek, struck out over the moor at so brisk a dog trot that his short, fat legs seemed fairly to twinkle.

CHAPTER XI

BY THE side of the little chattering stream that flowed through the bit of woodland where Mr. Nippers and his associates had come upon them, they found Dollops, with his legs drawn up, his arms folded across his knees and his forehead resting upon them, sleeping serenely over the embers of a burnt-out fire. He was still "making music," but of a kind which needed no assistance from a mouth harmonica to produce it.

They awoke him and told him of the sudden change in the programme and of the need for haste in carrying it out.

"Oh, so help me! Them Apaches, eh? And that foreign josser, Count What's-his-name, too?" said he, rubbing his eyes and blinking sleepily. "Right you are, guv'ner! Gimme two seconds to get the cobwebs out of my thinking-box and I'm ready to face marching orders as soon as you like. My hat! though, but this *is* a startler. I can understand wot them Apache johnnies has got against you, sir, of course; but wot that Mauravanian biscuit is getting after you for beats me. Wot did you ever do to the blighter, guv'ner? Trip him up in some little bit of crooked business, sir, and 'did him down,' as the 'Mericans say?"

"Something like that," returned Cleek. "Don't waste time in talking. Simply get together such things as we shall need and let us be off about our business as soon as possible."

Dollops obeyed instructions upon both points — obeyed them, indeed, with such alacrity that he shut up like an oyster forthwith, dived into the caravan and bounced out

again, and within five minutes of the time he had been told
of the necessity for starting, had started, and was forging
away with the others over the dark, still moor and facing
cheerily the prospect of a thirty-mile walk to Cumberland-
shire.

All through the night they pressed onward thus — the
two men walking shoulder to shoulder and the boy at their
heels — over vast stretches of moorland where bracken and
grass hung heavy and glittering under their weight of dew;
down the craggy sides of steep gullies where the spring
freshets had quickened mere trickles into noisy water-
splashes that spewed over the rocks, to fall into chuckling,
froth-filled pools below; along twisting paths; through the
dark, still woodland stretches, and thence out upon the wild,
wet moor again, with the wind in their faces and the sky all
a-prickle with steadily dimming stars.   And by and by the
mist-wrapped moon dropped down out of sight, the worn-
out night dwindled and died, and steadily brightening Glory
went blushing up the east to flower the pathway for the
footfalls of the Morning.

But as yet the farthermost outposts of Cumberland were
miles beyond the range of vision, so that the long tramp
was by no means ended, and, feeling the necessity for covering as much ground as possible while the world at large was
still in what Dollops was wont to allude to as " the arms of
Murphy's house," the little party continued to press onward persistently.

By four o'clock they were again off the moors and in the
depths of craggy gorges; by five they were on the borders of
a deep, still tarn, and had called a halt to light a fire and get
things out of the bag which Dollops carried — things to eat
and to drink and to wear — and were enjoying a plunge in
the ice-cold water the while the coffee was boiling; and by
six — gorged with food and soothed by tobacco — they
were lying sprawled out on the fragrant earth and blinking

drowsily while their boots were drying before the fire. And after that there was a long hiatus until Cleek's voice rapped out saying sharply, "Well, I'll be dashed! Rouse up there, you lazy beggars. Do you know that it's half-past twelve and we've been sleeping for hours?"

They knew it then, be assured, and were up and on their way again with as little delay as possible. Rested and refreshed, they made such good time that two o'clock found them in the Morcam Abbey district, just over the borders of Cumberland, and, with appetites sharpened for luncheon, bearing down on a quaint little hostlery whose signboard announced it as the Rose and Thistle.

"Well, there's hospitality if you like," said Cleek, as, at their approach, a cheery-faced landlady bobbed up at an open window and, seeing them, bobbed away again and ran round to welcome them with smiles and curtseys delivered from the arch of a vine-bowered door.

"Welcome, gentlemen, welcome," beamed she as they came up and joined her. "But however in the world did you manage to get over here so soon? — the train not being due at Shepperton Old Cross until five-and-twenty past one, and that a good mile and a quarter away as the crow flies. However, better too early than too late — Major Norcross and Lady Mary being already here and most anxious to meet you."

As it happened that neither Cleek nor Mr. Narkom had any personal acquaintance with the lady and gentleman mentioned, it was so clearly a case of mistaken identity that the superintendent had it on the tip of his tongue to announce the fact, when there clashed out the sound of a door opening and shutting rapidly, a clatter of hasty footsteps along the passage, and presently there came into view the figure of a bluff, hearty, florid-faced man of about five-and-forty, who thrust the landlady aside and threw a metaphorical bombshell by exclaiming excitedly:

"My dear sir, I never was so delighted. Talk about English slowness. Why, this is prompt enough to satisfy a Yankee. I never dispatched my letter to you until late yesterday afternoon, Mr. Narkom, and — by the way, which *is* Mr. Narkom, and which that amazing Mr. Cleek? Or, never mind — perhaps that clever johnnie will be coming later; you can tell me all about that afterward. For the present, come along. Let's not keep Lady Mary waiting — she's anxious. This way, please."

Here — as Mr. Narkom had lost no time in acknowledging his identity, it being clear that no mistake had been made after all — here he caught the superintendent by the arm, whisked him down the passage, and throwing open the door at the end of it, announced excitedly, "All right, Mary. The Yard's answered — the big reward's caught 'em, as I knew it would — and here's Narkom. That chap Cleek will come by a later train, no doubt."

The response to this came from an unexpected quarter. Of a sudden the man he had left standing at the outer door, under the impression that he was in no way connected with the superintendent, but merely a gentleman who had reached the inn at the same time, came down the passage to the open door, brushed past him into the room, and announced gravely, "Permit me to correct an error, please, Major. The 'man Cleek' is not coming later — he is here, and very much at your and Lady Mary Norcross' service, believe me. I have long known the name of Major Seton Norcross as one which stands high in the racing world — as that, indeed, of the gentleman who owns the finest stud in the kingdom and whose filly, Highland Lassie, is first favourite for the forthcoming Derby — and I now have the honour of meeting the gentleman himself, it seems."

The effect of this was somewhat disconcerting. For, as he concluded it, he put out his hand and rested it upon Mr. Narkom's shoulder, whereat Lady Mary half rose from her seat, only to sit down again suddenly and look round at her liege lord with uplifted eyebrows and lips slightly parted. Afterward she declared of the two men standing side by side in that familiar manner: "One reminded me of an actor trying to play the part of a person of distinction, and the other of a person of distinction trying to play the part of an ordinary actor and not quite able to keep what he really was from showing through the veneer of what he was trying to be."

The major, however, was too blunt to bottle up his sentiments at any time, and being completely bowled over in the present instance put them into bluff, outspoken, characteristic words.

"Oh, gum games!" he blurted out. "If you really are Cleek ——"

"I really am. Mr. Narkom will stand sponsor for that."

"But, good lud, man! Oh, look here, you know, this is all tommyrot! What under God's heaven has brought a chap like you down to this sort of thing?"

"Opinions differ upon that score, Major," said Cleek quietly. "So far from being 'brought down,' it is my good friend, Mr. Narkom here, who has brought me *up* to it — and made me his debtor for life."

"Debtor nothing! Don't talk rubbish. As if it were possible for a gentleman not to recognize a gentleman!"

"It would not be so easy, I fear, if he were a good actor — and you have just done me the compliment of indirectly telling me that I must be one. It is very nice of you but — may we not let it go at that? I fancy from what I hear that I, too, shall soon be in the position to pay compliments, Major. I hear on every side that Highland Lassie is sure to carry off the Derby — in fact that, unless a miracle occurs, there'll be no horse 'in it' but her."

Here both the major and his wife grew visibly excited.

"Gad, sir!" exclaimed he, in a voice of deep despair. "I'm

afraid you will have to amend that statement so that it may read, 'unless a miracle occurs there will be *every* horse in it but her' — every blessed one from Dawson-Blake's Tarantula, the second favourite, down to the last 'also ran' of the lot."

"Good heavens! The filly hasn't 'gone wrong' suddenly, has she?"

"She's done more than 'gone wrong' — she's *gone altogether!* Some beastly, low-lived cur of a horse thief broke into the stables the night before last and stole her — stole her, sir, body and bones — and there's not so much as a hoofprint to tell what became of her."

"Well, I'm blest!"

"Are you? B'gad, then, you're about the only one who knows about it that is! For as if that wasn't bad enough, I've not only lost the best filly in England but the best trainer as well: and the brute that carried off the one got at the other at the same time, dash him!"

"What do you mean by 'got at' the trainer, Major? Did the man take a bribe and 'sell' you that way?"

"What, Tom Farrow? Never in God's world! Not that kind of a chap, by George! The man that offered Tom Farrow a bribe would spend the rest of the week in bed — gad, yes! A more faithful chap never drew the breath of life. God only knows when or how the thing happened, but Farrow was found on the moor yesterday morning — quite unconscious and at death's door. He had been bludgeoned in the most brutal manner imaginable. Not only was his right arm broken, but his skull was all but crushed in. There was concussion of the brain, of course. Poor fellow, he can't speak a word, and the chances are that he never will be able to do so again."

"Bad business, that," declared Cleek, looking grave. "Any idea of who may possibly have been the assailant? Local police picked up anything in the nature of a clue?"

"The local police know nothing whatsoever about it. I have not reported the case to them."

"Not reported —— H'm! rather unusual course, that, to pursue, isn't it? When a man has his place broken into, a valuable horse stolen, and his trainer all but murdered, one would naturally suppose that his first act would be to set the machinery of the law in motion without an instant's delay. That is, unless —— H'm! Yes! Just so."

"What is 'just so'?" inquired the major eagerly. "You seem to have hit upon some sort of an idea right at the start. Mind telling me what it is?"

"Certainly not. I could imagine that when a man keeps silent about such a thing at such a time there is a possibility that he has a faint idea of who the criminal may be and that he has excellent reasons for not wishing the world at large to share that idea. In other words, that he would sooner lose the value of the animal fifty times over than have the crime brought home to the person he suspects."

CHAPTER XII

LADY MARY made a faint moaning sound. The major's face was a study.

"I don't know whether you are a wizard or not, Mr. Cleek," he said, after a moment; "but you have certainly hit upon the facts of the matter. It is for that very reason that I have refrained from making the affair public. It is bad enough that Lady Mary and I should have our suspicions regarding the identity of the — er — person implicated without letting others share them. There's Dawson-Blake for one. If he knew, he'd move heaven and earth to ruin him."

"Dawson-Blake?" repeated Cleek. "Pardon, but will that be the particular Sir Gregory Dawson-Blake the millionaire brewer who achieved a knighthood in the last 'Honours List' and whose horse, Tarantula, is second favourite for the coming Derby?"

"Yes, the very man. He is almost what you might call a neighbour of ours, Mr. Cleek. His place, Castle Claverdale, is just over the border line of Northumberland and about five miles distant from Morcan Abbey. His stables are, if anything, superior to my own; and we both use the intervening moorland as a training ground. Also, it was Dawson-Blake's daughter that Lieutenant Chadwick played fast and loose with. Jilted her, you know — threw her over at the eleventh hour and married a chorus girl who had nothing to bless herself with but a pretty face and a long line of lodging-house ancestry. Not that Miss Dawson-Blake lost anything by getting rid of such a man before she committed the folly of tying herself to him for life, but her father never forgave Lieutenant Chadwick and would spend a million for the satisfaction of putting him behind bars."

"I see. And this Lieutenant Chadwick is — whom may I ask?"

"The only son of my elder and only sister, Mr. Cleek," supplied Lady Mary with a faint blush. "She committed the folly of marrying her music master when I was but a little girl, and my father died without ever looking at her again. Subsequently, her husband deserted her and went — she never learnt where, to the day of her death. While she lived, however, both my brother, Lord Chevelmere, and I saw that she never wanted for anything. We also supplied the means to put her son through Sandhurst after we had put him through college, and hoped that he would repay us by achieving honour and distinction. It was a vain hope. He achieved nothing but disgrace. Shortly after his deplorable marriage with the theatrical person for whom he threw over Miss Dawson-Blake — and who in turn threw him over when she discovered what a useless encumbrance he was — he was cashiered from the army, and has ever since been a hanger-on at race meetings — the consort of touts, billiard markers, card sharpers, and people of that sort. I had not seen him for six years, when he turned up suddenly in this neighbourhood three days ago and endeavoured to scrape acquaintance with one of the Abbey grooms."

"And under an assumed name, Mr. Cleek," supplemented the major somewhat excitedly. "He was calling himself John Clark and was trying to wheedle information regarding Highland Lassie out of my stable-boys. Fortunately, Lady Mary caught sight of him without being seen, and at once gave orders that he was to be turned off the premises, and never allowed to come near them again.

He was known, however, to be in this neighbourhood up to
dusk on the following evening, but he has never been seen
since Highland Lassie disappeared. You know now, perhaps, why I have elected to conduct everything connected
with this affair with the utmost secrecy. Little as we desire
to be in any way associated with such a man, we cannot but
remember that he is connected with us by ties of blood, and
unless Farrow dies of his injuries — which God forbid! we
will hush the thing up, cost what it may. All that I want
is to get the animal back — not to punish the man: if, indeed, he be the guilty party; for there is really no actual
proof of that. But if Dawson-Blake knew, it would be
different. He would move heaven and earth to get the
convict's 'broad arrow' on him and to bring disgrace upon
everybody connected with the man."

"H'm, I see!" said Cleek, puckering up his brows and
thoughtfully stroking his chin. "So that, naturally, there
is — with this added to the rivalry of the two horses — no
very good blood existing between Sir Gregory Dawson-
Blake and yourself?"

"No, there is not. If, apart from these things, Mr.
Cleek, you want my private opinion of the man, it can be
summed up in the word 'Bounder.' There is not one in-
stinct of the gentleman about him. He is simply a vulgar,
money-gilded, low-minded cad, and I wouldn't put it
beyond him to be mixed up in this disappearance of the filly
himself but that I know Chadwick was about the place; and
for there to be anything between Chadwick and him is as
impossible as it is for the two poles to come together, or for
oil to assimilate with water. That is the one thing in this
world that Dawson-Blake would not do under any circumstances whatsoever. Beyond that, I put nothing beneath
the man — nothing too despicable for him to attempt in the
effort to gain his own end and aim. He races not for the
sport of the thing, but for the publicity, the glory of

getting talked about, and of making the vulgar stare. He
wants the blue ribbon of the turf for the simple fame of
the thing; and he'd *buy* it if buying it were possible, and
either bribes or trickery could carry off the race."

"H'm! That's a sweeping assertion, Major."

"But made upon a basis of absolute fact, Mr. Cleek.
He has twice endeavoured to buy Farrow to desert me by
an offer of double wages and a pension; and, failing that,
only last week he offered my jockey £10,000 cash on the nail
to slip off over to France on the night before Derby Day,
and promised him a further five thousand if Tarantula
carried off the race."

"Oho!" said Cleek, in two different tones; and with a
look of supremest contempt. "So our Tinplate Knight is
that sort of a sportsman, is he, the cad? And having failed
to get hold of the *rider* —— H'm! Yes. It is possible
— perhaps. Chadwick's turning up at such a time might
be a mere coincidence — a mere tout's trick to get inside
information beforehand, or —— Well, you never can tell.
Suppose, Major, you give me the facts from the beginning.
When was the animal's loss discovered — and how? Let
me have the full particulars, please."

The major sighed and dropped heavily into a chair.

"For an affair of such far-reaching consequences, Mr.
Cleek," he said gloomily, "it is singularly bald of what
might be called details, I am afraid; and beyond what I
have already told you there is really very little more to tell.
When or how the deed was committed, it is impossible to
decide beyond the indefinite statement that it happened
the night before last, at some time after half-past nine in the
evening, when the stable-boy, Dewlish, before going home,
carried a pail of water at Farrow's request into the building
where Highland Lassie's stall is located, and five o'clock
the next morning when Captain MacTavish strolled into the
stables and found the mare missing."

"A moment, please. Who is Captain MacTavish? And why should the gentleman be strolling about the Abbey stable-yard at five o'clock in the morning?"

"Both questions can be answered in a few words. Captain MacTavish is a friend who is stopping with us. He is a somewhat famous naturalist. Writes articles and stories on bird and animal life for the magazines. It is his habit to be up and out hunting for 'specimens' and things of that sort every morning just about dawn. At five he always crosses the stable yard on his way to the dairy where he goes for a glass of fresh milk before breakfast."

"I see. Captain a young man or an old one?"

"Oh, young, of course. About two or three and thirty, I should say. Brother of a deceased army pal of mine. Been stopping with us for the past two months. Very brilliant and very handsome chap — universal favourite wherever he goes."

"Thanks. Now just one more question before you proceed, please: About the trainer Farrow getting the stable-boy to carry in that pail of water. Would not that be a trifle unusual at such a time of the night?"

"I don't know. Yes — perhaps it would. I never looked at it in that light before."

"Very likely not. Stables would be closed and all the grooms, et cetera, off duty for the night at that hour, would they not?"

"Yes. That is, unless Farrow had reason for asking one of them to help him with something. That's what he did, by the way, with the boy, Dewlish."

"Just so. Any idea what he wanted with that pail of water at that hour of the night? He couldn't be going to 'water' one of the horses, of course, and it is hardly likely that he intended to take on a stableman's duties and wash up the place."

"Oh, gravy — no! He's a trainer, not a slosh-bucket.

I pay him eighteen hundred a year and give him a cottage besides."

"Married man or a single one?"

"Single. A widower. About forty. Lost his wife two years ago. Rather thought he was going to take another one shortly, from the way things looked. But of late he and Maggie McFarland don't seem, for some reason or another, to be hitting it off together so well as they did."

"Who's Maggie McFarland, please?"

"One of the dairymaids. A little Scotch girl from Nairn who came into service at the Abbey about a twelvemonth ago."

"H'm! I see. Then the filly isn't the only 'Highland Lassie' in the case, it would seem. Pardon? Oh, nothing. Merely a weak attempt to say something smart, that's all. Don't suppose that Maggie McFarland could by any possibility throw light upon the subject of that pail of water, do you, Major?"

"Good lud, no! Of course she couldn't. What utter rot. But see here — come to think of it now, perhaps *I* can. It's as like as not that he wanted it to wash himself with before he went over to the shoer's at Shepperton Old Cross with Chocolate Maid. I forgot to tell you, Mr. Cleek, that ever since Dawson-Blake made that attempt to buy him off, Farrow became convinced that it wouldn't be safe to leave Highland Lassie unguarded night or day for fear of that cad's hirelings getting at her in some way or another, so he closed up his cottage and came to live in the rooms over the filly's stable, so as to be on the spot for whatever might or might not happen at any hour. He also bought a yapping little Scotch terrier that would bark if a match fell, and kept it chained up in the place with him. When the discovery of the filly's disappearance was made that dog was found still attached to its chain, but as dead as Maria Martin. It had been poisoned. There was a bit of meat lying beside the body and it was literally smothered in strychnine."

"Quite so. Keep strychnine about the place for killing rats, I suppose?"

"Yes, of course. They are a perfect pest about the granary and the fodder bins. But of course it wouldn't be lying round loose — a deadly thing like that. Besides, there never was any kept in that particular section of the stables, so the dog couldn't have got hold of it by accident. Then there's another thing I ought to tell you, Mr. Cleek: Highland Lassie never was stabled with the rest of the stud. We have always kept her in one especial stable. There are just two whacking big box stalls in the place. She occupies one and Chocolate Maid the other. Chocolate Maid is Lady Mary's personal property — a fine, blooded filly that will make a name for herself one of these days, I fancy. Dark-coated and smooth as a piece of sealskin, the beauty. To-day she is the only animal in that unlucky place. Yes, come to think of it, Mr. Cleek," he added with a sort of sigh, "that is probably what the poor fellow wanted the pail of water for: to wash up and ride her over to the forge at Shepperton Old Cross."

"Singular time to choose for such a proceeding, wasn't it, Major? After half-past nine o'clock at night."

"It would be if it were any other man and under any other circumstances. But remember! It is but three weeks to Derby Day and every hour of daylight is worth so much gold to us. Farrow knew that he could not spare a moment of it for any purpose; and he is most particular over the shoeing. Will see it done himself and direct the operation personally. Sort of mania with him. Wouldn't let the best man that ever lived take one of the horses over for him. Go himself, no matter what inconvenience it put him to. Farrier at Shepperton Old Cross knows his little 'fads and fancies' and humours them at all times. Would open the forge and fire up for him if it were two o'clock in the morning."

"I see. And did he take Chocolate Maid over there on that night, after all?"

"Yes. Lady Mary and I attended a whist drive at Farmingdale Priory that evening; but her ladyship was taken with a violent headache and we had to excuse ourselves and leave early. It would be about a quarter to eleven o'clock when we returned to the Abbey and met Farrow riding out through the gates on Chocolate Maid. We stopped and spoke to him. He was then going over to the shoer's with the mare."

"How long would it take him to make the journey?"

"Oh, about five-and-twenty minutes — maybe half an hour: certainly not more."

"So then it would be about quarter-past eleven when he arrived at the farrier's? I see. Any idea at what time he got back?"

"Not the ghost of one. In fact, we should never have known that he ever did get back — for nobody heard a sound of his return the whole night long — were it not that when Captain MacTavish crossed the stableyard at five o'clock in the morning and, seeing the door ajar, looked in, he found Chocolate Maid standing in her stall, the dog dead, and Highland Lassie gone. Of course, Chocolate Maid being there after we had passed Farrow on the road with her was proof that he did return at some hour of the night, you know: though when it was, or why he should have gone out again, heaven alone knows. Personally, you know, I am of the opinion that Highland Lassie was stolen while he was absent; that, on returning he discovered the robbery and, following the trail, went out after the robbers, and, coming up with them, got his terrible injuries that way."

"H'm! Yes! I don't think! What 'trail' was he to find, please, when you just now told me that there wasn't so much as a hoofprint to tell the tale? Or was that an error?"

"No, it wasn't. The entire stableyard is paved with red tiles, and we've had such an uncommon spell of dry weather lately that the earth of the surrounding country is baked as hard as a brickbat. An elephant couldn't make a foot-mark upon it, much less a horse. But, gravy, man! instead of making the thing clearer, I'm blest if you're not adding gloom to darkness, and rendering it more mysterious than ever. What under the four corners of heaven could Farrow have followed, then, if the 'trail' is to be eliminated entirely?"

"Maybe his own inclination, Major — maybe nothing at all," said Cleek, enigmatically. "If your little theory of his returning and finding Highland Lassie stolen were a thing that would hold water I am inclined to think that Mr. Tom Farrow would have raised an alarm that you could hear for half a mile, and that if he had started out after the robbers he would have done so with a goodly force of fol-lowers at his heels and with all the lanterns and torches that could be raked and scraped together."

"Good lud, yes! of course he would. I never thought of that. Did you, Mary? His whole heart and soul were bound up in the animal. If he had thought that anything had happened to her, if he had known that she was gone, a pitful of raging devils would have been spirits of meekness beside him. Man alive, you make my head whiz. For him to go off over the moor without word or cry at such a time —— I say, Mr. Cleek! For God's sake, what do you make of such a thing as that at such a time, eh?"

"Well, Major," replied Cleek, "I hate to destroy any man's illusions and to besmirch any man's reputation, but —*que voulez vous?* If Mr. Tom Farrow went out upon that moor after the mare was stolen, and went without giving an alarm or saying a word to anybody, then in my private opinion your precious trainer is nothing in the world but a precious double-faced, double-dealing, dishonourable blackguard, who treacherously sold you to the enemy and got • just what he deserved by way of payment."

Major Norcross made no reply. He simply screwed up his lips until they were a mere pucker of little creases, and looked round at his wife with something of the pain and hopeless bewilderment of an unjustly scolded child.

"You know, Seton, it was what Captain MacTavish sug-- gested," ventured she, gently and regretfully. "And when two men of intellect——" Then she sighed and let the rest go by default.

"Demmit, Mary, you don't mean to suggest that I haven't any, do you?"

"No, dear; but——"

"Buts be blowed! Don't you think I know a man when I run foul of him? And if ever there was a square-dealing, honest chap on this earth —— Look here, Mr. Cleek. Gad! you may be a bright chap and all that, but you'll have to give me something a blessed sight stronger than mere suspicion before you can make me believe a thing like that about Tom Farrow."

"I am not endeavouring to make you believe it, Major. I am merely showing you what would certainly be the absolute truth of the matter *if* Tom Farrow had done what you suggested, and gone out on that moor alone and without a word or a cry when he discovered that the animal was stolen. But, my dear sir, I incline to the belief that he never did go out there after any person or any living thing whatsoever."

"Then, dash it, sir, how in thunder are you going to explain his being there at all?"

"By the simple process, Major, of suggesting that he was on his way back to the Abbey at the time he encountered his unknown assailant. In other words, that he had not only never returned to the place after you and her ladyship saw him leaving it at a quarter to eleven, but was never permitted to do so."

"Oh, come, I say! That's laying it on too thick. How. the dickens can you be sure of such a thing as that?"

"I'm not. I am merely laying before you the only two things possible to explain his presence there. One or the other of them is the plain and absolute truth. If the man went out there *after* the filly was stolen he is a scoundrel and a liar. If he is innocent, he met with his injuries on the way back to his quarters above Highland Lassie's stall."

"But the other animal? But Chocolate Maid? How could she have got back to the stable, then? She couldn't have found her way back alone after Farrow was assaulted — at least, she could, of course, but not in the condition she was in when found next morning. She had no harness of any sort upon her. Her saddle was on its peg. She was in her box — tied up, b'gad! and the door of the box was closed and bolted; so that if by any chance —— Hullo! I say! What on earth are you smiling in that queer way for? Hang it, man! do you believe that I don't know what I'm talking about?"

"Oh, yes, Major. It isn't that kind of a smile. I have just discovered that four and four make eight when you add them up properly; and the smile is one of consequent satisfaction. A last question, please. At what time in the morning was Farrow found lying unconscious upon the moor?"

"Somewhere between six and seven o'clock. Why?"——

"Oh, nothing in particular. Who found him? Captain MacTavish?"

"No. Maggie McFarland. She was just coming back from milking when —— Hang it, man! I wish you wouldn't smile all up one side of your face in that confounded manner. It makes me think that you must have something up your sleeve."

"Well, if I have, Major, suppose you drive me over to the stables and give me a chance to take it out?" suggested Cleek, serenely. "A little 'poking about' sometimes does wonders, and a half hour in Highland Lassie's quarters may pick the puzzle to pieces a great deal sooner than you'd believe. Or, stop! Perhaps, on second thought, it will be better for you and her ladyship to go on ahead, as I shall want to have a look at Tom Farrow's injuries as well, so it will be best to have everything prepared in advance, in order to save time. No doubt Mr. Narkom and I can get a conveyance of some sort here. At any rate — h'm! it is now a quarter to three, I see — at any rate, you may certainly expect us at quarter-past five. You and her ladyship may go back quite openly, Major. There will be no need to attempt to throw dust in Sir Gregory Dawson-Blake's eyes any longer by keeping the disappearance of the animal a secret. If he's had a hand in her spiriting away, he knows, of course, that she's gone; but if he hasn't — oh, well, I fancy I know who did, and that she will be in the running on Derby Day after all. A few minutes in Highland Lassie's stable will settle that, I feel sure. Your ladyship, my compliments. Major, good afternoon. I hope if night overtakes us before we get at the bottom of the thing you can manage to put us up at the Abbey until to-morrow that we may be on the spot to the last?"

"With pleasure, Mr. Cleek," said Lady Mary; and bowed him out of the room.

CHAPTER XIII

IT WAS precisely ten minutes past five o'clock and the long-lingering May twilight was but just beginning to gather when the spring cart of the Rose and Thistle arrived at the Abbey stables, and Cleek and Mr. Narkom descending therefrom found themselves the centre of an interested group composed of the major and Lady Mary, the countryside doctor, and Captain MacTavish.

The captain, who had nothing Scottish about him but his name, was a smiling, debonnaire gentleman with flaxen hair and a curling, fair moustache; and Cleek, catching sight of him as he stood leaning, in a carefully studied pose, against the stable door-post with one foot crossed over the other, one hand in his trousers pocket and the other swinging a hunting crop whose crook was a greyhound's head wrought in solid silver, concluded that here was, perhaps, the handsomest man of his day, and that, in certain sections of society, he might be guaranteed to break hearts by the hundred. It must be said of him, however, that he carried his manifold charms of person with smooth serenity and perfect poise; that, if he realized his own beauty, he gave no outward evidences of it. He was calm, serene well-bred, and had nothing of the "Doll" or the "Johnny" element in either his bearing or his deportment. He was at once splendidly composed and almost insolently bland.

"Pleased to meet you, Mr. Cleek. Read a great deal about you one way and another," he said, when the major made the introduction — a performance which the captain evidently considered superfluous as between an army officer

131

and a police detective. "Sorry I shan't be able to remain and study your interesting methods, however. Should have been rather pleased to do so, otherwise."

"And I for my part should have been pleased to have you do so, Captain, I assure you," replied Cleek, the first intonation of his voice causing the captain to twitch up his head and stare at him as if he were a monstrosity. "Shall you be leaving us, then, before the investigation is concluded?"

"Well, I'm blest! Why, how in the world — oh — er — yes. Obliged to go. Wire from London this afternoon. Regiment sails for India in two days. Beastly nuisance. Shall miss the Derby and all that. By the way, Norcross, if this chap succeeds in finding the filly in time for the race, that little bet of ours stands, of course?"

"Of course," agreed the major. "Ready, are you, Mr. Cleek? Right you are — come along." And he forthwith led the way into the stable where Chocolate Maid, like a perfect horse in French bronze, stood munching hay in her box as contentedly as if there were no such things in the world as touts and swindlers and horse thieves, and her companion of two days ago still shared the quarters with her.

"Gad! but she's a beauty and no mistake, Major," said Cleek as he went over and, leaning across the low barrier of the enclosure, patted the mare's shoulder and smoothed her glossy neck. "I don't wonder that you and her ladyship have such high hopes for her future. The creature seems well-nigh perfect."

"Yes, she is a pretty good bit of horseflesh," replied he, "but not to be compared with Highland Lassie in speed, wind, or anything. There *she* is, Mr. Cleek; and it's as natural as life, the beauty!"

Speaking, he waved his hand toward a framed picture of the missing animal — a coloured gift plate which had been given away with the Easter number of *The Horseman*, and which Farrow had had glazed and hung just over her box.

Cleek, following the direction of the indicating hand, looked up and saw the counterfeit presentment of a splendidly proportioned sorrel with a splash of white on the flank and a white "stocking" on the left forefoot.

"A beauty, as you say, Major," agreed he, "but do you know that I, for my part, prefer the charms of Chocolate Maid? May be bad judgment upon my part but — there you are. What a coat! What a colour! What splendid legs, the beauty! Mind if I step in for a moment and have a look at her?"

The major did not, so he went in forthwith and proceeded to look over the animal's points — feeling her legs, stroking her flanks, examining her hoofs. And it was then and then only that the major remembered about the visit to the farrier's over at Shepperton Old Cross and began to understand that it was not all simple admiration of the animal, this close examination of her.

"Oh, by Jove! I say!" he blurted out as he made — with Cleek — a sudden discovery; his face going first red and then very pale under the emotions thus engendered. "She *hasn't* any new shoes on, has she? So she can't have been taken to the farrier's after all."

"No," said Cleek, "she can't. I half suspected that she hadn't, so — well, let it go. Let's have a look round Highland Lassie's box, please. H'm! Yes! Very nice; very splendid — everything of the best and all in apple pie order. By the way, Major, you surely don't allow harness to be washed and oiled in here?"

"Certainly not! What in the world could have put such an idea into your head?"

"Merely that bit of rag and that dirty sponge tucked in the corner over there and half covered by the bedding."

The major went over and touched the things with the toe of his boot.

"It's one of those imps of stable-boys, the young vandals!" he declared, as he kicked the rag and the sponge out of the box and across the stable floor. "It's well for them that Farrow isn't about or there would be some cuffed ears for that sort of presumption, the young beggars! Hullo! Found something else?"

"No," said Cleek. "That is, nothing of any importance. Merely a bit torn from an old handbill — see? It probably got mixed up with the bedding. It's of no account, anyhow." Here he gave his hand a flirt as if flinging the bit of paper over the low barrier of the box, instead of which he cleverly "palmed" it and afterward conveyed it unsuspected to his pocket. "You were right in what you declared this afternoon, Major; for a case of such far-reaching effects it is singularly bald in the matter of detail. At all events there's no more to be discovered here. By the way, Doctor, am I privileged to go up and see the patient? I should like to do so if I may."

"By all means, sir, by all means," replied the doctor. "I am happy to inform you that his condition has considerably improved since my visit at noon, Mr. Cleek, and I have now every hope that he may pull through all right."

"Excellent!" said Cleek. "But I think I shouldn't let that good news go abroad just yet a while, Doctor. If you haven't taken anybody into your confidence regarding it as yet, don't do so. You haven't, have you?"

"No. That is, nobody but those who are now present. I told the major and her ladyship on their return this afternoon, of course. And — naturally — Captain MacTavish. He was with me at the time I made the examination, which led me to arrive at the conclusion that the man would survive."

"Ah!" said Cleek — and the curious, one-sided smile went slowly up his cheek. "Oh, well, everything is all right among friends, of course, but I shouldn't let it go any farther. And now, if you please, let us go up to Farrow's room."

They went up forthwith — Lady Mary alone refraining from joining the group — and a moment or two later Cleek found himself standing beside the bed of the unconscious trainer.

He was a strong, sturdily built man, this Tom Farrow, upon whose integrity the major banked so heavily in his warm, trustful, outspoken way; and if the face is any index to the mind — which, in nine cases out of ten, it isn't! — that trustfulness and confidence were not misplaced. For Farrow's was a frank, open countenance which suggested a clear conscience and an honest nature, even though it was now pale and drawn with the lines 'hat come of suffering and injury.

At Cleek's request the doctor removed the bandages and allowed him to inspect the wound at the back of the head.

"H'm! Made with a heavy implement shaped somewhat after the fashion of a golf stick and almost as heavy as a sledge hammer," he commented. "Arm broken, too. Probably that was done first, and the man struck again after he was on the ground and unable to defend himself. There are two blows, you see: this one just above the ear, and that crushing one at the back of the head. That's all I care to see, Doctor, thank you. You may replace the bandages."

Nevertheless, although he asserted this, it was noticeable that his examination of the stricken trainer did not end here; for while the doctor was busy replacing the bandages he took the opportunity to lift the man's hands and inspect them closely — parting the fingers and looking at the thin, loose folds of skin between them. A few minutes later, the bandages being replaced and the patient turned over to the nurse in charge, the entire party left the room and filed down the stairs together.

"Any ideas, Mr. Cleek?" questioned the major, eagerly.

"Yes, plenty of them," replied he. "I rather fancy we shall not have to put you to the trouble of housing us at the

Abbey to-night, Major. The case is a shallower one than I fancied at first. Shouldn't be surprised if we cleared it all up inside of the next two hours."

"Well, I'll be — dithered!" exclaimed the major, aghast. "Do you mean to tell me that you've got at the bottom of the thing? That you've found something that leads you to suspect where the animal is?"

"More than suspect, Major. I know where she is. By half-past seven o'clock to-night — if you want me to make you a promise — I'll put her bridle into your hands and she will be at the other end of it!"

"You will?"

"I certainly will, Major — my word for it."

"Well, of all the dashed —— I'm done! I'm winded! I'm simply scooped dry! Where on earth did you get your clues, man? You never did anything but walk about that I could see; and now to declare —— I say, MacTavish, did you hear that? Did you hear what he has promised — eh?"

"I heard," responded the captain with a laugh. "But I'll believe when I see. I say, Mr. Inspector, where did you find the secret? Hidden between Farrow's fingers or wrapped around Chocolate Maid's legs?"

"Both," said Cleek serenely. "Tell you something else if you care to hear it. I know who poisoned the dog the other night. Farrow did it himself."

The major's exclamation of indignation was quite lost in the peal of the captain's laughter.

"Hawkshaw out-Hawkshawed!" cried he derisively. "Find out that, too, from Farrow's fingers?"

"Oh, no — that would be impossible. He washed them before he went out that night and they've been washed by the nurse several times since. I found it out from the dog himself — and he's not the only dog in this little business, believe me — though I'm willing to stake my reputation and my life upon it that neither one nor the other of them had any hand in spiriting away the missing horse."

"Who did, then, Mr. Cleek? who did?"

"Tom Farrow and Tom Farrow alone, Major," began Cleek — and then stopped suddenly, interrupted by a painful circumstance.

By this time they had reached the foot of the stairs and were filing out into the stable again, and there by the open door Lady Mary Norcross was standing endeavouring to soothe and to comfort a weeping girl — Maggie McFarland, the dairymaid from Nairn.

"Oh, but say he winna dee — say he winna!" she was crying out distressfully. "If I thoct the sin o' that wad added to the sair conscience o' me." Then with a sudden intaking of the breath, as if drowning, and a sudden paleness that made her face seem ivory white, she cowered away, with hands close shut, and eyes wide with fright as she looked up and saw the gentlemen descending.

"It winna matter — it winna matter: I can come again, my leddy!" she said in a frightened sort of whisper which rose suddenly to a sort of wailing cry as she faced round and ran like a thing pursued.

Cleek glanced round quietly and looked at Captain MacTavish. He was still his old handsome, debonnaire, smiling self; but there was a look in his eyes which did not make them a very pleasant sight at present.

"Upon my word, Seton, I cannot make out what has come over that silly girl," said Lady Mary as her liege lord appeared. "She came here begging to be allowed to go up and see Farrow and to be assured that he would live, and then the moment you all put in an appearance she simply dashed away, as you saw. I really cannot understand what can be the matter with her."

"Don't bother about that just now, Mary; don't bother about anything, my dear, but what this amazing man has promised," exclaimed the major excitedly. "Do you know, he has declared that if we give him until half-past seven to-night ——"

Here Cleek interrupted.

"Your pardon, Major — I amend that," he said. "I know all about the horse and it will not now take so long as I thought to know all about the 'dog' as well. Give me one hour, Major — just one, gentlemen, all — and I will give you the answer to the riddle — every part of it: dog's part as well as horse's — here on this spot, so surely as I am a living man. Major, all I ask of you is one thing. Let me have a couple of your grooms out there on the moor inside of the next fifteen minutes, please. May I have them?"

"Certainly, Mr. Cleek — as many as you want."

"Two will do, thanks. Two are enough for fair play in any little bout and — not going to stop and see the finish, Captain? It will all be over in an hour."

"Sorry, but I've got my packing to attend to, my man."

"Ah, to be sure. Oh, well, it doesn't matter. You know the proverb: 'If the mountain will not come to Mahomet, why, Mahomet must go to the mountain,' of course," said Cleek. "I'll just slip round to the dairy and have a glass of milk to brace me up for the business and then — in one hour — in just one by the watch — you shall have the answer to the riddle — *here*."

Then, with a bow to Lady Mary, he walked out of the stable and went round the angle of the building after Maggie McFarland.

CHAPTER XIV

HE LIVED up to the letter of his promise.

In an hour he had said when he walked out, and it was an hour to the very tick of the minute when he came back.

Mr. Narkom knowing him so well, knowing how, in the final moments of his *coups*, he was apt to become somewhat spectacular and theatrical, looked for him to return with a flourish of trumpets and carry all before him with a whirlwind rush; so that it came in the nature of a great surprise, when with the calmness of a man coming in to tea he entered the stable with a large stone bottle in one hand and an hostler's sponge in the other.

"Well, gentlemen, I am here, you see," he said with extreme calmness. "And " — indicating the bottle — "have brought something with me to do honour to the event. No, not to drink — it is hardly that sort of stuff. It is Spirit of Wine, Major. I found it over in Farrow's cottage and have brought it with me — as he, poor chap, meant to do in time himself. There are some wonderful things in Tom Farrow's cottage, Major; they will pay for looking into, I assure you. Pardon, Mr. Narkom? A criminal? Oh, no, my friend — a martyr!"

"A martyr?"

"Yes, your ladyship; yes, Major — a martyr. A martyr to his love, a martyr to his fidelity. As square a man and as faithful a trainer as ever set foot in a stableyard— that's Tom Farrow. I take off my hat to him. The world can do with more of his kind."

"But, my dear sir, you said that it was he that spirited away the animal; that it was he and he alone who was responsible for her disappearance."

"Quite so — and I say it again. Gently, gently, Major — I'll come to it in a minute. Personally I should like to put it off to the last, it's such a fine thing for a finish, by Jove! But — well it can't be done under the circumstances. In other words, there is a part of this little business this evening which I must ask Lady Mary not to stop to either hear or see; but as she is naturally interested in the matter of Highland Lassie's disappearance I will take up that matter first and ask her to kindly withdraw after the filly has been restored."

"Gad! you've found her, then? You've got her?"

"Yes, Major, I've got her. And as I promised that I would put her bridle into your hand with the animal herself at the other end of it, why — here you are!"

Speaking, he walked across to the box where the brown filly was tethered, unbolted it, unfastened the animal and led her out.

"Here you are, Major," he said, as he tendered him the halter. "Take hold of her, the beauty; and may she carry off the Derby Stakes with flying colours."

"But, good lud, man, what on earth are you talking about? This is Chocolate Maid—this is Lady Mary's horse."

"Oh, no, Major, oh, no! Chocolate Maid is in the stable at Farrow's cottage — hidden away and half starved, poor creature, because he couldn't go back to feed and look after her. This is your bonny Highland Lassie — dyed to look like the other and to throw possible horse nobblers and thieves off the scent. If you doubt it, look here."

He uncorked the bottle, poured some of the Spirit of Wine on the sponge and rubbed the animal's brown flank. The dark colour came away, the sorrel hide and the white splotch began to appear, and before you could say Jack

Robinson, the major and Lady Mary had their arms about the animal's neck and were blubbing like a couple of children.

"Oh, my bully girl! Oh, my spiffing girl! Oh, Mary, isn't it clinking, dear? The Lassie — the Highland Lassie — her own bonny self."

"Yes, her own bonny self, Major," said Cleek "and you'd never have had a moment's worry over her if that faithful fellow upstairs had been suffered to get back here that night and to tell you about it in the morning. I've had a little talk with — oh, well, somebody who is in a position to give me information that corroborates my own little 'shots' at the matter (I'll tell you all about that later on), and so am able to tell you a thing or two that you ought to have known before this! I don't know whether Lieutenant Chadwick's coming here and prying about had any wish to do harm to the horse at the back of it or not. I only know that Farrow thought it had, and he played this little trick to block the game and to throw dust into the eyes of anybody that attempted to get at her. What he did then was to dye her so that she might be mistaken for Chocolate Maid, then to take Chocolate Maid over to his own stable and hide her there until the time came to start for Epsom. That's what he wanted the pail of water for, Major — to mix the dye and to apply it. I half suspected it from the beginning, but I became sure of it when I found that scrap of paper in the bedding of the box. It was still wet — a bit of the label from the dye-bottle which came off in the operation. Between the poor chap's fingers I found stains of the dye still remaining. Spirit of Wine would have removed it, but washing in water wouldn't. Pardon, your ladyship? When did I begin to suspect that Farrow was at the bottom of it? Oh, when first I heard of the poisoned dog. Nobody ever heard it bark when the poisoner approached the stables. That, of course, meant that the person who administered the poison must have been some one with whom it was familiar, and also some one who was already inside the place, since even the first approaching step of friend or foe would have called forth one solitary bark at least. Farrow didn't do the thing by halves, you see. He meant it to look like a genuine case of horse stealing to outsiders, and killing the dog gave it just that touch of actuality which carries conviction. As for the rest — the major must tell you that in private, your ladyship. The rest of this little matter is for men alone."

Lady Mary bowed and passed out into the fast coming dusk; and, in the stable the major, Cleek and Narkom stood together, waiting until she was well beyond earshot.

"Now, Major, we will get down to brass tacks, as oui American cousins say," said Cleek, when that time at length came. "You would like to know, I suppose, how poor Farrow came by his injuries and from whose hand. Well, you shall. He was coming back from his cottage after stabling the real Chocolate Maid there when the thing happened; and he received those injuries for rushing to the defence of the woman he loved, and attempting to thrash the blackguard who had taken advantage of her trust and belief in him to spoil her life forever. The woman was, of course, Maggie McFarland. The man was your charming guest, Captain MacTavish!"

"Good God! MacTavish? MacTavish?"

"Yes, Major — the gallant captain who received such a sudden call to rejoin his regiment as soon as he knew that Tom Farrow was likely to recover and to speak. Perhaps you can understand now why Farrow and the girl no longer seemed to 'hit it off together as formerly.' The gallant captain had come upon the boards. Dazzled by the beauty of him, tricked by the glib tongue of him, deluded into the belief that she had actually 'caught a gentleman' and that he really meant to make her his wife and take her away to

India with him, when he went, the silly, innocent, confiding little idiot became his victim and threw over a good man's love for a handful of Dead Sea Fruit."

"Never for one instant had Tom Farrow an idea of this; but the night before last as he crossed the moor — he knew! In the darkness he stumbled upon the truth. He heard her crying out to the fellow to do her justice, to keep his word and make her the honest wife he had promised that she should be, and he heard, too, the man's characteristic reply. You can guess what happened, Major, when you know Tom Farrow. In ten seconds he was up and at that fellow like a mad bull.

"The girl, terrified out of her life, screamed and ran away, seeing the brave captain laying about him with his heavy, silver-headed hunting crop as she fled. She never saw the end of the fight — she never dared; but in the morning when there was no Tom Farrow to be seen, she went out there on the moor and found him. She would have spoken then had she dared, poor creature, but the man's threat was an effective one. If she spoke he would do likewise. If she kept silent she might go away and her disgrace be safely hidden. Which she chose, we know."

"The damned hound!"

"Oh, no, Major, oh, no — that's too hard on hounds. The only houndlike thing about that interesting gentleman was that he made an attempt to 'get to cover' and to run away. I knew that he would — I knew that that was his little dodge when he made that little excuse about having to pack up his effects. He saw how the game was running and he meant to slip the cable and clear out while he had the chance."

"And you let him do it? — you never spoke a word, but let the blackguard do it? Gad, sir, I'm ashamed of you!"

"You needn't be, Major, on that score at least. Please remember that I asked for a couple of grooms to be stationed on the moor I gave them their orders and then went on to Farrow's cottage alone. If they have followed out those orders we shall soon see."

Here he stepped to the door of the stable, put his two forefingers between his lips and whistled shrilly. In half a minute more the two grooms came into the stable, and between them the gallant captain, tousled and rather dirty, and with his beautiful hair and moustache awry.

"Got him, my lads, I see," said Cleek.

"Yes, sir. Nabbed him sneakin' out the back way like you thought he would, sir, and bein' as you said it was the major's orders, we copped him on the jump and have been holdin' of him for further orders ever since."

"Well, you can let him go now," said Cleek, serenely. "And just give your attention to locking the door and lighting up. Major, Doctor, Mr. Narkom, pray be seated. The dear captain is going to give you all a little entertainment and the performance is about to begin. As good with your fists as you are with a metal-headed hunting crop, Captain?"

"None of your dashed business what I'm good at," replied the captain. "Look here, Norcross ——"

"You cut that at once!" roared the major. "If you open your head to me, I'll bang it off you, you brute."

"Well, then you, Mr. Policeman ——"

"Ready for you in a minute, Captain; don't get impatient," said Cleek, as he laid aside his coat and began to roll up his sleeves. "Rome wasn't built in a day — though beauty may be wrecked in a minute. You'll have the time of your life this evening. You are really too beautiful to live, Captain, and I'm going to come as near to killing you as I know how without actually completing the job. You see, that poor little Highland lassie hasn't a father or brother to do this business for her, so she's kindly consented to my taking it on in her behalf. I'm afraid I shall break that lovely nose of yours, my gay gallant — and I don't give a damn if I do! A brute that spoils a woman's life deserves to go through the world with a mark to record it, and I'm going to put one on you to the best of my ability. All seated, gentlemen? Right you are. Now then, Captain, come on. Come on — you *swine!* "

It was twenty minutes later.

Lady Mary Norcross — deep in the obligatory business of dressing for dinner — had just taken up a powder puff and was assiduously dabbing the back of her neck, when the door behind her opened softly and the voice of her liege lord travelled across the breadth of the room, saying:

"Mary! May I come in a minute, dear? I just want to get my cheque book out of your writing desk — that's all."

"Yes, certainly. Come in by all means," gave back her ladyship. "I'm quite alone. Springer has finished with me, and oh! Good heavens! Seton! My dear, my *dear!*"

"All right. Don't get frightened. It isn't mine. And it isn't his, either — much of it. We've been having a little 'set to' at the stable, and I got it hugging a policeman."

"Seton!"

"Yes — I know it's awful, but I simply couldn't help it. Demmit it, Mary, don't look so shocked — I'd have *kissed* the beggar as well, if I thought I could acquire the trick of that heavenly 'jab with the left' that way. I haven't had such a beautiful time since the day I was twenty-one, darling; he fights like a blooming *angel*, that chap."

"What chap? What on earth are you talking about?"

"That man Cleek. Weeping Widows! It was the prettiest job you ever saw. We're sending the beggar over to the hospital — and —— Tell you all about it when I get back. Can't stop just now, dear. Bye, bye!"

Then the door closed with a smack, and man and cheque book were on their way downstairs.

CHAPTER XV

I T IS a recognized fact in police circles that crime has a
curious propensity for indulging in periodical outbursts
of great energy, great fecundity, and then lapsing into a
more or less sporadic condition for a time — like a gorged
tiger that drowses, and stirs only to lick its chops after a
hideous feast. So that following the lines of these fixed
principles the recent spell of criminal activity was succeeded
by a sort of lull, and the next two weeks were idle ones for
Cleek.

Idle but idyllic — from his point of view; for he was back
in the little house in the pleasant country lands now, with
his walled garden, his ferns and his flowers, and the full glory
of tulip-time was here.

And soon another "glory" would be here as well.

In twelve more days *she* would be back in England. In
twelve more days he and Dollops would move out, and Ailsa
Lorne would move in, and this little Eden in the green and
fragrant meadowlands would have another tenant from
that time forth.

But hers would not be a lonely tenancy, however; for
"Captain Horatio Burdage" had recently written to Mrs.
Condiment that, as the Sleeping Mermaid seemed likely
to prove an unprofitable investment after all and to bring
her little reward for her labours, he purposed relinquishing
it and recalling "Old Joseph" to him; and with that end in
view had already secured for the good lady a position as
companion-housekeeper to one Miss Ailsa Lorne, who, in
the early part of June, would call upon her at her present

quarters and personally conduct her and the deaf-and-dumb maid-of-all-work to their future ones.

Here, then, in this bower of bloom, would this dear girl of his heart await the coming of that glorious day when the last act of restitution had been made, the last Vanishing Cracksman debt wiped off the slate, and he could go to her — clean-handed at last — to ask the fulfilment of her promise.

Remembering that, it was a sheer delight to be free from all Yard calls for a time that he might give his whole attention to the work of getting the place ready for her; and day after day he was busy in the high-walled old-world garden — digging, planting, pruning — that when she came it might be brimming over with flowers.

But although he devoted himself mind and body to this task and lived each day within the limits of that confining wall, he had not wholly lost touch with the world at large, for each morning the telephone — installed against the time of Ailsa's tenancy — put him into communication with Mr. Narkom at the Yard, and each night a newspaper carried in to him by Dollops kept him abreast of the topics of the times.

It was over that telephone he received the first assurance that his haste in getting out of Yorkshire had not been an unnecessary precaution, his suspicions regarding the probable action of the Nosworths not ill grounded, for Mr. Narkom was able to inform him that carefully made inquiries had elicited the intelligence that, within two days after the Round House affair, men who were undoubtedly foreigners were making diligent inquiries throughout the West Riding regarding the whereabouts of two men and a boy who had been travelling about in a two-horsed caravan.

"That sudden bolt of ours was a jolly good move, old chap," said the superintendent, when he made this announcement. "It did the beggars absolutely. Shouldn't be a bit surprised if they'd chucked the business as a bad job and gone back to the Continent disgusted. At any rate, none of my plain-clothes men has seen hide nor hair of one of the lot since, either in town or out. Waldemar, too, seems to have hooked it and can't be traced; so I reckon we've seen the last of him."

But Cleek was not so sure of that. He had his own ideas as to what this disappearance of the Apaches meant, and did not allow himself to be lulled into any sense of security by it. There were more ways than one in which to catch a weasel, he recollected, and determined not to relax his precautions in the smallest iota when next the Yard's call for his services should come.

That it would come soon he felt convinced as the days advanced that rounded out the end of his second week of freedom from it; and what form it would take when it did come was a matter upon which he could almost have staked his life, so sure he felt of it.

For a time of great national excitement, great national indignation, had arrived, and the press had made him acquainted with all the circumstances connected therewith. As why not, when the whole country was up in arms over it and every newspaper in the land headlined it in double caps and poured forth the story in full detail?

It had its genesis in something which had happened at Gosport in the preceding week, and happened in this startling manner:

In the waterway between Barrow Island and the extreme end of the Royal Clarence Victualling Yard there had been found floating the body of a man of about five-and-thirty years of age, fully and fashionably clothed and having all those outward signs which betoken a person of some standing.

It was evident at once that death must have been the result of accident, and that the victim had been unable to swim, for the hands were encased in kid gloves, the coat was tightly buttoned, and a pair of field-glasses in a leather case still hung from the long shoulder-strap which supported the weight of them. The victim's inability to swim was established by the fact that he had made no effort to rid himself of these hampering conditions, and was clinging tightly to a foot-long bit of driftwood, which he must have clutched at as it floated by.

It was surmised, therefore, that the man must have fallen into the water in the dark — either from the foreshore or from some vessel or small boat in which he was journeying at the time — and had been carried away by the swift current and drowned without being missed, the condition of the body clearly establishing the fact that it had been in the water for something more than a fortnight when found. Later it was identified by one of the deck hands of the pleasure steamer which cruises round the Isle of Wight daily as being that of a man he had seen aboard that vessel on one of its night trips to Alum Bay between two and three weeks previously; and still later it was discovered that a boatman in that locality had been hired to take a gentleman from the Needles to a yacht "lying out to sea" that selfsame night, and that the gentleman in question never turned up.

What followed gave these two circumstances an appalling significance. For when the body was carried to the mortuary, and its clothing searched for possible clues to identification, there was found upon it a sealed packet addressed simply "A. Steinmüller, Königstrasse 8," and inside that packet there were two unmounted photographs of the exterior of Blockhouse Fort and the Southsea Fort, a more or less accurate ground-plan drawing of the interior of the Portsmouth Dockyard, together with certain secret information relative to supplies and to the proposed armament of cruisers now undergoing alteration and reëquipment.

The wrath and amazement engendered by that discovery,

however, were as nothing compared with the one which so swiftly followed.

Brought up before the Admiral Superintendent and the Board, John Beachman, the dock master — who alone knew these things outside of the Admiralty — was obliged to admit that one person, and one only — his eldest son — was in a position to obtain admission to the safe in which he kept his private papers, and that son was engaged to a young lady whom he had met during a holiday tour on the Continent.

"English or foreign?" he was asked; to which he replied that she was English — or, at least, English by birth, although her late father was a German. He had become naturalized before his death, and was wholly in sympathy with the country of his adoption. He did not die in it, however. Circumstances had caused him to visit the United States, and he had been killed in one of the horrible railway disasters for which that country was famous. It was because the daughter was thus left orphaned, and was so soon to become the wife of their son, that he and Mrs. Beachman had taken her into their home in advance of the marriage. They did not think it right that she should be left to live alone and unprotected, considering what she was so soon to become to them; so they had taken her into the home, and their son had arranged to sleep at an hotel in Portsmouth pending the date of the wedding. The lady's name was Hilmann — Miss Greta Hilmann. She was of extremely good family, and quite well-to-do in her own right. She had never been to Germany since the date of the engagement. She had relatives there, however; one in particular — a Baron von Ziegelmundt and his son Axel. The son had visited England twice — once many months back, and the last time some seven or eight weeks ago. They liked him very much — the bridegroom-elect especially so. They had become very great friends indeed. No,

Axel von Ziegelmundt was no longer in England. He had left it something like a month ago. He was on a pleasure trip round the world, he had heard, but had no idea where he had gone when he left Portsmouth.

Two hours after this statement was made, if the populace could have got hold of young Harry Beachman it would have torn him to pieces; for it was then discovered that the drowned man was no less a person than this Herr Axel von Ziegelmundt, and that they had not only spent the greater part of that particular day shut up in the former's room in the Portsmouth hotel, but had been together up to the very moment when the excursion steamer had started on its moonlight trip to Alum Bay and to the bringing about of that providential accident which had prevented the State affairs of an unsuspecting nation from being betrayed to a secret foe.

What followed was, in the face of this, of course, but natural. John Beachman was suspended immediately, and his son's arrest ordered. It served no purpose that he denied indignantly the charge of being a traitor, and swore by every sacred thing that the hours spent in his room at the hotel were passed in endeavouring to master the intricacies of the difficult German card game, Skaat, and that never in all their acquaintance had one word touching upon the country or the country's affairs passed between Axel von Ziegelmundt and himself, so help him God! It was in vain, also, that Greta Hilmann — shouting hysterically her belief in him and begging wildly that if he must be put into prison she might be taken with him "and murdered when you murder him if he is to be court-martialled and shot, you wretched blunderers!" — it was in vain that Greta Hilmann clung to him and fought with all her woman's strength to keep the guard from laying hands upon him or to tear her from his side; the outraged country demanded him, and took him in spite of all. Nor did it turn the current of

sympathy in his direction that, crazed when they tore him
from her, this frantic creature had gone from swoon to
swoon until her senses left her entirely, and the end was —
tragedy.

The full details were never forthcoming. The bare facts
were that she was carried back to Beachman's house in a
state of hysteria bordering close upon insanity, and that
when, under orders from the Admiralty, that house and all
its contents were impounded pending the fullest inquiry
into the dock master's books and accounts, the Admiral
Superintendent and the appointed auditor entered into
possession, her condition was found to be so serious that it
was decided not to insist upon her removal for a day or two
at least. A nurse was procured from the naval hospital
and put in charge of her; but at some period during the
fourth night of that nurse's attendance — and when she,
worn out by constant watching, slept in her chair — the
half-delirious patient arose, and, leaving a note to say that
life had lost all its brightness for her, and if they cared
to find her they might look for her in the sea, vanished entirely. She could scarcely have hit upon a worse thing for
the evil repute of her lover's name or her own. For those
who had never known her personally were quick to assert
that this was proof enough of how the thing had been managed. In short, that she, too, was a spy, and that she had
adopted this subterfuge to get back to Germany before the
scent grew hot and the law could lay a hand upon her.
Those who had known her took a more merciful view so far
as she was concerned, but one which made things look all
the blacker for her lover. What could her desperation and
her utter giving up all hope even before the man was put on
trial mean if it was not that she knew he was guilty, knew
he would never get off with his life, and that her suicide was
a tacit admission of this ?

CHAPTER XVI

MEANWHILE public indignation ran high, the investigation of the dock master's books, papers, and accounts proceeded *in camera*, and all England waited breathlessly for the result to be made known.

Thus matters stood when on Thursday night at half-past seven o'clock — exactly one week after the discovery of that packet on the body of the drowned man — an amazing thing happened, a thing which smacked almost of magic, and put to shame all that had gone before in the way of mystery, surprise, and terror.

The wildest storm that had been known on that coast for years had been raging steadily ever since daybreak and was raging still. A howling wind, coming straight over the Channel from France, was piling ink-black seas against an ink-black shore, and all the devils of the pit seemed to be loose in the noisy darkness.

In the suspended dock master's house the Admiral Superintendent, Sir Charles Fordeck, together with his private secretary, Mr. Paul Grimsdick, and the auditor, Mr. Alexander MacInery, who had been continuing their investigations since morning, were now coming within sight of the work's end — the only occupants of a locked and guarded room, outside of which a sentry was posted, while round about the house in the stormy outer darkness other guards patrolled ceaselessly. Over the books Sir Charles and the auditor bent at one end of the room; at the other Paul Grimsdick tapped on his typewriter and made transcripts from the shorthand notes beside him. It was at this instant, just when the clock on the mantel was beginning to chime the half-hour after seven, that such a crash of thunder ripped out of the heavens that the very earth seemed to tremble with the force of it, and the three men fairly jumped in their seats.

"Gad! that was a stunner, if you like!" exclaimed Sir Charles with a laugh. "Something went down that time, or I miss my guess."

Something had "gone down" — gone down in black and white, too, at that — and before another half-hour had passed the mystery and the appalling nature of that something was made known to him and to his two companions.

The operator at the central telegraph office, sitting beside a silent instrument with the key open deciphering a message which a moment before had come through, jumped as they had jumped when that crash of thunder sounded; then without hint or warning up spoke the open instrument, beginning a sentence in the middle and chopping it off before it was half done.

"Hullo! that deflected something — crossed communication or I'm a Dutchman!" he said, and bent over to "take it." In another moment he got more of a shock than twenty thunderbolts could possibly have given him. For, translated, that interrupted communication ran thus:

". . and eight-inch guns. The floating conning tower's lateral plates of . . . "

And there, as abruptly as it began, the communication left off.

"Good God! There's another damned German spy at it!" exclaimed the operator, jumping from his seat and grabbing for his hat. "Gawdermity, Hawkins, take this instrument and watch for more. Somebody's telegraphin' naval secrets from the dockyard, and the storm's 'tapped' a wire somewhere and sent the message to us!" Then he flung himself out into the storm and darkness and ran and ran and ran.

But the mystery of the thing was all the greater when the facts came to be examined. For those two parts of sentences were found to be verbatim copies of the shorthand notes which Mr. Paul Grimsdick had just taken down. These notes had never left the sight of the three men in the guarded room of that guarded house for so much as one second since they were made. No one but they had passed either in or out of that room during the whole seven days of the inquiry. There was no telegraph instrument in the room — in the house — or within any possible reach from it. Yet somebody in that building — somebody who could only know the things by standing in that room and copying them, for never once had they been spoken of by word of mouth — some invisible, impalpable, superhuman body was wiring State secrets from it. How? And to whom?

Naturally, this state of affairs set the whole country by the ears and evoked a panicky condition which was not lessened by the Press' frothing and screaming.

Thus matters stood on the evening of Wednesday, the twenty-second of May, and thus they still stood on the morning of the twenty-third, when the telephone rang and Dollops rushed into Cleek's bedroom crying excitedly and disjointedly:

"Mr. Narkom, sir. Ringing up from his own house. Wants you in a hurry. National case, he says, and not a minute to lose."

Cleek was out of bed and at the instrument in a winking; but he had no more than spoken the customary "Hello!" into the receiver, when the superintendent's voice cut in cyclonically and swept everything before it in a small tornado of excited words.

"Call of the Country, dear chap!" he cried. "That

infernal dockyard business at Portsmouth. Sir Charles Fordeck just sent through a call for you. Rush like hell! Don't stop for anything! Train it over to Guildford if you have to charter a special. Meet you there — in the Portsmouth Road — with the limousine — at seven-thirty. We'll show 'em — by God, yes! Good-bye!"

Then "click!" went the instrument as the communication was cut off, and away went Cleek, like a gunshot, on a wild rush for his clothes.

The sun was but just thrusting a crimson arc into view in the transfigured east when he left the house — on a hard run; for part at least of the way must be covered afoot, and the journey was long — but by four o'clock it was almost as bright as midday, and the possibility of securing a conveyance for the rest of the distance was considerably increased by that fact; by five, he *had* secured one, and by seven he was in the Portsmouth Road at Guildford munching the sandwiches Dollops had thoughtfully slipped into his pocket and keeping a sharp lookout for the coming of the red limousine.

It swung up over the rise of the road and came panting toward him at a nerve-racking pace while it still lacked ten minutes of being the appointed half-hour, and so wild was the speed at which Lennard, in his furious interest, was making it travel that Cleek could think of nothing to which to liken it but a red streak whizzing across a background of leaf-green with splatters of mud flying about it and an owl-eyed demon for pilot.

It pulled up with a jerk when it came abreast of him, but so great was Lennard's excitement, so deep seated his patriotic interest in the business he had in hand, he seemed to begrudge even the half-minute it took to get his man aboard; and before you could have turned around twice the car was rocketing on again at a demon's pace.

"Gad! but he's full of it, the patriotic beggar!" said Cleek with a laugh, as he found himself deposited in Narkom's lap instead of on the seat beside him, so sudden was the car's start the instant he was inside. "It might give our German friends pause, don't you think, Mr. Narkom, if they could get an insight into the spirit of the race as a fighting unit?"

"It'll give 'em hell if they run up against it — make no blooming error about that!" rapped out the superintendent too "hot in the choler" to be choice of words. "It's a nasty little handful to fall foul of when its temper is up; and this damned spy business, done behind a mask of friendship in times of peace ——Look here, Cleek! If it comes to the point, just give me a gun with the rest. I'll show the Government that I can lick something beside insurance stamps for my country's good — by James, yes!"

"Just so," said Cleek, with one of his curious, crooked smiles. He was used to these little patriotic outbursts on the part of Mr. Narkom whenever the German bogey was dragged out by the Press. "But let us hope it will not come to that. It would be an embarrassment of riches so far as our friends the editors are concerned, don't you think, to have two wars on their hands at the same time? And I see by papers that the long-threatened Mauravanian revolution has broken out at last. In short, that our good friend Count Irma has made his escape from Sulberga, put himself at the head of the Insurgents, and is organizing a march on the capital ——"

Here he pulled himself up abruptly, as if remembering something, and, before Mr. Narkom could put in a word, launched into the subject of the case in hand and set him thinking and talking of other things.

CHAPTER XVII

IT HAD gone nine by all the reliable clocks in town when the wild race to the coast came to an end, and after darting swallowlike through the wind-swept streets of Portsmouth, the limousine, mud splashed and disreputable, rushed up to the guarded entrance of the suspended dock master's house at Portsea; and precisely one and a quarter minutes thereafter Cleek stood in the presence of the three men most deeply concerned in the clearing up of this mystifying affair.

He found Sir Charles Fordeck, a dignified and courtly gentleman of polished manners and measured speech, although now, quite naturally, labouring under a distress of mind which visibly disturbed him. He found Mr. Paul Grimsdick, his secretary, a frank-faced, straight-looking young Englishman of thirty; Mr. Alexander MacInery, a stolid, unemotional Scotsman of middle age, with a huge knotted forehead, eyebrows like young moustaches, and a face like a face of granite; and he found, too, reason to believe that each of these was, in his separate way, a man to inspire confidence and respect.

"I can hardly express to you, Mr. Cleek, how glad I am to meet you and to have you make this quick response to my appeal," said the Admiral Superintendent, offering him a welcoming hand. "I feel that if any man is likely to get to the bottom of this mysterious business you are that man. And that you should get to the bottom of it — quickly, at whatever cost, by whatever means — is a thing to be desired not only in the nation's interest, but for the honour of myself and my two colleagues."

"I hardly think that your honour will be called into question, Sir Charles," replied Cleek, liking him the better for the manliness which prompted him in that hour of doubt and difficulty to lay aside all questions of position, and by the word "colleague" lift his secretary to the level of himself, so that they might be judged upon a common plane as men, and men alone. "It would be a madman indeed who would hint at anything approaching treason with regard to Sir Charles Fordeck."

"No madder than he who would hint it of either of these," said Sir Charles, laying a hand upon the shoulder of the auditor and the secretary, and placing himself between them. "I demand to be judged by the same rule, set upon the same plane with them. We three alone were in this house when that abominable thing happened; we three alone had access to the records from which that information was wired. It never, for so much as the fraction of one second, passed out of our keeping or our sight; if it was wired at all it must have been wired from this house, from that room, and in that case, one or other of us must positively have been the person to do so. Well, *I* did not; MacInery did not; Grimsdick did not. And yet, as you know, the 'wiring' was done — we should never stand a chance of knowing to whom, nor by whom, but for the accident which deflected the course of the message."

"H'm! Yes! I don't think," commented Cleek reflectively. "It won't wash, that theory; no, decidedly it won't wash. Pardon?   Oh, no, Sir Charles, I am not casting any doubt upon the telegraph operator's statement of the manner in which he received the message; it is his judgment that is at fault, not his veracity. Of course, there have been cases — very rare ones, happily — of one wire automatically tapping another through, as he suggested, there being a break and an overlapping of the broken wire on to the sound one; but in the present instance there isn't a ghost of a chance of such a thing having happened. In other words, Sir Charles, it is as unsound in theory as it is false in fact. Mr. Narkom has been telling me on the way here that the operator accounted for the sudden starting of the message to the falling of a storm-snapped wire upon an uninjured one, and for its abrupt cessation to the slipping off of that broken wire under the influence of the strong gale. Now, as we entered the town and proceeded through it, I particularly noted the fact that no broken wires were anywhere visible, nor was there sight or sign of men being engaged in repairing one."

"Ah, yes," agreed Sir Charles, a trifle dubiously, "that may be quite so, Mr. Cleek; but, if you will pardon my suggesting it, is there not the possibility of a flaw in your reasoning upon that point? The wire in question may not have been located in that particular district through which you were travelling."

"I don't think there is any chance of my having made an error of that sort, Sir Charles," replied Cleek, smiling. "Had I been likely to do so, our friend the telegraph operator would have prevented it. He recognized at once that the communication was coming over the wire from the dockyard, I am told; and I have observed that every one of the dockyard wires is intact. I fancy when we come down to the bottom of it we shall discover that it was not the dockyard wire which 'tapped' a message from some other, but that the dockyard wire was being 'tapped' itself, and that the storm, causing a momentary interruption in the carrying on of that 'tapping' process, allowed a portion of the message to slip past and continue to the wire's end — the telegraph office."

"Good lud! Then in that case ——"

"In that case, Mr. Narkom, there can be no shadow of a doubt that that message was sent by somebody in this house — and over the dockyard's own private wire."

"But how, Mr. Cleek — in the name of all that is wonderful, how?"

"Ah, that is the point, Sir Charles. I think we need not
go into the matter of who is at the bottom of the whole
affair, but confine ourselves to the business of discovering
how the thing was done, and how much information has
already gone out to the enemy. I fancy we may set our
minds at rest upon one point, however, namely, the identity of the person whose hand supplied the drawing found
upon the body of the drowned man. That hand was a
woman's; that woman, I feel safe in saying, was Sophie
Borovonski, professionally known to the people of the
underworld as 'La Tarantula.'"

"I never heard of her, Mr. Cleek. Who is she?"

"Probably the most beautiful, unscrupulous, reckless,
dare-devil spy in all Europe, Sir Charles. She is a Russian
by birth, but owns allegiance to no country and to no
crown. Together with her depraved brother Boris, and her
equally desperate paramour, Nicolo Ferrand, she forms one
of the trio of paid bravos who for years have been at the
beck and call of any nation despicable enough to employ
them; always ready for any piece of treachery or dirty work,
so long as their price is paid — as cunning as serpents, as
slippery as eels, as clever as the devil himself, and as patient.
We shall not go far astray, gentlemen, if we assert that the
lady's latest disguise was that of Miss Greta Hilmann."

"Good God! Young Beachman's fiancée?"

"Exactly, Sir Charles. I should not be able to identify
her from a photograph were one obtainable, which I doubt
— she is far too clever for that sort of thing — but the evidence is conclusive enough to satisfy me, at least, of the
lady's identity."

"But how — how?"

"Mr. Narkom will tell you, Sir Charles, that from our
time of starting this morning to our arrival here we made

but one stop. That stop was at the Portsmouth mortuary before we appeared at this house. I wished to see the body of the man who was drowned. I have no hesitation, Sir Charles, in declaring that that man's name is not, and never was, Axel von Ziegelmundt. The body is that of Nicolo Ferrand, 'La Tarantula's' clever lover. The inference is obvious. 'Miss Greta Hilmann's' anguish and despair were real enough, believe me (that is why it deceived everybody so completely). It is not, however, over the frightful position of young Beachman that she sorrowed, but over the death of Ferrand. Had he lived, I believe she has daring enough to have remained here and played her part to the end, but she either lost her nerve and her mental balance — which, by the way, is not in the least like her under any circumstances whatsoever — or some other disaster of which we know nothing overtook her and interfered with her carrying on the work in conjunction with her brother."

"Her brother?"

"Yes. He would be sure to be about. They all three worked in concert. Gad! if I'd only been here before the vixen slipped the leash — if I only had! Let us have the elder Mr. Beachman in, if you please, Sir Charles; there's a word or so I want to have with him. You've had him summoned, of course!"

"Yes, he and the telegraph operator as well; I thought you might wish to question both," replied he. "Grimsdick, go — or, no! I'll go myself. Beachman ought to know of this appalling thing; and it is best that it should be broken by a friend."

Speaking, he left the room, coming back a few minutes later in company with the telegraph operator and the now almost hysterical dock master. He waited not one second for introduction or permission or anything else, that excited father, but rushed at Cleek and caught him by the hand.

"It's my boy and you're clearing him — God bless you!" he exclaimed, catching Cleek's hand and wringing it with all his strength. "It isn't in him to sell his country; I'd have killed him with my own hand years ago, if I thought it was. But it wasn't — it never was! My boy! my boy! my splendid, loyal boy!"

"That's right, old chap, have it out. Here on my shoulder, if you want to, daddy, and don't be ashamed of it!" said Cleek, and reached round his arm over the man's shoulder and clapped him on the back. "Let her go, and don't apologize because it's womanish. A man without a strain of the woman in him somewhere isn't worth the powder to blow him to perdition. We'll have him cleared, daddy — gad, yes! And look here! When he is cleared you take him by the ear and tell him to do his sweethearting in England, the young jackass, and to let foreign beauties alone; they're not picking up with young Englishmen of his position for nothing, especially if they are reputed to have money of their own and to be connected with titled families. If you can't make him realize that by gentle means, take him into the garden and bang it into him — hard."

"Thank you, sir; thank you! I can see it now, Mr. Cleek. Not much use in shouting 'Rule Britannia' if you're going to ship on a foreign craft, is there, sir? But anybody would have been taken in with her — she seemed such a sweet, gentle little thing and had such winning ways. And when she lost her father, the wife and I simply couldn't help taking her to our hearts."

"Quite so. Ever see that 'father,' Mr. Beachman?"

"Yes, sir, once; the day before he sailed — or was supposed to have sailed — for the States."

"Short, thick-set man was he? Carried one shoulder a little lower than the other, and had lost the top of a finger on the left hand?"

"Yes, sir; the little finger. That's him to a T."

"Boris Borovonski!" declared Cleek, glancing over at Sir Charles. "No going to the States for that gentleman with a 'deal' like this on hand. He'd be close by and in constant touch with her. Did she have any friends in the town, Mr. Beachman?"

"No, not one. She appeared to be of a very retiring disposition, and made no acquaintances whatsoever. The only outside person I ever knew her to take any interest in was a crippled girl who lived with her bedridden mother and took in needlework. Greta heard of the case, and went to visit them. Afterward she used to carry work to them frequently, and sometimes fruit and flowers."

"Ever see that bedridden woman or that cripple girl?"

"No, sir, never. Harry and I would be busy here most of the days, so she always went alone."

"Did she ever ask Mrs. Beachman to accompany her?"

"Not that I ever heard of, sir. But it would have been to no purpose if she had. The wife is a very delicate woman; she rarely ever goes anywhere."

"Hum-m-m! I see! So, then, you really do not know if there actually was a woman or a girl at all? Any idea where the persons were supposed to live?"

"Yes. They hired a room on the top floor of a house adjoining the Ocean Billow Hotel, sir. At least, Reggie — that's my youngest son, Mr. Cleek — saw Greta go in there and look down from one of the top floor windows one day when he was on his way home from school. He spoke to her about it at the dinner table that night, and she said that that was where her 'pensioners lived.'"

"Pretty good neighbourhood that, by Jove! for people who were 'pensioners' to be living in," commented Cleek. "The Ocean Billow Hotel is a modern establishment — lifts, electric lights, liveried attendants, and caters to people of substance and standing."

"Yes," admitted Beachman. "When I was suspended, sir, during the examination and this house taken over by Sir Charles, I took Mrs. Beachman and Reggie there, and we have remained at the place, nominally under guard, ever since. You see, being convenient and in a straight line, so to speak, it offered extra advantages in case of my being summoned here at a moment's notice."

"H'm! Yes! I see!" said Cleek, stroking his chin. "In a straight line from here, eh? House next door would, of course, offer the same advantages; and from a room on the top floor a wire-tapping device —— Yes, just so! I think, Sophie, I think I smell a very large mouse, my dear, and I shan't be surprised if we've hit upon the place of reception for your messages the very first shot."

"Messages, Mr. Cleek? Messages?" interposed Sir Charles. "You surely do not mean to infer that the woman telegraphed messages from this house? Do you forget, then, that there is no instrument, no wire, attached to the place?"

Cleek puckered up his brows. For the moment he had forgotten that fact.

"Still, there are wires passing over it, Sir Charles," he said presently; "and if a means of communication with those were established, the 'tapper' at the other end could receive messages easily. She is a devil of ingenuity is Sophie. I wouldn't put it beyond her and her confederates to have rigged up a transmitting instrument of some sort which the woman could carry on her person and attach to the wire when needed."

Here Sir Charles threw in something which he felt to be in the nature of a facer.

"Quite so," he admitted. "But do not forget, Mr. Cleek, that the deflected message was sent last night, and that the woman was not then in this house."

CHAPTER XVIII

THE queer little one-sided smile cocked up the corner of Cleek's mouth. " Sure of that, Sir Charles?" he inquired placidly. " Sure that she was not? I am told, it is true, that she left the note saying she was going to drown herself, and disappeared four nights ago; I am also told that since the date of Mr. Beachman's suspension this place has been under constant guard night and day, but I have *not* been told, however, that any of the guards saw her leave the place. No, no, no! Don't jump to conclusions so readily, gentlemen. She will be out of it now, — out and never likely to return; the news of that miscarried message would warn her that something was wrong, and she would be 'up and out of it' like a darting swallow. The question is, how and when did she get out? Let's have in the guard and see."

The sentries were brought in one after the other and questioned. At no time since they were first put on guard, they declared — at *no time*, either by day or by night — had any living creature entered or left the house up to now, except the Admiral Superintendent, his secretary, the auditor, and the nurse who had been summoned to look after the stricken girl. To that they one and all were willing to take solemn oath.

There is an old French proverb which says: "He that protests too much leads to the truth in spite of himself." It was the last man to be called who did this.

"No, sir, nobody passed, either in or out, I'll take my dying oath to that," asserted he, his feelings riled up by the thought that this constant questioning of his statement was a slur upon his devotion to his duty. "There aren't nobody going to hint as I'm a slacker as don't know what he's a-doing of, or a blessed mug that don't obey orders; no, sir — no fear! Sir Charles's orders was, 'Nobody in or out' and nobody in or out it was; my hat! yuss! Why, sir " — turning to the dock master — "you must 'a' known; he must 'a' told you. I wouldn't allow even young Master Reggie in last night when he came a-pleading to be let in to get the school books he'd left behind."

"When he *what?*" almost roared the dock master, fairly jumping. "Good lord, Marshall, have you gone off your head? Do you mean to claim that you saw my boy here — last night?"

"Certainly, sir. Just after that awful clap of thunder it was — say about eight or ten minutes after; and what with that and the darkness and the way the wind was howling, I never see nor heard nothing of him coming till I got to the door, and there he was — in them light-coloured knickers and the pulled-down wideawake hat I'd seen him wear dozens of times — with his coat collar turned up and a drippin' umbrella over his head, making like he was going up the steps to try and get in. 'Who's there?' as I sings to him, though I needn't, for the little light was streaking out through the windows showed me what he was wearing and who it was well enough. 'It's me — Master Reggie, Marshall,' he says. 'I've come to get my school books. I left 'em behind in the hurry, and father says he's sure you'll let me go in and get 'em.' 'Oh, does he?' says I. 'Well, I'm surprised at him and at you, too, Master Reggie, a-thinking I'd go against orders. Word is that nobody gets in; and nobody *does*, even the king hisself, till them orders is changed. So you just come away from that door, and trot right away back to your pa,' I says to him, 'and ask him from me what kind of a sentry he thinks Bill Marshall is.'

Which sets him a-snivelling and a-pleading till I has to take
him by the shoulder, and fair drag him away before I could
get him to go as he'd been told."

"Well done, Sophie!" exclaimed Cleek. "Gad! what a
creature of resource the woman is, and what an actress she
would make, the vixen! No need to ask you if your son
really did come over here last night, Mr. Beachman; your
surprise and indignation have answered for you."

"I should think it would, by George!" rapped out the
dock master. "What sort of an insane man must you have
thought me, Marshall, to credit such a thing as that? As if
I'd have been likely to let a delicate fifteen-year-old boy
go out on an errand of any kind in a beast of a storm like
last night's, much less tell him that he was to ask a sentry,
in my name, to disobey his orders. Good God! gentlemen,
it's simply monstrous! Why, look here, Sir Charles; look
here, Mr. Cleek! Even if I'd been guilty of such a thing,
and the boy was willing to go out, he couldn't have done
it to save his life. The poor little chap met with an accident last night and he's been in bed ever since. He was
going down the stairs on his way to dinner when that terrific
clap of thunder came, and the blessed thing startled him so
much that, in the pitch darkness, he missed his footing,
fell clear to the bottom of the staircase, and broke his collar
bone."

"Poor little lad! Too bad, too bad!" sympathized Sir
Charles, feelingly, and, possibly, would have said more but
that Cleek's voice broke in softly, but with a curiously sharp
note underlying its sleekness.

"In the pitch darkness, Mr. Beachman?" it inquired.
"The pitch darkness of a public hotel *at dinner time*? Isn't
that rather extraordinary?"

"It would be, under any other circumstances, sir, but
that infernal clap of thunder interfered in some way with
the electric current, and every blessed light in the hotel went

smack out — whisk! like that! — and left the place as black as a pocket. Everybody thought for the moment that the wires must have fused, but it turned out that there was nothing the matter with them — only that the current had been interrupted for a bit — for the lights winked on again as suddenly as they had winked out."

"By Jupiter!" Cleek cracked out the two words like the snapping of a whip lash, then quickly turned round on his heel and looked straight and intently at the telegraph operator.

"Speak up — quick!" he said in the sharp staccato of excitement. "I am told that when that crash came and the diverted message began there was a force that almost knocked you off your stool. Is that true?"

"Yes, sir," the man replied, "perfectly true. It was something terrific. The Lord only knows what it would have been if I'd been touching the instrument."

"You'd have been as dead as Julius Cæsar!" flung back Cleek. "No wonder she cut away to see what was wrong, the vixen! No wonder the lights went out! Mr. Narkom, the limousine — quick! Come along, Sir Charles; come along, Mr. Beachman — come along at once!"

"Where, Mr. Cleek — where?"

"To the top floor of the house next door to the Ocean Billow Hotel, Sir Charles, to see 'Miss Greta Hilmann's' precious pensioners," he made answer, rather excitedly. "Unless I am wofully mistaken, gentlemen, one part of this little riddle is already solved, and the very elements have conspired to protect England to become her foeman's executioner."

He was not mistaken — not in any point with regard to that house and the part it had played in this peculiar case — for, when they visited it and demanded in the name of the law the right to enter and to interview "the bedridden woman and the crippled girl who occupied the top floor," they were met with the announcement that no such persons dwelt there, nor had ever done so.

"It is let to an invalid, it is true," the landlady, a motherly, unsuspecting old soul, told them when they made the demand. "But it is a gentleman, not a lady. A professional gentleman, I believe — artist or sculptor, something of that sort — and never until last night has anybody been with him but his niece, who makes occasional calls. Last night, however, a nephew came — just for a moment; indeed, it seemed to me that he had no more than gone upstairs before he came down again and went out. Pardon? No, nobody has called to-day, neither has the gentleman left his room. But he often sleeps until late."

He was sleeping forever this time. For when they came to mount the stairs and force open the door of the room, there, under a half-opened skylight, a dead man lay, one screwed-up, contracted hand still clutching the end of a flex, which went up and out to the telegraph wires overhead. On a table beside the body a fused and utterly demolished telegraph instrument stood; and it was evident from the scrap of flex still clinging to this that it had once formed part of that which the dead hand held; that it had snapped somehow, and that the man was attempting to re-attach it to the instrument when death overtook him.

"Gentlemen, the wire tapper — Boris Borovonski!" said Cleek, as he bent over and looked at him. "Step here, Mr. Beachman, and tell me if this is not the man who played the part of 'Miss Greta Hilmann's' interesting papa."

"Yes, yes!" declared the dock master excitedly, after he, too, had bent over and looked into the dead face. "It is the very man, sir, the very one! But who — but why — but how?" He then looked upward in a puzzled way to where the flex went up and out through the skylight and, threading through a maze of wires, hooked itself fast to one.

"Electrocuted," said Cleek, answering that inquiring

glance. "A few thousand volts — a flash of flame through heart and head and limbs, and then this! See his little game, Mr. Narkom? See it, do you, Sir Charles? He was taking the message from the tapped wire with that flex, and the fragment that reached the telegraph office only got through when the flex snapped. The furious gale did that, no doubt, whipping it away from its moorings, so to speak, and letting the message flash on before he could prevent it.

"Can't you read the rest when you look up and see that other wire — the thick one with the insulated coating torn and frayed by contact with the chimney's rough edge? It is not hard to reconstruct the tragedy when one sees that. When the flex snapped he jumped up and grabbed it, and was in the very act of again attaching it to the instrument when he became his own executioner. Look for yourself. The wild wind must either have blown the flex against the bared wire of the electric light or the bared wire against the flex — that we shall never know — and in the winking of an eye he was annihilated.

"No wonder the lights in the hotel went out, Mr. Beachman. The whole strength of the current was short-circuited through this man's body, and it crumpled him up as a glove crumples when it is cast in the fire. But the dead hand, which had recovered the broken flex, still held it, you see, and no more of the 'tapped' message went down the dockyard wire. So long as that message continued, so long as the instrument which sent it continued to send it, it was 'received' here — a mere silent, unrecorded, impotent thrill locked up in the grip of a dead man's hand.

"And look there — the pile of burnt paper beside the fused instrument and the cinder of a matchbox against it. The force which obliterated life in him infused it into the 'dipped' heads of those little wooden sticks, and flashed them into flame. So long as there was anything for that flame to feed upon it continued its work, you see, and Sophie Borovonski found nothing to take away with her, after all. Gentlemen, the State secrets that were stolen will remain England's own — the records were burnt, and the dead cannot betray."

CHAPTER XIX

IT HAD gone two o'clock. The morning's work was done, a hasty luncheon disposed of, and the investigators were back in the dockmaster's house discussing the curious features of the case again.

"And now, gentlemen," said Cleek, "to the unsolved part of the riddle — the mysterious manner in which the messages were sent from this house. For sent from here they undoubtedly were, and by Sophie Borovonski; but the question of how still remains to be discovered."

"I make it that it's the devil's own work, Mr. Cleek," said MacInery, "and that there must have been some accident connected with it, the same as with the taking off of the wire-tapping chap."

"Hardly that, I'm afraid," replied Cleek. "I think it was accident which put a *stop* to the proceedings here, not one which created them. We now know perfectly well that the woman was in this house — undiscovered and unsuspected for days; and you may safely lay your life that she wasn't idle, wasn't stopping here for nothing. The pile of papers burnt shows very clearly that considerable intelligence had been forwarded to her brother, so it is safe to infer that she was wiring it to him constantly."

"But how was it possible for her to obtain that information?" queried Sir Charles. "I again declare to you most solemnly, Mr. Cleek, that no one entered or left the room, that no word was spoken that could be said to have any bearing upon secret matters, so nothing could possibly be overheard; and how could the woman read documents which were never out of our sight for a minute? Granted that she had some means of wiring intelligence to her brother — indeed, we now know that to have been the case — how under God's heaven did she obtain that intelligence?"

"Well, that's a facer, certainly, Sir Charles; but with such a past-mistress of ingenuity as she — well, you never know. Sure she couldn't possibly have managed to get into the room and hide herself somewhere, you think?"

"I am positive she couldn't. The thing isn't possible. There's no place where she *could* have hidden. Come in and see."

He unlocked the door and, followed by the rest, led the way into the room where the inquiry into the dockmaster's affairs had been held. A glance about it was sufficient to corroborate Sir Charles's statement.

On one side stood a large fireproof safe, closely locked; on the other were two windows — iron-grilled and with inside shutters of steel; at one end was a large flat-topped table, at which Sir Charles and MacInery had conducted their investigation of the books, et cetera, and at the other a smaller writing-table, upon which stood a typewriter set on a sound-deadening square of felt, and over which hung a white-disked electric bulb. There were five chairs, and not another mortal thing. No cupboard, no wardrobe, no chest — nothing under heaven in which a creature any bigger than a cat could have hidden.

"You see," said Sir Charles, with a wave of the hand, "she couldn't have hidden in here, neither could she have hidden outside and overheard, for nothing was said that could have been of any use to her."

"Quite confident of that?"

"Oh, I can answer for that, Mr. Cleek," put in young Grimsdick. "We were so careful upon that point that Sir Charles never dictated even the smallest thing that he

wanted recorded; merely passed over the papers and said:
'Copy that where I have marked it'; and to save my table
from being overcrowded, I scratched down the marked
paragraphs in shorthand, and prepared to transcribe them
on the typewriter later. Why, sir, look here; the diabolical
part of the mystery is that those two fragments of sentences
flashed out at the telegraph office at the time of that frightful peal of thunder, and at that very instant I was in the act
of transcribing them on the typewriter."

"Hello! Hello!" rapped out Cleek, twitching round
sharply. "Sure of that, are you — absolutely sure?"

"Beyond all question, Mr. Cleek. Sir Charles will tell
you that the thunder-clap was so violent and so sudden that
both he and Mr. MacInery fairly jumped. As for me, I was
so startled that I struck a wrong letter by mistake and had
to rub out a word and type it over again. Come and see.
The paper is still on my table, and I can show you the erasure and the alteration. Now, nobody could have seen that
paper, at that particular time; not a solitary word had been
spoken with regard to it, and it wasn't more than half a
minute before that Sir Charles himself had taken it out of
the safe. Look, sir, here's the paper and here's the place
where I erased the word — see?"

Cleek walked over to the typewriter and looked at the
paper, saw the erasure, lifted it, looked at other typed sheets
lying under it, and then knotted up his brows.

"H'm!" he said reflectively, and looked farther. "You've
got a devilish hard touch for a man who does this sort of
thing constantly, and ought therefore to be an adept in the
art of typewriting evenly. And there are other errors and
erasures. Look here, my friend, I don't believe you're
used to this machine."

"No, sir, I'm not. I'm not accustomed to a shift key.
My own machine hasn't one."

"Your own! By Gad! What are you using this machine for, then, if you've got one of your own? And why didn't you bring your own when you came here on important business like this?"

"I did; but as we found this one already here I started in on it; and when I found it difficult to work, I went out to get my own, which I'd left in the outer room, just as I'd taken it from the carrier who brought it over. But the careless beggar must have handled it as if it were a trunk, for the spring was broken, the carriage wouldn't work, and two of the type bars were snapped off."

"By *Jupiter!*" Cleek's voice struck in so suddenly and with such vehemence that it was almost a bark, like that of a startled terrier, and Mr. Narkom, knowing the signs, fairly jumped at him.

"You've found out something, *I* know!" he cried. "What is it, old chap — eh?"

"Let me alone, let me alone!" flung back Cleek, irritably. "I want the dockmaster! I want him at once! Where *is* the man? Oh, there you are, Mr. Beachman. Speak up — quickly. Was that 'Hilmann' woman ever allowed to enter this room? Did she ever make use of this typewriter at any time?"

"Yes, sir — often," he replied. "She was one of the best and most careful typists I ever saw. Used to attend to all my correspondence for me and —— Good God, man, what are you doing? Don't you know that that thing's Government property?"

For Cleek, not waiting for him to finish what he was saying, had suddenly laid hands on the machine, found it screwed fast to the table and, catching up the nearest chair, was now smashing and banging away at it with all his force.

"Government destruction, you mean!" he gave back sharply. "Didn't I tell you she was a very demon of ingenuity, stupid? Didn't I say —— Victory! Now then, look here — all of you! Here's a pretty little contrivance, if you like."

He had battered the typewriter from its fastenings and sent it crashing to the floor, a wreck, not ten seconds before; now, his hand, which, immediately thereafter, had been moving rapidly over the surface of the sound-deadening square of felt beneath, whisked that, too, from the table, and let them all see the discovery he had made.

Protruding from the surface of that table and set at regular intervals there were forty-two needle points of steel — one for each key of the typewriter — which a moment before had pierced the felt's surface just sufficient to meet the bottom of the "key" above it, and to be driven downward when that key was depressed.

Spectacular as ever in these times, he faced about and gave his hand an outward fling.

"Gentlemen, the answer to the riddle," he said. "You have been supplying her with the needed information yourselves. A ducat to a door knob, every time a letter was struck on this machine its exact duplicate was recorded somewhere else. Get a saw, Mr. Beachman, and let us see to what these steel points lead."

They led to a most ingenious contrivance, as it turned out. A highly sensitive spiral spring attached to an "arm" of thin, tough steel beneath the surface of the table communicated with a rigid wire running down the wall behind one of that table's back legs and, passing thence through a small gimlet-hole in the floor, descended and disappeared.

Following that wire's course, they, too, descended until, in the fulness of time, the end was reached in a far corner of the cellar underneath the building.

There, behind an upturned empty cask, they came upon yet another wire, which wound upward, and was found afterward to travel out and up beside the "leader" until it joined the private wire of the dockyard just outside the

dormer window of what had once been Miss Greta Hilmann's bedroom. And to these wires — the one descending and the other ascending from behind that empty cask
in the cellar — there was a singular contrivance attached.
To one, a plain, everyday instrument for dispatching tele-
grams by the Morse system; to the other, a curious little
keyboard which was an exact counterpart of the keyboard
to the typewriter upstairs; and besides this there lay some
remnants of food from the store cupboard of the house, and
a sheaf of paper leaves covered with typewritten characters.

"Gentlemen, the absolute end of the riddle at last," said
Cleek, as he took up one of those leaves. "Look at them —
Government secrets every one. And I, like an ass, forgot
to remember that Nicolo Ferrand was one of the cleverest
mechanicians and one of the craftiest 'wire workers' that
the underworld boasts. Look, Sir Charles; look, Mr.
Narkom. Every touch of a letter on the keyboard of the
typewriter upstairs registered its exact duplicate on this
infernal contrivance down here, and fast as it was recorded,
that vixen wired it on to Boris Borovonski. Can't you
understand now why she left her post and flew to him?
The shock which killed him and travelled with lessened
force down the wire to the telegraph operator was felt here,
and the instrument she used was, in all probability, dis-
abled. She knew then, of course, that something had happened to her brother, and in a panic flew to find out what.

"But even the shrewdest slip up sometimes and overlook
things. Her foolish slip lay in this: that she forgot to
take with her these original drafts of the intelligence she
had wired to the dead man."

"Ah, weel," said Mr. Alexander MacInery, who, like a
true Scotsman, never liked to be found at the small end of
the horn upon any occasion, "after all, 'tis no more than I
expected. I said it was accident that was at the bottom of
it, and accident it's turned out to be."

"No doubt," agreed Cleek, with one of his peculiar smiles. "But, personally, I always like to think that there's a Power above, and when men — *and* nations — have played the game squarely —— Shan't we be going upstairs, Sir Charles? Mr. Narkom and I have a long ride back to town, and the afternoon is on the decline."

It was still farther on that road, however, before he was able to actually tear himself away from the dockyard and be off home; for there were those little legal necessities which are the penalty of dealing with Government affairs to be attended to; there was the boring business of meeting high officials, and listening to compliments and congratulations, and he was really glad when the limousine, answering to orders, rolled up, the final good-byes were said, and he and Mr. Narkom swung off townward together.

But despite the fact that he had just carried to a successful conclusion a case which would go far to enhance his reputation and to hasten the day for which he had so long and so earnestly worked, Cleek was singularly uncommunicative, markedly abstracted, as they rode back through the streets of Portsmouth Town on their way to the highroad; and had the superintendent been more observant and less wrapped up in the glory that was to be theirs as the result of the day's adventure, he might have discovered that, while his ally seemed to be dozing stupidly when he was not leaning back in a corner and smoking, he was all the time keeping a close watch of the crowded streets through which they were speeding as if looking for some one or something he expected to see. Nor did he relax this peculiar system of vigilance even after the town itself had dropped away into the far distance, and the car was scudding along over the broad stretches and the less-frequented thoroughfares of the open country.

"I shall not go all the way back with you, if you don't

mind, Mr. Narkom," he said, breaking silence abruptly, as they raced along. "Just set me down at the place where you picked me up this morning, please, and I will do the rest of the journey by train."

"Cinnamon! Why?"

"Oh, just a mere whim of mine, that's all. No — don't press me for an explanation, please. 'Where ignorance is bliss," et cetera. Besides, I'm a whimsical beggar at best, you know — and who bothers to inquire why a donkey prefers thistles to hay? So just drop me down when we reach the outskirts of Guildford, if you will be so kind."

Mr. Narkom was discreet enough to drop the subject at that and to make no further allusion to the matter until they came, in the fulness of time, to the place in question. Here he called Lennard to a halt, and Cleek alighted — not furtively, nor yet in haste — and, standing beside the car, reached in and shook hands with him.

"Until you want me again," he smiled in his easy, off-hand way. "And if that turns out to be a long time off 1 shan't be sorry. Meanwhile, if you wish to do me a favour, look about for a limousine of another make and a quite different colour. I've an odd idea that this one is fast coming to the end of its career of usefulness. Good-bye. All right, Lennard — let her go."

Then the door of the car closed with a smack, and he was off and away — so openly and at such a leisurely pace that it was clear he had neither need nor desire to effect a get-away unobserved.

"Well, I'll be dashed!" was Mr. Narkom's unspoken comment upon the proceeding — for, under his hat, he had come to the conclusion that Cleek had, in some way, by some unconfessed means, learned that Waldemar or the Apache had come back into the game and were again on his heels, but had said nothing for fear of worrying him. "Walking off as cool as you please and never the first attempt to come any of his old Vanishing Cracksman's dodges. Amazing beggar! What's he up to now, I wonder?"

It is just possible that could he have followed he would have wondered still more, for Cleek was bearing straight down upon the populous portions of the town, and about ten minutes after they two had parted, struck into the High Street, walked along it for a short distance, studying the signs over the various buildings until, sighting one which announced that it was the Guildford Office of the Royal British Life Assurance Society, he crossed the street, and with great deliberation passed in under it, and disappeared from sight.

It was one of the contradictory points of his singularly contradictory character, that whereas he had chafed under the delay in getting away from the Royal dockyard at Portsea because he was eager to get back to his work in the little old walled garden, and all his thoughts were with the flowers he was preparing for *her*, in the end he did not see the place until after the moon was up, and all hope of gardening for that day had to be abandoned entirely, yet — he came back to Dollops whistling and as happy as a sandboy.

He was up with the first cock crow next morning, and dawn found him plying fork and rake and trowel among the flowers, and positively bubbling over with enthusiasm; for the budding roses were just beginning to show colour and to give promise of full bloom for the day of days — and more than that he did not ask of heaven.

Indeed, it was written that he might not, for the balance had again swung over, the call of Nature again sounded, and the Great Mother, taking him to her bosom, had again merged the Man in the Idealist and cradled him into forgetfulness of all spells but hers. So that all through the day he went in and out among his flowers whistling and singing and living in a sort of ecstasy that ran on like a dream without end.

On the morrow the little garden was all finished and ready, and nothing now remained but to sit in idleness and wait.

CHAPTER XX

MAY had smiled itself out and June had blushed itself in — the most wondrous June, in Cleek's eyes, the world had ever seen. For the long waiting was over, the old order of things had changed, the little house in the meadowlands had its new tenant, and *she* was in England again.

It did not fret him, as it otherwise might have done, that he and Dollops had been obliged to go back to the old business of lodging a week here and a week there in the heart of the town, rather than within reach of the green trees and the fragrant meadows he loved, for always there was the chance of stealing out to meet her in the glorious countrylands when the evening came, or of a whole day with her in the woods and fields when a whole day could be spared; and to a nature such as his these things were recompense enough.

Not that many days could be spared at present, for, although nothing had been seen or heard of Waldemar or the Apaches for weeks on end, these were strenuous times for Mr. Narkom and the forces of the Yard, and what with the Coronation of his Majesty close at hand, and every train discharging hordes of visitors into London day in and day out, and crooks of every description — homemade as well as imported — from the swell mobsman down to the common lag making it the Mecca of an unholy pilgrimage — they had their hands filled to overflowing, and were worked to their utmost capacity.

The result, so far as Cleek was concerned, scarcely needs recording. It was not in him to be guilty of that form of snobbishness which is known as "standing on his dignity" at such a time — when the man who had stood his friend was in need of help, indeed, might lose his official head if he were found wanting in such a crisis — so that, naturally, he came to Mr. Narkom's assistance and took a hand in the "sorting out" process in the manner — yes, and at times, in the uniform, too — of the ordinary constable, and proved of such invaluable aid in the matter of scenting out undesirables and identifying professional crooks that things speedily fell into a more orderly shape, and he had just begun to look forward to a resumption of those happy days of wandering in the woods with Ailsa when out of the lull of coming peace there fell an official bombshell.

It took the form of a cablegram — a belated cipher communication from the police of America to the police of Great Britain — which on being decoded, ran thus:

"Just succeeded in tracing 218. Sailed ten days ago on *Tunisian* — Allan Line — from Canada, under name of Hammond. Woman with him. Handsome blonde. Passing as sister. Believed to be 774."

Now as this little exchange of courtesies relative to the movements of the noted figures of the underworld is of almost daily occurrence between the police systems of the two countries in question, Mr. Narkom had only to consult his Code Book to get at the gist of the matter; and when he did get at it, his little fat legs bent under him like a couple of straws, his round little body collapsed into the nearest chair, and he came within a hair's breadth of having a "stroke."

For the *Tunisian*, as it happened, had docked and discharged her passengers exactly thirteen hours before, so that it was safe to declare that the persons to whom those numerals alluded had unquestionably slipped unchallenged past the guardians of the port, and were safely housed at this minute within the intricacies of that vast brick-and-mortar puzzle, London; yet here they were registered in the Code Book, thus:

"No. 218 — Nicholas Hemmingway, popularly known as 'Diamond Nick.' American. Expert swindler, confidence man and jewel thief. Ex-actor and very skilful at impersonation. See Rogues' Gallery for portrait.

"No 774 — Ella Plawsen, variously known to members of the light-fingered fraternity as 'Dutch Ella' and 'Lady Bell.' German-American. Probably the most adroit female jewel thief in existence. Highly educated, exceedingly handsome, and amazingly plausible and quick witted. Usually does the 'society dodge.' Natural blonde, and about twenty-five years old. No photograph obtainable."

Within forty-five minutes after Mr. Narkom had mastered these facts he had rushed with them to Cleek, and there was a vacancy in the list of special constables from that time forth.

"Slipped in, have they?" said Cleek when he heard. "Well, be sure of one thing, Mr. Narkom: they will not have gone to a hotel — at least in the beginning — they are far too sharp for that. Neither will they house themselves in any hole and corner where their sallying forth in fine feathers to make their little clean-up would occasion comment and so lead to a clue. Indeed, I shouldn't be surprised if they were far too shrewd to remain together in any place, but will elect to operate singly, appear to have no connection whatsoever, while they are here, and to have a sort of 'happy reunion' elsewhere after their little job has been pulled off successfully. But in any case, when we find them — if we ever do — depend upon it they will be located in some quiet, respectable, secluded district, one of the suburbs, for instance, and living as circumspectly as the most prudish of prying neighbours could desire.

"Let us then go in for a series of 'walking tours' about the outlying districts, Mr. Narkom, and see if we can't stumble

over something that will be worth while. It is true I've
never met nor even seen Hemmingway, but I fancy I should
know if a man were made up or not for the rôle in which he
appears. I did, however, brush elbows with Dutch Ella
once. It was that time I went over to New York on that
affair of the Amsterdam diamonds. *You* remember? When
I 'split' the reward with the fellow from Mulberry Street,
whose daughter wanted to study music as a profession and
he couldn't afford to let her. I hobnobbed with some acquaintances of the — er — old days, over there, and went
one night to the big French Ball at the Academy of Music,
where, my companion of the night told me, there would be
'a smashing big clean-up, as half the swell crooks in town
would be there — for business.'

"They were, I dare say, for he kept pointing out this one
and that to me and saying, 'That's so and so!' as they danced
past us. I shouldn't know any of them again, so far as
looks are concerned, for the annual French Ball in New
York is a masked ball, as you are, perhaps, aware; and I
shouldn't know 'Dutch Ella' any better than the rest, but
for one thing — although I danced with her."

"Danced with her, Cleek? Danced?"

"Yes. For the purpose of 'getting a line on her shape,' so
to speak, for possible future reference. I couldn't see her
face, for she was masked to the very chin; but there's a
curious, tumor-like lump, as big as a hen's egg, just under
her right shoulder-blade, and there's the scar of an acid
burn on the back of her left hand that she'll carry to her
grave. I shall know that scar if ever I see it again. And
if by any chance I should run foul of a woman bearing one
like it, and that woman should prove to have also a lump
under the right shoulder-blade —— Come along! Let's
get out and see if we can find one. 'Time flies,' as the an-
archist said when he blew up the clock factory. Let's tod-
dle."

They "toddled" forthwith, but on a fruitless errand, as it proved. Nevertheless, they "toddled" again the next day as hopefully as ever; and the next after that, and the next again, yet at the end of the fourth they were no nearer any clue to the whereabouts of Dutch Ella and Diamond Nick than they had been in the beginning. If, as Cleek sometimes fancied, they had not merely passed through England on their way to the Continent, but were still here, housed like hawks in a safe retreat from which they made predatory excursions under the very noses of the police, there was nothing to signalize it. No amazing jewel theft, no affair of such importance as one engineered by them would be sure to be, had as yet been reported to the Yard; and for all clue there was to their doings or their whereabouts one might as well have set out to find last summer's roses or last winter's snow as hope to pick it up by any method as yet employed.

Thus matters stood when on the morning of the fifth day Cleek elected to make Hampstead Heath and its environments the scene of their operations, and at nine o'clock set forth in company with the superintendent to put them into force in that particular locality, with the result that by noontime they found themselves in the thick of as pretty a riddle as they had fallen foul of in many a day.

It came about in this way:

Turning out of St. Uldred's road into a quiet, tree-shaded avenue running parallel with the historic heath, somewhere in the neighbourhood of the Vale of Health district, they looked up to discover that there was but one building in the entire length of the thoroughfare — a large, imposing residence set back from the road proper, and encircled by a high stone wall with curiously wrought iron gates leading into the enclosure — and that before that building two copper-skinned, turbaned, fantastically clothed Hindus were doing sentry duty in a manner peculiar unto themselves — the one standing as motionless as a bronze image before the barred gateway, and the other pacing up and down before him like a clockwork toy that had been well wound up.

"The Punjab for a ducat!" declared Cleek as he caught sight of them. "And the insignia of the Ranee of Jhang, or I'm a Dutchman. I knew the old girl was over here for the coronation, to be sure, but I'd no idea of stumbling over some of her attendants in this quarter, by Jip! Not putting up out here of late, is she, Mr. Narkom?"

"No. She's still at Kensington. And what the dickens those johnnies are keeping guard over that place for beats us. Know it, don't you? It's the residence of Sir Mawson Leake — Leake & Leake, you know: Jewellers, Bond Street. Fine old place, isn't it? Inherited it from his father, as he did the business, and —— What's that? No, not a young man — not a young man by any means. Grown children — two sons. One by his first wife, and —— Hullo! that's a rum trick, by James! See that, did you, old chap?"

"See what? The manner in which that clockwork johnnie stopped in his tracks and eyed us as we passed?"

"No. The woman. All muffled up to the eyes — and in weather like this. Just stepped out of the house door, saw those two niggers, and then bolted back indoors as if the Old Boy was after her."

"Caught sight of us, very likely. You know what high-class Brahmans are where Europeans are concerned. It will be the old Ranee herself, three to one, paying a morning visit to the jeweller in reference to some of her amazing gems. That would explain the presence of the sentries. She travels nowhere without a guard."

"To be sure," admitted the superintendent, and walked on, dropping the matter from his mind entirely.

Ten minutes later, however, it was brought back to it in

a rather startling manner; for, upon rounding the end of the thoroughfare along which they had been walking, and coming abreast of an isolated building (which was clearly the stable of the house they had recently passed), they were surprised to hear the sound of a muffled cry within, to catch a whiff of charcoal smoke as the door was flung wildly open by the same muffled female Mr. Narkom had observed previously, and something more than merely startled to have her rush at them the instant she caught sight of them, crying out distractedly:

"I was afraid of it, I knew it! I knew that he would! Oh, help me, gentlemen — help me for the love of God! I can't lift him. I can't drag him out — he is too heavy for me! My husband! In there! In *there !* He'll die if you don't get him out!"

They understood then, and for the first time, what she was driving at, and rushed past her into the stable — into what had once been designed for a coachman's bedroom — to find an apartment literally reeking with the fumes that poured out from a charcoal furnace on the floor, and beside that the body of a man — inert, crumpled up, fast sinking into that hopeless state of unconsciousness which precedes asphyxiation by charcoal.

In the winking of an eye Cleek had caught up the deadly little firebrick furnace and sent it crashing through the plugged-up window into the grounds behind, letting a current of pure air rush through the place; then, while Narkom, with one hand over his mouth and nostrils, and the other swinging a pair of handcuffs by their chain, was doing a like thing with another window in the front wall, he gathered up the semi-conscious man, swung him sacklike over his shoulder, carried him out into the roadway, and propped him up against the side of the stable, while he chafed his hands and smacked his cheeks and, between times, fanned him with his hatbrim and swore at him for a "weak-backed, marrowless thing to call itself a man, and yet go in for the poltroon's trick of suicide!"

The woman was still there, squeezing her hands and sobbing hysterically, but although she had not as yet uncovered her face, it did not need that to attest the fact that she was no Hindu, but white like the man she had spoken of as her husband, and at the very first words she uttered when she saw that he was beyond danger, both Cleek and Narkom knew them for what they were — Sir Mawson and Lady Leake.

"Mawson, how could you!" she said reproachfully, going to him the very instant he was able to get on his feet, and folding him to her in an agonized embrace. "I suspected it when you left the house — but, oh, how could you?"

"I don't know," he made answer, somewhat shamefacedly yet with a note of agony in his voice that made one pity him in spite of all. "But it seemed too horrible a disgrace to be lived through. And now I shall have to face it! Oh, my God, Ada, it is too much to ask a man to bear! They are there, on guard, those Hindus, protecting me and mine until the Ranee's steward comes to receive the Ladder of Light, as promised, at ——"

"Sh-h!" she struck in warningly, remembering the presence of the others, and clapping her hand over his mouth to stay any further admission; for she had heard Cleek repeat after her husband — but with a soft significant whistle — "The Ladder of Light!" and supplement that with, "Well, I'm dashed!" and turned round on him instantly with a forced smile upon her lips but the look of terror still lingering in her fast-winking eyes.

"It is rude of me, gentlemen, to forget to thank you for your kind assistance, and I ask your forgiveness," she said. "I owe you many, many thanks and I am endeavouring to express them. But as this is merely a little family affair, I am sure you will understand."

Cleek hears that the fabulous " Ladder of Light" is back
in London again

Young Mawson overhears his parents discussing the problem of the
jewel. " He is extravagant to the point of insanity," said Sir Mawson

It was a polite dismissal. Narkom pivoted his little fat body on his heel, and prepared to take it. Cleek didn't.

"Your pardon, but the Ladder of Light can never be regarded as a family affair in *any* English household whatsoever," he said, blandly. "I can give you its exact history if you wish it. It is a necklace said to have once been the property of the Queen of Sheba and worn by her at the court of King Solomon. It is made up of twelve magnificent steel-white diamonds, cut semi-square, and each weighing twenty-eight and one half carats. They are joined together by slender gold links fitting into minute holes pierced through the edge of each stone. It is valued at one million pounds sterling and is the property of the Ranee of Jhang, who prizes it above all other of her marvellous and priceless jewels. She is not a pleasant old lady to cross, the Ranee. She would be a shrieking devil if anything were to happen to that necklace, your ladyship."

She had been slowly shrinking from him as the history of the Ladder of Light proceeded; now she leaned back against her husband, full of surprise and despairing terror, and stared and stared in a silence that was only broken by little fluttering breaths of alarm.

"It is uncanny!" she managed to say at last. "You know of that? Of the necklace? You know even me? — us? — and yet I have not uncovered my face nor given you my name. Are you then gifted with clairvoyance, Mr. — Mr. ——"

"Cleek," he gave back, making her a polite bow. "Cleek is the name, Lady Leake. Cleek of Scotland Yard."

"That man? Dear God! that amazing man?" she cried, her whole face lighting up, her drooping figure springing erect, revitalized.

"At your ladyship's service," he replied. "We are out this morning — Superintendent Narkom and I — in quest of what is probably the most skilful and audacious pair of jewel thieves in the world — just the one particular pair in all the universe to whom a loot so valuable as the Ladder of Light would offer the strongest kind of an appeal. So, if by any chance, something has occurred which threatens the safety of that amazing necklace — and you and Sir Mawson are in a position to know the facts —— Come! Take me into your confidence, and — perhaps! Who knows?"

Before he had fairly finished speaking, Lady Leake caught up his hand, and, holding it fast squeezed in both her own, looked up at him with bright, wet eyes.

"It must have been heaven itself that sent you to us this morning," she cried. "If any man in the world *can* help us, I believe in my soul that you are the man. Mawson, you hear, dearest? It is Mr. Cleek. The wonderful Mr. Cleek. Why didn't we think of *him* before? Tell him, Mawson — tell him everything, my dear."

Sir Mawson acted upon the suggestion instantly.

"Mr. Cleek, I beg, I implore you to come to our assistance!" he exclaimed in a very transport of excitement. "Lady Leake is right. If any man *can*, you are he! You ask if anything has happened with regard to that accursed necklace and if I can give you any information on the subject? To both questions, yes! It is gone! It is lost! It is stolen!"

"What's that? Stolen? The Ladder of Light? Good heavens! When? Where? How?"

"Yesterday — from my keeping! From my house! And God have mercy on me, I have every reason to believe that the thief is my eldest son!"

CHAPTER XXI

IT WAS a full minute later and in all that minute's length no one had spoken, no one had made a single sound.

The shock, the shame, of such a confession, telling, as it did, why he had attempted to destroy himself, had crumpled the man up, taken all the vitality out of him. He faced round and leaned his bent arm against the wall of the stable, hid his face in the crook of it, and Cleek, pitying him, let him have that minute all to himself. Then:

"Come," he said, very gently, going over to him and patting him on the shoulder. "Buck up! Buck up! There's nothing in all the world so deceptive as appearances, Sir Mawson; perhaps, when I've heard the facts —— Well, haven't I told you that I am out for a pair of expert jewel thieves, and that that necklace is just the sort of thing they'd be likely to make play for? How do you know, then, that they didn't?"

"I wish I could believe that, I wish I could even hope it," he gave back miserably. "But you don't know the facts, Mr. Cleek."

"To be sure I don't; and they're what I'm after. Let's have them, please. To begin with, how came the Ladder of Light to be in your possession at all?"

"It was brought to me yesterday — for repairing — by the Ranee's own *major domo*. Not a mere *eice*, Mr. Cleek, but the most trusted of all her henchmen. Three of the narrow gold links which hold the stones together had worn thin and needed strengthening. It was four o'clock in the afternoon when he arrived, and the Ranee, he said, had selected our house for the work on the recommendation of royalty. There was several hours' work on the thing — I saw that the instant I examined it. But I was appalled by the fearful responsibility of having a jewel of such fabulous value on the premises — with people constantly coming in and going out — and determined, therefore, to take it home and do the repairs myself. I informed the Ranee's *major domo* of that resolution, and demanded of him a guard of the Ranee's own attendants to accompany me on the journey and to keep watch over my house until he should come in person to receive the necklace to-day.

"He accorded me this willingly; departed — still retaining possession of the jewel, for I would not have it left with me at any cost — returned with the guard an hour later, handed me the case containing the necklace, and I left for home a few minutes after five — and the Hindu guard with me. On arriving ——"

"One moment, please," interposed Cleek. "Did you examine the case to see if the Ladder of Light was still there before you started?"

"Yes, Mr. Cleek. I have no very great faith in Hindus at any time, so you may be sure I took that precaution the instant the man placed the case in my hands. The necklace was there. I even went further. Before leaving my place of business I submitted the stones to chemical test to be sure that no substitution had been made. They were absolutely genuine; so that there can be no shadow of doubt that it was the Ladder of Light itself I carried home with me. On arriving at my residence I stationed the two Hindu guards at the front gate, entered the house, and was upon the point of going immediately to my study to subject the stones to yet another chemical test — to make sure that no trickery had been practised upon me by the Hindus on the journey — when I was unexpectedly pounced upon in

the main hallway by my son, Henry, who was in a greatly
excited state and attempted to renew the subject of our
unpleasant interview of the day before."

Here Sir Mawson's voice grew curiously thick and un-
steady. He paused a moment as if ashamed to go on, then
stiffened himself and continued.

"Mr. Cleek," he said, agitatedly, "it is necessary that I
should tell you, at this point, something with regard to
those who make up the members of my household."

"You needn't. I have already heard. Lady Leake is, I
believe, your second wife, and you have two sons."

"No — three," he corrected. "Henry, my eldest, who is
twenty-four and is the only survivor of the children of my
first and most unhappy marriage; Curzon, who is just
entering his twenty-first year, and Bevis, who has not yet
turned seven, and is, of course, still in the nursery. I may
as well admit to you, Mr. Cleek, that my first marriage was
a failure; that it was none of my own choosing, but was
consummated in deference to the will and wishes of my
parents. We were utterly unsuited to each other, my first
wife and I, and it is, no doubt, only natural that the son
she left me when death delivered us both from an irksome
bondage should reflect in himself some of those points of
difference which made our union a mistake.

"Don't misunderstand me, however. He is very dear to
me — dear, too, to his stepmother, who loves him as her
own, and the one strong feature in his character is the love
he gives her in return. Then, too, he is my first born, my
heir, and no man fails to love that first child that ever
called him father."

"No man could fail to love this particular one at all
events, Mr. Cleek," put in her ladyship. "Wild, reckless,
extravagant — yes! But at heart, the dearest boy!"

"Just so!" interposed Cleek. "But let us get on, please.
So this 'dearest boy' had an unpleasant interview with you

the day before yesterday, did he, Sir Mawson? What was it about?"

"The usual thing — money. He is extravagant to the point of insanity. I've paid his debts until my patience is quite worn out, hoping against hope that he will reform. At that interview, however, he asked for a thing I would *not* listen to —£200 to settle a gambling debt at his club: to take up an I. O. U. that would get him blacklisted as a defaulter if it were not met. 'Then get blacklisted!' I said to him, 'if there's no other way to cut you off from the worthless lot you associate yourself with. You'll not get one farthing from me to settle any such disgraceful thing as a gambling debt, rest assured of that!" Then I walked out of the room and left him, and that was the last I saw of him until he pounced upon me in the hall yesterday when I was going to my study with the case containing the Ranee's necklace.

"That was the subject he wanted to renew. He'd been to town, he said, and had had a talk with the man to whom he had given the I. O. U., 'and dad, if you'll only do it just this once — just this one last *once!*' he was saying when I interrupted him. 'I've no time to listen now, and no inclination. I've important business to attend to,' I said, then waved him aside and went into the study and locked the door while I attended to the matter of applying the acid test to the diamonds for the second time.

"Meanwhile, he had gone up to Lady Leake's boudoir to implore her to use her influence with me, and he was still there when, after the stones had again answered to the acid test, I carried the necklace up there (to leave it in her charge for the brief time it would take me to prepare the tools and materials for the work in hand) and told her all about it. But I didn't know that at the time, Mr. Cleek, for he was sitting in a deep, cushioned armchair at the far end of the room, and the tall back of that chair was turned toward me. Indeed, I hadn't the faintest suspicion that there was anybody but Lady Leake and myself in the room until he got up suddenly and said, 'Dad, you aren't too busy to listen now! Won't you let me ask you what I was going to do downstairs? Won't you, dad? Please!'

"Of course he had heard what I had said, Mr. Cleek — although I never gave a thought to that at the time — and as Lady Leake had, womanlike, taken the gorgeous necklace out of the case, held it up to her neck and was then viewing herself in her dressing mirror, it followed that he also saw. But how could I dream of there being anything in that to regret, and he a son of mine? It was only — afterward — when it came back to my memory —— Good God! it is too horrible to think of even now, much less to talk about!"

"Steady, steady, Sir Mawson!" sounded Cleek's soothing voice. "Brakes on! Sidetrack your emotions if you can and stick to the mainline! Well, what followed?"

"I have no very clear recollection, Mr. Cleek, for just then Lady Leake chose to add her entreaties to his, and to ask me if I would permit her to draw her next quarter's pin money in advance and let her take up the I. O. U. for him. But I was so furious at the thought of his skulking in like a beggar and a cad, and trying to 'bleed' her, that I flew into a violent rage, ordered him out of the room instantly, and forbade his stepmother to lend or give him one farthing either then or at any time thereafter. 'There will be no gambler's I. O. U.'s taken up for you by anybody in this house,' I flung at him. 'If you are in debt, get out of it in your own way and as best you can!'

"I think that even then I was conscious of a sense of gratification at the way he took that ultimatum, Mr. Cleek, for instead of whining like a whipped cur, he pulled himself up straight and strong, clicked his heels together, and said very quietly, 'All right, sir, I'll take you at your word.

Thank you for past favours. Good-bye!' and then walked out of the room. That was the last I have seen or heard of him."

"H'm! Leave the house, did he?"

"Yes — but not then. That was a few minutes before seven. A servant saw him on the top landing coming out of his own room with something wrapped up in a parcel, after that. And another, who was busy cleaning up in the lower hall, saw him come down and go out at ten minutes past."

"And in the meantime, the Ladder of Light had vanished?"

"Yes. After Henry had left the boudoir I had a few minutes' heated argument with Lady Leake; then, remembering the work I had in hand, I left the necklace in her charge and hurried away to rig up a temporary workshop. It was about twenty minutes past seven when I finished doing that, and went back to Lady Leake's boudoir to get the jewel. I found her in a state of the wildest excitement, flying about the room like an insane woman and searching everywhere. The necklace was gone! Only for one single minute of time had it been out of her sight, yet in that minute it had vanished, utterly and completely, and there was not a trace of it to be found anywhere."

"H'm! Just so! Case gone, too, Sir Mawson?"

"No! That was still there, lying on her dressing-table, but it was empty."

"I see. So, then, it could not have been that that was wrapped up in the parcel your son was seen carrying. Anybody in that room after Sir Mawson left you, your ladyship?"

"Not a living soul, Mr. Cleek."

"Could no one have stolen it without your knowledge?"

"That would be impossible. I locked the door the instant Sir Mawson left me."

"Ah, then, of course! Another question, please. Sir Mawson has spoken of there being 'one single minute' when the necklace was not directly under your eyes. When was that?"

"When I left the room, Mr. Cleek."

"Oho! Then you did leave it, eh?"

"Yes. It was thoughtless of me, of course; but I only ran down to the foot of the staircase, when I remembered, and ran back in a perfect panic. Still I had locked the door in going out even then and the key was in my hand. It was still locked when I returned, but in that one single minute the necklace had disappeared. I was gratifying my woman's vanity by holding it up to my throat and viewing myself in the glass just an instant before, and I remember perfectly, laying it down on the velvet lining of its open case at the time I recollected the matter which caused me to leave the room."

"May I ask what that matter was?"

"Yes. A service I had promised to perform for Miss Eastman."

"Miss Eastman? Who is she?"

"My son's fiancée. She and her father are visiting us at present. Curzon met and became engaged to Miss Eastman on the occasion of her last visit to England, and this time her father is accompanying her."

"Her last *visit*? Then the lady and her father are not English?"

"Oh, dear, no — Americans. They came over less than a week ago. Pardon? No, I do not at the moment recall the name of the vessel, Mr. Cleek, but whichever one it was it seems to have been a very ill-conditioned affair and gave them a very bad crossing, indeed. That is why I had to render Miss Eastman the service of which I spoke — the sudden recollection of which caused me to lay down the necklace and hurry from the room. I had forgotten all about it until I happened to see the roll of lint on my dressing-table."

"Lint, Lady Leake? What on earth had lint to do with the matter?"

"I had bought it for Miss Eastman when I was in town this morning. She asked me to, as she had used her last clean bandage yesterday. She had a very bad fall on shipboard, Mr. Cleek, and injured her left hand severely!"

Narkom made a curious sort of gulping sound, whipped out his handkerchief and began to dab his bald spot, and looked round at Cleek out of the tail of his eye. But Cleek neither moved nor spoke nor made any sign — merely pushed his lower lip out over his upper one and stood frowning at the stable door.

And here — just here — a strange and even startling thing occurred. With just one hoarse "Toot-toot!" to give warning of its coming, a public taxi swung round the curve of the road, jerked itself up to a sudden standstill within a rope's cast of the spot where the four were standing, and immediately there rang forth a rollicking, happy youthful voice crying out, as the owner of it stood up and touched an upright forefinger to his numbered cap, in jolly mimicry of the Hanson cabman of other days: "Keb, sir? Keb, mum? Keb! Keb!" and hard on the heels of that flung out a laughing, "Hullo, mater? Hullo, dad? you dear old Thunder Box! I say! 'How does this sort of thing get you?' as Katie Eastman says. Buttons all over me, like a blooming Bobby! What?"

And it needed no more than that to assure Cleek and Mr. Narkom that in the bright-eyed, bonny-faced, laughing young fellow who jumped down from the driver's seat at this, and stood up straight and strong, and displayed his taxicabman's livery unabashed and unashamed, they were looking upon Sir Mawson Leake's eldest son and — heir!

"Henry!" The voice was Lady Leake's, and there was

pain and surprise and joy and terror all jumbled up in 'it curiously, as she ran to him. "Henry! Is it really *you?*" "'Sure thing!' — to quote Katie again. Just took a spin over to show myself off. Plenty of brass trimmings! What? I thought, dad, you'd like to be sure that I really am done with the clubs at last. Not because they blacklisted me — for they didn't — but because — oh well, *you* know. No taxicabmen need apply — that sort of thing. I'll be invited to resign from every blessed one of them tomorrow, and there's not a chap connected with any one of 'em who'd be seen taking a match from me to light his cigarette with after this. All the same, though, I go out of them with a clean slate, and that's all I cared about. I did get that two hundred after all, pater. Curzon and Katie raised it for me between them — out of their own private accounts, you know — and as driving a car is the only thing I really do understand, I'm earning the money to pay them back this way."

"That's the stuff, by Jupiter! That's the stuff!" rapped out Cleek, impulsively. "You ought to have known from the first, Sir Mawson, that they don't make thieves of this sort of material?"

"Thieves? What do you mean by thieves? And who the dickens are you, anyway? I say, dad, who's this johnnie? What's he driving at? What does he mean by talking about thieves?"

"The necklace — the Ranee's necklace! The Ladder of Light!" bleated Sir Mawson feebly. "It is gone! It is lost! It went when *you* went. There has been no trace of it since." Then he joined Lady Leake, and plucked at the boy's sleeve, and between them out came the whole miserable story.

"And you think that I stole it? You dare to think that?" flung out his son, jerking back from him and brushing aside Lady Leake's solicitous hand. "Very well, then.

think what you jolly well please! I'm done with the lot of you!"

And after that — the Deluge! Speaking, he turned on his heel and rushed back to his taxi, wrenched open its door, revealing what none of them had suspected before, because of the drawn curtains: that the vehicle was occupied — and sang out in a fine fury, "Pull up the blinds, Curz. Come out, old chap. Come out, Major! Come out, Katie — all of you — at once! There isn't going to be any 'jolly lark,' any 'pleasant surprise,' any 'killing of the fatted calf.' This isn't a comedy — it's a tragedy! Hop out lively — the lot of you! I'm done with my father, and I've got to get back to my place in the ranks as fast as I can fly. I'll pay you back, Katie. I'll pay you back, Curz, old chap! Yes, by God! I will if I drive this thing night and day without sleeping!"

Then came a sudden banging of the taxi's door, a hoot from the horn as he jumped back to his seat and sounded a warning note, and in the winking of an eye he was off and away, and there in the road stood a stout, pleasant-faced old gentleman, a youth with a budding moustache, and a bright-faced, fairylike little lady of about eighteen, all three of whom were standing stock still and staring after the vanishing taxi in the blankest of blank amazement. Of a sudden, however:

"My goodness, popper, I guess Curzon and I have sort of muffed it somehow!" the little lady said, forlornly.

"I guess you have, honey — I guess you have. Anyhow, something's gone bust, that's a sure thing! Let's go and ask Sir Mawson what it's all about."

"Yes, let us by all means," put in the younger man. "Come on!"

Mr. Narkom, who heard these things, drew closer to Cleek, looked up at him anxiously, and contrived to whisper an inquiry which fell only upon his ally's ears.

"Found out anything, old chap?"

"Yes. From their words it is clear that Sir Mawson has taken nobody in the house — even his son, Curzon — into his confidence regarding the lost necklace."

"I don't mean that — I'm alluding to the others. Found out anything about *them?*"

"Yes, and a very important thing, too: They are *not* Diamond Nick and Dutch Ella. Not in the least like them, neither are they disguised. Also, Miss Eastman's injury is only a sprained wrist, it appears. You observe she does not even attempt to cover the back of her hand. I'm afraid, Mr. Narkom, you've been barking up the wrong tree."

CHAPTER XXII

BY THIS time the major, his daughter, and young Curzon Leake, full of deep and earnest solicitude for the long-erring Henry, and fairly bristling with questions and entreaties, had crossed the intervening space and were at Sir Mawson's side; but as the details of what was said and done for the next ten minutes have no bearing upon the case in hand, they may well be omitted from these records. Suffice it then, that, on the plea of "having some very important business with these gentlemen, which will not permit of another moment's delay," and promising to "discuss the other matter later on," Sir Mawson managed to get rid of them, with the story of the lost necklace still unconfessed, and was again free to return to the subject in hand.

"Of course, I can understand your reluctance, with those Indian chaps about, to take anybody into your confidence regarding the loss of the jewel, Sir Mawson," said Cleek, as soon as the others were well out of hearing; "but sometimes a policy of silence is wise, and sometimes it is a mistake. For instance: if any of a man's servants should know of a circumstance which might have a bearing upon a robbery they are not likely to mention it if they don't even know that a robbery has been committed. However, we shall know more about that after I've been over the ground and poked about a bit. So, if you and her ladyship will be so kind, I should like to have a look indoors, particularly in Lady Leake's boudoir, as soon as possible."

Upon what trivial circumstances do great events sometimes hinge! Speaking, he turned toward the curve of the

204

road to go back to the guarded gates of the house which he had so recently passed, when Lady Leake's hand plucked nervously at his sleeve.

"Not that way! Not for worlds, with those Hindus on the watch!" she exclaimed agitatedly. "Heaven knows what they might suspect, what word they might send to the Ranee's steward, if they saw us returning to the house without having seen us leave it. Come! there is another and a safer way. Through the grounds and round to the door of the music room, at the back of the building. Follow me."

They followed forthwith, and in another moment were taking that "other way" with her, pushing through a thick plantation, crossing a kitchen garden, cutting through an orchard, and walking rapidly along an arboured path, until they came at last to the final obstacle of all — a large rock garden — which barred their progress to the smooth, close-clipped lawn at whose far end the house itself stood. This rock garden, it was plain from the course she was taking, it was Lady Leake's intention to skirt, but Cleek, noting that there was a path running through the middle of it, pointed out that fact.

"One moment!" he said. "As time is of importance, would not this be the shorter and the quicker way?"

"Yes," she gave back, without, however, stopping in her progress around the tall rocks which formed its boundary. "But if we took it we should be sure to meet Bevis. That is his especial playground, you know, and if he were to see his father and me we shouldn't be able to get rid of him again. No! Don't misunderstand, Mr. Cleek. I am not one of those mothers who find their children a nuisance in their nursery stage. Bevis is the dearest little man! But he is so full of pranks, so full of questions, so full of life and high spirits — and I couldn't stand that this morning. Besides, he has no one to play with him to-day. This is Miss Miniver's half holiday. Pardon? Yes — his nursery governess. She won't be back until three. I only hope he will stay in the rock garden and amuse himself with his pirates' cave until then."

"His ——"

"Pirates' cave. Miss Miniver took him to a moving-picture show one day. He saw one there and nothing would do him but his father must let him have one for himself; so the gardeners made one for him in the rock garden and he amuses himself by going out on what he calls 'treasure raids' and carries his spoils in there."

"His spoils, eh? H'm! I see! Pardon me, Lady Leake, but do you think it is possible that this affair we are on may be only a wild goose chase after all? In other words, that, not knowing the value of the Ranee's necklace, your little son may have made that a part of his spoils and carried it off to his pirates' cave?"

"No, Mr. Cleek, I do not. Such a thing is utterly impossible. For one thing, the boudoir door was locked, remember; and, for another, Bevis had been bathed and put to bed before the necklace was lost. He could not have got up and left his room, as Miss Miniver sat with him until he fell asleep."

"H'm!" commented Cleek. "So that's 'barking up the wrong tree' for a second time. Still, of course, the necklace couldn't have vanished of its own accord. Hum-m-m! Just so! Another question, your ladyship: You spoke of running down to the foot of the stairs with the lint for Miss Eastman and running back in a panic when you remembered the necklace. How, then, did you get the lint to Miss Eastman, after all?"

"I sent it to her with apologies for not being able to do the bandaging for her."

"Sent it to her, your ladyship? By whom?"

"Jennifer — one of the servants."

"Oho!" said Cleek, in two different tones. "So then you

did unlock the door of your boudoir for a second time, and
somebody other than Sir Mawson and your stepson *did* see
the inside of the room, eh?"

"Your pardon, Mr. Cleek, but you are wrong in both
surmises. Jennifer was the servant who was working in
the lower hall at the time — the one who says he saw Henry
leave the house at ten minutes past seven. The instant I
reached the foot of the stairs and thought of the necklace,
I called Jennifer to me, gave him the lint with orders to take
it at once to Miss Eastman's maid with the message mentioned, and then turned round and ran back to my boudoir
immediately."

"H'm! I see. I suppose, your ladyship, it isn't possible that this man Jennifer might, in going to carry that
message —— But no! I recollect: the door of your boudoir was locked. So even if he had managed to outstrip
you by going up another staircase ——"

"Oh, I see what you mean!" she declared, as they reached
the edge of the lawn and set out across it. "But, Mr. Cleek,
such a thing would not bear even hinting at, so far as Jennifer is concerned. He is the soul of honesty, for one thing;
and, for another, he couldn't have outstripped me, as you
put it, had I returned at a snail's pace. He is very old,
and near-sighted. There! look! That is he, over there,
sweeping the leaves off the terrace. You can see for yourself how impossible it would be for him to run upstairs."

Cleek did see. Looking in the direction indicated, he
saw an elderly man employed as stated, whose back was
bowed, and whose limping gait betokened an injury which
had left him hopelessly lame.

"His leg had to be amputated as the result of being run
over by an omnibus in the streets of London," explained
her ladyship, "and, in consequence, he wears a wooden one.
He has been in the employ of the family for more than forty
years. Originally he was a gardener, and, after his accident,

Sir Mawson was for pensioning him off so that he could end his days in quiet and comfort. But he quite broke down at the thought of leaving the old place, and as he wouldn't listen to such a thing as being paid for doing nothing, we humoured his whim and let him stay on as a sort of handy man. I am sorry to say that Bevis, little rogue, takes advantage of his inability to run, and plays no end of pranks upon him. But he adores the boy, and never complains."

Cleek, who had been studying the man fixedly with his narrowed eyes — and remembering what had been said of Diamond Nick's skill at impersonation, the while they were crossing the lawn — here twitched his head, as if casting off a thought which annoyed him, and turned a bland look upon Lady Leake.

"One last question, your ladyship," he said. "I think you said that Jennifer was cleaning the hall at the time your stepson left the house; and, as, presumably, you wouldn't overwork a crippled old chap like that, how happened it that he was still at his labours at ten minutes past seven o'clock in the evening? That's rather late to be cleaning up a hall, isn't it?"

"Yes, much *too* late," she acknowledged. "But it couldn't be helped in the present instance. The gasfitters didn't finish their work as early as we had hoped, and as he couldn't begin until they *had* finished, he was delayed in starting."

"The gasfitters, eh? Oho! So you had those chaps in the house yesterday, did you?"

"Yes. There had been an unpleasant leakage of gas in both the music room and the main hall, for two or three days, and as the men had to take down the fixtures to get to the seat of the trouble, Jennifer improved the opportunity to give the chandelier and the brackets a thorough cleaning, since he couldn't of course start to clear up the mess the workmen made until after they had finished and gone.

But — Mr. Cleek! *They* couldn't have had anything to do with the affair, for they left the house at least ten minutes before the Ladder of Light came into it. So, naturally —— This is the door of the music room, gentlemen. Come in, please."

⸜ The invitation was accepted at once, and in another half minute Cleek and Mr. Narkom found themselves standing in a wonderful white-and-gold room, under a huge crystal chandelier of silver and cut glass, and looking out through an arched opening, hung with sulphur-coloured draperies, into a sort of baronial hall equipped with armour and tapestries, and broad enough to drive a coach through without danger to its contents.

From this hall, as they discovered, when Lady Leake led them without delay toward the scene of the necklace's mysterious vanishment, a broad, short flight of richly carpeted stairs led to a square landing, and thence another and a longer flight, striking off at right angles, communicated with the passage upon which her ladyship's boudoir opened.

"It was here that I stood, Mr. Cleek, when I recollected about the necklace as I called Jennifer to me," she explained, pausing on the landing at the foot of this latter flight of stairs just long enough to let him note, over the broad rail of the banister, that the great hall was clearly visible below. "He was there, just under you, drying the globes of the music-room chandelier when I called to him. Now come this way, please, and you will see how impossible it is for any one to have entered and left the boudoir during my brief absence without my seeing or hearing."

It was; for the door of the boudoir, which was entirely detached from the rest of the suite occupied by herself and her husband, was immediately opposite the head of the staircase and clearly visible from the landing at its foot.

She unlocked this one solitary door, and let them see that the only other means of possibly entering the room was by way of a large overhanging bay window overlooking the grounds. But this was a good twenty feet above the surface of the earth and there was not a vine nor a tree within yards and yards of it, and as the space beneath was so large and clear that no one could have manipulated a ladder without the certainty of discovery, Cleek saw at a glance that the window might be dismissed at once as a possible point of entry.

Nor did anything else about the room offer a hint more promising. All that he saw was just what one might have expected to see in such a place under such circumstances as these.

On the dressing-table, surrounded by a litter of silver and cut-glass toilet articles, lay the case which had once contained the famous necklace, wide open and empty. Over the back of a chair — as if it had been thrown there under the stress of haste and great excitement — hung a negligée of flowered white silk trimmed with cascades of rich lace, and across a sofa at the far end of the room, a dinner gown of gray satin was carefully spread out, with a pair of gray silk stockings and gray satin slippers lying beside it.

"Everything is exactly as it was, Mr. Cleek, at the time the necklace disappeared," explained her ladyship, noting the manner in which his glances went flickering about the room, skimming the surface of all things but settling on none. "Everything, that is, but that negligée there."

"Wasn't that in the room, then?"

"Oh, yes, but it wasn't on the chair; it was on me. I had come up to dress for dinner a short time before Henry made his appearance — indeed, I had only just taken off my street costume and started to dress when he rapped at the door and implored me to let him come in and speak to me for a minute or two. 'For God's sake, mater!' was the way he put it, and as haste seemed to be of vital importance, I slipped on my negligée and let him in as quickly as I could.

Afterward, when Sir Mawson came in with the wonderful necklace ——"

She stopped abruptly, and her voice seemed to die away in her throat; and when she spoke again it was in a sort of panic.

"Mr. Cleek!" she cried, "*Mr. Cleek!* What is it? What's the matter? Good heavens, Mawson, has the man gone out of his mind?"

In the circumstances the question was an excusable one. A moment before, she had seen Cleek walk in the most casual manner to the chair where the lace-clouded negligée hung, had seen him pick it up to look at the chair seat under it, and was collectedly proceeding with the account of the events of yesterday, when, without hint or warning, he suddenly yapped out a sound that was curiously like a dog that had mastered the trick of human laughter, flung the negligée from him, dropped on his knees, and was now careering round the room like a terrier endeavouring to pick up a lost scent — pushing aside tables, throwing over chairs, and yapping, yapping.

"Cleek, old chap!" It was Narkom that spoke, and the hard, thick hammering of his heart made his voice shake. "Good lud, man! in the name of all that's wonderful ——"

"Let me alone!" he bit in, irritably. "Of all the asses! Of all the blind, mutton-headed idiots!" then laughed that curious, uncanny laugh again, scrambled to his feet and made a headlong bolt for the door. "Wait for me — all of you — in the music room," he threw back from the threshold. "Don't stir from it until I come. I want that fellow Jennifer! I want him *at once!*"

And here, turning sharply on his heel with yet another yapping sound, he bolted across the passage, ran down the staircase like an escaping thief, and by the time the others could lock up the boudoir and get down to the music room, there wasn't a trace of him anywhere.

CHAPTER XXIII

IT WAS a full half hour later, and Sir Mawson and Lady Leake and Mr. Maverick Narkom were in the throes of the most maddening suspense, when the door of the music room flashed open and flashed shut again, and Cleek stood before them once more — quite alone still, but with that curious crooked smile which to Narkom stood for so much, looping up the corner of his mouth and mutely foreshadowing the riddle's spectacular end.

"Cleek, dear chap!" The superintendent's voice was sharp and thin with excitement. "You've found out something, then?"

"I hope, Mr. Narkom, I have found out everything," he replied with a marked emphasis on the word hope. "But as we are told when in doubt or in difficulty to 'look above' for a way out, permit me to follow that advice before proceeding any further with the subject."

Here he stepped to the centre of the room, twitched back his head, and, with chin upslanted and eyes directed toward the ceiling, moved slowly round in a narrow circle for a moment or two.

But of a sudden he came to a sharp standstill, rapped out a short, queer little laugh, and, altering these mysterious tactics, looked down and across the room at Sir Mawson Leake.

"I think the Ranee did not look to the security of those slim gold links a day too soon, Sir Mawson," he said. "It is too much to ask a man to risk his whole fortune on the tenacity of a bit of age-worn wire as you have done, and if

I were in your shoes I'd tell the old girl's *major domo* when he comes for the necklace, to get it repaired somewhere else — and be dashed to him."

"Good! Wouldn't I, in a twinkling, if I could only lay hands on the wretched thing again. But I haven't it, as you know."

"Quite true. But you are going to have it — presently. I know where it is!"

"Mr. Cleek!"

"Gently, gently, my friends. Don't go quite off your heads with excitement. I repeat, I know where it is. I have found it and —— Mr. Narkom! Look sharp! A chair for Lady Leake — she's tottering. Steady, steady, your ladyship; it will only complicate matters to lose a grip on yourself now; and you have kept up so brave a front all through, it would be a pity to break down at the end."

"I am not breaking down. I am quite all right. Please go on, Mr. Cleek — please do. I can stand anything better than this. Are you sure you have found it? Are you *sure?*"

"Absolutely. I have had a nice little talk with old Jennifer, and a very satisfactory visit to Master Bevis Leake's interesting 'pirates' cave' and —— Gently, gently, Sir Mawson; gently, all of you. Don't jump to conclusions too quickly. No, your ladyship, I did not find the necklace in that cave, and for the simple reason that it is not and never has been there — in short, neither your son Bevis nor the servant, Jennifer, has the least idea in the world *where* it is. I have, however, and if in return for handing it over to him, Sir Mawson will give me his promise to take that boy, Henry, back and give him another chance, he shall have it in his hands ten seconds afterward."

"I promise! I promise! I promise!" broke in Sir Mawson, almost shouting in his excitement. "I give you my word, Mr. Cleek, I give you my solemn oath."

"Right you are," said Cleek in reply. Then he twitched forward a chair, stepped on the seat of it, reached up into the midst of the chandelier's glittering cut-glass lustres, snapped something out from their sparkling festoons, and added serenely, " Favour for favour: there you are, then!" as he dropped the Ladder of Light into Sir Mawson's hands.

And all in a moment, what with Lady Leake laughing and crying at one and the same time, her liege lord acting pretty much as if he had suddenly gone off his head, and Mr. Maverick Narkom chiming in and asserting several times over that he'd be jiggered, there was the dickens and all to pay in the way of excitement.

"Up in the chandelier!" exclaimed Lady Leake when matters had settled down a bit. "Up there, where it might have remained unnoticed for months, so like is it to the strings of lustres. But how? But when? Oh, Mr. Cleek, who in the world put it there? And why?"

"Jennifer," he made answer. "No, not for any evil purpose, your ladyship. He doesn't know even yet that it was there, or that he ever in all his life held a thing so valuable in his hands. All that he does know in connection with it is that while he was cleaning those lustres out there in the hallway yesterday afternoon between four and five o'clock your son Bevis, out on one of his 'treasure raids,' paid him a visit, and that long after, when the old fellow came to replace the lustres on the chandelier, he discovered that one string was missing.

" 'I knowed the precious little rascal had took it, sir, of course,' was the way he put it in explaining the matter to me; 'and I felt sure I'd be certain to find it in his pirates' cave. But Lord bless you, it turned out as he hadn't took it there at all, as I found out a goodish bit afterward, when her ladyship comes down to the landing at the top of the first flight of stairs, calls me up to give me the lint for Miss

Eastman, and then gives a jump and a cry, like she'd just recollected something, and runs back upstairs as fast as she could fly. For when I looks down, there was the missing string of lustres lying on the landing right where her ladyship had been standing, and where he, little rascal, had went and hid it from me. So I picks it up and puts it back in its place on the chandelier just as soon as I'd taken the lint to Miss Eastman like her ladyship told me.'

"In that, Lady Leake, lies the whole story of how it came to be where you saw me find it. Jennifer is still under the impression that what he picked up on that landing was nothing more than the string of twelve cut-glass lustres joined together by links of brass wire which is at this moment hanging among the 'treasures' in your little son's pirates' cave."

"On the landing? Lying on the landing, do you say, Mr. Cleek?" exclaimed her ladyship. "But heavens above, how could the necklace ever have got there? Nobody could by any possibility have entered the boudoir after I left it to run down to the landing with the lint. You saw for yourself how utterly impossible such a thing as that would be."

"To be sure," he admitted. "It was the absolute certainty that nobody in the world could have actually forced the key to the solution upon me. Since it was possible for only one solitary person to have entered and left that room since Sir Mawson placed the necklace in your charge, clearly then that person was the one who carried it out. Therefore, there was but one conclusion, namely, that when your ladyship left that room the Ladder of Light left it with you: on your person, and —— Gently, gently, Lady Leake; don't get excited, I beg. I shall be able in a moment to convince you that my reasoning upon that point was quite sound, and to back it up with actual proof.

"If you will examine the necklace, Sir Mawson, you will

see that it has not come through this adventure uninjured; in short, that one of the two sections of its clasp is missing, and the link that once secured that section to the string of diamonds has parted in the middle. Perhaps a good deal which may have seemed to you sheer madness up to this point will be clearly explained when I tell you that when I lifted Lady Leake's negligée from that chair a while ago I found this thing clinging to the lace of the right sleeve."

"Good heavens above! Look, Ada, look! The missing section of the clasp."

"Exactly," concurred Cleek. "And when you think of where I found it I fancy it will not be very difficult to reason out how the necklace came to be where Jennifer picked it up. On your own evidence, Lady Leake, you hastily laid it down on your dressing-table, when the sight of the lint bandage recalled to your mind your promise to Miss Eastman, and from that moment it was never seen again. The natural inference then is so clear I think there can hardly be a doubt that when you reached over to pick up that bandage the lace of your sleeve caught on the clasp, became entangled, and that when you left the room you carried the Ladder of Light with you. The great weight of the necklace swinging free as you ran down the staircase would naturally tell upon that weak link, and no doubt when you leaned over the banister at the landing to call Jennifer, that was, so to speak, the last straw. The weak link snapped, the necklace dropped away, and the thick carpet entirely muffled the sound of its fall. As for the rest ——"

The loud jangling of the door bell cut in upon his words. He pulled out his watch and looked at it.

"That will be the Ranee's *major domo*, I fancy, Sir Mawson," he observed, "and with your kind permission Mr. Narkom and I will be going. We have, as I have already told you, a little matter of importance still to attend to in the interest of the Yard, and although I haven't the slightest idea we shall be able to carry it to a satisfactory conclusion for a very long time — if ever — we had better be about it. Pardon? Reward, your ladyship? Oh, but I've had that: Sir Mawson has given me his promise to let that bonny boy have another chance. That was all I asked, remember. There's good stuff in him, but he stands at the crossroads, and face to face with one of life's great crises. Now is the time when he needs a friend. Now is the time for his father to *be* a father; and opportunity counts for so much in the devil's gamble for souls. Get to him, daddy — get to him and stand by him — and you'll have given me the finest reward in the world."

And here, making his adieus to Lady Leake, whose wet eyes followed him with something of reverence in them, and shaking heartily the hand Sir Mawson held out, he linked arms with Narkom, and together they passed out, leaving a great peace and a great joy behind them.

"Gad, what an amazing beggar you are!" declared the superintendent, breaking silence suddenly as soon as they were at a safe distance from the house. "You'll end your days in the workhouse, you know, if you continue this sort of tactics. Fancy chucking up a reward for the sake of a chap you never saw before, and who treated you like a mere nobody. Why, man alive, you could have had almost any reward — a thousand pounds if you'd asked it — for finding a priceless thing like that."

"I fancy I've helped to find something that is more priceless still, my friend, and it's cheap at the price."

"But a thousand pounds, Cleek! a thousand pounds! God's truth, man, think what you could do with all that money — think what you could buy!"

"To be sure; but think what you *can't!* Not one day of lost innocence, not one hour of spoilt youth! It isn't because they have a natural tendency toward evil that *all* men go wrong. It is not what they possess but what they lack that's at the bottom of the downfall of four fifths of them. Given such ingredients as a young chap suffering under a sense of personal injury, a feeling that the world's against him, that he has neither a home nor a friend to stand by him in his hour of need, and the devil will whip up the mixture and manufacture a criminal in less than no time. It is easier to save him while he's worth the saving than it is to pull him up after he has gone down the line, Mr. Narkom, and if by refusing to accept so many pounds, shillings, and pence, a man can do the devil out of a favourable opportunity —— Oh, well, let it go at that. Come on, please. We are still as far as ever from the 'game' we set out to bag, my friend; and as this district seems to be as unpromising in that respect as all the others — where next?"

CHAPTER XXIV

"I'M BOTHERED if I know," returned Narkom helplessly. "Gad! I'm at my wits' end. We seem to be as far as ever from any clue to that devilish pair and unless you can suggest something ——" He finished the sentence by taking off his hat, and looking up at Cleek hopefully, and patting his bald spot with a handkerchief which diffused a more or less agreeable odour of the latest Parisian perfume.

"H'm!" said Cleek, reflectively. "We might cross the Heath and have a look round Gospel Oak, if you like. It's a goodish bit of a walk and I've no idea that it will result in anything, I frankly admit, but it is one of the few places we have *not* tried, so we might have a go at that if you approve."

"By James! yes. The very thing. There's always a chance, you know, so long as it's a district we've never done. Gospel Oak it is, then. And look here — I'll tell you what. You just stop here a bit and wait for me, old chap, while I nip back to the house and ask Sir Mawson's permission to use his telephone — to ring up the Yard as usual, you know, and tell them in what quarter we're operating, in case there should be reason to send anybody out to find me in a hurry. Back with you in no time and then we'll be off to Gospel Oak like a shot."

"Right you are. I'll stop here under the trees and indulge in a few comforting whiffs while you are about it. Get along!"

Narkom paused a moment to grip his cuff between finger

tips and palm, and run his coat sleeve round the shiny surface
of his "topper," then shook out his handkerchief and returned it to his pocket, jerked down his waistcoat and gave
it one or two sharp flicks with the backs of his nails, and
before a second diffusion of scent had evaporated, or the
whimsical twist it called to Cleek's lips had entirely vanished, the scene presented nothing more striking than an
ordinary man leaning back against a tree and engaged in
scratching a match on the side of an ordinary wooden matchbox.   The Yard's Gentleman had gone.

It was full ten minutes later when he lurched into view
again, coming down the garden path at top speed, with one
hand on his hat's crown and the other holding the flapping
skirts of his frock coat together, and Cleek could tell from
the expression of his round, pink face that something of importance had occurred.

It had — and he blurted it out in an outburst of joyous
excitement the moment they again stood together.   The
search for Dutch Ella and Diamond Nick was at an end.
The police of Paris had cabled news of their location and
arrest that very morning in the French capital, and would
hold them under lock and key until the necessary prelimi-
naries were over, relative to their deportation as undesirables, and their return to Canada.

"The news arrived less than an hour ago," he finished,
"and that wideawake young beggar, Lennard, thought it
was so important that I ought to know it as soon as possible,
so he hopped on to the limousine and put off as fast as
he could streak it.   He's up here in this district now — this
minute — hunting for us.   Come on! let's go and find him.
By James! it's a ripping end to the business — what?"

"That depends," replied Cleek without much enthusiasm.
"Which limousine is Lennard using to-day?   The new
blue one?'

"Cinnamon, no!   That won't be delivered until the day

after to-morrow. So it will be the good old red one, of course. Will it matter?"

"Come and see!" said Cleek, swinging out of the grounds into the public highway again, and walking fast. "At all events, an ounce of certainty is worth a pound of suspicion, and this little *faux pas* will decide the question. They are no fools, those Apaches; and Waldemar knows how to wait patiently for what he wants."

"Waldemar? The Apaches? Good lud, man, what are you talking about? You are not worrying over that business again, I hope. Haven't I told you over and over again that we couldn't find one trace of them anywhere in London — that they cleared out bag and baggage after that fruitless trip to Yorkshire? The whole truth of the matter, to my way of thinking, is that they awoke then to the fact that you had 'dropped' to their being after you, and knowing you weren't to be caught napping, gave it up as a bad job."

"Or altered their tactics and set out to follow some one else."

"Some one else? Good lud, don't talk rubbish. What good would following some one else do if they were after you?"

"Come and see," said Cleek again, and would say no more, but merely walked on faster than ever — up one thoroughfare and down another — flicking eager glances to right and to left in search of the red limousine.

In the thick of the High Street they caught sight of it at last, tooling about aimlessly, while Lennard kept constant watch on the crowd of shoppers that moved up and down the pavement.

"Cut ahead and stop it and we shall see what we *shall* see, Mr. Narkom. I'll join you presently," said Cleek, and he stood watching while the superintendent forged ahead in the direction of the limousine; and continued watching even after he saw him reach it and bring it to a halt, and stand at the kerb talking earnestly with Lennard.

But of a sudden the old crooked smile looped up the corner of his mouth; he stood at attention for a moment or two, breathing hard through his nostrils, and moving not at all until, abruptly starting into activity, he walked rapidly down the pavement and joined Narkom.

"Well?" queried the superintendent, looking up at him quizzically. "Come to any decision, old chap?"

"Yes — and so will you in a second. Don't turn — don't do anything hastily. Just look across the street, at the jeweller's window, opposite, and tell me what you think of it."

Narkom's swift, sidelong glance travelled over the distance like a gunshot, arrowed through the small collection of persons gathered about the shop window inspecting the display of trinkets, and every nerve in his body jumped.

"Good God! Waldemar!" he said, under his breath.

"Exactly. I told you he knew how to wait. Now look farther along the kerb on this side. The closed carriage waiting there. It was dawdling along and keeping pace with him when I saw it first. The man on the box is a fellow named Serpice — an Apache. *Chut!* Be still, will you? — and look the other way. They will do me no harm — *here*. It isn't their game, and, besides, they daren't. It is too public, too dangerous. It will be done, when it *is* done, in the dark — when I'm alone, and none can see. And Waldemar will not be there. He will direct, but not participate. But it won't be to-day nor yet to-night, I promise you. I shall slip them this time if never again."

The superintendent spoke, but the hard hammering of his heart made his voice scarcely audible.

"How?" he asked. "How?"

"Come and see!" said Cleek for yet a third time. Then with an abruptness and a swiftness that carried everything before it, he caught Narkom by the arm, swept him across the street, and without hint or warning tapped Waldemar upon the shoulder.

"Ah, bon jour, Monsieur le Comte," he said airily, as the Mauravanian swung round and looked at him, blanching a trifle in spite of himself. "So you are back in England, it seems? Ah, well, we like you so much — tell his Majesty when next you report — that this time we shall try to keep you here."

Taken thus by assault, the man had no words in which to answer, but merely wormed his way out of the gathering about him and, panic stricken, obliterated himself in the crowd of pedestrians teeming up and down the street.

"You reckless devil!" wheezed Narkom as he was swept back to the limousine in the same cyclonic manner he had been swept away from it. "You might have made the man savage enough to do something to you, even in spite of the publicity, by such a proceeding as that."

"That is precisely what I had hoped to do, my friend, but you perceive he is no fool to be trapped into that. We should have had some excuse for arresting him if he had done a thing of that sort, some charge to prefer against him, whereas, as matters stand, there's not one we can bring forward that holds good in law or that we could *prove* if our lives depended upon it. You see now, I hope, Mr. Narkom, why you have seen nothing of him lately?"

"No — why?"

"You have not used the red limousine, and he has been lying low ready to follow that, just as I suspected he would. If he couldn't trace where Cleek goes to meet the red limousine, clearly then the plan to be adopted must be to follow the red limousine and see where it goes to meet Cleek, and then to follow that much-wanted individual when he parts from you and makes his way home. That is the thing the fellow is after. To find out where I live and to 'get' me some night out there. But, my friend, 'turn about is fair play' the world over, and having had his inning at hunting me, I'm going in for mine at hunting him. I'll get him; I'll trap him into something for which he can be turned over to the law — make no mistake about that."

"My hat! What do you mean to do?"

"First and foremost, make my getaway out of the present little corner," he replied, "and then rely upon your assistance in finding out where the beggar is located. We're not done with him even for to-day. He will follow — either he or Serpice: perhaps both — the instant Lennard starts off with us."

"You are going back with us in the limousine, then?"

"Yes — part of the way. Drive on, Lennard, until you can spot a plain-clothes man, then give him the signal to follow us. At the first station on the Tube or the Underground, pull up sharp and let me out. You, Mr. Narkom, alight with me and stand guard at the station entrance while I go down to the train. If either Waldemar or an Apache makes an attempt to follow, arrest him on the spot, on any charge you care to trump up — it doesn't matter so that it holds him until my train goes — and as soon as it has gone, call up your plain-clothes man, point out Serpice to him, and tell him to follow and to stick to the fellow until he meets Waldemar, if it takes a week to accomplish it, and then to shadow his precious countship and find out where he lives. Tell him for me that there's a ten-pound note in it for him the moment he can tell me where Waldemar is located; and to stick to his man until he runs him down. Now, then, hop in, Mr. Narkom, and let's be off. The other chap will follow, be assured. All right, Lennard. Let her go!"

Lennard 'let her go' forthwith, and a quarter of an hour later saw the programme carried out in every particular, only that it was not Waldemar who made an attempt to follow when the limousine halted at the Tube station and Cleek jumped out and ran in (the count was far too shrewd for that); it was a rough-looking Frenchman who had just previously hopped out of a closed carriage driven by a fellow countryman, only to be nabbed at the station doorway by Narkom, and turned over to the nearest constable on the charge of pocket picking.

The charge, however, was so manifestly groundless that half a dozen persons stepped forward and entered protest; but the superintendent was so pig-headed that by the time he could be brought to reason, and the man was again at liberty to take his ticket and go down in the lift to the train, the platform was empty, the train gone, and Cleek already on his way.

A swift, short flight under the earth's surface carried him to another station in quite another part of London; a swift, short walk thence landed him at his temporary lodgings in town, and four o'clock found him exchanging his workaday clothes for the regulation creased trousers and creaseless coat of masculine calling costume, and getting ready to spend the rest of the day with *her*.

CHAPTER XXV

THE sky was all aflame with the glory of one of late June's gorgeous sunsets when he came up over the long sweep of meadowland and saw her straying about and gathering wild flowers to fill the vases in the wee house's wee little drawing-room, and singing to herself the while in a voice that was like honey — thin but very, very sweet — and at the sight something seemed to lay hold of his heart and quicken its beating until it interfered with his breathing, yet brought with it a curious sense of joy.

"Good afternoon, Mistress of the Linnets!" he called out to her as he advanced (for she had neither seen nor heard his coming) with the big sheaf of roses he had brought held behind him and the bracken and kingcups smothering him in green and gold up to the very thighs.

She turned at the sound, her face illumined, her soft eyes very bright — those wondrous eyes that had lit a man's way back from perdition and would light it onward and upward to the end — and greeted him with a smile of happy welcome.

"Oh, it is you at last," she said, looking at him as a woman looks at but one man ever. "Is this your idea of 'spending the afternoon' with one, turning up when tea is over and twilight about to begin? Do you know, I am a very busy young woman these days" — blushing rosily — "and might have spent a whole day in town shopping but that Dollops brought me word that I might look for you? But, of course —— No! I shan't say it. It might make you vain to hear that you had the power to spoil my day."

"Not any vainer than you have made me by telling me
other things," he retorted with a laugh. "I am afraid I
have spoiled a good many days for you in my time, Ailsa.
But, please God, I shall make up for them all in the brightness of the ones that are to come. I couldn't help being
late to-day — I'll tell you all about that presently — but
may I offer something in atonement? Please, will you add
these to your bouquet and forgive me?"

"Roses! Such beauties! How good of you! Just smell!
How divine!"

"Meaning the flowers or their donor?" — quizzically.
"Or, no! Don't elucidate. Leave me in blissful ignorance.
You have hurt my vanity quite enough as it is. I was
deeply mortified — cut to the quick, I may say, if that will
express my sense of grovelling shame any clearer — when
I arrived here and saw what you were doing. Please,
mum" — touching his forelock and scraping his foot backward after the manner of a groom — "did I make such a
bad job of my work in that garden that when you want a
bouquet you have to come out here and gather wild flowers?
I put fifty-eight standard roses on that terrace just under
your bedroom window, and surely there must be a bloom
or two that you could gather?"

"As if I would cut one of them for anything in the
world!" she gave back, indignantly. Then she laughed,
and blushed and stepped back from his impetuous advance.
"No — please! You fished for that so adroitly that you
landed it before I thought. Be satisfied. Besides, Mrs.
Condiment is at her window, and I want to preserve as much
as possible of her rapidly depreciating estimate of me. She
thinks me a very frivolous young person, 'to allow that
young Mr. Hamilton to call so frequent, miss, and if you'll
allow me to say it, at such unseemly hours. I don't think
as dear Captain Burbage would quite approve of it if he
knew.'"

"Gad! that's rich. What a mimic you are. It was the dear old girl to the life. She hasn't an inkling of the truth, then?"

"Not one. She doesn't quite approve of you, either. 'I likes to see a gent more circumpec, miss, and a trifle more reserved when he's gettin' on his thirties. Muckin' about with a garden fork and such among a trumpery lot of roses, and racin' here, there, and everywhere over them medders after ferns and things, like a schoolboy on a holiday, aren't what I calls dignified deportment in full-grown men, and in my day they didn't use to do it!' Sometimes I am in mortal terror that she intends to give me notice and to leave me bag and baggage; for she is always saying that she's 'sure dear Captain Burbage couldn't have known what he was a-doing of, poor, innocent, kind-hearted gentleman — and him so *much* of a gent, too, and so wonderful quiet and sedate!'"

"Poor old girl!" said Cleek, laughing. "What a shock to her if she knew the truth. And what on earth *would* you do if she were to chance to get a peep at Dollops? But then, of course, there's no fear of that — the young beg-gar's too careful. I told him never to come near the house when he carries any notes."

"And he never does. Always leaves them under the stone in the path through the woods. I go there, of course, twice every day, and I never know that he has been about until I find one. I am always glad to get them, but to-day's one made me very, very happy indeed."

"Because I told you you might expect me?"

"Yes. But not that alone. I think I cried a little and I *know* I went down on my knees — right there — out in those woods, when I read those splendid words, 'There is but one more debt to be paid. The "some day" of my hopes is near to me at last.'"

Her voice died off. He uncovered his head, and a still-

ness came that was not broken by any sound or any movement, until he felt her hand slip into his and remain there.

"Walk with me!" he said, closing his fingers around hers
and holding them fast. "Walk with me always. My
God! I love you so!"

"Always!" she made answer in her gentle voice; and with
her hand shut tight in his, passed onward with him — over
the green meadows and into the dim, still woods, and out
again into the flower-filled fields beyond, where all the sky
was golden after the fierce hues of the sunset had drained
away into the tender gleam of twilight, and there was not
one red ray left to cross the path of him.

"You have led me this way from the first," he said,
breaking silence suddenly. "Out of the glare of fire,
through the dark, into peaceful light. I had gone down to
hell but for you — but that you stooped and lifted me.
God!" — he threw back his head and looked upward,
with his hat in his hand and the light on his face — "God,
forget me if ever I forget that. Amen!" he added, very
quietly, very earnestly; then dropped his chin until it
rested on his breast, and was very still for a long time.

"Yes," he said, taking up the thread of conversation
where it had been broken so long a time ago, "there is but
one more debt to be cleared off: the value of the Princess
Goroski's tiara. A thousand pounds will wipe that off —
it was not a very expensive one — and I could have had
that sum to-day if I had thought of myself alone. Mr.
Narkom thinks me a fool. I wonder what you will think
when you hear?" And forthwith he told her.

"If you are again 'fishing'," she replied with a quizzical
smile, "then again you are going to be successful. I think
you a hero. Kiss me, please. I am very, very proud of
you. And that was what made you late in coming, was
it?"

"Not altogether that. I might have been earlier but that we ran foul of Waldemar and the Apaches again, and I had to lose time in shaking them off. But I ought not to have told you that. You will be getting nervous. It was a shock to Mr. Narkom. He was so sure they had given up the job and returned home."

"I, too, was sure. I should have thought that the rebellion would have compelled that, in Count Waldemar's case at least," she answered, gravely. "And particularly in such a grave crisis as his country is now called upon to face. Have you seen to-day's papers? They are full of it. Count Irma and the revolutionists have piled victory on victory. They are now at the very gates of the capital; the royal army is disorganized, its forces going over in hordes to the insurgents; the king is in a very panic and preparing, it is reported, to fly before the city falls."

"A judgment, Alburtus, a judgment!" Cleek cried with such vehemence that it startled her. "Your son drinks of the cup you prepared for Karma's. The same cup, the same result: dethronement, flight, exile in the world's wildernesses, and perhaps — death. Well done, Irma! A judgment on you, Mauravania. You pay! You pay!"

"How wonderful you are — you seem to know everything!" declared Ailsa. "But in this at least you appear to be misinformed, dear. I have been reading the reports faithfully and it seems that death was not the end of all who shared in Queen Karma's exile and flight. Count Irma is telling a tale which is calling recruits to the standard of the revolutionists hourly. The eldest son — the Crown Prince Maximilian — is still alive. The count swears to that; swears that he has seen him; that he knows where to find him at any moment. The special correspondent of the *Times* writes that everywhere the demand is for the Restoration, the battle cry of the insurgents 'Maximilian!' and the whole country ringing with it."

"I can quite believe it," he said, with one of his queer, crooked smiles. "They are an excitable people, the Mauravanians, but, unfortunately, a fickle one as well. It is up to-day and down to-morrow with them. At present the cry is for Maximillian; this time next month it may be for Irma and a republican form of government, and — Maximillian may go hang for all they want of him. Still, if they maintain the present cry — and the House of Alburtus falls — and the followers of Irma win —— But what's the use of bothering about it? Let us talk of things that have a personal interest for us, dear. Give me to-morrow, if you can. I shall have a whole day's freedom for the first time in weeks. The water lilies are in bloom in the upper reaches of the Thames and my soul is simply crying for the river's solitudes, the lilies, the silence, and *you!* I want you — all to myself — up there, among God's things. Give me the day, if you can."

She gave him not one but many, as it turned out; for that one day proved such a magic thing that she was only too willing to repeat it, and as the Yard had no especial need of him, and the plain-clothes man who had been set upon Waldemar's track had as yet nothing to report, it grew to be a regular habit with him to spend the long days up in the river solitudes with Ailsa, picnicking among the swans, and to come home to Dollops at night tired, but very happy.

It went on like this for more than ten days, uninterruptedly; but at length there came a time when an entry in his notebook warned him that there was something he could not put off any longer — something that must certainly be attended to to-morrow, in town, early — and he went to bed that night with the melancholy feeling that the next day could only be a half holiday, not a whole one, and that his hours with her would be few.

But when that to-morrow came he knew that even these

were to be denied him; for the long-deferred call of the Yard had come, and Narkom, ringing him up at breakfast time, asked for an immediate meeting.

"In town, dear chap, as near to Liverpool Street and as early as you can possibly make it."

"Well, I can't make it earlier than half-past ten. I've got a little private business of my own to attend to, as it happens, Mr. Narkom," he replied. "I'd put it off if I could, but I can't. To-day before noon is the last possible hour. But look here! I can meet you at half-past ten in Bishopsgate Street, between St. Ethelburga's Church and Bevis Narks, if that will do. Will, eh? All right. Be on the lookout for me there, then. What? The new blue limousine, eh? Right you are. I'm your man to the tick of the half hour. Good-bye!"

And he was, as it turned out. For the new blue limousine (a glistening, spic-span sixty-horsepower machine, perfect in every detail) had no more than come to a standstill at the kerb in the exact neighbourhood stated at the exact half hour agreed upon, when open whisked the door, and in jumped Cleek with the swiftness and agility of a cat.

CHAPTER XXVI

"GOOD morning, my friend. I hope I haven't taken you too much by surprise," he said, as the limousine sprang into activity the instant he closed the door, and settled himself down beside the superintendent.

"Not more than usual, dear chap. But I shall never get quite used to some of your little tricks. Gad! You're the most abnormally prompt beggar that ever existed, I do believe. You absolutely break all records."

"Well, I certainly came within a hair's breadth of losing my reputation this morning, then," he answered cheerily, as he fumbled in his pockets for a match. "It was a hard pull to cover the distance and get through the business in time, I can tell you, with the brief margin I had. But fortunately —— Here! Take charge of that, will you? And read it over while I'm getting a light."

"That" was a long legal-looking envelope which he had whisked out of his pocket and tossed into Narkom's lap.

"'Royal British Life Assurance Society,'" repeated he, reading off the single line printed on the upper left-hand corner of the envelope. "What the dickens —— I say, is it a policy?"

"Aha!" assented Cleek, with his mouth full of smoke. "The medico who put me through my paces, some time ago, reported me sound in wind and limb, and warranted not to bite, shy, or kick over the traces, and I was duly ordered to turn up at the London office before noon on a given day to sign up (and pay down) and receive that interesting document, otherwise my application would be void, et cetera.

This, as it happens, is the 'given day' in question; and as the office doesn't open for business before ten A. M., and there wasn't the least likelihood of my being able to get back to it before noon, when you were calling for me — 'there you have the whole thing in a nutshell,' as the old woman said when she poisoned the filberts."

Meanwhile, Narkom had opened the envelope and glanced over the document it contained. He now sat up with a jerk and voiced a cry of amazement.

"Good Lord, deliver us!" he exclaimed. "In favour of Dollops!"

"Yes," said Cleek. "He's a faithful little monkey and — I've nothing else to leave him. There's always a chance, you know — with Margot's lot and Waldemar's. I shouldn't like to think of the boy being forced back into the streets if — anything should happen to me."

"Well, I'll be —— What a man! What a man! Cleek, my dear, dear friend — my comrade — my pal ——"

"Chuck it! Scotland Yard with the snuffles is enough to make the gods shriek, you dear old footler! Why, God bless your old soul, I —— Brakes on! Let's talk about the new limousine. She's a beauty, isn't she? Locker, mirror: just like the old red one, and —— Hello! I say, you are taking me into the country, I perceive; we've left the town behind us."

"Yes; we're bound for Darsham."

"Darsham? That's in Suffolk, isn't it? And about ninety-five miles from Liverpool Street Station, as the crow flies. So our little business to-day is to be an out-of-town affair, eh? Well, let's have it. What's the case? Burglary?"

"No — murder. Happened last night. Got the news over the telephone this morning. Nearly bowled me over when I heard it, by James! for I saw the man alive — in town — only the day before yesterday. It's a murder of a peculiarly cunning and cleverly contrived character, Cleek, with no apparent motive, and absolutely no clue as to what means the assassin used to kill his victim, nor how he managed to get in and out of the place in which the crime was committed. There isn't the slightest mark on the body. The man was not shot, not stabbed, not poisoned, nor did he die from natural causes. There is no trace of a struggle, yet the victim's face shows that he died in great agony, and was beyond all question the object of a murderous attack."

"Hum-m!" said Cleek, stroking his chin. "Sounds interesting, at all events. Let's have the facts of the case, please. But first, who was the victim? Anybody of importance?"

"Of very great importance — in the financial world," replied Narkom. "He is — or, rather, was — an American multi-millionaire; inventor, to speak by the card, of numerous electrical devices which brought him wealth beyond the dreams of avarice, and carried his fame all over the civilized world. You will, no doubt, have heard of him. His name is Jefferson P. Drake."

"Oho!" said Cleek, arching his eyebrows. "That man, eh? Oh, yes, I've heard of him often enough — very nearly everybody in England has by this time. Chap who conceived the idea of bettering the conditions of the poor by erecting art galleries that were to be filled and supported out of the rates and, more or less modestly, to be known by the donor's name. That's the man, isn't it?"

"Yes, that's the man."

"Just so. Stop a bit! Let's brush up my memory a trifle. Of English extraction, wasn't he? And, having made his money in his own native country, came to that of his father to spend it? Had social aspirations, too, I believe; and, while rather vulgar in his habits and tastes, was exceedingly warm-hearted — indeed, actually lovable — and made up for his own lack of education by spending barrels of money upon that of his son. Came to England something more than a year ago, if I remember rightly; bought a fine old place down in Suffolk, and proceeded forthwith to modernize it after the most approved American ideas — steam heat, electric lights, a refrigerating plant for the purpose of supplying the ice and the creams and the frozen sweets so necessary to the American palate; all that sort of thing, and set out forthwith to establish himself as a sumptuous entertainer on the very largest possible scale. That's the 'lay of the land,' isn't it?"

"Yes, that's it precisely. The estate he purchased was Heatherington Hall, formerly Lord Fallowfield's place. The entail was broken ages ago, but no Fallowfield ever attempted to part with the place until his present lordship's time. And although he has but one child, a daughter, I don't suppose that he would have been tempted to do so, either, but that he was badly crippled — almost ruined, in fact — last year by unlucky speculations in the stock market, with the result that it was either sell out to Jefferson P. Drake or be sold out by his creditors. Naturally, he chose the former course. That it turned out to be a most excellent thing for him you will understand when I tell you that Drake conceived an almost violent liking for him and his daughter, Lady Marjorie Wynde, and not only insisted upon their remaining at Heatherington Hall as his guests in perpetuity, but designed eventually to bring the property back into the possession of the original 'line' by a marriage between Lady Marjorie and his son."

"Effective if not very original," commented Cleek, with one of his curious one-sided smiles. "And how did the parties most concerned view this promising little plan? Were they agreeable to the arrangement?"

"Not they. As a matter of fact, both have what you may call a 'heart interest' elsewhere. Lady Marjorie, who, although she is somewhat of a 'Yes, papa,' and 'Please, papa,' young lady, and could, no doubt, be induced to sacrifice herself for the family good, is, it appears, engaged to a young lieutenant who will one day come in for money, but hasn't more than enough to pay his mess bills at present, I believe. As for young Jim Drake — why, matters were even worse with *him*. It turns out that he'd found the girl *he* wanted before he left the States, and it took him just about twenty seconds to make his father understand that he'd be shot, hanged, drawn, quartered, or even reduced to mincemeat, before he'd give up that girl or marry any other, at any time or at any cost, from now to the Judgment Day."

"Bravo!" said Cleek, slapping his palms together. "That's the spirit. That's the boy for my money, Mr. Narkom! Get a good woman and stick to her, through thick and thin, at all hazards and at any cost. The jockey who 'swaps horses' in the middle of a race never yet came first under the wire nor won a thing worth having. Well, what was the result of this plain speaking on the young man's part? Pleasant or unpleasant?"

"Oh, decidedly unpleasant. The father flew into a rage, swore by all that was holy, and by a great deal that wasn't, that he'd cut him off 'without one red cent,' whatever that may mean, if he ever married that particular girl; and as that particular girl — who is as poor as Job's turkey, by the way — happened by sheer perversity of fortune to have landed in England that very day, in company with an eminent literary person whose secretary she had been for some two or three years past, away marched the son, took out a special license, and married her on the spot."

"Well done, independence! I like that boy more than ever, Mr. Narkom. What followed? Did the father relent, or did he invite the pair of them to clear out and hoe their own row in future?"

"He did neither; he simply ignored their existence.

Young Drake brought his wife down to Suffolk and took rooms at a village inn, and then set out to interview his father. When he arrived at the Hall he was told by the lodgekeeper that strangers weren't admitted, and, on his asking to have his name sent in, was informed that the lodgekeeper had 'never heard of no sich person as Mr. James Drake — that there wasn't none, and that the master said there never had been, neither' — and promptly double-locked the gates. What young James Drake did after that it appears that nobody knows, for nobody saw him again until this morning; and it was only yesterday, I must tell you, that he made that unsuccessful attempt to get into the place to see his father. *He* says, however, that he spent the time in going over to Ipswich and back in the hope of seeing a friend there to whom he might apply for work. He says, too, that when he got there he found that that friend — an American acquaintance — had given up his rooms the day before, and rushed off to Italy in answer to a cable from his sister; or so, at least, the landlady told him."

"Which, of course, the landlady can be relied upon to corroborate if there is any question regarding the matter? Is there?"

"Well, he seems to think that there may be. He's the client, you must know. It was he that gave me the details over the telephone, and asked me to put you on the case. As he says himself, it's easy enough to prove about his having gone to Ipswich to see his friend, but it isn't so easy to prove about his coming back in the manner he did. It seems he was too late for any return train, that he hadn't money enough left in the world to waste any by taking a private conveyance, so he walked back; and that, as it's a goodish stretch of country, and he didn't know the way, and couldn't at night find anybody to ask, he lost himself more than once, with the consequence that it was daylight when he got back to the inn, where his frightened wife sat awaiting him, never having gone to bed nor closed an eye all night, poor girl, fearing that some accident had befallen him. But, be that as it may, Cleek, during those hours he was absent his father was mysteriously murdered in a round box of a room in which he had locked himself, and to which, owing to structural arrangements, it would seem impossible for anything to have entered; and, as young Drake rightly says, the worst of it is that the murder followed so close upon the heels of his quarrel and promised disinheritance, that his father had no time to alter the will which left him sole heir to everything; so that possibly people will talk."

"Undoubtedly," agreed Cleek. "And yet you said there was no motive and absolutely no clue. M' yes! I wonder if I shall like this independent young gentleman quite so well after I have seen him."

"Oh, my dear fellow! Good heavens, man, you can't possibly think of suspecting him. Remember, it is he himself who brings the case — that the Yard would never have had anything to do with it but for him."

"Quite so. But the local constabulary would; and the simplest way to blind a jackass is to throw dust in his eyes. They are natural born actors, the Americans; they are good schemers and fine planners. Their native game is 'bluff,' and they are very, very careful in the matter of detail."

Then he pinched up his chin and sat silent for a moment, watching the green fields and the pleasant farmlands as the limousine went pelting steadily on.

CHAPTER XXVII

"SUPPOSE, now, that you have succeeded in putting the cart before the horse, Mr. Narkom," Cleek said suddenly, "you proceed to give me, not the ramifications of the case, but the case itself. You have repeatedly spoken of the murder having taken place in some place which is difficult of access and under most mystifying circumstances. Now, if you don't mind, I should like to hear what those circumstances are."

"All right, old chap, I'll give you the details as briefly as possible. In the first place, you must know that Heatherington Hall is a very ancient place, dating back, indeed, to those pleasant times when a nobleman's home had to be something of a fortress as well, if he didn't want to wake up some fine morning and find his place 'sacked,' his roof burnt over his head, and himself and his lady either held for ransom or freed from any possibility of having 'headaches' thereafter. Now, a round tower with only one door by which to enter, and no windows other than narrow slits, through which the bowmen could discharge their shafts at an attacking party without exposing themselves to the dangers of a return fire, was the usual means of defence adopted — you'll see dozens of them in Suffolk, dear chap, but whether for reasons of economy or merely to carry out some theory of his own, the first lord of Heatherington Hall did not stick to the general plan.

"In brief, instead of building a tall tower rising from the ground itself, he chose to erect upon the roof of the west wing of the building a lower but more commodious one than was customary. That is to say, that while his tower was less than half the height of any other in the country, its circumference was twice as great, and, by reason of the double supply of bowman's slits, equally as effective in withstanding a siege; and, indeed, doubly difficult to assault, as before an invading force could get to the door of the place it would have to fight its way up through the main building to reach the level of it.

"Now, owing to the peculiarity of its construction — it is not more than eighteen feet high — the fact that it contained but one circular room, and all those bowman slits in the walls of it, this unusual 'tower' gained an equally unusual name for itself, and became known everywhere as the 'Stone Drum of Heatherington,' and is even mentioned by that name in the *Inquisitio Eliensis* of the "Domesday Book," which, as you doubtless know, is the particular volume of that remarkable work which records the survey, et cetera, of the counties of Cambridge, Hertford, Essex, Norfolk, Suffolk, and Huntingdon."

"I see," said Cleek, with an amused twinkle in his eye. "You are getting on, Mr. Narkom. We shall have you lecturing on archæology one of these fine days. But to return to our mutton — or, rather, our stone drum — was it in that place, then, that the murder was committed?"

"Yes. It is one of the few, very few, parts of the building to which Mr. Jefferson P. Drake did nothing in the way of modernizing, and added nothing in the way of 'improvements.' That, probably, was because, as it stood, it offered him a quiet, secluded, and exclusive retreat for the carrying on of his experiments; for wealth had brought with it no inclination to retire, and he remained to the last in the lists of the world's active forces. As a general thing, he did not do much in the way of burning the midnight oil, but conducted most of his experiments in the daytime. But last night was an exception. It may be that the news of his son's appeal to the lodgekeeper that afternoon had upset him, for he was restless and preoccupied all the evening, Lord Fallowfield says — or, at least, so young Drake reports him as having said — and instead of retiring with the rest of the house party when bedtime came and his Japanese valet carried up his customary carafe of ice-water ———"

"Oh, he has a Japanese valet, has he? But, of course, in these days no American gentleman with any pretence to distinction whatsoever would be without one. Go on, please. His Japanese valet carried up the ice-water, and — then what?"

"Then he suddenly announced his intention of going into the Stone Drum and working for a few hours. Lord Fallowfield, it appears, tried his best to dissuade him, but to no purpose."

"Why did he do that? Or don't you know?"

"Yes. I asked that very question myself. I was told that it was because his lordship saw very plainly that he was labouring under strong mental excitement, and he thought that rest would be the best thing for him in the circumstances. Then, too, his lordship and he are warmly attached to each other. In fact, the earl was as fond of him as if he had been a brother. As well he ought to be, by James! when you recollect that before he got the idea into his head of marrying his son to Lady Marjorie he added a codicil to his will bequeathing the place to Lord Fallowfield, together with all the acres and acres of land he had added to it, and all the art treasures he had collected, absolutely free from death duties."

"Oho!" said Cleek, then smiled and pinched his chin and said no more.

"Well, it appears that when his lordship found that he couldn't make the stubborn old johnnie change his mind, he accompanied him to the Stone Drum, together with the valet, to see that everything was as it should be, and that nothing was wanting that might tend to the comfort and convenience of a night worker. When there was nothing more that could be done, the valet was dismissed, his lord-ship said good-night to his friend and left him there alone, hearing, as he passed along the railed walk over the roof of the wing to the building proper (a matter of some twenty-odd feet) the sound of the bolt being shot, the bar put on, and the key being turned as Mr. Drake locked himself in.

"What happened from that moment, Cleek, nobody knows. At seven o'clock this morning the valet, going to his master's room with his shaving-water, found that he had never gone to bed at all, and, on hastening to the Stone Drum, found that a light was still burning within and faintly illuminating the bowman's slits; but although he knocked on the door and called again and again to his mas-ter, he could get no answer. Alarmed, he aroused the entire household; but despite the fact that a dozen persons en-deavoured to get word from the man within, not so much as a whisper rewarded them. The bolt was still 'shot,' the bar still on, the key still turned on the inner side of the door, so they could force no entry to the place; and it was never until the village blacksmith had been called in and his sledge had battered down the age-weakened masonry in which that door was set that any man knew for certain what that burning light and that unbroken silence por-tended. When, however, they finally got into the place there lay the once famous inventor at full length on the oaken floor close to the barred door, as dead as George Washington, and with never a sign of what killed him either on the body or in any part of the place. Yet the first look at his distorted features was sufficient to prove that he had died in agony, and the position of the corpse showed clearly that when the end came he was endeavouring to get to the door."

"Heart failure, possibly," said Cleek.

"Not a hope of it," replied Narkom. "A doctor was sent for immediately; fortunately one of the most famous surgeons in England happened to be in the neighbourhood at the time — called down from town to perform an operation. He is willing, so young Mr. Drake tells me, to stake his professional reputation that the man's heart was as sound as a guinea; that he had not imbibed one drop of anything poisonous; that he had not been asphyxiated, as, of course, he couldn't have been, for the bowman's slits in the wall gave free ventilation to the place, if nothing more; that he had not been shot, stabbed, or bludgeoned, but, nevertheless, he had died by violence, and that violence was not, and could not be, attributed to suicide, for there was everything to prove to the contrary. In short, that whatever had attacked him had done so unexpectedly and while he was busy at his work-table, for there was the chair lying on its back before it, just as it had fallen over when he jumped up from his seat, and there on the 'working plan' he was drawing up was the pen lying on a blob of India ink, just as it had dropped from his hand when he was stricken. Some murderous force had entered that room, and passed out of it again, leaving the door barred, bolted, and locked upon the inside. Some weapon had been used, and yet no weapon was there and no trace upon the body to indicate what its character might be. Indeed, everything in the room was precisely as it had been when Lord Fallowfield walked out last night and left him, beyond the fact of the overturned chair and a little puddle of clear water lying about a yard or so from the work-table and, owing to the waxing and polishing, not yet absorbed by the wood of the floor. As no one could account for the presence of that, and as it was the only thing there which might offer a possible clue to the mystery, the doctor took a small sample of that water and analyzed it. It was simply plain, everyday, common, or garden pure water, and nothing more, without the slightest trace of any foreign matter or of any poisonous substance in it whatsoever. There, old chap, that's the 'case' — that's the little riddle you're asked to come down and solve. What do you make of it, eh?"

"Tell you better when I've seen Mr. James Drake and Lord Fallowfield and — the doctor," said Cleek, and would say no more than that for the present.

CHAPTER XXVIII

IT WAS somewhere in the neighbourhood of half-past three when the opportunity to interview those three persons was finally vouchsafed him; and it may be recorded at once that the meeting did some violence to his emotions. In short, he found Mr. James Drake (far from being the frank-faced, impulsive, lovable young pepper-pot which his actions and words would seem to stand sponsor for) a rather retiring young man of the "pale and studious" order, absolutely lacking in personal magnetism, and about the last person in the world one would expect to do the "all for love" business of the average hero in the manner he had done. On the other hand, he found the Earl of Fallowfield an exceedingly frank, pleasant-mannered, rather boyish-looking gentleman, whose many attractions rendered it easy to understand why the late Mr. Jefferson P. Drake had conceived such a warm affection for him, and was at such pains to have him ever by his side. It seemed, indeed, difficult to believe that he could possibly be the father of Lady Marjorie Wynde, for his manner and appearance were so youthful as to make him appear to be nothing closer than an elder brother. The doctor — that eminent Harley Street light, Mr. John Strangeways Hague — he found to be full of Harley Street manners and Harley Street ideas, eminently polite, eminently cold, and about as pleased to meet a detective police officer as he would be to find an organ-grinder sitting on his doorstep.

"Have you come to any conclusions as to the means of death, Doctor?" asked Cleek after he had been shown into the Stone Drum, where the body of the dead man still lay and where the local coroner and the local J. P. were conducting a sort of preliminary examination prior to the regulation inquest, which must, of course, follow. "The general appearance would suggest asphyxia, if asphyxia were possible."

"Which it is not," volunteered Doctor Hague, with the geniality of a snowball. "You have probably observed that the many slits in the wall permit of free ventilation; and asphyxia with free ventilation is an impossibility."

"Quite so," agreed Cleek placidly. "But if by any chance those slits could have been closed from the outside — I observe that at some period and for some purpose Mr. Drake has made use of a charcoal furnace" — indicating it by a wave of the hand — "and apparently with no other vent to carry off the fumes than that supplied by the slits. Now if they were closed and the charcoal left burning, the result would be an atmosphere charged with carbon monoxide gas, and a little more than one per cent. of that in the air of a room deprived of ventilation would, in a short time, prove fatal to any person breathing that air."

The doctor twitched round an inquiring eye, and looked him over from head to foot.

"Yes," he said, remembering that, after all, there were Board Schools, and even the humblest might sometimes learn, parrot-like, to repeat the "things that are in books." "But we happen to know that the slits were not closed and that neither carbon oxide nor carbon monoxide was the cause of death."

"You have taken samples of the blood, of course, to establish that fact beyond question, as one could so readily do?" ventured Cleek suavely. "The test for carbon monoxide is so simple and so very certain that error is impossible. It combines so tensely, if one may put it that way, with the blood, that the colouring of the red corpuscles is utterly overcome and destroyed."

"My good sir, those are elementary facts of which I do not stand in need of a reminder."

"Quite so, quite so. But in my profession, Doctor, one stands in constant need of 'reminders.' A speck, a spot, a pin-prick — each and all are significant, and —— But is this not a slight abrasion on the temple here?" bending over and, with his glass, examining a minute reddish speck upon the dead man's face. "Hum-m-m! I see, I see! Have you investigated this thing, Doctor? It is interesting."

"I fail to see the point of interest, then," replied Doctor Hague, bending over and examining the spot. "The skin is scarcely more than abraded — evidently by the finger nail scratching off the head of some infinitesimal pustule."

"Possibly," agreed Cleek, "but on the other hand, it may be something of a totally different character — for one thing, the possible point at which contact was established between the man's blood and something of a poisonous character. An injection of cyanide of potassium, for instance, would cause death, and account in a measure for this suggestion of asphyxia conveyed by the expression of the features."

"True, my good sir; but have the goodness to ask yourself who could get into the place to administer such hypodermic? And, if self-administered, what can have become of the syringe? If thrown from one of the bowman's slits, it could only have fallen upon the roof of the wing, and I assure you that was searched most thoroughly long before your arrival. I don't think you will go so far as to suggest that it was shot in, attached to some steel missile capable of making a wound; for no such missile is, as you see, embedded in the flesh nor was one lying anywhere about the floor. The cyanide of potassium theory is ingenious, but I'm afraid it won't hold water."

"Hold water!" The phrase brought Cleek's thoughts harking back to what he had been told regarding the little puddle of water lying on the floor, and of a sudden his eyes narrowed, and the curious one-sided smile travelled up his cheek.

"No, I suppose not," he said, replying to the doctor's remark. "Besides, your test tubes would have settled that when it settled the carbon monoxide question. Had cyanide been present, the specimens of blood would have been clotted and blue."

Of a sudden it seemed to dawn upon the doctor that this didn't smack quite so much of Board School intelligence as he had fancied, and, facing round, he looked at Cleek with a new-born interest.

"I beg your pardon," he said, "but I don't think I caught your name, Mr. — er — er ——"

"Cleek, Doctor; Hamilton Cleek, at your service."

"Good Lord! That is, I — er — er — my dear sir, my dear Mr. Cleek, if there is any intelligence I can possibly supply, pray command me."

"With pleasure, Doctor, and thank you very much indeed for the kind offer. I have been told that there was a little puddle of water on the floor at the time the murder was discovered, also that you took a sample of it for analysis. As I don't see any sign of that puddle now, would you mind telling me what that analysis established. I have heard, I may tell you, that you found the water to contain no poisonous substance; but I should be obliged if you can tell me if it was water drawn from a well or such as might have been taken from a river or pond."

"As a matter of fact, my dear Mr. Cleek, I don't think it came from any of the three."

"Hum-m-m! A manufactured mineral water, then?"

"No, not that, either. If it had been raining and there was any hole or leak in this roof, I should have said it was rain water that had dripped in and formed a little puddle on the floor. If it had been winter, I should have said it was the result of melted snow. As a matter of fact, I incline more to the latter theory than to any other, although it is absurd, of course, to think of snow being obtainable anywhere in England in the month of July."

"Quite so, quite so — unless — it doesn't matter. That's all, thank you, Doctor, and very many thanks."

"A word, please, Mr. Cleek," interposed the doctor as he turned to move away and leave him. "I am afraid I was not very communicative nor very cordial when you asked me if I had any idea of the means employed to bring about the unfortunate man's death; may I hope that you will be better mannered than I, Mr. Cleek, if I ask you if you have? Thanks, very much. Then, have you?"

"Yes," said Cleek. "And so, too, will you, if you will make a second blood test, with the specimens you have, at a period of about forty-eight hours after the time of decease. It will take quite that before the presence of the thing manifests itself under the influence of any known process or responds to any known test. And even then it will only be detected by a faintly alcoholic odour and excessively bitter taste. The man has been murdered — done to death by that devil's drug woorali, if I am not mistaken. But who administered it and *how* it was administered are things I can't tell you yet."

"Woorali! Woorali! That is the basis of the drug curarin, produced by Roulin and Boussingault in 1828 from a combination of the allied poisons known to the savages of South America and of the tropics by the names of corroval and vao, is it not?"

"Yes. And a fiend's thing it is, too. A mere scratch from anything steeped in it is enough to kill an ox almost immediately. The favourite 'native' manner of using the hellish thing is by means of a thorn and a blowpipe. But no such method has been employed in this case. No thorn nor, indeed, any other projectile has entered the flesh, nor is there one lying anywhere about the floor. Be sure I looked, Doctor, the instant I suspected that woorali had been used. Pardon me, but that must be all for the present. I have other fish to fry."

CHAPTER XXIX

THE "frying" of them took the shape of first going outside and walking round the Stone Drum, and then of stepping back to the door and beckoning Narkom and Lord Fallowfield and young James Drake out to him.

"Anybody in the habit of sitting out here to read or paint or anything of that sort?" he asked abruptly.

"Good gracious, no!" replied Lord Fallowfield. "Whatever makes you ask such a thing as that, Mr. Cleek?"

"Nothing, only that I have found four little marks disposed of at such regular distances that they seem to have been made by the four legs of a chair resting, with a rather heavy weight upon it, on the leads of the roof and immediately under one of the bowman's slits in the Stone Drum. A chair with casters, I should imagine, from the character of the marks. We are on a level with the sleeping quarters of the servants in the house proper, I believe, and chairs with casters are not usual in servants' bedrooms in most houses. Are they so here?"

"Certainly not," put in young Drake. "Why, I don't believe there is a chair with casters on the whole blessed floor. Is there, Lord Fallowfield? You ought to know."

"Yes, there is, Jim. There are three in fact; they all are in the old armoury. Been there a dog's age; and they so matched the old place your poor father never had them taken out."

"The 'old armoury'? What's that, your lordship, may I ask?"

"Oh, a relic of the old feudal times, Mr. Cleek. You see,

on account of the position of the Stone Drum, the weapon room, or arming-room, had to be up here on a level with the wing roof, instead of below stairs, as in the case of other 'towers.' That's the place over there — the window just to the left of the door leading into the building proper. It is full of the old battle flags, knights' pennants, shields, cross-bows, and the Lord knows what of those old days of primitive warfare. We Fallowfields always preserved it, just as it was in the days of its usefulness, for its historical interest and its old association with the name. Like to have a look at it?"

"Very much indeed," replied Cleek, and two minutes later he was standing in the place and revelling in its air of antiquity.

As Lord Fallowfield had declared, the three old chairs which supplied seating accommodation were equipped with casters, but although these were the prime reason for Cleek's visit to the place, he gave them little more than a passing glance, bestowing all his attention upon the ancient shields and the quaint old cross-bows with which the walls were heavily hung in tier after tier almost to the groined ceiling.

"Primitive times, Mr. Narkom, when men used to go out with these jimcrack things and bang away at each other with skewers!" he said, taking one of them down and examining it in a somewhat casual manner, turning it over, testing its weight, looking at its catch, and running his fingers up and down the propelling string. "Fancy a chap with one of these things running up against a modern battery or sailing out into a storm of shrapnel! Back to your hook, grandfather" — hanging it up again — "times change and we with time. By the way, your lordship, I hope you will be better able to give an account of *your* whereabouts last night than I hear that Mr. Drake here is able to do regarding his."

"I? Good heavens, man, what do you mean?" flung out his lordship, so taken aback by the abruptness of the remark that the very breath seemed to be knocked out of him. "Upon my soul, Mr. Cleek ——"

"Gently, gently, your lordship. You must certainly realize that in the circumstances the same necessity must exist for you to explain your movements as exists for Mr. Drake. I am told that in the event of the elder Mr. Drake's death this property was to come to you wholly unencumbered by any charge or any restrictions whatsoever."

"Good God! So it was. Upon my soul, I'd forgotten all about that!" exclaimed his lordship with such an air that he was either speaking the absolute truth or was a very good actor indeed.

"Jim! My boy! Oh, good heavens! I never gave the thing a thought — never one! No, Mr. Cleek, I can give no account of my movements other than to say that I went to bed directly I left the Stone Drum. Or — yes. I can prove that much, by George! I can, indeed. Ojeebi was with me, or, at least, close at my heels at the time, and he saw me go into my room, and must have heard me lock the door."

"Ojeebi? Who is he?"

"My father's Japanese valet," put in young Drake. "Been with him for the past five years. If he tells you that he saw Lord Fallowfield go into his room and lock the door after him, you can rely upon that as an absolute and irrefutable truth. 'Whitest' little yellow man that ever walked on two feet; faithful as a dog, and as truthful as they make 'em."

"And they don't make 'em any too truthful, as a rule, in his country, by Jove!" said Cleek. "Still, of course, as he could not possibly have anything to gain —— Call him up, will you, and let us hear what he has to say with regard to Lord Fallowfield's statement."

Young Drake rang for a servant, issued the necessary order, and some five or six minutes later a timid little yellow man with the kindest face and the most gentle step a man could possess came into the room, his soft eyes reddened with much weeping, and tear-stains marking his sallow cheeks.

"Oh, Mr. Jim! Oh, Mr. Jim! the dear, kind old 'boss'! He gone! he gone!" he broke out disconsolately as he caught sight of his late master's son, and made as if to prostrate himself before him.

"That's all right, Ojeebi — that's all right, old man!" interrupted young Drake, with a smothered "blub" in his voice and a twitching movement of his mouth. "Cut it out! I'm not iron. Say, this gentleman wants to ask you a few questions, Ojeebi; deliver the goods just as straight as you know how."

"Me, Mr. Jim? Gentleman want question me?" The small figure turned, the kindly face lifted, and the sorrowful eyes looked up into Cleek's unemotional ones.

"Yes," said he placidly; and forthwith told him what Lord Fallowfield claimed.

"That very true," declared Ojeebi. "The lord gentleman he right ahead of me. I see him go into his room and hear him lock door. That very true indeed."

"H'm! Any idea of the time?"

"Yes — much idea. Two minutes a-past twelve. I see clock as I go past Lady Marj'ie's room."

"What were you doing knocking about that part of the house at that hour of the night? Your room's up here in the servant's quarters, isn't it?"

"Yes, sir. But I go take ice-water to the boss's room. Boss never go to bed nights without ice-water handy, sir. 'Merican boss never do."

"Yes! Quite so, quite so! Where did you get the ice rom — and how? Chop it from a big cake?"

"No, sir. It always froze to fit bottle. I get him from'
the ice-make room downstairs."

"He means the refrigerating room, Mr. Cleek," explained
young Drake. "You know, I take it, what a necessary
commodity we Americans hold ice to be. Indeed, the dear
old dad wouldn't think a dinner was a dinner without ice-
water on the table, and ice-cream for the final course. And
as there was no possibility of procuring a regular and ade-
quate supply in an out-of-the-way spot like this, he had a
complete artificial ice-making plant added to the place, and
overcame the difficulty in that way. That is what Ojeebi
means by the 'ice-make room.' What he means about its
being frozen to fit the bottles is this: The ice which is to
be used for drinking purposes is manufactured in forms
or vessels which turn it out in cubes, so that whenever
it is wanted all that a servant has to do is to go to the
plant, and the man in charge supplies him with all the cubes
required."

"Ah, I see," said Cleek, and stroked his chin. "Well,
that's all, I reckon, for the time being. Ojeebi has certainly backed up your statement to the fullest, your lordship, so we can dispense with him entirely. And now, if I
have your permission, gentlemen, I should like to feel myself privileged to go poking about the house and grounds for
the next hour or so in quest of possible clues. At the end
of that time I will rejoin you here, and shall hope to have
something definite to report. So if you don't mind my
going —— Thanks very much. Come along, Mr. Narkom. I've a little something for you to do, and — an hour
will do it, or I'm a dogberry."

With that he took his departure from the armoury and,
with the superintendent following, went down through the
house to the grounds and out into the screen of close crowding, view-defying trees.

Here he paused a minute to pull out his notebook and

scribble something on a leaf, and then to tear out that leaf and put it into Mr. Narkom's hand.

"Rush Lennard off to the post-office with that, will you? and have it wired up to town as soon as possible," he said. "Prepay the reply, and get that reply back to me as soon as telegraph and motor can get it here."

Then he swung off out of the screen of the trees and round the angle of the building, and set about hunting for the refrigerating plant.

CHAPTER XXX

I T WAS five and after when the superintendent, pale and shaking with excitement, came up the long drive from the Hall gates and found Cleek lounging in the doorway of the house, placidly smoking a cigarette and twirling a little ball of crumpled newspaper in his hand.

"Right was I, Mr. Narkom?" he queried smilingly.

"Good God, yes! Right as rain, old chap. Been carrying it for upward of a twelvemonth, and no doubt waiting for an opportunity to strike."

"Good! And while you have been attending to your little part of the business I've been looking out for mine, dear friend. Look!" said Cleek, and opened up the little ball of paper sufficiently to show what looked like a cut-glass scent bottle belonging to a lady's dressing-bag close stoppered with a metal plug sealed round with candle wax. "Woorali, my friend; and enough in it to kill an army. Come along — we've got to the bottom of the thing, let us go up and 'report.' The gentlemen will be getting anxious."

They were; for on reaching the armoury they found young Drake and Lord Fallowfield showing strong traces of the mental strain under which they were labouring and talking agitatedly with Lady Marjorie Wynde, who had, in the interim, come up and joined them, and was herself apparently in need of something to sustain and to strengthen her; for Ojeebi was standing by with an extended salver, from which she had just lifted to her lips a glass of port.

"Good God! I never was so glad to see anybody in my life, gentlemen," broke out young Drake as they appeared.

"It's beyond the hour you asked for — ages beyond — and my nerves are almost pricking their way through my skin. Mr. Cleek — Mr. Narkom — speak up, for heaven's sake. Have you succeeded in finding out anything?"

"We've done better than that, Mr. Drake," replied Cleek, "for we have succeeded in finding out everything. Look sharp there, Mr. Narkom, and shut that door. Lady Marjorie looks as if she were going to faint, and we don't want a whole houseful of servants piling in here. That's it. Back against the door, please; her ladyship seems on the point of crumpling up."

"No, no, I'm not; indeed, I'm not!" protested Lady Marjorie with a forced smile and a feeble effort to hold her galloping nerves in check. "I am excited and very much upset, of course, but I am really much stronger than you would think. Still, if you would rather I should leave the room, Mr. Cleek ——"

"Oh, by no means, your ladyship. I know how anxious you are to learn the result of my investigations. And, by that token, somebody else is anxious, too — the doctor. Call him in, will you, Mr. Drake? He is still with the others in the Stone Drum, I assume."

He was; and he came out of it with them at young Drake's call, and joined the party in the armoury.

"Doctor," said Cleek, looking up as he came in, "we've got to the puzzle's unpicking, and I thought you'd be interested to hear the result. I was right about the substance employed, for I've found the stuff and I've nailed the guilty party. It was woorali, and the reason why there was no trace of a weapon was because the blessed thing melted. It was an icicle, my friend, an icicle with its point steeped in woorali, and if you want to know how it did its work — why, it was shot in there from the cross-bow hanging on the wall immediately behind me, and the person who shot it in was so short that a chair was necessary to get up to the bowman's slit when —— No, you don't, my beauty! There's a gentleman with a noose waiting to pay his respects to all such beasts as you!"

Speaking, he sprang with a sharp, flashing movement that was like to nothing so much as the leap of a pouncing cat, and immediately there was a yap and a screech, a yell and a struggle, a click of clamping handcuffs, and a scuffle of writhing limbs, and a moment later they that were watching saw him rise with a laugh, and stand, with his hands on his hips, looking down at Ojeebi lying crumpled up in a heap, with gyves on his wrists and panic in his eyes, at the foot of the guarded door.

"Well, my pleasant-faced, agreeable little demon, it'll be many a long day before the spirits of your ancestors welcome you back to Nippon!" Cleek said as the panic-stricken Jap, realizing what was before him, began to shriek and shriek until his brain and nerves sank into a collapse and he fainted where he lay. "I've got you and I've got the woorali. I went through your trunk and found it — as I knew I should from the moment I clapped eyes upon you. If the laws of the country are so lax that they make it possible for you to do what you have done, they also are stringent enough to make you pay the price of it with your yellow little neck!"

"In the name of heaven, Mr. Cleek," spoke up young Drake, breaking silence suddenly, "what can the boy have done? You speak as if it were he that murdered my father; but, man, why should he? What had he to gain? What motive could a harmless little chap like this have for killing the man he served?"

"The strongest in the world, my friend — the greed of gain!" said Cleek. "What he could not do in your father's land it is possible for him to do in this one, which foolishly allows its subjects to insure even the life of its ruler without his will, knowledge, or consent. For nearly a twelvemonth this little brute has been carrying a heavy insurance upon the life of Jefferson P. Drake; but, thank God, he'll never live to collect it. What's that, Doctor? How did I find that out? By the simplest means possible, my dear sir.

"For a reason which concerns nobody but myself, I dropped in at the Guildford office of the Royal British Life Assurance Society in the latter part of last May, and upon that occasion I marked the singular circumstance that a Japanese was then paying the premium of an already existing policy. Why I speak of it as a singular circumstance, and why I let myself be impressed by it, lie in the fact that, as the Japanese regard their dead ancestors with absolute veneration and the privilege of being united with them a boon which makes death glorious, life assurance is not popular with them, since it seems to be insulting their ancestors and makes joining them tainted with the odour of baser things. Consequently, I felt pretty certain that it was some other life than his own he was there to pay the regularly recurring premium upon. The chances are, Doctor, that in the ordinary run of things I should never have thought of that man or that circumstance again. But it so happens that I have a very good memory for faces and events, so when I came down here to investigate this case, and in the late Mr. Drake's valet saw that Japanese man again — voila! I should have been an idiot not to put two and two together.

"The remainder, a telegram inquiring if an insurance upon the life of Jefferson P. Drake, the famous inventor, had been effected by anybody but the man himself, settled the thing beyond question. As for the rest, it is easy enough to explain. Your remark that the little puddle found upon the floor of the Stone Drum appeared to you to bear a distinct resemblance to the water resulting from melted snow, added to what I already knew regarding the refrigerating plant installed here, put me on the track of the ice; and as the small spot on the temple was of so minute a character, I knew that the weapon must have been pointed. A pointed weapon of ice leaves but one conclusion possible, Doctor. I have since learned from the man in charge of the refrigerating plant that this yellow blob of iniquity here was much taken by the icicles which the process of refrigeration caused to accumulate in the place and upon the machine itself during rotation, and that last night shortly after twelve o'clock he came down and broke off and carried away three of them. How I came to know what motive power he employed to launch the poisoned shaft can be explained in a word. Most of the weapons — indeed, all but one — hanging on the wall of this armoury are lightly coated with dust, showing that it must be a week or more since any housemaid's work was attended to in this particular quarter. One of them is not dusty. Furthermore, when I took it down for the purpose of examining it I discovered that, although smeared with ink or paint to make it look as old as the others, the bowstring was of fresh catgut, and there was a suspicious dampness about the 'catch,' which suggested either wet hands or the partial melting, under the heat of living flesh, of the 'shaft,' which had been an icicle. That's all, Doctor; that's all, Mr. Drake; that's quite all, Lord Fallowfield. A good, true-hearted young chap will get both the girl he wants and the inheritance which should be his by right; a good, true friend will get back the ancestral home he lost through misfortune and has regained through chance, and a patient and faithful lady will, in all probability, get the man she loves without now having to wait until he comes into a dead man's shoes. Lady Marjorie, my compliments. Doctor, my best respects, and gentlemen all — good afternoon."

And here with that weakness for the theatrical which was his besetting sin, he bowed to them with his hat laid over his heart, and walked out of the room.

CHAPTER XXXI

"NO, MR. NARKOM, no. As an instrument of death the icicle is *not* new," said Cleek, answering the superintendent's question as the limousine swung out through the gates of Heatherington Hall and faced the long journey back to London. "If you will look up the records of that energetic female, Catherine de Medici, Queen of France, you will find that she employed it in that capacity upon two separate occasions; and coming down to more modern times, you will also find that in the year 1872 the Russian, Lydia Bolorfska, used it at Galitch, in the province of Kostroma, to stab her sleeping husband. But as a projectile, it *is* new — as a *successful* projectile, I mean — for there have been many attempts made, owing to its propensity to dissolve after use, to discharge it from firearms, but never in one single instance have those attempts resulted in success. The explosion has always resulted in shivering and dispersing it in a shower of splinters as it leaves the muzzle of the weapon. There can be no doubt, however, that could it be propelled in a perfectly horizontal position, the power behind it would, in spite of its brittle nature, drive it through a pine board an inch thick. But, as I have said, the motive power always defeats the object by landing it against the target in a mass of splinters."

"I see. And the Jap got over that by employing a crossbow; and that, of course, did the trick."

"No. I doubt if he would have been able to put enough power behind that to drive it into the man's body with deadly effect, if, indeed, he could make it enter it at all.

Where Ojeebi scored over all others lay in the fact that with his plan there was no necessity to have the icicle enter the victim's body at all. He required nothing more than just sufficient power of propulsion to break the skin and establish contact with the blood, and then that hellish compound on the point of the projectile could be depended upon to do the rest. It did, as you know, and then dropped to the floor and melted away, leaving nothing but a little puddle of water behind it."

"But, Cleek, my dear chap, how do you account for the fact that when the doctor came to analyze that water he found no trace of the poison in it?"

"He did, Mr. Narkom, only that he didn't recognize it. Woorali is extremely volatile, for one thing, and evaporates rapidly. For another, there was a very small quantity used — a very small quantity necessary, so malignant it is — and the water furnished by the melting icicle could dilute that little tremendously. It would not be able to obliterate all trace of it, however, but the infinitesimal portion remaining would make spring water give the same answer in analysis as that given by the water resulting from melted snow. It was when Doctor Hague mentioned the fact that if it wasn't for the utter absurdity of looking for such a substance in England in July, he should have said it *was* melted snow, that I really got my first clue. Later, however, when —— But come, let's chuck it! I've had enough of murder and murderers for one day — let's talk of something else. Our new 'turnout,' here, for instance. You have 'done yourself proud' this time and no mistake — she certainly *is* a beauty, Mr. Narkom. By the way, what have you done with the old red one? Sold it?"

"Not I, indeed. I know a trick worth two of that. I send it out, empty, every day, in the hope of having those Apache johnnies follow it, and have a plain-clothes man trailing along behind in a taxi, ready to nip in and follow them if they do. But they don't — that is, they haven't up to the present; but there's always hope, you know."

"Not in that direction, I'm afraid. Waldemar's a better general than that, believe me. Knowing that we have discovered his little plan of following the red limousine just as we discovered his other, of following me, he will have gone off on another tack, believe me."

"Scotland! You don't think, do you, that he can possibly have found out anything about the new one and has set in to follow *this?*"

"No, I do not. As a matter of fact I fancy he has started to do what he ought to have done in the beginning — that is, to keep a close watch on the criminal news in the papers day by day, and every time a crime of any importance crops up, pay his respects to the theatre of it and find out who is the detective handling the case. A ducat to a doughnut he'd have been on our heels down here to-day if this little business of the Stone Drum had been made public in time to get into the morning papers. He means to have me, Mr. Narkom, if having me is possible; and he's down to the last ditch and getting desperate. Yesterday's cables from Mauravania are anything but reassuring."

"I know. They say that unless something happens very shortly to turn the tide in Ulric's favour and quell the cries for 'Restoration,' the King's downfall and expulsion are merely a matter of a few days at most. But what's that got to do with it that you suggest its bearing upon any need for haste on Waldemar's part?"

"Only that, with matters in such a state, he cannot long defer his return to the army of his country and the defence of its king," replied Cleek, serenely. "And every day he loses in failing to pay his respects to your humble servant in the manner he desires to do increases the strain of the situation and keeps him from the service of his royal master."

"Well, I wish to God something would happen to blow him and his royal master and their blooming royal country off the map, dammem!" blazed out Narkom, too savage to be choice of words. "We've never had a moment's peace, you and I, since the dashed combination came into the game. And for what, I should like to know? Not that it's any use asking *you*. You're so devilish close-mouthed a man might as well ask questions of a ton of coal for all answer he may hope to get. I shall always believe, however, that you did something pretty dashed bad to the King of Mauravania that time you were over there on that business about the Rainbow Pearl, to make the beggar turn against you, as I believe he *has*."

"Then, you will always believe what isn't true," replied Cleek, lighting a fresh cigarette. "I simply restored the pearl and his Majesty's letter to the hands of Count Irma, and did not so much as see the King while I was there. Why should I? — a mere police detective, who had been hired to do a service and paid for it like any other hireling. I took my money and I went my way; that's all there was about it. If it has pleased Count Waldemar to entertain an ugly feeling of resentment toward me, I can't help that, can I now?"

"Oh, then, it's really a personal affair between you and him, after all?"

"Something like that. He doesn't approve of my — er — knowing things that I do know; and it would be the end of a very promising future for him if I told. Here — have a cigarette and smoke yourself into a better temper. You look savage enough to bite a nail in two."

"I'd bite it in four if it looked anything like that Waldemar johnnie, by James!" asserted the superintendent, vigorously. "And if ever he lays a hand on *you* —— Look here, Cleek: I know it sounds un-English, very Continental, rotten 'soft' from one man to another, but — dammit,

Cleek, I love you! I'd go to hell for you! I'd die fighting for you! Do you understand?"

"Perfectly," said Cleek; then he put out his hand and took Mr. Narkom's in a hard, firm grip, and added, gently: "My friend, my comrade, my *pal!* Side by side — together — to the end." And the car ran on for a good half mile before either spoke again.

CHAPTER XXXII

"MR. NARKOM!"

It was an hour later, and Cleek's voice broke the silence abruptly. He had taken out his notebook and had been scribbling in it for some little time, but now, as he spoke, he tore out the written leaf and passed it over to the superintendent.

"Mr. Narkom, I refused, in the beginning, to give you the address of the little house at which I was located. Here it is. Put it in your pocketbook against future need, will you?"

"Yes, certainly. But cinnamon! old chap, what good is it to me now when you've left the place?"

"You will understand, perhaps, when I tell you that Miss Lorne is its present occupant. It was for that I took it in the beginning. There may come a need to communicate with her; there may come a need for her to communicate with you. There's always a chance, you know, that a candle may be put out when the wind blows at it from all directions; and if anything should happen — I mean if — er — anything having a bearing upon me personally that you think she *ought* to be told should come to pass — well, just go to her at once, will you? — there's a dear friend. That's the address (don't lose it) and full directions how to get there speedily. I am giving it to you now, as we shall soon be in town again and I shall leave you directly we arrive there. I'm in haste to get back to Dollops and see if between us we can't hit upon some plan, he and I, to get at the whereabouts of Waldemar. That plain-clothes

man of yours is like the butler with the bottle of cider —
he 'doesn't seem to get any forrarder.' "

"Kibblewhite!" blurted out the superintendent, sitting
up sharply. "Well, of all the born jackasses, of all the
mutton-heads in this world ———"

"Well, he doesn't seem to be very bright, I must say."

"He? Lud! I wasn't talking about *him;* I was talking
about myself. I had something to tell you to-day, and this
blessed business drove it clean out of my head. Kibblewhite had the dickens and all of a time trying to get at that
chap Serpice, as you may remember?"

"I do — in a measure. Succeeded in finding out, finally,
that the carriage he drove was one he hired from a liveryman by the month, I think was the last report you gave
me; but couldn't get any further with the business because
Serpice took it into his head not to call for the carriage again
and made off, this Kibblewhite chap didn't know where,
and appears never to have found a means of discovering."

"No; he didn't. But ten days ago he got word from the
liveryman that Serpice had just turned up and was about to
make use of the carriage again; and off Kibblewhite cut,
hotfoot, in the hope of being able to follow him. No go,
however. By the time he arrived at the stable Serpice
had already gone; so there was nothing left for the poor
disappointed chap to do but to go out on the hunt and see
if he couldn't pick him up somewhere in the streets."

"Which he didn't, of course?"

"Excuse me — which he *did*. But it was late in the
afternoon and he was coming back to the stable with the
carriage empty. Also, it was in the thick of the traffic at
Ludgate Circus, and Kibblewhite was so afraid the fellow
might mix himself up in it and give him the slip that he
took a chance shot to prevent it. Nipping up the officer on
point, he made himself and his business known, and, in a
winking, in nips the constable, hauls Mr. Serpice up sharp,

and arrests him for driving a public vehicle without a license."

"Well played, Kibblewhite!" approved Cleek. "That, of course, meant that the fellow would be arrested and have to give his address and all the rest of it?"

"So Kibblewhite himself thought; but what does the beggar do but turn the tables on him in the most unexpected manner by absolutely refusing to do anything of the kind, and, as he did *not* have a license, and would not call anybody to pay his fine, the magistrate finished the business by committing him to *jail* for ten days in default. And here's the thing I was ass enough to forget: His ten days' imprisonment was up this morning; Kibblewhite, in disguise, was to be outside the jail to follow him when he was discharged and see where he went, and he told me to look for him to turn up at the Yard before six this evening with a full report of the result of his operations."

"Bravo!" said Cleek, leaning back in his seat, with a sigh of satisfaction. "I've changed my mind about leaving you, Mr. Narkom; we will go on to the Yard together. As, in all probability, after ten days without being able to communicate with his pals or with Waldemar, our friend Serpice will be hot to get to them at once and explain the cause of his long absence, the chances are that Kibblewhite will have something of importance to report at last."

He had, as they found out when, in the fulness of time, they arrived at the Yard and were told that he was waiting for them in the superintendent's office, and in his excitement he almost threw it at them, so eager he was to report.

"I've turned the trick at last, Superintendent," he cried. "The silly josser played straight into my hands, sir. The minute he was out of jail he made a beeline for Soho, and me after him, and there he 'takes to earth' in a rotten little restaurant in the worst part of the district; and when I nips over and has a look inside, there he was shakin' hands with

a lot of Frenchies of his own kind, and them all prancin'
about and laughin' like they'd gone off their bloomin'
heads. I sees there aren't no back door to the place, and I
knows from that that he'd have to come out the same way as
he went in, so off I nips over to the other side of the street
and lays in wait for him.

"After about ten minutes or so, out he comes — him and
another of the lot — moppin' of his mouth with his coat-
sleeve, and off they starts in a great hurry, and me after
them. They goes first to a barber shop, where the man I
was followin' nips in, has a shave, a hair-cut and a wash-up,
while the chap that was with him toddles off and fetches
him a clean shirt and a suit of black clothes. In about
fifteen minutes out my man comes again, makin' a tolerable
respectable appearance, sir, after his barberin' and in his
clean linen and decent clothes. Him and his mate stands
talkin' and grinnin' for a minute or so, then they shakes
hands and separates, and off my man cuts it, westward.

"Sir, I sticks to him like a brother. I follers him smack
across to the Strand and along that to the Hotel Cecil, and
there the beggar nips in and goes up the courtyard as bold
as you please, sends up his name to a gent, the gent sends
down word for him to be showed up at once, and in that way
I spots my man. For when I goes up to the clerk and shows
my badge and asks who was the party my johnnie had
asked for, he tells me straight and clear: 'Gentleman he's
making a suit of clothes for — Baron Rodolf de Mont-
ravenne, an Austrian nobleman, who has been stopping here
for weeks!'"

Cleek twitched round his eye and glanced at Narkom.

" 'Things least hidden are best hidden,' " he quoted,
smiling. "The dear count knows a thing or two, you perceive. You have done very well indeed, Kibblewhite. Here
is your ten-pound note and many thanks for you services.
Good evening."

Kibblewhite took the money and his departure immediately; but so long as he remained within hearing distance — so long as the echo of his departing steps continued to sound — Cleek remained silent, and the curious crooked smile made a loop in his cheek. But of a sudden:

"Mr. Narkom," he said, quietly "I shan't be found in any of my usual haunts for the next few days. If, however, you should urgently need me, call at the Hotel Cecil and ask for Captain Maltravers — and call in disguise, please; our friend the count is keen. Remember the name. Or, better still, write it down."

"But, good God! Cleek, such a risk as that ——"

"No — please — don't attempt to dissuade me. I want that man, and I'll get him if getting him be humanly possible. That's all. Thanks very much. Good-bye."

Then the door opened and shut, and by the time Mr. Narkom could turn round from writing down the name he had been given, he was quite alone in the room.

CHAPTER XXXIII

"**N**UM-BAH Nine-ninety-two — Captain Maltravers, please. Nine-ninety-two. Num-bah Nine-ninety-two!"

Thrice the voice of the page — moving and droning out his words in that perfunctory manner peculiar unto the breed of hotel pages the world over — sounded its dreary monotone through the hum of conversation in the rather crowded tearoom without producing the slightest effect; then, of a sudden, the gentleman seated in the far corner reading the daily paper — a tall, fair-haired, fair-moustached gentleman with "The Army" written all over him in capital letters — twitched up his head, listened until the call was given for the fourth time, and, thereupon, snapped his fingers sharply, elevated a beckoning digit, and called out crisply: "Here, my boy — over here — this way!"

The boy went to him immediately, extended a small, circular metal salver, and then, lifting the thumb which held in position the hand-written card thereon, allowed the slip of pasteboard to be removed.

"Gentleman, sir — waiting in the office," he volunteered.

"Captain Maltravers" glanced at the card, frowned, rose with it still held between his fingers, and within the space of a minute's time walked into the hotel's public office and the presence of a short, stout, full-bearded "dumpling" of a man with the florid complexion and the country-cut clothes of a gentleman farmer, who half sat and half leaned upon the arm of a leather-covered settle nervously tapping with the ferule of a thick walking-cane, a boot whose exceedingly high sole and general construction mutely stood sponsor for a withered and shortened leg.

"My dear Yard; I am delighted to see you!" exclaimed the "captain" as he bore down on the little round man and shook hands with him heartily. "Grimshaw told me that you would be coming up to London shortly, but I didn't allow myself to hope that it would be so soon as this. Gad! it's a dog's age since I've seen you. Come along up to my own room and let us have a good old-fashioned chat. Key of Nine-ninety-two, please, clerk. Thanks very much. Come along, Yard — this way, old chap!"

With that he linked his arm in his caller's, bore him clumping and wobbling to the nearby lift, and thence, in due course, to the door of number Nine-ninety-two and the seclusion which lay behind it. He was still chattering away gayly as the lift dropped down out of sight and left them, upon which he shut the door, locked it upon the inside, and stopping long enough to catch up a towel and hang it over the keyhole, turned on his heel and groaned.

"What! am I not to have even a two days' respite, you indefatigable *machine?*" he said, as he walked across the room and threw himself into a chair with a sigh of annoyance. "Think! it was only this morning that I ventured upon the first casual bow of a fellow guest with the dear 'Baron'; only at luncheon we exchanged the first civil word. But the ice was broken and I should have had him 'roped in' by teatime — I am sure of it. And now you come and nip my hopes in the bud like this. And in a disguise that a fellow as sharp as he would see through in a wink if he met you."

"It was the best I could do, Cleek — I'm not a dabster in the art of making up, as you know." Mr. Narkom's voice was, like his air, duly apologetic. "Besides, I hung around until I saw him go out before I ventured in; although I was on thorns the whole blessed time. I had to see you, old

chap — I simply had to — and every minute was of importance. I shouldn't have ventured to come at all if it hadn't
been imperative."

"I'm sure of that," said Cleek, recovering his good
humour instantly. "Don't mind my beastly bad temper
this afternoon, there's a good friend. It's a bit of a disappointment, of course, after I'd looked forward to a clear
field just as soon as Waldemar should return, but —— It is
you, first and foremost, at all times and under all circumstances. Other matters count as nothing with me when
you call. Always remember that."

"I do, old chap. It's because I do that I went to the
length of promising Miss Larue that I'd lay the case before
you."

"Miss Larue? A moment, please. Will the lady to
whom you refer be Miss Margaret Larue, the celebrated
actress? The one in question who treated me so cavalierly
last August in that business regarding the disappearance
of that chap James Colliver?"

"Yes. He was her brother, you recollect, and — don't
get hot about it, Cleek. I know she treated you very badly
in that case, and so does she, but ——"

"She treated me abominably!" interposed Cleek, with
some heat. "First setting me on the business, and then
calling me off just as I had got a grip on the thing and was
within measuring distance of the end. I can't forgive that;
and I never could fathom her reason for it. If it was as
you yourself suggested at the time, because she shrank from
the notoriety that was likely.to accrue to her from letting
everybody in the world know that 'Jimmy the Shifter' was
her own brother, she ought to have thought of that in the
beginning — when she acknowledged it so openly — instead
of making such an ass of me by her high-handed proceeding
of calling me off the scent at its hottest, as if I were a tame
puppy to be pulled this way and that with a string. I ob-

ject to being made a fool of, Mr. Narkom; and there's no denying the fact that Miss Larue treated me very badly in that James Colliver case — very badly and very cavalierly indeed."

Unquestionably Miss Larue had. Even Mr. Narkom had to admit that; for the facts which lay behind these heated remarks were not such as are calculated to make any criminal investigator pleased with his connection therewith. Clearly set forth, those facts were as follows:

On the nineteenth day of the preceding August, James Colliver had disappeared, as suddenly and as completely and with as little trace left behind as does a kinematograph picture when it vanishes from the screen.

Now the world at large had never heard of James Colliver until he did disappear, and it is extremely doubtful if it would have done so even then but that circumstances connected with his vanishment brought to light the startling disclosure that the worthless, dissolute hulk of a man who was known to the habitués of half the low-class public houses in Hoxton by the pseudonym of "Jimmy the Shifter" was not only all that time and drink had left of the once popular melodramatic actor Julian Monteith, but that he was, in addition thereto, own brother to Miss Margaret Larue, the distinguished actress who was at that moment electrifying London by her marvellous performance of the leading rôle in *The Late Mrs. Cavendish.*

The reasons which impelled Miss Larue to let the public discover that her real name was Maggie Colliver, and that "Jimmy the Shifter" was related to her by such close ties of blood, were these: *The Late Mrs. Cavendish* was nearing the close of its long and successful run at the Royalty, and its successor was already in rehearsal for early production. That successor was to be a specially rewritten version of the old-time favourite play *Catharine Howard; or, The Tomb, the Throne, and the Scaffold,* with Miss Larue, of course, in the part of the ambitious and ill-fated Catharine. Preparations were on foot for a production which would be splendidly elaborate as to scenery and effects, and absolutely accurate as to detail. For instance, the costume which Henry VIII had worn at the time of his marriage with Catharine Howard was copied exactly, down to the minute question of the gaudy stitchery on the backs of the gloves and the toes of the shoes; and permission had been obtained to make the mimic betrothal ring which the stage "Henry" was to press upon the finger of the stage "Catharine" an exact replica of the real one, as preserved among the nation's historic jewels. Not to be outdone in this matter of accuracy, Miss Larue naturally aimed to have the dresses and the trinkets she wore as nearly like those of the original Catharine as it was possible to obtain. As her position in the world of art was now so eminent and had brought her into close touch with the elect, it was not difficult for the lady to borrow dresses, and even jewels, of the exact period from the heirlooms treasured by members of the nobility, that these might be copied in mimic gems for her by the well-known theatrical and show supply company of Henry Trent & Son, Soho.

To this firm, which was in full charge of the preparation of dresses, properties, and accessories for the great production, was also entrusted the making of a "cast" of Miss Larue's features and the manufacture therefrom of a wax head with which it was at first proposed to lend a touch of startling realism to the final scene of the execution of Catharine on Tower Hill, but which was subsequently abandoned after the first night as being unnecessarily gruesome and repulsive.

It was during the course of the final rehearsals for this astonishing production, and when the army of supers who had long been drilling for it at other hours was brought for the first time into contact with the "principals," that Miss

Larue was horrified to discover among the members of that "army" her dissolute brother, "Jimmy the Shifter."

For years — out of sheer sympathy for the wife who clung to him to the last, and the young son who was growing up to be a fine fellow despite the evil stock from which he had sprung — Miss Larue had continuously supplied this worthless brother with money enough to keep him, with the strict proviso that he was never to come near any theatre where she might be performing, nor ever at any time to make known his relationship to her. She now saw in this breaking of a rule, which heretofore he had inviolably adhered to, clear evidence that the man had suddenly become a menace, and she was in great haste to get him out of touch with her colleagues before anything could be done to disgrace her.

In so sudden and so pressing an emergency she could think of no excuse but an errand by which to get him out of the theatre, and of no errand but one — the stage jewels which Messrs. Trent & Son were making for her. She therefore sat down quickly at the prompt table, and, drawing a sheet of paper to her, wrote hurriedly:

Messrs. Trent & Son:
GENTLEMEN — Please give the bearer my jewels — or such of them as are finished, if you have not done with all — that he may bring them to me immediately, as I have instant need of them. Yours faithfully,
MARGARET LARUE.

This she passed over to the stage manager, with a request to "Please read that, Mr. Lampson, and certify over your signature that it is authentic, and that you vouch for having seen me write it." After which she got up suddenly, and said as calmly as she could: "Mr. Super Master, I want to borrow one of your men to go on an important errand to Trent & Son for me. This one will do," signalling out her brother. "Spare him, please. This way, my man — come quickly!"

With that she suddenly caught up the note she had written — and which the stage manager had, as requested, certified — and, beckoning her brother to follow, walked hurriedly off the stage to a deserted point in the wings.

"Why have you done this dreadful thing?" she demanded in a low, fierce tone as soon as he came up with her. "Are you a fool as well as a knave that you come here and risk losing your only support by a thing like this?"

"I wanted to see you — I had to see you — and it was the only way," he gave back in the same guarded tone. "The wife is dead. She died last night, and I've got to get money somewhere to bury her. I'd no one to send, since you've taken Ted away and sent him to school, so I had to come myself."

The knowledge that it was for no more desperate reason than this that he had forced himself into her presence came as a great relief to Miss Larue. She hastened to get rid of him by sending him to Trent & Son with the note that she had written, and to tell him to carry the parcel that would be handed to him to the rooms she was occupying in Portman Square — and which she made up her mind to vacate the very next day — and there to wait until she came home from rehearsal.

He took the note and left the theatre at once, upon which Miss Larue, considerably relieved, returned to the duties in hand, and promptly banished all thought of him from her mind.

It was not until something like two hours afterward that he was brought back to mind in a somewhat disquieting manner.

"I say, Miss Larue," said the stage manager as she came off after thrice rehearsing a particularly trying scene, and, with a weary sigh, dropped into a vacant chair at his table, "aren't you worried about that chap you sent with the note to Trent & Son? There's been time for him to go and return twice over, you know; and I observe that he's not back yet. Aren't you a bit uneasy?"

"No. Why should I be?"

"Well, for one thing, I should say it was an extremely risky business unless you knew something about the man. Suppose, for instance, he should make off with the jewels? A pretty pickle you'd be in with the parties from whom you borrowed them, by Jove!"

"Good gracious, you don't suppose I sent him for the originals, do you?" said Miss Larue with a smile. "Trent & Son *would* think me a lunatic to do such a thing as that. What I sent him for was, of course, merely the paste replicas. The originals I shall naturally go for myself."

"God bless my soul! The paste replicas, do you say?" blurted in Mr. Lampson excitedly. "Why, I thought — Trent & Son will be sure to think so themselves under the circumstances! They can't possibly think otherwise."

"'Under the circumstances'? 'Think otherwise'?" repeated Miss Larue, facing round upon him sharply. "What do you mean by that, Mr. Lampson? Good heavens! not that they could possibly be mad enough to give the man the originals?"

"Yes, certainly! Good Lord! what else can they think — what else can they give him? They sent the paste duplicates here by their own messenger this morning! They are in the manager's office — in his safe — at this very minute; and I was going to bring them round to you as soon as the rehearsal is over!"

Consternation followed this announcement, of course. The rehearsal was called to an abrupt halt. Mr. Lampson and Miss Larue flew round to the front of the house in a sort of panic, got to the telephone, and rang up Trent & Son, who confirmed their worst fears. Yes, the man had arrived with the note from Miss Larue something over an hour ago, and they had promptly handed him over the original jewels. Not all of them, of course, but those which they had finished duplicating and of which they had sent the replicas to the theatre by their own messenger that morning. Surely that was what Miss Larue meant by the demand, was it not? No other explanation seemed possible after they had sent her the copies and — Good Lord! hadn't heard about it? Meant the imitations? Heavens above, what an appalling mistake! What was that? The man? Oh, yes; he took the things after Mr. Trent, senior, had removed them from the safe and handed them over to him, and he had left Mr. Trent's office directly he received them. Miss Larue could ascertain exactly what had been delivered to him by examining the duplicates their messenger had carried to the theatre.

Miss Larue did, discovering, to her dismay, that they represented a curious ruby necklace, of which the original had been lent her by the Duchess of Oldhampton, a stomacher of sapphires and pearls borrowed from the Marquise of Chepstow, and a rare Tudor clasp of diamonds and opals which had been lent to her by the Lady Margery Thraill.

In a panic she rushed from the theatre, called a taxi, and, hoping against hope, whirled off to her rooms at Portman Square. No Mr. James Colliver had been there. Nor did he come there ever. Neither did he return to the squalid home where his dead wife lay; nor did any of his cronies nor any of his old haunts see hide or hair of him from that time. Furthermore, nobody answering to his description had been seen to board any train, steamship, or sailing-vessel leaving for foreign parts, nor could there be found any hotel, lodging-house, furnished or even unfurnished apartment into which he had entered that day or upon any day thereafter.

In despair, Miss Larue drove to Scotland Yard and put the matter into the hands of the police, offering a reward of

£1,000 for the recovery of the jewels; and through the medium of the newspapers promised Mr. James Colliver that she would not prosecute, but would pay that £1,000 over to *him* if he would return the gems, that she might restore them to their rightful owners.

Mr. James Colliver neither accepted that offer nor gave any sign that he was aware of it. It was then that Scotland Yard, in the person of Cleek, stepped in to conduct the search for both man and jewels; and within forty-eight hours some amazing circumstances were brought to light.

First and foremost, Mr. Henry Trent, who said he had given the gems over to Colliver, and that the man had immediately left the office, was unable, through the fact of his son's absence from town, to give any further proof of that statement than his own bare word; for there was nobody but himself in the office at the time, whereas the door porter, who distinctly remembered James Colliver's entrance into the building, as distinctly remembered that up to the moment when evening brought "knocking-off time" James Colliver had never, to his certain knowledge, come out of it!

The next amazing fact to be unearthed was that one of the office cleaners had found tucked under the stairs leading up to the top floor a sponge, which had beyond all possible question been used to wipe blood from something and had evidently been tucked there in a great hurry. The third amazing discovery took the astonishing shape of finding in an East End pawnbroker's shop every one of the missing articles, and positive proof that the man who had pledged them was certainly not in the smallest degree like James Colliver, but was evidently a person of a higher walk in life and more prosperous in appearance than the missing man had been since the days when he was a successful actor.

These circumstances Cleek had just brought to light when Miss Larue, having found the gems, determined to drop the case, and refused thereafter so much as to discuss it with any living soul.

That her reason for taking this unusual step had something behind it which was of more moment than the mere fact that the jewels had been recovered and returned to their respective owners there could hardly be a doubt; for from that time onward her whole nature seemed to undergo a radical change, and, from being a brilliant, vivacious, cheery-hearted woman whose spirits were always of the highest and whose laughter was frequent, she developed suddenly into a silent, smileless, mournful one, who shrank from all society but that of her lost brother's orphaned son, and who seemed to be oppressed by the weight of some unconfessed cross and the shadow of some secret woe.

Such were the facts regarding the singular Colliver case at the time when Cleek laid it down — unprobed, unsolved, as deep a mystery in the end as it had been in the beginning — and such they still were when, on this day, at this critical time and after an interval of eleven months, Mr. Maverick Narkom came to ask him to pick it up again.

"And with an element of fresh mystery added to complicate it more than ever, dear chap," he declared, rather excitedly. "For, as the father vanished eleven months ago, so yesterday the son, too, disappeared. In the same manner — from the same point — in the selfsame building and in the same inexplicable and almost supernatural way! Only that in this instance the mystery is even more incomprehensible, more like 'magic' than ever. For the boy is known to have been shown by a porter into a room almost entirely surrounded by glass — a room whose interior was clearly visible to two persons who were looking into it at the time — and then and there to have completely vanished without anybody knowing when, where, or how."

CHAPTER XXXIV

"**W**HAT'S that?" rapped out Cleek, sitting up sharply. His interest had been trapped, just as Mr. Narkom knew that it would. "Vanished from a glass-room into which people were looking at the time? And yet nobody saw the manner of his going, do you say?"

"That's it precisely. But the most astonishing part of the business is the fact that, whereas the porter can bring at least three witnesses to prove that he showed the boy into that glass-room, and at least one to testify that he heard him speak to the occupant of it, the two watchers who were looking into the place at the time are willing to swear on oath that he not only did not enter the place, but that the room was absolutely vacant at the period, and remained so for at least an hour afterward. If that isn't a mystery that will want a bit of doing to solve, dear chap, then you may call me a Dutchman."

"Hum-m-m!" said Cleek reflectively. "How, then, am I to regard the people who give this cross testimony — as lunatics or liars?"

"Neither, b'gad!" asseverated Narkom, emphatically. "I'll stake my reputation upon the sanity and the truthfulness of every mother's son and every father's daughter of the lot of them! The porter who says he showed the boy into the glass-room I've known since he was a nipper — his dad was one of my Yard men years ago — and the two people who were looking into the place at the time, and who swear that it was absolutely empty and that the lad *never* came into it —— Look here, old chap, I'll let you into a bit of family history. One of them is a distant relative of Mrs. Narkom — an aunt, in fact, who's rather down in the world, and does a bit of dressmaking for a living. The other is her daughter. They are two of the straightest-living, most upright, and truly religious women that ever drew the breath of life, and they wouldn't, either of 'em, tell a lie for all the money in England. There's where the puzzle of the thing comes in. You simply have *got* to believe that that porter showed the boy into that room, for there are reliable witnesses to prove it, and he has no living reason to lie about it; and you have *got* to believe that those two women are speaking the truth when they say that it was empty at that period and remained empty for an hour afterward. Also — if you will take on the case and solve at the same time the mystery attending the disappearance of both father and son — you will have to find out where that boy went to, through whose agency he vanished, and for what cause."

"A tall order that," said Cleek with one of his curious, one-sided smiles. "Still, of course, mysteries which are humanly possible of creation are humanly possible of solution, and — there you are. Who is the client? Miss Larue? If so, how is one to be sure that she will not again call a halt, and spoil a good 'case' before it is halfway to completion?"

"For the best of reasons," replied Narkom earnestly. "Hers is not the sole 'say' in the present case. Added to which, she is now convinced that her suspicions in the former one were not well grounded. The truth has come out at last, Cleek. She stopped all further inquiry into the mysterious disappearance of her brother because she had reason to believe that the elder Mr. Trent had killed him for the purpose of getting possession of those jewels to tide over a financial crisis consequent upon the failure of some heavy speculations upon the stock market. She held her peace and closed up the case because she loves and is engaged to be married to his son, and she would have lost everything in the world sooner than hurt his belief in the honour and integrity of his father."

"What a ripping girl! Gad, but there *are* some splendid women in the world, are there not, Mr. Narkom? What has happened, dear friend, to change her opinion regarding the elder Mr. Trent's guilt?"

"The disappearance of the son under similar circumstances to that of the father, and from the same locality. She knows now that the elder Mr. Trent can have no part in the matter, since he is at present in America, the financial crisis has been safely passed, and the son — who could have no possible reason for injuring the lad, who is, indeed, remarkably fond of him, and by whose invitation he visited the building — is solely in charge and as wildly anxious as man can be to have the abominable thing cleared up without delay. He now knows why she so abruptly closed up the other case, and he is determined that nothing under heaven shall interfere with the prosecution of this one to the very end. It is he who is the client, and both he and his fiancée will be here presently to lay the full details before you."

"Here!" Cleek leaned forward in his chair with a sort of lunge as he flung out the word, and there was a snap in his voice that fairly stung. "Good heavens above, man! They mustn't come here. Get word to them at once and stop them."

"It wouldn't be any use trying, I'm afraid, old chap; I expect they are here already. At all events, I told them to watch from the other side of the way until they saw me enter, and then to come in and go straightway to the public tearoom and wait until I brought you to them."

"Well, of all the insane —— Whatever prompted you to do a madman's trick like that? A public character like Miss Larue, a woman whom half London knows by sight, who will be the target for every eye in the tearoom, and the news of whose presence in the hotel will be all over the place in less than no time! Were you out of your head?"

"Good lud! Why, I thought I'd be doing the very thing that would please you, dear chap," bleated the superintendent, despairingly. "It seemed to me such a natural thing for an actress to take tea at a hotel — that it would look so innocent and open that nobody would suspect there was anything behind it. And you always say that things least hidden are hidden the most of all."

Cleek struck his tongue against his teeth with a sharp, clicking sound indicative of mild despair. There were times when Mr. Narkom seemed utterly hopeless.

"Well, if it's done, it's done, of course; and there seems only one way out of it," he said. "Nip down to the tearoom as quickly as possible, and if they are there bring them up here. It's only four o'clock and there's a chance that Waldemar may not have returned to the hotel yet. Heaven knows, I hope not! He'd spot you in a tick, in a weak disguise like that."

"Then why don't you go down yourself and fetch them up, old chap? He'd never spot *you*. Lord! your own mother wouldn't know you from Adam in this spiffing get-up. And it wouldn't matter a tinker's curse then if Waldemar was back or not."

"It would matter a great deal, my friend — don't deceive yourself upon that point. For one thing, Captain Maltravers is registered at the office as having just arrived from India after a ten years' absence, and ten years ago Miss Margaret Larue was not only unknown to fame, but must have been still in pinafores, so how was he to have made her acquaintance? Then, too, she doesn't expect to see me without you, so I should have to introduce myself and stop to explain matters — yes, and even risk her companion getting excited and saying something indiscreet, and those are rather dangerous affairs in a public tearoom, with everybody's eyes no doubt fixed upon the lady. No, you must attend to the matter yourself, my friend; so nip off and be about it. If the lady and her companion are there, just whisper them to say nothing, but follow you immediately. If they are not there, slip out and warn them not to come. Look sharp — the situation is ticklish!"

And just how ticklish Mr. Narkom realized when he descended and made his way to the public tearoom. For the usual four o'clock gathering of shoppers and sightseers was there in full force, the well-filled room was like a hive full of buzzing bees who were engaged in imparting confidences to one another, the name of "Margaret Larue" was being whispered here, there and everywhere, and all eyes were directed toward a far corner where at a little round table Margaret Larue herself sat in company with Mr. Harrison Trent engaged in making a feeble pretence of enjoying a tea which neither of them wanted and upon which neither was bestowing a single thought.

Narkom spotted them at once, made his way across the crowded room, said something to them in a swift, low whisper, and immediately became at once the most envied and most unpopular person in the whole assembly; for Miss Larue and her companion arose instantly and, leaving some pieces of silver on the table, walked out with him and robbed the room of its chief attraction.

All present had been deeply interested in the entire proceeding, but none more so than the tall, distinguished looking foreign gentleman seated all alone at the exactly opposite end of the room from the table where Miss Larue and her companion had been located; for his had been the tensest kind of interest from the very instant Mr. Narkom had made his appearance, and remained so to the last.

Even after the three persons had vanished from the room,

he continued to stare at the doorway through which they
had passed, and the rather elaborate tea he had ordered
remained wholly untouched. A soft step sounded near him
and a soft voice broke in upon his unspoken thoughts.

"Is not the tea to Monsieur's liking?" it inquired with all
the deference of the Continental waiter. And that awoke
him from his abstraction.

"Yes — quite, thank you. By the way, that was Miss
Larue who just left the room, was it not, Philippe?"

"Yes, Monsieur — the great Miss Larue: the most famous
of all English actresses."

"So I understand. And the lame man who came in and
spoke to her — who is he? Not a guest of the hotel, I am
sure, since I have never seen him here before."

"I do not know, Monsieur, who the gentleman is. It
shall be the first I shall see of him ever. It may be, however, that he is a new arrival. They would know at the
office, if Monsieur le Baron desires me to inquire."

"Yes — do. I fancy I have seen him before. Find out
for me who he is."

Philippe disappeared like a fleet shadow. After an
absence of about two minutes, he came back with the
desired intelligence.

"No, Monsieur le Baron, the gentleman is not a guest,"
he announced. "But he is visiting a guest. The name is
Yard. He arrived about a quarter of an hour ago and sent
his card in to Captain Maltravers, who at once took him up
to his room."

"Captain Maltravers? So! That will be the military
officer from India, will it not?"

"Yes, Monsieur; the one with the fair hair and moustache
who lunched to-day at the table adjoining Monsieur le
Baron's own."

"Ah, to be sure. And 'passed the time of day' with me,
as they say in this peculiar language. I remember the

gentleman perfectly. Thank you very much. There's something to pay you for your trouble."

"Monsieur le Baron is too generous! Is there any other
service ——"

"No, no — nothing, thank you. I have all that I re-
quire," interposed the "Baron" with a gesture of dismissal.

And evidently he had; for five minutes later he walked
into the office of the hotel, and said to the clerk, "Make out
my bill, please — I shall be leaving England at once," and
immediately thereafter walked into a telephone booth, consulted his notebook, and rang up 253480 Soho, and, on getting it, began to talk rapidly and softly to some one who
understood French.

Meantime Mr. Narkom, unaware of the little powder
train he had unconsciously lighted, had gone on up the stairs
with his two companions — purposely avoiding the lift that
he might explain matters as they went — piloted them safely
to the suite occupied by "Captain Maltravers," and at the
precise moment when "Baron Rodolf de Montravanne"
walked into the telephone booth, Cleek was meeting Miss
Larue for the first time since those distressing days of eleven
months ago, and meeting Mr. Harrison Trent for the first
time ever.

CHAPTER XXXV

CLEEK found young Trent an extremely handsome man of about three-and-thirty; of a highly strung, nervous temperament, and with an irritating habit of running his fingers through his hair when excited. Also, it seemed impossible for him to sit still for half a minute at a stretch; he must be constantly hopping up only to sit down again, and moving restlessly about as if he were doing his best to retain his composure and found it difficult with Cleek's calm eyes fixed constantly upon him.

"I want to tell you something about that bloodstained sponge business, Mr. Cleek," he said in his abrupt, jerky, uneasy manner. "I never heard a word about it until last night, when Miss Larue confessed her former suspicions of my dear old dad, and gave me all the details of the matter. That sponge had nothing to do with the affair at all. It was I that tucked it under the staircase where it was found, and I did so on the day before James Colliver's disappearance. The blood that had been on it was mine, not his."

"I see," said Cleek, serenely. "The explanation, of course, is the good, old tried-and-true refuge of the story-writers — namely, a case of nose-bleeding, is it not?"

"Yes," admitted Trent. "But with this difference: mine wasn't an accidental affair at all — it was the result of getting a jolly good hiding; and I made an excuse to get away and hop out of town, so that the dad wouldn't know about it nor see how I'd been battered. The fact is, I met one of our carmen in the upper hall. He was as drunk as a lord, and when I took him to task about it and threatened him with discharge, he said something to me that I thought needed a jolly sight more than words by way of chastisement, so I nipped off my coat and sailed into him. It turned out that he was the better man, and gave me all that I'd asked for in less than a minute's time; so I shook hands with him, told him to bundle off home and sleep himself sober, and that if he wouldn't say anything about the matter I wouldn't either, and he could turn up for work in the morning as usual. Then I washed up, shoved the sponge under the staircase, and nipped off out of town; because, you know, it would make a deuced bad impression if any of the other workmen should find out that a member of the firm had been thrashed by one of the employees — and Draycott had done me up so beautifully that I was a sight for the gods."

The thing had been so frankly confessed that, in spite of the fact of having in the beginning been rather repelled by him, Cleek could not but experience a feeling of liking for the man. "So that's how it happened, is it?" he said, with a laugh. "It is a brave man, Mr. Trent, that will resist the opportunity to make himself a hero in the presence of the lady he loves; and I hope I may be permitted to congratulate Miss Larue on the wisdom of her choice. But now, if you please, let us get down at once to the details of the melancholy business we have in hand. Mr. Narkom has been telling me the amazing story of the boy's visit to the building and of his strange disappearance therein, but I should like to have a few further facts, if you will be so kind. What took the boy to the building, in the first place? I am told he went there upon your invitation, but I confess that that seems rather odd to me. Why should a man of business want a boy to visit him during business hours?"

"Good Lord, man! I couldn't have let him see what he wanted to see if he didn't come during business hours, could

I? But that's rather ambiguous, so I'll make haste to put it plainer. Young Stan — his Christian name is Stanley, as I suppose you know — young Stan is mad to learn the business of theatrical property making, and particularly that of the manufacture of those wax effigies, et cetera, which we supply for the use of drapers in their show windows; and as he is now sixteen and of an age to begin thinking of *some* trade or profession for the future, I thought it would save Miss Larue putting up a jolly big premium to have him taught outside if we took him into our business free, so I invited him to come and look round and see if he thought he'd like it when he came to look into the messy details.

"Well, he came rather late yesterday afternoon, and I'd taken him round for just about ten or a dozen minutes when word was suddenly brought to me that the representative of one of the biggest managers in the country had just called with reference to an important order, so, of course, I put back to the office as quickly as I could foot it, young Stan quite naturally following me, as he didn't know his way about the place alone, and, being a modest, retiring sort of boy, didn't like facing the possibility of blundering into what might prove to be private quarters, and things of that sort. He said as much to me at the time.

"Well, when I got back to the office, I soon found that the business with my visitor was a matter that would take some time to settle — you can't give a man an estimate all on a jump, and without doing a bit of figuring, you know — so I told young Stan that he might cut off and go over the place on his own, if he liked, as it had been arranged that, when knocking-off time came, I was to go back with him to Miss Larue's flat, where we all were to have supper together. When I told him that, he asked eagerly if he might go up to the wax-figure department, as he was particularly anxious to see Loti at work, and so ——"

"Loti!" Cleek flung in the word so sharply that Trent gave a nervous start. "Just a moment, please, before you go any further, Mr. Trent. Sorry to interrupt, but, tell me, please: is the man who models your show-window effigies named Loti, then? Is, eh? Hum-m! Any connection by chance with that once famous Italian worker in wax, Giuseppe Loti — chap that used to make those splendid wax tableaux for the Eden Musée in Paris some eighteen or twenty years ago?"

"Same chap. Went all to pieces all of a sudden — clear off his head for a time, I've heard — in the very height of his career, because his wife left him. Handsome French woman — years younger than he — ran off with another chap and took every blessed thing of value she could lay her hands upon when — but maybe you've heard the story?"

"I have," said Cleek. "It is one that is all too common on the Continent. Also, it happened that I was in Paris at the time of the occurrence. And so you have that great Giuseppe Loti at the head of your waxwork department, eh? What a come-down in the world for him! Poor devil! I thought he was dead ages ago. He dropped out suddenly and disappeared from France entirely after that affair with his unfaithful wife. The rumour was that he had committed suicide; although that seemed as improbable as it now turns out to be, in the face of the fact that on the night after his wife left him he turned up at the Café Royal and publicly —— No matter! Go on with the case, please. What about the boy?"

"Let's see, now, where was I?" said Trent, knotting up his brow. "Oh, ah! I recollect — just where he asked me if he could go up and see Loti at work. Of course, I said that he could; there wasn't any reason why I shouldn't, as the place is open to inspection always, so I opened the door and showed him the way to the staircase leading up to the glass-room, and then went to the speaking-tube and called up to

Loti to expect him, and to treat him nicely, as he was the nephew of the great Miss Larue and would, in time, be mine also."

"Was there any necessity for taking that precaution, Mr. Trent?"

"Yes. Loti has developed a dashed bad temper since last autumn and is very eccentric, very irritable — not a bit like the solemn, sedate old johnnie he used to be. Even his work has deteriorated, I think, but one daren't criticise it or he flies into a temper and threatens to leave."

"And you don't wish him to, of course — his name must stand for something."

"It stands for a great deal. It's one of our biggest cards. We can command twice as much for a Loti figure as for one made by any other waxworker. So we humour him in his little eccentricities and defer to him a great deal. Also, as he prefers to live on the premises, he saves us money in other ways. Serves for a watchman as well, you understand."

"Oh, he lives on the premises, does he? Where? In the glass-room?"

"Oh, no; that would not be possible. The character as well as the position of that renders it impossible as a place of habitation. He uses it after hours as a sort of sitting-room, to be sure, and has partly fitted it up as one, but he sleeps, eats, and dresses in a room on the floor below."

"Not an adjoining one?"

"Oh, no; an adjoining room would be an impossibility. Our building is an end one, standing on the corner of a short passage which leads to nothing but a narrow alley running along parallel with the back of our premises, and the glass-room covers nearly the entire roof of it. As a matter of fact, Mr. Cleek, although we call it that at the works, the term Glass Room is a misnomer. In reality, it's nothing more nor less than a good sized 'lean-to' greenhouse that the dad bought and had taken up there in sections, and its rear elevation rests against the side wall of a still higher building than ours, next door — the premises of Storminger the carriage builder, to be exact. But look here: perhaps I can make the situation clearer by a rough sketch. Got a lead pencil and a bit of paper, anybody? Oh, thanks very much, dear. One can always rely upon *you*. Now, look here, Mr. Cleek — this is the way of it. You mustn't mind if it's a crude thing, because, you know, I'm a rotten bad draughtsman and can't draw for nuts. But all the same, this will do at a pinch."

Here he leaned over the table in the centre of the room and, taking the pencil and the blank back of the letter which Miss Larue had supplied, made a crude outline sketch thus:

"There you are," he said suddenly, laying the crude drawing on the table before Cleek, and with him bending over it. "You are supposed to be looking at the houses

from the main thoroughfare, don't you know, and, therefore, at the front of them. This tall building on the left
marked 1 is Storminger's; the low one, number 2, adjoining,
is ours; and that cagelike-looking thing, 3, on the top of it,
is the glass-room. Now, along the front of it here, where
I have put the long line with an X on the end, there runs a
wooden partition with a door leading into the room itself,
so that it's impossible for anybody on the opposite side of
the main thoroughfare to see into the place at all. But
that is not the case with regard to people living on the
opposite side of the short passage (this is here, that I've
marked 4), because there's nothing to obstruct the view
but some rubbishy old lace curtains which Loti, in his en-
deavour to make the place what he calls homelike, would
insist upon hanging, and *they* are so blessed thin that anybody can look right through them and see all over the place.
Of course, though, there are blinds, which he can pull down
on the inside if the sun gets too strong; and when they are
down, nobody can see into the glass-room at all. Pardon?
Oh, we had it constructed of glass, Mr. Narkom, because of
the necessity for having all the light obtainable in doing the
minute work on some of the fine tableaux we produce for
execution purposes. We are doing one now — The Relief
of Lucknow — for the big exhibition that's to be given next
month at Olympia and —— The place marked 6 at the
back of our building? Oh, that's the narrow alley of which
I spoke. We've a back door opening into it, but it's prac-
tically useless, because the alley is so narrow one can't drive
a vehicle through it. It's simply a right of way that can't
legally be closed and runs from Croom Street on the right
just along as far as Sturgiss Lane on the left. Not fifty
people pass through it in a day's time.

"But to come back to the short passage, Mr. Cleek. Observe, there are no windows at all on the side of our building, here: Number 2. There were, once upon a time, but we

had them bricked up, as we use that side for a 'paint frame' with a movable bridge so that it can be used for the purpose of painting scenery and drop-curtains. But there *are* windows in the side of the house marked 5; and directly opposite the point where I've put the arrow there is one which belongs to a room occupied by a Mrs. Sherman and her daughter — people who do 'bushel work' for wholesale costume houses. Now, it happens that at the exact time when the porter says he showed young Stan into the glass-room those two women were sitting at work by that window, and, the blinds not being drawn, could see smack into the place, and are willing to take their oath that there was no living soul in it."

"How do they fix it as being, as you say, 'the exact time,' Mr. Trent? If they couldn't see the porter come up to the glass-room with the boy, how can they be sure of that?"

"Oh, that's easily explained: There's a church not a great way distant. It has a clock in the steeple which strikes the hours, halves, and quarters. Mrs. Sherman says that when it chimed half-past four she was not only looking into the glass-room, but was calling her daughter's attention to the fact that, whereas some few minutes previously she had seen Loti go out of the place, leaving a great pile of reference plates and scraps of material all over the floor, and he had never, to her positive knowledge, come back into it, there was the room looking as tidy as possible, and, in the middle of it, a table with a vase of pink roses upon it, which she certainly had not seen there when he left."

"Hallo! Hallo!" interjected Cleek rather sharply. "Let's have that again, please!" and he sat listening intently while Trent repeated the statement; then, of a sudden, he gave his head an upward twitch, slapped his thigh, and, leaning back in his seat, added with a brief little laugh, "Well, of all the blithering idiots! And a simple little thing like that!"

"Like what, Mr. Cleek?" queried Trent, in amazement. "You don't surely mean to say that you can make anything important out of a table and a vase of flowers? Because, I may tell you that Loti is mad on flowers, and always has a vase of them in the room somewhere."

"Does he, indeed? Natural inclination of the artistic temperament, I dare say. But never mind, get on with the story. Mrs. Sherman fixes the hour when she noticed this as half-past four, you say? How, then, does the porter who showed the boy into the glass-room fix it, may I ask?"

"By the same means precisely — the striking of the church clock. He remembers hearing it just as he reached the partition door, and was, indeed, at particular pains to take out his watch to see if it tallied with it. Also, three of our scene painters were passing along the hall at the foot of the short flight of steps leading up to the glass-room at the time. They were going out to tea; and one of them sang out to him laughingly, 'Hallo, Ginger, how does that two-shilling turnip of yours make it? Time for tea at Buckingham Palace?' for he had won the watch at a singing contest only the night before, and his mates had been chaffing him about it all day. In that manner the exact time of his going to the door with the boy is fixed, and with three persons to corroborate it. A second later the porter saw the boy push open the swing-door and walk into the place, and as he turned and went back downstairs he distinctly heard him say, 'Good afternoon, sir. Mr. Trent said I might come up and watch, if you don't mind.'"

"Did he hear anybody reply?"

"No, he did not. He heard no one speak but the boy."

"I see. So, then, there is no actual proof that Loti *was* in there at the time, which, of course, makes the testimony of Mrs. Sherman and her daughter appear reliable when they say that the room was empty."

"Still the boy was there if Loti wasn't, Mr. Cleek.

There's proof enough that he did go into the place even though those two women declare that the room was empty."

"Quite so, quite so. And when two and two don't make four, 'there's something rotten in the state of Denmark.' What does Loti himself say with regard to the circumstance? Or hasn't he been spoken to about it?"

"My hat, yes! I went to him about it the very first thing. He says the boy never put in an appearance, to *his* knowledge; that he never saw him. In fact, that just before half-past four he was taken with a violent attack of sick headache, the result of the fumes rising from the wax he was melting to model figures for the tableau, together with the smell of the chemicals used in preparing the background, and that he went down to his room to lie down for a time and dropped off to sleep. As a matter of fact, he was there in his room sleeping when, at half-past six, I went for the boy, and, finding the glass-room vacated, naturally set out to hunt up Loti and question him about the matter."

"When you called up to the glass-room through the speaking-tube, to say that the boy was about to go up, who answered you — Loti ?"

"Yes."

"At what time was that? Or can't you say positively?"

"Not to the fraction of a moment. But I should say that it was about four or five minutes before the boy got there — say about five-and-twenty minutes past four. It wouldn't take him longer to get up to the top of the house, I fancy, and he certainly did not stop at any of the other departments on the way."

"Queer, isn't it, that the man should not have stopped to so much as welcome the boy after you had been at such pains to tell him to be nice to him? Does he offer any explanation on that score?"

"Yes. He says that, as his head was so bad, he knew that he would probably be cross and crotchety; so as I had asked him to be kind, he thought the best thing he could do was to leave a note on the table for the boy, telling him to make himself at home and to examine anything he pleased, but to be sure not to touch the cauldron in which the wax was simmering, as it tilted readily and he might get scalded. He was sorry to have to go, but his head ached so badly that he really had to lie down for a while.

"That note, I may tell you, was lying on the table when I went up to the glass-room and failed to find the boy. It was that which told me where to go in order to find Loti and question him. I'll do him the credit of stating that when he heard of the boy's mysterious disappearance he flung his headache and his creature comforts to the winds and joined in the eager hunt for him as excitedly and as strenuously as anybody. He went through the building from top to bottom; he lifted every trapdoor, crept into every nook and corner and hole and box into which it might be possible for the poor little chap to have fallen. But it was all useless, Mr. Cleek — every bit of it! The boy had vanished, utterly and completely; from the minute the porter saw him pass the swing-door and go into the glass-room we never discovered even the slightest trace of him, nor have we been able to do so since. He has gone, he has vanished, as completely as if he had melted into thin air, and if there is any ghost of a clue to his whereabouts existing ——"

"Let us go and see if we can unearth it," interrupted Cleek, rising. "Mr. Narkom, is the limousine within easy reach?"

"Yes, waiting in Tavistock Street, dear chap. I told Lennard to be on the lookout for us."

"Good! Then if Miss Larue will allow Mr. Trent to escort her as far as the pavement, and he will then go on alone to his place of business and await us there, you and I will leave the hotel by the back way and join him as soon as possible. Leave by the front entrance if you be so kind; and — pardon, one last word, Mr. Trent, before you go. At the time when this boy's father vanished in much the same way, eleven months ago, you had, I believe, a door porter at your establishment name Felix Murchison. Is that man still in your employ?"

"No, Mr. Cleek. He left about a week or so after James Colliver's disappearance."

"Know where he is?"

"Not the slightest idea. As a matter of fact, he suddenly inherited some money, and said he was going to emigrate to America. But I don't know if he did or not. Why?"

"Oh, nothing in particular — only that I shouldn't be surprised if the person who supplied that money was the pawnbroker who received in pledge the jewels which your father handed over to James Colliver, and that the sum which Felix Murchison 'inherited' so suddenly was the £150 advanced upon those gems."

"How utterly absurd! My dear Mr. Cleek, you must surely remember that the pawnbroker said the chap who pawned the jewels was a gentlemanly appearing person, of good manners and speech, and Murchison is the last man in the world to answer to that description. A great hulking, bull-necked, illiterate *animal* of that sort, without an H in his vocabulary and with no more manners than a pig!"

"Precisely why I feel so certain *now* that the pawnbroker's 'advance' was paid over to *him*," said Cleek, with a twitch of the shoulder. "Live and learn, my friend, live and learn. Eleven months ago I couldn't for the life of me understand why those jewels had been pawned at all; to-day I realize that it was the only possible course. Miss Larue, my compliments. Au revoir." And he bowed her out of the room with the grace of a courtier, standing well out of sight from the hallway until the door had closed behind her

and her companion and he was again alone with the superintendent.

"Now for it! as they used to say in the old melodramas,"
he laughed, stepping sharply to a wardrobe and producing,
first, a broad-brimmed cavalry hat, which he immediately
put on, and then a pair of bright steel handcuffs. "We
may have use for this very effective type of wristlets, Mr.
Narkom; so it's well to go prepared for emergencies. Now
then, off with you while I lock he door. That's the way to
the staircase. Nip down it to the American bar. There's a
passage from that leading out to the Embankment Gar-
dens. A taxi from there will whisk us along Savoy Street,
across the Strand and up Wellington Street to Tavistock
in less than no time; so we may look to be with Lennard
inside of another ten minutes."

"Righto!" gave back the superintendent. "And I can
get rid of this dashed rig as soon as we're in the limousine.
But, I say; any ideas, old chap — eh?"

"Yes, two or three. One of them is that this is going to
be one of the simplest cases I ever tackled. Lay you a
sovereign to a sixpence, Mr. Narkom, that I solve the riddle
of that glass-room before they ring up the curtain of any
theatre in London to-night. What's that? Lying? No,
certainly not. There's been no lying in the matter at all;
it isn't a case of that sort. The pawnbroker did not lie; the
porter who says he showed the boy into the room did not
lie; and the two women who looked into it and saw nothing
but an empty room did not lie either. The only thing that
did lie was a vase of pink roses — a bunch of natural An-
aniases that tried to make people believe that they had
been blooming and keeping fresh ever since last August!"

"Good Lord! you don't surely think that that Loti
chap ——"

"Gently, gently, my friend; don't let yourself get excited.
Besides, I *may* be all at sea, for all my cocksureness. I

don't think I am, but — one never knows. I'll tell you one thing, however: The man with whom Madame Loti eloped had, for the purpose of carrying on the intrigue, enlisted as a student under her husband, and gulled the poor fool by pretending that he wished to learn waxwork making, when his one desire was to make love to the man's worthless wife. When they eloped, and Loti knew for the first time what a dupe he had been, he publicly swore, in the open room of the Café Royal, that he would never rest until he had run that man down and had exterminated him and every living creature in whose veins his blood flowed. The man was an English actor, Mr. Narkom. He posed under the *nom de théâtre* of Jason Monteith — his real name was James Colliver! Step livelier, please — we're dawdling!"

CHAPTER XXXVI

THEY that climb the highest have the farthest to fall. It was after five o'clock when the limousine arrived at the premises of Trent & Son, and Cleek, guided by the junior member of the firm and accompanied by Superintendent Narkom, climbed the steep stairs to the housetop and was shown into the glass-room.

His first impression, as the door swung inward, was of a scent of flowers so heavy as to be oppressive; his second, of entering into a light so brilliant that it seemed a very glare of gold, for the low-dropped sun, which yellowed all the sky, flooded the place with a radiance which made him blink, and it was some little time before his eyes could accustom themselves to it sufficient to let him discover that the old Italian waxworker was there, busy on his latest tableau.

Cleek blinked and looked at the old man, serenely at first, then blinked and looked again, conscious of an overwhelming sense of amazement and defeat for just one fraction of a minute, and that some of his cocksure theories regarding the case had suddenly been knocked into a cocked hat.

No wonder Mr. Harrison Trent had spoken of deterioration in the art of this once celebrated modeller. No wonder!

The man was not Giuseppe Loti at all! — not that world-famed worker in wax who had sworn in those bitter other days to have the life of the vanished James Colliver.

CHAPTER XXXVII

CLEEK'S equanimity did not desert him, however. It was one of his strong points that he always kept his mental balance even when his most promising theories were deracinated. He therefore showed not the slightest trace of the disappointment with which this utterly unexpected discovery had filled him, but, with the most placid exterior imaginable, suffered himself to be introduced to the old waxworkér, who was at the time working assiduously upon the huge tableau-piece designed for the forthcoming Indian Exhibition, a well-executed assembly of figures which occupied a considerable portion of the rear end of the glass-room, and represented that moment when the relief force burst through the stockade at Lucknow and came to the rescue of the beleaguered garrison.

"A couple of gentlemen from Scotland Yard, Loti, who have come to look into the matter of young Colliver's disappearance," was the way in which Trent made that introduction. "You can go on with your work; they won't interfere with you."

"Welcome, gentlemen — most welcome," said Loti, with that courtesy which Continental people never quite forget; then nodded, and went on with his work as he had been told, adding, with a mournful shake of the head: "Ah! a strange business that, signori; an exceedingly strange business."

"Very," agreed Cleek off-handedly and from the other end of the room. "Rippin' quarters, these, signor; and now that I've seen 'em I don't mind confessing that my pet theory has gone all to smash and I'm up a gum-tree, so to speak. I'd an idea, you know, that there might be a sliding-panel or a trapdoor which you chaps here might have overlooked, and down which the boy might have dropped, or maybe gone on a little explorin' expedition of his own, don't you know, and hadn't been able to get back."

"Well, of all the idiotic ideas — ," began Trent, but was suffered to get no further.

"Yes, isn't it?" agreed Cleek, with his best blithering-idiot air. "I realize that, now that I see your floor's of concrete. Necessary, I suppose, on account of the chemicals and the inflammable nature of the wax? You could have a rippin' old flare-up here if that stuff was to catch fire from a dropped match or anything of that sort — eh, what? Blest if I can see" — turning slowly on his heel and looking all round the room —"a ghost of a place where the young nipper could have got. It's a facer for me. But, I say" — as if suddenly struck with an idea — "you don't think that he nipped something valuable and cut off with it, do you? Didn't miss any money or anything of that sort which you'd left lying about, did you, Mr. — er — Lotus, eh?"

"Loti, if you please, signor. I had indeed hoped that my name was well known enough to— *Pouffe!* No, I miss nothing — I miss not so much as a pin. I am told he shall not have been that kind of a boy." And then, with a shake of the head and a pitying glance toward the author of these two asinine theories regarding the strange disappearance, returned to his work of putting the finishing touches to a recumbent figure representing a dead soldier lying in the foreground of the tableau.

"Oh, well, you never can tell what boys will do; and it's an old saying that 'a good booty makes many a thief,'" replied Cleek airily. "Reckon I'll have to hunt up something a bit more promising, then. Don't mind my poking about a bit, do you?"

"Not in the slightest, signor," replied the Italian, and glanced sympathizingly up at Trent and gave his shoulders a significant shrug, as if to say: "Is this the best that Scotland Yard can turn out?" when Cleek began turning over costume plates and looking under books and scraps of material which lay scattered about the floor, and even took to examining the jugs and vases and tumblers in which the signor's bunches of cut flowers were placed. There were many of them — on tables and chairs and shelves, and even on the platform of the tableau itself — so many, in fact, that he was minded, by their profusion, of what Trent had said regarding the old waxworker's great love of flowers.

He looked round the room, in an apparently perfunctory manner, but in reality with a photographic eye for its every detail, finding that it agreed in every particular with the description which Trent had given him.

There were the cheap lace curtains all along the glazed side which overlooked the short passage leading down to the narrow alley, but they were of so thin a quality, and so scantily patterned, that the mesh did not obstruct the view in any manner, merely rendering it a trifle hazy; for he could himself see from where he stood the window in the side of the house opposite, and, seated at that window, Mrs. Sherman and her daughter, busy at their endless sewing.

And there, too, were the blinds — strong blue linen ones running on rings and cords — with which, as he had been told, it was possible to arrange the light as occasion required. They were fashioned somewhat after the manner of those seen in the studios of photographers — several sectional ones overhead and one long one for that side of the room which overlooked the short passage; and, as showing how minute was Cleek's inspection for all its seeming indifference, it may be remarked that he observed a peculiarity regarding that long blind which not one person in a hundred would have noticed. That is to say, that, whereas, when one looks at a window from the interior of a room, one in-variably finds that the blinds are against the glass, and that the curtains are so hung as to be behind them when viewed from the street, here was a case of the exactly opposite arrangement being put into force; to wit: It was the lace curtains which hung against the window panes and the big blind which was next the room, so that, if pulled down, a person standing within would see no lace curtains at all, while at the same time they would remain distinctly visible to anybody standing without.

If this small discrepancy called for any comment, Cleek made none audibly; merely glanced at the blind and glanced away again, and went on examining the books and the vases of flowers, and continued his apparently aimless wandering about the room.

Of a sudden, however, he did a singular thing, one which was fraught with much significance to Mr. Narkom, who knew the "signs" so well. His wandering had brought him within touching distance of the busy waxworker, who, just at that moment, half turned and stretched forth his hand to pick up a tool which had fallen to the floor, the act of recovering which sent his wrist protruding a bit be-yond the cuff of his working-blouse. What Narkom saw was the quick twitch of Cleek's eye in the direction of that hand, then its swift travelling to the man's face and trav-elling off again to other things; and he knew what was coming when his great ally began to pat his pockets and rummage about his person as if endeavouring to find some-thing.

"My luck!" said Cleek, with an impatient jerk of the head. "Not a blessed cigarette with me, Mr. Narkom; and you know what a duffer I am if I can't smoke when I'm trying to think. I say — nip out, will you, and get me a packet? There!" — scribbling something on a leaf from his notebook and pushing it into the superintendent's hand — "that's the brand I like. It's no use bringing me any other. Look 'em up for me, will you? There's a good friend."

Narkom made no reply, but merely left the room with the paper crumpled in his shut hand and went downstairs as fast as he could travel. What he did in the interval is a matter for further consideration. At present it need only be said that had any one looked across the short passage some eight or ten minutes after his departure Narkom might have been seen standing in the background of the room at whose window Mrs. Sherman and her daughter still sat sewing.

Meanwhile Cleek appeared to have forgotten all about the matter which was the prime reason for his presence in the place and to have become absorbingly interested in the business of tableau making, for he plied the old Italian with endless questions relative to the one he was engaged in constructing.

"Jip! You don't mean to tell me that you make the whole blessed thing yourself, do you — model the figures, group 'em, paint the blessed background, and all?" said he, with yokel-like amazement. "You *do?* My hat! but you're a wonder! That background's one of the best I've ever clapped eyes on. And the figures! I could swear that that fellow bursting in with a sword in his hand was alive if I didn't know better; and as for this dead johnnie here in the foreground that you're working on, he's a marvel. What do you stuff the blessed things with? Or don't you stuff 'em at all?"

"Oh, yes, signor, they are stuffed, all of them. There is a wicker framework covered with canvas; and inside cotton waste, old paper, straw."

"You don't mean it! Well, I'm blest! Nothing but waste stuff and straw? Why, that fellow over there — the Sepoy chap with the gun in his hands —— Oh, good Lord!

just my blessed luck! I hope to heaven I haven't spoilt anything!" For, in leaning over to indicate the figure alluded to, he had blundered against the edge of the low platform, lost his balance, and sprawled over so awkwardly and abruptly that, but for the fact that the figure of the dead soldier was there for his hand to fall upon in time to check it, he must have pitched headlong into the very heart of the tableau, and done no end of damage. Fortunately, however, not a figure had been thrown down, and even the "dead soldier" had stood the shock uncommonly well, not even a dent showing, though Cleek had come down rather heavily and his palm had struck smack on the figure's chest.

"Tut! tut! tut! tut!" exclaimed the Italian with angry impatience. "Oh, do have a little care, signor! The bull in a china-shop is alone like this." And he turned his back upon this stupid blunderer, even though Cleek was profuse in his apologies, and looked as sorry as he declared. After a time, however, he went off on another tack, for his quick-travelling glance had shown him Mr. Narkom in the house across the passage, and he turned on his heel and walked away rapidly.

"Tell you what it is: it's this blessed glare of light that's accountable," he said. "A body's likely to stumble over anything with the light streaming into the place in this fashion. What you want in here is a bit of shade — like this."

Here he crossed the room hastily and, reaching up, pulled down the long window blind with a sudden jerk. But before either Trent or the Italian could offer any objection to this interference with the conditions under which the wax-worker chose to conduct his labours, he seemed, himself, to realize that the proceeding did not mend matters, and, releasing his hold upon the blind, let the spring of the roller carry it up again to its original position. As he did this he said with a peculiarly asinine air:

"That's a bit worse than the other, by Jip! Makes the blessed place too dashed dark altogether; so it's not the light that's to blame after all."

"I should have thought even a fool might have known that!" gave back the waxworker, almost savagely. "The light is poor enough as it is. Look for yourself. It is only the afterglow — and even that is already declining. *Pouffe!*" And here, as if in disgust too great for words, he blew the breath from his lips with a sharp, short gust, and facing about again went back to his work on the tableau.

Cleek made no response; nor yet did Trent. By this time even he had begun to think that accident more than brains must have been at the bottom of the man's many successes; that he was, in reality, nothing more than a blundering muddler; and, after another ten minutes of putting up with his crazy methods, had just made up his mind to appeal to Narkom for the aid of another detective, when the end which was all along being prepared came with such a rush that it fairly made his head swim.

All that he was ever able clearly to recall of it was that there came a sudden sound of clattering footsteps rushing pell-mell up the staircase; that the partition door was flung open abruptly to admit Mr. Maverick Narkom, with three or four of the firm's employees pressing close upon his heels; that the superintendent had but just cried out excitedly, "Yes, man, *yes!*" when there arose a wild clatter of falling figures, a snarl, a scuffle, a cry, and that, when he faced round in the direction of it, there was the Lucknow tableau piled up in a heap of fallen scenery and smashed waxworks, and in the middle of the ruin there was the "signor" lying on his back with a band of steel upon each wrist, and over him Cleek, with a knee on the man's chest and the look of a fury in his eyes, crying aloud: "Come out of it! Come out of it, you brute-beast! Your little dodge has failed!"

And hard on the heels of that shock Mr. Trent received

another. For of a sudden he saw Cleek pluck a wig from the man's head and leave a white line showing above the place where the joining paste once had met the grease paint with which the fellow's face was coloured, and heard him say as he tossed that wig toward him and rose, "Out of your own stage properties, Mr. Trent — borrowed to be returned like this."

"Heaven above, man," said Trent in utter bewilderment, "what's the meaning of it all? Who is that man, then, since it's clear he's not Loti?"

"A very excellent actor in his day, Mr. Trent; his name is James Colliver," replied Cleek. "I came to this place fully convinced that Loti had murdered him; I now know that he murdered Loti, and that to that crime he has added a yet more abominable one by killing his own son!"

"It's a lie! It's a lie! I didn't! I didn't! I never saw the boy!" screeched out Colliver in a very panic of terror. "I've never killed any one. Loti sold out to me! Loti . went back to France. I pawned the jewels to get the money to pay him to go."

"Oh, no, you didn't, my friend," said Cleek. "You performed that operation to shut Felix Murchison's mouth — the one man who could swear, and did swear, that James Colliver never left this building on the day of his disappearance, and who probably would have said more if you hadn't made it worth his while to shut his mouth and to disappear. You and I know, my friend, that Loti was the last man on this earth with whom you could come to terms upon anything. He had publicly declared that he would have your life, and he'd have kept his word if you hadn't turned the tables and killed him. You stole his wife, and you were never even man enough to marry her even though she had borne you a son and clung to you to the end, poor wretch! You killed Loti, and you killed your own son. No doubt he is better off, poor little chap, to be dead and gone rather than to live with the shadow of illegitimacy upon him; and no doubt, either, that when he came up here yesterday to meet Giuseppe Loti, he saw what I saw to-day, and knew you as I knew you then — the scar on the wrist, which was one of the marks of identification given me at the time I was sent to hunt you up! And you killed him to shut his mouth."

"I didn't! I didn't!" he protested wildly. "I never saw him. He wasn't here. The women in the house across the way will swear that they saw the empty room."

"Not now!" declared Cleek, with emphasis. "I've convinced them to the contrary. Mr. Trent, let a couple of your men come over here and take charge of this fellow, please, and I will convince you as well. That's right, my lads. Lay hold of the beggar and don't let him get a chance to make a dash for the stairs. Got him fast, have you? Good! Now then, Mr. James Colliver, *this* is what those deluded women saw — this little dodge, which is going to help Jack Ketch to come into his own."

Speaking, he walked rapidly across to the long blind, pulled it down to its full length, then with a wrench tore it wholly from the roller and whirled it over, so that they who were within could now see the outer side.

It bore, painted upon it, a perfect representation of the interior of the glass-room, even to the little spindle-legged table with a vase of pink roses upon it which *now* stood at that room's far end.

"A clever idea, Colliver, and a good piece of painting," he said. "It took me in once — last August — just as it took in Mrs. Sherman and her daughter yesterday. The mistiness of the lace curtains falling over it lent just the effect of 'distance' that was required to perfect the illusion and to prevent anybody from detecting the paint. As for the boy —— Gently, lads, gently! Don't let the beggar in his struggles make you step on that 'dead soldier.' Under the thick coating of wax a human body lies — the boy's!

Hullo! Gone off his balance, eh, at the knowledge that the game is entirely up?" This as Colliver, with a terrible cry, collapsed suddenly and fell to the floor shrieking and grovelling. "They are a cowardly lot these brute-beast men when it comes to the wall and the final corner. Mr. Trent, break this to Miss Larue as gently as you can. She has suffered a great deal, poor girl, and it is bound to be a shock. She doesn't know that the woman he called his wife never really was his wife; she doesn't know about Loti or his threat. If she had she'd have told me, and I might have got on the trail in the first case instead of waiting to pick it up like this."

He paused and held up his hand. Through all this Colliver had not once ceased grovelling and screaming; but it was not his cries that had drawn that gesture from Cleek. It was the sound of some one racing at top speed up the outer stairs, and with it the jar of many excited voices mingled in a babble of utter confusion.

The door of the glass-room swung inward abruptly, and the head bookkeeper looked in, with a crowd of clerks behind him.

"Mr. Trent, sir, whatever is the matter? Is anybody hurt? I never heard such screams. The whole place is ringing with them and there's a crowd gathering about the door."

Cleek left the junior partner to explain the situation, stepped to the side of the glass-room, looked down, saw that the statement was quite true, and — stepped sharply back again.

"We shall have to defer removing our prisoner until it gets dark, I fancy, Mr. Narkom," he said, serenely. "And with Mr. Trent's permission we will make use of the door leading into the alley at the back when that time comes. Bookkeeper!"

"Yes, sir?"

"You might explain to the constable on duty in the neighbourhood — if he comes to inquire, that is — the cause of the disturbance, and that Scotland Yard is in charge and Superintendent Narkom already on the premises. That's all, thank you. You may close the door and take your colleagues below. Hullo! our prisoner seems to be subsiding into something akin to gibbering idiocy, Mr. Trent. Fright has turned his brain, apparently. Let us make use of the respite from his shrieks. You will, of course, wish to hear how I got on the track of the man, and what were the clues which led up to the solving of the affair. Well, you shall. Sit down, and while we are waiting for the darkness to come I'll give you the complete explanation."

CHAPTER XXXVIII

COLLIVER, who had now sunk into a state of babbling incoherence, lay on his face in the wreck of the tableau, rolling his head from side to side and clasping and unclasping his manacled hands.

Trent turned his back upon the unpleasant sight and, placing three chairs at the opposite end of the room, dropped into one and lifted an eager countenance to Cleek.

"Tell me first of all," he asked, "how under heaven you came to suspect how the disappearance of the boy was managed? It seems like magic, to me. When in the world did you get the first clue to it, Mr. Cleek?"

"Never until I heard of those two women looking into this room and seeing the vase of pink roses standing on a spindle-legged table in the centre of it," he replied. "You see, even in the old days when I had the other case in hand and was searching for a clue to Colliver's disappearance, never had any one mentioned the name of Loti to me. I knew, of course, that you made wax figures here, but I never heard until this afternoon that Loti was the man who was employed to model them. I also knew about the existence of the glass-room and its position, for I had been at the pains of inspecting it from the outside. That came about in this way: Just before Miss Larue closed up the case of James Colliver I had obtained the first actual clue to his movements after he left Mr. Trent, senior, and came out of the office.

"That clue came from the door porter, Felix Murchison. What careful 'pumping' got out of him was that when James

Colliver left the office he had asked him, Murchison, which was the way to the place where they made the waxworks, as he'd heard that they were making a head of Miss Larue to be used in the execution scene of Catharine Howard, and he'd like to have a look at it. Murchison said that he told him the figures were made in a glass-room on the top of the house, and directed him how to reach it. He went up the stairs, and that was the last that was seen of him.

"Naturally when I heard that I thought I'd like to see the exterior of the building to ascertain if there was any opening, door or window, by which he could have left the upper floor without coming down the main staircase. That led me to beg permission of the people in the house across the passage there to look from one of the side windows, and so gave me my first view of the glass-room. What I saw was exactly what Mrs. Sherman and her daughter saw yesterday — namely, that spick and span room with the table in the centre and the vase of pink roses standing on it.

"Need I go further than to say that when I heard of those women seeing a room that was badly littered a few minutes before suddenly become a tidy one with a table and a vase of roses standing in the middle of it, without anybody having come into the place for the purpose of making the change, I instantly remembered my own experience and suspected a painted blind?

"When I entered this room to-day and saw the peculiar position of that blind I became almost certain I had hit upon the truth, and sent Mr. Narkom to the house across the way to test it. That's why I pulled the blind down. Why I stumbled and nearly fell into the tableau was because I had a faint suspicion of the horrible truth when I noticed how abominably thick the neck, hands, and ankles of that 'dead soldier' were; and I wanted to test the truth or falseness of the 'straw stuffing' assertion by actual touch, particularly as I felt sure that the presence of all these strongly scented flowers was for the purpose of covering less agreeable odours should the heat of the weather cause decomposition to set in before he could dispose of the body. I don't think he ever was mad enough to intend letting the thing remain a part of the tableau. I fancy he would have found an excuse to get it out somehow and to make away with it entirely, as, no doubt, he did with the body of Loti.

"What's that, Mr. Narkom? No, I don't think that Murchison had any actual hand in the crime or really knew the identity of the man. I fancy he must have gone up to tell the fictitious Loti that he knew James Colliver had entered that glass-room and never come out of it, and Colliver, of course, had to shut his mouth by buying him off and sending him out of the country. That is why he took yet another disguise and pawned the jewels. He had to get the money some way. As for the rest, I imagine that when Colliver went up to the room to see that wax head, and Loti caught sight of him, the old Italian jumped on him like a mad tiger; and, seeing that it was Loti's life or his own, Colliver throttled him. When that was done, the necessity for disposing of the body arose, and the imposture was the actual outcome of a desire to save his own neck. That's all, I think, Mr. Narkom; so you may revise your 'notes' and mark down the Colliver case as 'solved' at last and the mystery of it cleared up after all."

Three hours of patient waiting had passed and gone. The darkness had fallen, the streets were still, save for the faint hum of life coming from districts afar, and the time for action had come at last. Cleek rose and put on his hat.

"I think we may safely venture to remove our prisoner now, Mr. Narkom," he said, "and if you will slip out the back way and get Lennard to bring the limousine around to the head of that narrow alley ——"

"They're there already, dear chap. I stationed Lennard

there when I went across to look into that business about
the painted blind. It seemed the least conspicuous place
for him to wait."

"Excellent! Then, if you will run on ahead and have the
door of it open for me and everything ready so that we may
whisk him in and be off like a shot, and Mr. Trent will let
one of these good chaps here run down to the man's room
and fetch him a hat, I'll attend to his removal."

"Here's one here, sir, that'll do at a pinch and save time,"
suggested one of the men, picking up a cavalryman's hat
from the wreck of the ruined tableau and dusting it by slapping it against his thigh. "I don't think he'll resist much,
sir; he seems to have gone clear off his biscuit and not to
know enough for that; but if you'd like me and my mate to
lend a hand ——"

"No, thanks; I shall be able to manage him myself, I
fancy," said Cleek, serenely. "Get him on his feet, please.
That's the business! Now then, Mr. Narkom nip off; I'm
following."

Mr. Narkom "nipped off" without an instant's delay, and
two minutes later saw him slipping out through the rear
door of the building with Cleek and the jabbering, unre-
sisting prisoner at the bottom of the last flight of stairs not
twenty yards behind.

But the passage of the next half minute saw something of
more moment still; for, as Narkom ran on tiptoe up the dim
alley to the waiting limousine standing at its western end,
and unlatching the vehicle's door, swung it open to be ready
for Cleek, out of the stillness there roared suddenly the
shrill note of a dog-whistle, and all in a moment there was
— mischief.

A crowd of quick-moving Apache figures sprang up from
sheltering doors and, scudding past him, headed full tilt
down the narrow alley, calling out as they ran that piercing
"La, la, loi!" which is the war cry of their kind.

A blind rage — all the more maddening in that it was impotent, since he had neither weapon to defend nor the power to slay — swept down upon the superintendent as he realized the import of that mad rush, and, ducking down his head, he bolted after them, into the thick of them — punching, banging, slogging, shouting, swearing — an incarnate Passion, the Epitome of Man's love for Man — a little fat Fury that was all a whirl of flying fists as it swept onward and that seemed to go absolutely insane at what he looked up the alley and saw.

"Get back, Cleek! Get back, for God's sake!" he yelled, in a very panic of fear and dismay; then cleft his way with beating arms and kicking feet through the hampering crowd, arrowed out of its midst, and bore down upon the cavalry-hatted figure that had stepped out of the dark doorway of Trent & Son's building and was standing flattened against the rear wall of it.

He reached out his hand and made a blind clutch at it, and, while he was yet far out of reaching distance of it, faced round and made a wild effort to cover it with his short, fat body and his arms outflung, like a crucifix, and looked at the Apaches and swore without one thought of being profane.

"Me, you damned devils! Me, me, not him! Not him, damn you! damn you! damn you!" he cried, hoarse-throated and — said no more!

The scuttling crowd came up with him, broke about him, swept past him. A loud explosion sounded; a flare of light broke full against the cavalry hat; a stifling odour of picric acid filled the air and gripped the throat, and with its coming, man and hat slid down the wall and dropped at its foot a crumpled heap that never in this world would stand erect again.

"Killed! Killed!" half-cried, half-groaned the superintendent, staggering a bit as the crowd flew on up the alley, and vanished around the corner of the street into which it merged. "Oh, my God! After all my care; after all my love for him! Killed like a dog. Oh, Cleek! Oh, Cleek! The dearest friend — the finest pal — the greatest detective genius of the age!" And then, swinging his arm up and across his eyes and holding it there, made a queer choking sound behind the sheltering crook of it.

But of a sudden a voice spoke up from the darkness of the open door near by and said quietly:

"That's the finest compliment I ever had paid me in all my life, Mr. Narkom. Don't worry over me, dear friend; I'm still able to sit up and take nourishment. The Apaches have saved the public executioner a morning's work. Colliver has parted with his brains forever; and may God have mercy on his soul!"

"Cleek!" Mr. Narkom scarcely knew his own voice, such a screaming thing it was. "Cleek, dear chap, is it you?"

"To be sure. Come inside here if you doubt it. Come quickly; there's a crowd of quite a different sort coming: the report of that bomb has aroused the neighbourhood; and I have quite enough of crowds for one evening, thank you."

Narkom was inside the building before you could have said Jack Robinson, "pump-handling" Cleek with all his might and generally deporting himself like a man gone daft.

"I thought they'd finished you! I thought they'd 'done you in.' It was the Apache, you know — and that infernal scoundrel Waldemar: he must have found out somehow," he said excitedly. "But we've got it on him at last, Cleek: he's come within the law's reach after all."

"To be sure; but I doubt if the law will be able to find him, Mr. Narkom. He will have left the country before the trap was actually sprung, believe me; or failing that, will be well on his way out of it."

"But perhaps not absolutely out of it, dear chap. There

are the ports, you know; and so long as he is on English soil —— Come and see! Come and see! We may be able to head him off. Let's get out by way of the front of the building, Cleek, and if I can once get to the telegraph and wire to the coast — and he hasn't yet sailed —— Come on! come on! Or no: wait a moment. That's a constable out there, asking for information. I'll nip out and let him know that the Yard's on the case and give him a few orders about reporting it. Wait for me at the front door, old chap. With you in a winking."

He stepped out into the alley as he spoke and mingled with the gathering crowd.

But Cleek did not stir. The alley was no longer dark for, with the gathering of the crowd, lights had come and he stood for many minutes staring into it and breathing hard and the colour draining slowly out of his face until it was like a thing of wax.

Outside in the narrow alley the gathering of curious ones which the sound of the explosion and the sight of a running policeman had drawn to the place was every moment thickening, and with the latest addition to it there had come hurrying into the narrow space a morbid-minded newsboy with the customary bulletin sheet pinned over his chest.

"The *Evening News!* Six o'clock edition!" that bulletin was headed, and under that heading there was set forth in big black type:

END OF THE MAURAVANIAN REVOLUTION
FALL OF THE CAPITAL
FLIGHT OF THE DEPOSED KING
OVERWHELMING SUCCESS OF IRMA'S TROOPS.

"Mr. Narkom," said Cleek, when at the end of ten minutes the superintendent came bustling back, hot and eager to begin the effort to head off Count Waldemar. "Mr.

Narkom, dear friend, the days of trouble and distress are over and the good old times you have so often sighed for have come back. Look at that newsboy's bulletin. Waldemar is too late in all things and — we have seen the last of him forever."

EPILOGUE

THE AFFAIR OF THE MAN WHO WAS FOUND

MR. MAVERICK NARKOM glanced up at the calendar hanging on the office wall, saw that it recorded the date as August 18th, and then glanced back to the sheet of memoranda lying on his desk, and forthwith began to scratch his bald spot perplexedly.

"I wonder if I dare do it?" he queried of himself in the unspoken words of thought. "It seems such a pity when the beggar's wedding day is so blessed near — and a man wants his last week of single blessedness all to himself, by James — if he can get it! Still, it's a case after his own heart; the reward's big and would be a nice little nest egg to begin married life upon. Besides, he's had a fairly good rest as it is, when I come to think of it. Nothing much to do since the time when that Mauravanian business came to an end. I fancy he rather looked to have something come out of that in the beginning from the frequent inquiries he made regarding what that johnnie Count Irma and the new Parliament were doing; but it never did. And now, after all that rest — and this a case of so much importance —— Gad! I believe I'll risk it. He can't do any more then decline. Yes, by James! I will."

His indecision once conquered, he took the plunge instantly; caught up the desk telephone, called for a number, and two minutes later was talking to Cleek, thus:

"I say, old chap, don't snap my head off for suggesting such a thing at such a time, but I've a most extraordinary case on hand and I hope to heaven that you will help me out with it. What's that? Oh, come, now, that's ripping of you, old chap, and I'm as pleased as Punch. What? Oh, get along with you! No more than you'd do for me under the same circumstances, I'll be sworn. Yes, to-day — as early as possible. Right you are. Then could you manage to meet me in the bar parlour of a little inn called the French Horn, out Shere way, in Surrey, about four o'clock? Could, eh? Good man! Oh, by the way, come prepared to meet a lady of title, old chap — she's the client. Thanks very much. Good-bye."

Then he hung up the receiver, rang for Lennard, and set about preparing for the journey forthwith.

And this, if you please, was how it came to pass that when Mr. Maverick Narkom turned up at the French Horn that afternoon he found a saddle horse tethered to a post outside, and Cleek, looking very much like one of the regular habitués of Rotten Row who had taken it into his mind to canter out into the country for a change, standing in the bar parlour window and looking out with appreciative eyes upon the broad stretch of green downs that billowed away to meet the distant hills.

"My dear chap, how on earth do you manage it?" said the superintendent, eying him with open approval, not to say admiration. "I don't mean the mere putting on the clothes and *looking* the part — I've seen dozens in my time who could do that right enough, but the beggars always 'fell down' when it came to the acting and the talking, while you — I don't know what the dickens it is nor how you manage to get it, but there's a certain something or other in your bearing, your manner, your look, when you tackle this sort of thing that I always believed a man had to be born to and couldn't possibly acquire in any other way."

"There you are wrong, my dear friend. It *is* possible, as you see. That is what makes the difference between the mere actor and the real *artiste*," replied Cleek, with an air of conceited self-appreciation which was either a clever illusion or an exhibition of great weakness. "If one man might not do these things better than another man, we should have no Irvings to illuminate the stage, and acting would drop at once from its place among the arts to the undignified level of a tawdry trade. And now, as our American cousins say, 'Let's come down to brass tacks.' What's the case and who's the lady?"

"The widow of the late Sir George Essington, and grandmother of the young gentleman in whose interest you are to be consulted."

"Grandmother, eh? Then the lady is no longer young?"

"Not as years go, although, to look at her, you would hardly suspect that she is a day over five-and-thirty. The Gentleman with the Hour Glass has dealt very, very lightly with her. Where he has failed to be considerate, however, the ladies, who conduct certain 'parlours' in Bond Street, have come to the rescue in fine style."

"Oh, she is that kind of woman, is she?" said Cleek with a pitch of the shoulders. "I have no patience with the breed! As if there was anything more charming than a dear, wrinkly old grandmother who bears her years gracefully and fusses over her children's children like an old hen with a brood of downy chicks. But a grandmother who goes in for wrinkle eradicators, cream of lilies, skin-tighteners, milk of roses, and things of that kind — faugh! It has been my experience, Mr. Narkom, that when a woman has any real cause for worrying over the condition of her face, she usually has a just one to be anxious over that of her soul. So this old lady is one of the 'face painters,' is she?"

"My dear chap, let me correct an error: a grandmother her ladyship may be, but she is decidedly not an old one. I believe she was only a mere girl when she married her late husband. At any rate, she certainly can't be a day over forty-five at the present moment. A frivolous and a recklessly extravagant woman she undoubtedly is — indeed, her extravagances helped as much as anything to bring her husband into the bankruptcy court before he died — but beyond that I don't think there's anything particularly wrong with her 'soul.'"

"Possibly not. There's always an exception to every rule," said Cleek. "Her ladyship may be the shining exception to this unpleasant one of the 'face painters.' Let us hope so. English, is she?"

"Oh, yes — that is, her father was English and she herself was born in Buckinghamshire. Her mother, however, was an Italian, a lineal descendant of a once great and powerful Roman family named di Catanei."

"Which," supplemented Cleek, with one of his curious one-sided smiles, "through an ante-papal union between Pope Alexander VI and the beautiful Giovanna de Catanei — otherwise Vanozza — gave to the world those two arch-poisoners and devils of iniquity, Cæsar and Lucretia Borgia. Lady Essington's family tree supplies a mixture which is certainly unique: a fine, fruity English pie with a rotten apple in it. Hum-m-m! if her ladyship has inherited any of the beauty of her famous ancestress — for in 1490, when she flourished, Giovanna de Catanei was said to be the most beautiful woman in the world — she should be something good to look upon."

"She is," replied Narkom. "You'll find her, when she comes, one of the handsomest and most charming women you ever met."

"Ah, then she has inherited some of the attractions and accomplishments of her famous forbears. I wonder if there has also come down to her, as well, the formula of those remarkable secret poisons for which Lucretia Borgia and her brother Cæsar were so widely famed. They were marvellous things, those Borgia decoctions — marvellous and abominable."

"Horrible!" agreed Narkom, a curious shadow of unrest coming over him at this subject rising at this particular time.

"Modern chemistry has, I believe, been quite unable to duplicate them. There is, for instance, that appalling thing the aqua tofana, the very fumes of which caused instant death."

"Aqua tofana was not a Bornean poison, my friend," said Cleek, with a smile. "It was discovered more than two hundred years after *their* time — in 1668, to be exact — by one Jean Baptiste de Gaudin, Signeur de St. Croix, the paramour and accomplice of that unnatural French fiend, Marie Marquise de Brinvilliers. Its discoverer himself died through dropping the glass mask from his face and inhaling the fumes while he was preparing the hellish mixture. The secret of its manufacture did not, however, die with him. Many chemists can, to-day, reproduce it. Indeed, I, myself, could give you the formula were it required."

"*You?* Gad, man! what don't you know? In heaven's name, Cleek, what caused you to dip into all these unholy things?"

"The same impulse which causes a drowning man to grip at a straw, Mr. Narkom — the desire for self-preservation. Remember what I was in those other days, and with whom I associated. Believe me, the statement that there is honour among thieves is a pleasant fiction and nothing more; for once a man sets out to be a professional thief, he and honour are no longer on speaking terms. I never could be wholly sure, with that lot; and my biggest *coups* were always a source of danger to me after they had been successfully completed. It became necessary for me to study *all* poisons, all secret arts of destruction, that I might guard against them and might know the proper antidote. As for the rest

— Sh! Mumm's a fine wine. Here comes the landlady with the tea. We'll drop the 'case' until afterward."

"Now tell me," said Cleek, after the landlady had gone and they were again in sole possession of the room, "what is it this Lady Essington wants of me? And what sort of a chap is this grandson in whose interest she is acting? Is he with her in this appeal to the Yard?"

"Certainly not, my dear fellow. Why, he's little more than a baby — not over three at the most. Ever hear anybody speak of the 'Golden Boy,' old chap?"

"What! The baby Earl of Strathmere? The little chap who inherited a title and a million through the drowning of his parents in the wreck of the yacht *Mystery?*"

"That's the little gentleman: the Right Honourable Cedric Eustace George Carruthers, twenty-seventh Earl Strathmere, variously known as the 'Millionaire Baby' and the 'Golden Boy.' His mother was Lady Essington's only daughter. She was only eighteen when she married Strathmere: only twenty-two when she and her husband were drowned, a little over a year ago."

"Early enough to go out of the world, that — poor girl!" said Cleek, sympathetically. "And to leave that little shaver all alone — robbed at one blow of both father and mother. Hard lines, my friend, hard lines! It is fair to suppose, is it not, that, with the death of his parents, the care and guidance of his little lordship fell to the lot of his grandmother, Lady Essington?"

"No, it did not," replied Narkom. "One might have supposed that it would, seeing that there was no paternal grandmother, but — well, the fact of the matter is, Cleek, that the late Lord Strathmere did not altogether approve of his mother-in-law's method of living (he was essentially a quiet, home-loving man and had little patience with frivolity of any sort), and it occasioned no surprise among those who knew him when it was discovered that he had made a will leaving everything he possessed to his little son and expressly stipulating that the care and upbringing of the boy were to be entrusted to his younger brother, the Honourable Felix Camour Paul Carruthers, who was to enjoy the revenue from the estate until the child attained his majority."

"I see! I see!" said Cleek, appreciatively. "Then that did her extravagant ladyship out of a pretty large and steady income for a matter of seventeen or eighteen years. Hum-m-m! Wise man — always, of course, provided that he didn't save the boy from the frying-pan only to drop him into the fire. What kind of a man is this brother — this Honourable Felix Carruthers — into whose hands he entrusted the future of his little son? I seem to have a hazy recollection of hearing that name, somewhere or somehow, in connection with some other affair. Wise choice, was it, Mr. Narkom?"

"Couldn't have been better, to my thinking. I know the Honourable Felix quite well: a steady-going, upright, honourable young fellow (he isn't over two or three-and-thirty), who, being a second son, naturally inherited his mother's fortune, and that being considerable, he really did not need the income from his little nephew's in the slightest degree. However, he undertook the charge willingly, for he is much attached to the boy; and he and his wife — to whom he was but recently married, by the way — entered into residence at his late brother's splendid property, Boskydell Priory, just over on the other side of those hills — you can see from the window, there — where they are at present entertaining a large house party, among whom are Lady Essington and her son Claude."

"Oho! Then her ladyship has a son, has she? The daughter who died was not her only child?"

"No. The son was born about a year after the daughter.

A nice lad — bright, clever, engaging; fond of all sorts of dumb animals — birds, monkeys, white mice — all manner of such things — and as tender-hearted as a girl. Wouldn't hurt a fly. Carruthers is immensely fond of him and has him at the Priory whenever he can. That, of course, means having the mother, too, which is a bit of a trial, in a way, for I don't believe that her ladyship and Mrs. Carruthers care very much for each other. But that's another story. Now, then, let's see — where was I? Oh, ah! about the house party at the Priory and Carruthers' fondness for the boy. You can judge of my surprise, my dear Cleek, when last night's post brought me a private letter from Lady Essington asking me to meet her here at this inn — which, by the way, belongs to the Strathmere estate and is run by a former servant at the Priory — and stating that she wished me to bring one of the shrewdest and cleverest of my detectives, as she was quite convinced there was an underhand scheme afoot to injure his little lordship — in short, she had every reason to believe that somebody was secretly attacking the life of the Golden Boy. She then went on to give me details of a most extraordinary and bewildering nature."

"Indeed? What were those details, Mr. Narkom?"

"Let her tell you for herself — here she is!" replied the superintendent, as a veiled and cloaked figure moved hurriedly past the window; and he and Cleek had barely more than pushed back their chairs and risen when that figure entered the room.

A sweep of her hand carried back her veil; and Cleek, looking round, saw what he considered one of the handsomest women he had ever beheld: a good woman, too, for all her frivolous life and her dark ancestry, if clear, straight-looking eyes could be taken as a proof, which he knew that they could *not;* for he had seen men and women in his day, as crafty as the fox and as dangerous as the serpent, who could look you straight in the eyes and never flinch; while others — as true as steel and as clean-lifed as saints — would send shifting glances flicking all round the room and could no more fix those glances on the face of the person to whom they were talking than they could take unto themselves wings and fly.

But good or ill, whichever the future might prove this lovely lady to be, one thing about her was certain: she was violently agitated, and nervousness was making her shake perceptibly and breathe hard, like a spent runner.

"It is good of you to come, Mr. Narkom," she said, moving forward with a grace which no amount of excitement could dispel or diminish — the innate grace of the woman *born* to her station and schooled by Mother Nature's guiding hand. "I had hoped that I might steal away and come here to meet you unsuspected. But, secretly as I wrote, carefully as I planned this thing, I have every reason to believe that my efforts are suspected and that I have, indeed, been followed. So, then, this interview must be a very hurried one, and you must not be surprised if it becomes necessary for me to run off without a moment's notice; for believe me, I am quite, quite sure that the Honourable Mr. Felix Carruthers is already following me."

"The Honourable — my dear Lady Essington, you don't mean to suggest that he — he of all men —— God bless my soul!"

"Oh, it may well amaze you, Mr. Narkom. It well-nigh stupefied me when I first began to suspect. Indeed, I can't do any more than suspect even yet. Perhaps it is he, perhaps that abominable woman he has married. You must decide that when you have heard. I perceive" — glancing over at Cleek — "you have been unable to bring a detective police officer to listen to what I have to say, but if you and your friend will listen carefully and convey the story to one in due course ——"

"Pardon, your ladyship, but my companion is a detective officer," interposed Narkom. "So if you will state the case at once he will be able to advise."

"A detective? You?" She flashed round on Cleek and looked at him in amazement, her lower lip indrawn, a look almost of horror in her eyes. One may not tell a lion that another lion is a jackass, though he masquerade in the skin of one. Birth spoke to Birth. She saw, she knew, she understood. "By what process could such as you — " she began; then stopped and made a slight inclination of the head. "Pardon," she continued; "that was rude. Your private affairs are of course your own, Mr. — er——"

"Headland, your ladyship," supplied Cleek. "My name is George Headland!" And Narkom knew from that that for all her grace and charm he neither liked nor trusted her soft-eyed ladyship.

"Thank you," said Lady Essington, accepting this self-introduction with a graceful inclination of the head. "No doubt Mr. Narkom has given you some idea of my reason for consulting you, Mr. Headland; but as time is very short let me give you the further details as briefly as possible. I am convinced beyond any shadow of a doubt that some one who has an interest in his death is secretly attacking the life of my little grandson; and I have every reason to believe that the 'some one' is either the Honourable Felix Carruthers or his wife."

"But to what purpose, your ladyship? People do not commit so desperate an act as murder without some powerful motive, either of gain or revenge, behind it, and from what I have heard, neither the uncle nor the aunt can have anything to win by injuring his little lordship."

"Can they not?" she answered, with a despairing gesture. "How little you know! Mrs. Carruthers is an ambitious woman, Mr. Headland, and, like all women of the class from which she was recruited, she aspires to a title. She was formerly an actress. The Honourable Felix married and took her from the theatre. It is abominable that a person of that type should be foisted upon society and brought into contact with her betters."

"Oho! that's where the shoe pinches, is it?" thought Cleek; but aloud he merely said: "The day has long passed, your ladyship, when the followers of Thespis have to apologize for their existence. There are many ladies of the stage in these times whose lives are exemplary and whose names call forth nothing but respect and admiration; and so long as this particular lady bore an unblemished reputation —— Did she?"

"Oh, yes. There was never a word against her in that respect. Felix would never have married her if there had been. But I believe in persons of that class remaining in their own circle, and not intruding themselves into others to which they were not *born*. She is an ambitious woman, as I have told you. She aspires to a title as *well* as to riches, and if little Lord Strathmere should die, her husband would inherit both. Surely that is 'motive' enough for a woman of that type. As for her husband ——"

"There, I am afraid, your suspicion confounds itself, your ladyship," interrupted Cleek. "I am told that the Honourable Mr. Carruthers is extremely fond of the boy; besides which, being rich in his own right, he has no reason to covet the riches of his brother's baby son."

"Pardon me: '*was* rich' is the proper expression, not 'is,' Mr. Headland. The failure, a fortnight or so ago, of the West Coast Diamond Mining Company, in which the greater part of his fortune was invested and of which he was the chairman, has sadly crippled his resources, and he has now nothing but the income from his nephew's estate to live upon."

"Hum-m-m! Ah! Just so!" said Cleek, pinching his chin. "Now I recollect what made the name seem familiar,

Mr. Narkom. I remember reading of the failure, and of the small hope that was held out of anything being saved from the wreckage. Still, the income from the Strathmere estate is enormous; and by dint of care, in the seventeen or eighteen years which must elapse before his little lordship comes of age ——"

"He will never come of age! He will be killed first — he is being killed now!" interposed Lady Essington, agitatedly. "Oh, Mr. Headland, help me! I love the boy — he is my own child's child. I love him as I never loved anything else in all the world; and if he were to die —— Dear God! what should I do? And he is dying: I tell you he is. And they won't let me go near him: they won't let me have him all to myself, these two! If his cries in the night wring my heart and I run to his nursery, one or the other of them is always there, and never for one moment will they let me hold him in my arms nor be with him alone."

"Hum-m-m! Cries out in the night, does he, your ladyship? What kind of cries? Those of fright or of pain?"

"Of pain — of excruciating pain: it would wring the heart of a stone to hear him, and, though there is never a spot of blood nor a sign of violence, he declares that some one comes in the night and sticks something into his neck — something which, in his baby way, he likens to 'a long, long needle that goes yite froo my neck and sets uvver needles prickin' and prickin' all down my arm.'"

"Hello! what's that? Let's have that again, please!" rapped out Cleek, before he thought; then recollected himself and added apologetically, "I beg your ladyship's pardon, but I am apt to get a little excited at times. Something like a needle being run into his neck, eh? And other needles continuing the sensation down the arm? Hum-m-m! Had a doctor called in?"

"No. I wished to, but neither the uncle nor aunt would let me do so. They say it is nothing—a mere 'growing pain'

which he will overcome in time. But it is not — I *know* it
is not! If it were natural, why did it never manifest itself
before the failure of that wretched diamond company?
Why did it wait to begin until after the Honourable Felix
Carruthers had lost his money? And why is it going on,
night after night, ever since? Why has he begun to fail in
health? — to change from a happy, laughing, healthy child
into a peevish, fretful, constantly complaining one? I tell
you they are killing him, those two; I tell you they are using
some secret diabolical thing which is sapping his very life;
and if ——"

She stopped and sucked her breath in with a little gasp of
fright, and, whisking down her veil, turned and made hurriedly for the door.

"I told you he guessed; I told you I should be followed!"
she said in a shaking voice. "He is coming — that man:
along the road there! look through the window and you will
see. Oh, come to my assistance, Mr. Headland! Find
some way to do it, for God's sake! Good-bye!"

Then the door opened and shut and she was gone, darting
out from the rear of the inn into the shelter of the scattered
clumps of furze bushes and the thick growth of bracken
which covered the downs, and running like a hare pursued.

"Well, what do you make of it, old chap?" asked Narkom
anxiously, turning to Cleek after ascertaining past all doubt
that the Honourable Felix Carruthers *was* riding up the road
toward the French Horn.

"Oh, a crime beyond doubt," he replied. "But whose I
am in no position to determine at present. A hundred
things might produce that stabbing sensation in the neck,
from the prick of a pin-point dipped in curare to a smear of
the 'Pope's balm,' that hellish ointment of the Borgias.
Hum-m-m! And so that's the Honourable Felix Carruthers, is it? Keep back from the window, my friend.
When you are out gunning for birds, it never does to raise

an alarm. And we should be hard put to it to explain our presence here at this particular time if he were to see you."

"My dear chap, you don't surely mean that you think *he* is really at the bottom of it?" began Narkom, in surprise; but before he could say a word further, *that* surprise was completely overwhelmed by another and a greater one. For the Honourable Felix had reined in and dismounted at the French Horn's door, and, with a clear-voiced, "No, don't put him up; I shan't be long, Betty. Just want a word or two with some friends I'm expecting," walked straightway into the bar parlour and advanced toward the superintendent with hand outstretched.

"Thank God, you got my letter in time, Mr. Narkom," he said, with a breath of intense relief. "Although I sent it by express messenger, it was after three o'clock and I was afraid you wouldn't. What a friend you are to come to my relief like this! I shall owe you a debt no money can repay. This then is the great and amazing Cleek, is it? I thank you, Mr. Cleek, I thank you from the bottom of my heart for accepting the case. Now we *shall* get to the bottom of the mystery, I am sure."

It was upon the tip of Narkom's tongue to inquire what he meant by all this; but Cleek, rightly suspecting that the letter to which he alluded had been delivered at the Yard after the superintendent's departure, jumped into the breach and saved the situation.

"Very good of you indeed to place such great reliance in me, Mr. Carruthers," he said. "We had to scramble for it, Mr. Narkom and I — the letter was so late in arriving — but, thank fortune, we managed to get here, as you see. And now, please, may I have the details of the case?"

He spoke guardedly, lest it should be upon some matter other than the interest of the "Golden Boy" and to prevent the Honourable Felix from guessing that he had already been approached upon that subject by Lady Essington. It was not some other matter, however. It was again the mystery of the secret attacks upon his little lordship he was asked to dispel; and the Honourable Felix, plunging forthwith into the details connected with it, gave him exactly the same report as Lady Essington had done.

"Come to the rescue, Mr. Cleek," he finished, rather excitedly. "Both my wife and I feel that you and you alone are the man to get at the bottom of this diabolical thing; and the boy is as dear to us as if he were our own. Help me to get proof — unimpeachable proof — of the hand which is engineering these diabolical attacks, that we may not only put an end to them before they go too far, but may avert the disgrace which publicity must inevitably bring."

"Publicity, Mr. Carruthers? What publicity are you in dread of, please?"

"That which could only bring shame to a dear, lovable young fellow if any hint of what I believe to be the truth should get out, Mr. Cleek," he replied. "To you I may confess it: I appeal to no medical man because I fear, for young Claude's sake, that investigation may lead to a discovery of the truth; for both my wife and I feel — indeed, we almost *know* — that it is his own grandmother, Lady Essington, who is injuring the boy and that it will not be long before she attempts to direct suspicion against *us*."

"Indeed? For what purpose?"

"To have us removed by the courts as not being fit to have the care of the child, and to get him transferred to her care, that she may enjoy the revenue from his estate."

"Phew!" whistled Cleek softly. "Well done, my lady!"

"We do our best to keep her from getting at him," went on the Honourable Felix, "but she succeeds in spite of us. His nursery was on the same floor as her rooms, but for greater safety I last night had him carried to my own bedchamber and double-locked all the windows and doors. I said to myself that nothing could get to him then; but — it did, just the same! In the middle of the night he woke up screaming and crying out that some one had come and stuck a long needle in his neck, and then for the first time — God! I nearly went off my head when I saw it — for the first time, Mr. Cleek, there was a mark upon him — three red raw little spots just over the collarbone on the left side of the neck, as if a bird had pecked him."

"Hum-m-m! And all the windows closed, you say?"

"All but one — the window of my dressing-room — but as that is barred so that nobody could possibly get in, I thought it did not matter, and so left it partly open for the sake of air."

"I see," said Cleek. "I see! Hum-m-m! A fortnight without any outward sign and then of a sudden three small raw spots! Indented in the centre are they, and much inflamed about the edges? Thanks! Quite so, quite so! And the doors locked and all the windows but one closed and secured on the inside, so that no human body —— What's that? Take the case? Certainly I will, Mr. Carruthers. You are entertaining a house party at present, I hear. Now if you can make it convenient to put me up in the Priory for a night or two, and will inform your guests that an old 'Varsity friend named — er — let's see! Oh, ah! Deland, that will do as well as any — Lieutenant Arthur Deland, home on leave from India — if you will inform your guests that that friend will join the house party to-morrow afternoon, I'll be with you in time for lunch, and will bring my man servant with me."

"Thank you! thank you!" said the Honourable Felix, wringing his hand. "I'll do exactly as you suggest, Mr. Cleek, and rooms shall be ready for you when you arrive."

And the matter being thus arranged, the Honourable Felix took his departure; and Cleek, calling the landlady to furnish him with pen, ink, and paper, sat down then and there to write a private note to Lady Essington, telling her to look out for Mr. George Headland to put in an appearance at the Priory in three days' time.

It was exactly half-past one o'clock when Lieutenant Arthur Deland, a big, handsome, fair-haired, fair-moustached fellow, with the stamp of the Army all over him, turned up at Boskydell Priory with an undersized Indian servant and an oversized kit and was presented to his hostess and to the several members of the house party, by all of whom he was voted a decided acquisition before he had been an hour under the Priory's roof.

It is odd how one's fancies sometimes go. He found the Honourable Mrs. Carruthers a sweet, gentle, dovelike little woman for whom he did not care in the least degree, and he found Lady Essington's son a rollicking, bubbling, overgrown boy of two-and-twenty, whom, in spite of frivolous upbringing and a rather pronounced brusqueness toward his mother, he fancied very much indeed. In fact, he "played right up" to Mr. Claude Essington, as our American cousins say; and Mr. Claude Essington, fancying him hugely, took him to his heart forthwith and blurted out his sentiments with almost small-boy candour.

"I say, Deland, you're a spiffing sort — I like you!" he said bluntly, after they'd played one or two sets of tennis with the ladies and done their "social duties" generally. "If things look up a bit and I'm able to go back to Oxford for the next term (and the Lord knows how I shall, if the mater doesn't succeed in 'touching' Carruthers for some money for we're jolly near broke and up to our eyes in debt), but if I do go back and you're in England still, I'll have you up for the May week and give you the time of your life. Oh, Lord! here's the mater coming now. Let's hook it. Come round to the stables, will you, and have a look at my collection. Pippin' lot — they'll interest you."

They did; for on investigation the "collection" proved to be made up of pigeons, magpies, parrakeets, white mice, monkeys, and even a tame squirrel, all of which came forth at their master's call and swarmed or flocked all over him.

"Now then, Dolly Varden, you keep your thieving tongs away from my scarfpin, old lady!" exclaimed this enthusiast to a magpie which perched upon his shoulder and immediately made a peck at the small pearl in his necktie. "Awfullest old thief and vagrant that ever sprouted a feather, this beauty," he explained to Cleek as he smoothed the magpie's head. "Steal your eye teeth if she could get at them, and goes off on the loose like a blessed wandering gypsy. Lost her for three days and nights a couple of weeks ago, and the Lord knows where the old vagrant put in her time. What's that? The white stuff on her beak? Blest if I know. Been pecking at a wall or something, I reckon, and — hullo! There's Carruthers and his little lordship strolling about hand in hand. Let's go and have a word with them. Strathmere's amazingly fond of my mice and birds."

With that he walked away with the mice and the monkeys and the squirrel clinging to him, and those of the birds that were not perched upon his shoulders or his hands circling round his head with a flurry of moving wings. Cleek followed. A word in private with the Honourable Felix was accountable for his appearance in the grounds with the boy, and Cleek was anxious to get a good look at him without exciting any possible suspicion in Lady Essington's mind regarding the "Lieutenant's" interest in him.

He was a bonny little chap, this last Earl of Strathmere, with a head and face that might have done duty for one of Raphael's "Cherubim" and the big "wonder eyes" that make baby faces so alluring.

"Strathmere, this is Lieutenant Deland, come all the way from India to visit us," said the Honourable Felix, as Cleek went down on his knees and spoke to the boy (examining him carefully the while). "Won't you tell him you are pleased to see him?"

"Pleased to see oo," said the boy, then broke into a shout of glee as he caught sight of young Essington with the animals and birds. "Pitty birdies! pitty mouses! Give! give!" he exclaimed eagerly, stretching forth his little hands.

"Certainly. Which will you have, old chap — magpie, parrakeet, pigeon, monkey, or mice?" said young Essington, gayly. "Here! take the lot and be happy!" Then he made as if to bundle them all into the child's arms, and might have succeeded in doing so, but that Cleek rose up and came between them and the boy.

"Do have some sense, Essington!" he rapped out sharply. "Those things may not bite nor claw you, but one can't be sure when they are handled by some one else. Besides, the boy is not well and he ought not to be frightened."

"Sorry, old chap — always puttin' my foot into it. But Strathmere likes 'em, don't you, bonny boy? and I didn't think."

"Take them back to the stables and let's have a go at billiards for an hour or two before tea," said Cleek, turning as Essington walked away, and looking after him with narrowed eyes and lips indrawn. When man and birds were out of sight, however, he made a sharp and sudden sound, and almost in a twinkling his "Indian servant" slipped into sight from behind a nearby hedge.

"Get round there and examine those birds after he's left them," said Cleek, in a swift whisper. "There's one — a magpie — with something smeared on its beak. Find out what it is and bring me a sample. Look sharp!"

"Right you are, sir," answered in excellent Cockney the undersized person addressed. "I'll spread one of me famous 'Tickle Tootsies' and nip in and ketch the bloomin' 'awk as soon as the josser's back is turned, guv'ner. I'm off, as the squib said to the match when it started blowin' of him up." Then the face disappeared again, and the child and the two men were again alone together.

"Good God, man!" exclaimed the Honourable Felix in a lowered voice of strong excitement. "You can't possibly believe that he — that dear, lovable boy —— Oh, it is beyond belief!"

"Nothing is 'beyond belief' in *my* line, my friend. Recollect that even Lucifer was an angel *once*. I know the means employed to bring about this" — touching softly the three red spots on his little lordship's neck — "but I have yet to decide how the thing is administered and by whom. Frankly I do not believe it is done with a bird's beak — though that, too, is possible, wild as it seems —but by this time to-morrow I promise you the riddle shall be solved. Sh-h! Don't speak — he's coming back. Take the boy into your own room to-night, but leave the door unfastened. I'm coming down to watch by him with you. Let him first be put into the regular nursery, however, then take him out without the knowledge of any living soul — of *any*. you hear? — and I will be with you before midnight."

That night two curious things happened: The first was that at a quarter to seven, when Martha, the nursemaid, coming up into the nursery to put his little lordship to bed, found Lieutenant Deland — who was supposed to be dressing for dinner at the time — standing in the middle of the room looking all about the place.

"Don't be startled, Nurse," he said, as he looked round and saw her. "Your master has asked me to design a new decoration for this room, and I'm having a peep about in quest of inspiration. Ah, Strathmere, 'Dustman's time,' I see. Pleasant dreams to you, old chap. See you in the morning when you're awake."

"Say good night to the gentleman, your lordship," said

the nurse, laying both hands on his shoulders and leading him forward, whereupon he began to whine sleepily:
"Want Sambo! Want Sambo!" and to rub his fists into
his eyes.

"Yes, dearie, Nanny'll get Sambo for your lordship after
your lordship has said good night to the gentleman," soothed
the nurse; and held him gently until he had done so.

"Good night, old chap," said Cleek. "Hello, Nurse, got
a sore finger, have you, eh? How did that happen? It
looks painful."

"It is, sir, though I can't for the life of me think whatever could have made a thing so bad from just scratching
one's finger, unless it could have happened that there was
something poisonous on the wretched magpie's claws. One
never can be sure where those nasty things go nor what they
dip into."

"The magpie?" repeated Cleek. "What do you mean
by that, Nurse? Have you had an unpleasant experience
with a magpie, then?"

"Yes, sir, that big one of Mr. Essington's: the nasty creature that's always flying about. It was a fortnight ago, sir.
Mistress' pet dog had got into the nursery and laid hold of
Sambo — which is his lordship's rag doll, sir, as he never will
go to sleep without — tore it well nigh to pieces did the dog;
and knowing how his lordship would cry and mourn if he
saw it like that, I fetched in my work-basket and started
to mend it. I'd just got it pulled into something like shape
and was about to sew it up when I was called out of the room
for a few minutes, and when I came back there was that
wretched Magpie that had been missing for several days
right inside my work-basket trying to steal my reels of cotton, sir. It had come in through the open window — like
it so often does, nasty thing. I loathe magpies and I believe that that one knows it. Anyway, when I caught up
a towel and began to flick at it to get it out of the room, it

turned on me and scratched or pecked my finger, and it's been bad ever since. ' Cook says she thinks I must have touched it against something poisonous after the skin was broken. Maybe I did, sir, but I can't think what."

Cleek made no comment; merely turned on his heel and walked out of the room.

The second curious thing occurred between nine o'clock and half-past, when the gentlemen of the party were lingering at the table over post-prandial liqueurs and cigars, and the ladies had adjourned to the drawing-room. A recollection of having carelessly left his kit-bag unlocked drew Cleek to invent an excuse for leaving the room for a minute or two and sent him speeding up the stairs. The gas in the upper halls had been lowered while the members of the household were below; the passages were dim and shadowy, and the thick carpet on halls and stairs gave forth never a murmur of sound from under his feet nor from under the feet of yet another person who had gone like he, but by a different staircase, to the floors above.

It was, therefore, only by the merest chance that he looked down one of the passages in passing and saw a swift-moving figure — a woman's — cross it at the lower end and pass hastily into the nursery of the sleeping boy. And — whether her purpose was a good or an evil one — it was something of a shock to realize that the woman who was doing this was the Honourable Mrs. Carruthers.

He locked the kit-bag, and went back to the dining-room just as the little gathering was breaking up, and Mr. Claude Essington, who always fed his magpies and his other pets himself, was bewailing the fact that he had "forgotten the beauties until this minute" and was smoothing out an old newspaper in which to wrap the scraps of cheese and meat he had sent the butler to the kitchen to procure.

The Honourable Felix looked up at Cleek with a question in his eye.

"No," he contrived to whisper in reply. "It was not anything poisonous — merely candle wax. The bird had flown in through the store-room window, and the housekeeper caught it carrying away candles one by one."

The Honourable Felix made no response, nor would it have been heard had he done so; for just at that moment young Essington, whose eye had been caught by something in the paper, burst out into a loud guffaw.

"I say, this is rich. Listen here, you fellows! Lay you a tenner that the chap who wrote this was a Paddy Whack, for a finer bull never escaped from a Tipperary paddock:

"'Lost: Somewhere between Portsmouth and London or some other spot on the way, a small black leather bag containing a death certificate and some other things of no value to anybody but the owner. Finder will be liberally rewarded if all contents are returned intact to

"'D. J. O'M., 425 Savile Row, West.'

"There's a beautiful example of English as she is advertised for you; and if —— Hullo, Deland, old chap, what's the matter with you?"

For Cleek had suddenly jumped up and, catching the Honourable Felix by the shoulder, was hurrying him out of the room.

"Just thought of something — that's all. Got to make a run; be with you again before bedtime," he answered evasively. But once on the other side of the door: "'Write me down an ass,'" he quoted, turning to his host. "No, don't ask any questions. Lend me your auto and your chauffeur. Call up both as quickly as possible. Wait up for me and keep your wife and Lady Essington and her son waiting up, too. I said to-morrow I would answer the riddle, did I not? Well, then, if I'm not the blindest bat that ever flew, I'll give you that answer to-night."

Then he turned round and raced upstairs for his hat and

coat, and ten minutes later was pelting off London-ward as fast as a £1,000 Panhard could carry him.

It was close to one o'clock when he came back and walked into the drawing-room of the Priory, accompanied by a sedate and bespectacled gentleman of undoubted Celtic origin whom he introduced as "Doctor James O'Malley, ladies and gentlemen, M.D., Dublin."

Lady Essington and her son acknowledged the introduction by an inclination of the head, the Honourable Felix and Mrs. Carruthers, ditto; then her ladyship's son spoke up in his usual blunt, outspoken way.

"I say, Deland, what's in the wind?" he asked. "What lark are you up to now? Felix says you've got a clinking big surprise for us all, and here we are, dear boy, all primed and ready for it. Let's have it, there's a good chap."

"Very well, so you shall," he replied. "But first of all let me lay aside a useless mask and acknowledge that I am not an Indian army officer — I am a simple police detective sometimes called George Headland, your ladyship, and sometimes ——"

"George Headland!" she broke in sharply, getting up and then sitting down again, pale and shaken. "And you came — you came after all! Oh, thank you, thank you! I know you would not confess this unless you have succeeded. Oh, you may know at last — you may know!" she added, turning upon the Honourable Felix and his wife. "I sent for him — I brought him here. I want to know and I *will* know whose hand it is that is striking at Strathmere's life — my child's child — the dearest thing to me in all the world. I don't care what I suffer, I don't care what I lose, I don't care if the courts award him to the veriest stranger, so that his dear little life is spared and he is put beyond all danger for good and all."

Real love shone in her face and eyes as she said this, and

It was the certainty of that which surprised Carruthers and his wife as much as the words she spoke.

"Good heavens! is this thing true!" The Honourable Felix turned to Cleek as he spoke. "Were you in her pay, too? Was she also working for the salvation of the boy?"

"Yes," he made answer. "I entered into her service under the name of George Headland, Mr. Carruthers — the service of a good woman whom I misjudged far enough to give her a fictitious name. I entered into yours by one to which I have a better right — Hamilton Cleek!"

"Cleek!" Both her ladyship and her son were on their feet like a flash; there was a breath of silence and then: "Well, I'm dashed!" blurted out young Essington. "Cleek, eh? the great Cleek? Scotland!" And sat down again, overcome.

"Yes, Cleek, my friend; Cleek, ladies and gentlemen all. And now that the mask is off, let me tell you a short little story which — no! Pardon, Mr. Essington, don't leave the room, please. I wish you, too, to hear."

"Wasn't going to leave it — only going to shut the door."

"Ah, I see. Allow me. It is now, ladies and gentlemen, exactly fourteen days since our friend Doctor O'Malley here, coming up from Portsmouth on his motorcycle after attending a patient who that day had died, was overcome by the extreme heat and the exertion of trying to fight off a belligerent magpie which flew out of the woods and persistently attacked him, and, falling to the ground, lost consciousness. When he regained it, he was in the Charing Cross Hospital, and all that he knew of his being there was that a motorist who had picked him and his cycle up on the road had carried him there and turned him over to the authorities. He himself was unable, however, to place the exact locality in which he was travelling at the time of the accident, otherwise we should not have had that extremely interesting advertisement which Mr. Essington read out this evening. For the doctor had lost a small black bag containing something extremely valuable, which he was carrying at the time and which supplies the solution to this interesting riddle. How, do you ask? Come with me — all of you — to Mr. Carruthers' room, where his little lordship is sleeping, and learn that for yourselves."

They rose at his word and followed him upstairs; and there, in a dimly lit room, the sleeping child lay with an old rag doll hugged up close to him, its painted face resting in the curve of his little neck.

"You want to know from where proceed these mysterious attacks — who and what it is that harms the child?" said Cleek as he went forward on tiptoe and, gently withdrawing the doll, held it up. "Here it is, then — this is the culprit: this thing here! You want to know how? Then by this means — look! See!" He thrust the blade of a pocket knife into the doll and with one sweep ripped it open, and dipping in his fingers drew from cotton wool and rags with which the thing was stuffed a slim, close-stoppered glass vial in which something that glowed and gave off constant sparks of light shimmered and burnt with a restless fire.

"Is this it, Doctor?" he said, holding the thing up.

"Yes! Oh, my God, yes!" he cried out as he clutched at it. "A wonder of the heavens, sure, that the child wasn't disfigured for life or perhaps kilt forever. A half grain of it — a half grain of radium, ladies and gentlemen — enough to burn a hole through the divvle himself, if he lay long enough agin it."

"Radium!" The word was voiced on every side, and the two women and two men crowded close to look at the thing. "Radium in the doll? Radium? I say, Deland — I mean to say, Mr. Cleek — in God's name, who could have put the cursed thing there?"

"Your magpie, Mr. Essington," replied Cleek, and with that brief preface told of Martha, the nurse, and of the torn doll and of the magpie that flew into the room while the girl was away.

"The wretched thing must have picked it up when the doctor fell and lost consciousness and the open bag lay unguarded," he said.   "And with its propensity for stealing and hiding things it flew with it into the nursery and hid it in the torn doll.   Martha did not see it, of course, when she sewed the doll up, but the scratch she received from the magpie presented a raw surface to the action of the mineral and its effect was instant and most violent.   What's that?   No, Mr. Carruthers — no one is guilty; no one has even tried to injure his lordship.   Chance only is to blame — and Chance cannot be punished.   As for the rest, do me a favour, dear friend, in place of any other kind of reward. Look to it that this young chap here gets enough out of the income of the estate to continue his course at Oxford and — that's all."

It was not, however; for while he was still speaking a strange and even startling interruption occurred.

A liveried servant, pushing the door open gently, stepped into the room bearing a small silver salver upon which a letter lay.

"Well, upon my word, Johnston, this is rather an original sort of performance, isn't it?" exclaimed Carruthers, indignant over the intrusion.

"I beg your pardon, sir, but I did knock," he apologized. "I knocked twice, in fact, but no one seemed to hear; and as I had been told it was a matter of more than life and death, I presumed.   Letter for Lieutenant Deland, sir.   A gentleman of the name of Narkom — in a motor, sir — at the door — asked me to deliver it at once and under any and all circumstances."

Cleek looked at the letter, saw that it was enclosed in a plain unaddressed envelope, asked to be excused, and stepped out into the passage with it.

That Narkom should have come for him like this — should have risked the upsetting of a case by appearing before he knew if it was settled or, indeed, likely to be — could mean but one thing: that his errand was one of overwhelming importance, of more moment than anything else in the world.

He tore off the envelope with hands that shook, and spread open the sheet of paper it contained.

There was but one single line upon it; but that line, penned in that hand, would have called him from the world's end.

"*Come to me at once. Ailsa,*" he read — and was on his way downstairs like a shot.

In the lower hall the butler stood, holding his hat and coat ready for him to jump into them at once.

"My — er — young servant — quick as you can!" said Cleek, grabbing the hat and hurrying into the coat.

"Already outside, sir — in the motor with the gentleman," the butler gave back; then opened the door and stepped aside, holding it back for him and bowing deferentially and the light of the hall, streaking out into the night, showed a flight of shallow steps, the blue limousine at the foot of them — with Lennard in the driver's seat and Dollops beside him — and standing on the lowest step of all Mr. Narkom holding open the car's door and looking curiously pale and solemn.

"What is it? Is she hurt? Has anything happened to her?" Cleek jumbled the three questions into one unbroken breath as he came running down the steps and caught at the superintendent's arm. Speak up! Don't stand looking at me like a dumb thing! Is anything wrong with Miss Lorne?"

"Nothing — nothing at all."

"Thank God! Then why? Why? For what reason has she sent for me? Where is she? Speak up!"

"In town. Waiting for you. At the Mauravanian embassy."

"At the —— Good God! How comes she to be *there?*"

"I took her. You told me if anything happened to you that I thought she ought to know —— Please get in and let us be off, sir — Sire — whichever it ought to be. I don't know the proper form of address. I've never had any personal dealings with royalty before."

The hand that rested on his arm tightened its grip the very instant that word royalty passed his lips. Now it relaxed suddenly, dropped away, and he scarcely recognized the voice that spoke next, so unlike to Cleek's it was, so thick was the tremulous note that pulsated through it.

"Royalty?" it repeated. "Speak up, please. What have you found out? What do you know of me that you make use of that term?"

"What everybody in the world will know by to-morrow. Count Irma has told! Count Irma has come, as the special envoy of the people, for Queen Karma's son! For the King they want! For you!" flung out Narkom, getting excited as he proceeded. "It's all out at last and — I know now. Everybody does. I'm to lose you. Mauravania is to take you from me after all. A palace is to have you — not the Yard. Get in, please, sir — Sire — your Majesty. Get in. They're waiting for you at the embassy. Get in and go! Good luck to you! God bless you! I mean that. It's just about going to break my heart, Cleek, but I mean it every word! Mind the step, Sire. Make room for me on the seat there, you two; and then off to the embassy as fast as you can streak it, Lennard. His Majesty is all ready to start."

"Not yet, please," a voice said quietly; then a hand reached out from the interior of the limousine, dropped upon Mr. Narkom's shoulder and, tightening there, drew him over the step and into the car. "Your old seat, my friend.

Here beside me. My memory is not a short one and my affections not fickle. All right *now*, Lennard. Let her go!"

Then the door closed with a smack, the limousine came round with a swing, and, just as in those other days when it was the Law that called, not the trumpet-peal from a throne, the car went bounding off at the good old mile-a-minute clip on its fly-away race for London.

It ended, that race, in front of the Mauravanian embassy; and Cleek's love for the spectacular must have come near to being surfeited that night, for the building was one blaze of light, one glamour of flags and flowers and festooned bunting; and looking up the steps, down which a crimson carpet ran across the pavement to the very kerbstone, he could see a double line of soldiers in the glittering white-and-silver of the Mauravanian Royal Guard — plumed and helmeted — standing with swords at salute waiting to receive him; and over the arched doorway the royal arms emblazoned, and above them — picked out in winking gas-jets — a wreath of laurel surrounding the monogram M. R., which stood for Maximilian Rex, aflame against a marble background.

"Here we are at last, sir," said Narkom as the car stopped (he had learned, by this time, that "Sire" belonged to the stage and the Middle Ages), and, alighting, held back the door that Cleek might get out.

Afterward he declared that that was the proudest moment of his life; for if it was not the proudest of Cleek's, his looks belied him. For, as his foot touched the crimson carpet, a band within swung into the stately measure of the Mauravanian National Anthem, an escort came down the hall and down the steps and lined up on either side of him, and if ever man looked proud of his inheritance, that man was he.

He went on up the steps and down the long hall with a
chorus of "Vivat Maximilian! Vivat le roi!" following
him and the sound of the National Anthem ringing in his
ears; then, all of a moment, the escort fell back, doors
opened, he found himself in a room that blazed with lights,
that echoed with the sound of many vivats, the stir of many
bodies, and looking about saw that he was surrounded by a
kneeling gathering and that one man in particular was at
his feet, sobbing.

He looked down and saw that that man was Irma, and
smiled and put out his hand.

The count bent over and touched it with his lips.

"Majesty, I never forgot! Majesty, I worked for it, fought
for it ever since that night!" he said. "I would have fought
for it ever if it need have been. But it was not. See, it was
not. It was God's will and it was our people's."

"My people's!" Cleek repeated, his head going back, his
eyes lighting with a pride and a happiness beyond all telling. "Oh, Mauravania! Dear land. Dear country. Mine
again!"

But hardly had the ecstasy of that thought laid its spell
upon him when there came another not less divine, and his
eyes went round the gathering in quest of one who should
be here — at his side — to share this glorious moment with
him.

She had come for that purpose — Narkom had said so.
Where was she, then? Why did she hold herself in the background at such a time as this?

He saw her at that very moment. The gathering had
risen and she with them — holding aloof at the far end of
the room. There was a smile on her lips, but even at that
distance he could see that she was very, very pale and that
there was a shadow of pain in her dear eyes.

"We both have battled for an ideal, Count," he said, with
a happy little laugh. "Here is mine. Here is what I have

fought for!" and crossing the room he went straight to Ailsa, with both hands outstretched to her and his face fairly beaming.

But it needed not the little shocked breath he heard upon all sides to dash that bright look from his face and to bring him to a sudden halt. For at his coming, Ailsa had dropped the deep curtsey which is the due of royalty, and was moving away from him backward, which is royalty's due also.

"Ailsa!" he said, moving toward her with a sharp and sudden step. "Ailsa, don't be absurd. It is too silly to think that forms should stand with you, too. Take my hand — take it!"

"Your Majesty ——"

"Take it, I tell you!" he repeated almost roughly. "Good God! do you think that this can make any difference? Take my hand! Do you hear?"

She obeyed him this time, but as her fingers rested upon his he saw that they were quite ringless — that the sign of their engagement had been removed — and caught her to him with a passionate sort of fierceness that was a reproach in itself.

"Could you think so meanly of me? Could you?" he cried. "Where is the ring?"

"In my pocket. I took it off when — I heard."

"Put it on again. Or, no! Give it to me and let me do that myself — here, before them all. Kings must have queens, must they not? You were always mine: you are always going to be. Even the day of our wedding is not to be changed."

"Oh, hush!" she made answer. "One's duty to one's country must always stand first with — kings."

"Must it? Kings after all are only men — and a man's first duty is to the one woman of his heart."

"Not with kings. There is a different rule, a different

law. Oh, let me go — please! I know, I fully realize, it would be different with you — if it were possible. But — it is the penalty one must pay for kingship, dear. Royalty must mate with royalty, not with a woman of the people. It is the law of all kingdoms, the immutable law."

It was. He had forgotten that; and it came upon him now with a shock of bitter recollection. For a moment he stood silent, the colour draining out of his face, the light fading slowly from his eyes; then, of a sudden, he looked over the glittering room and across its breadth at Irma.

"It would not be possible then?" he asked.

"Not as a royal consort, sir. The people's choice in that respect would lie with the hereditary princess of Danubia. I have already explained that to Mademoiselle. But if it should be your Majesty's pleasure to take a morganatic wife ——"

"Cut that!" rapped in Cleek's voice like the snap of a whiplash. "So, then, one is to sell one's honour for a crown; break a woman's life for a kingdom, and become a royal adulterer for the sake of a throne and sceptre!"

"But, Majesty, one's duty to one's country is a sacred thing."

"Not so sacred as one's redeemer, Count, and, under God, here is mine!" he threw back, heatedly. "Mauravania forgot once; she will forget again. She *must* forget! My lords and gentlemen, I decline her flattering offer. My only kingdom is here — in this dear woman's arms. Walk with me, Ailsa — walk with me always. You said you would. Walk with me, dear, as my queen *and* my wife."

And putting his arm about her and holding her close, and setting his back to the lights and the flags and the glittering Guard, he passed, with head erect, through the murmuring gathering and went down and out with her — to the blue limousine — to the Yard's service again — and to those better things which are the true crown of a man's life.

At the foot of the steps Narkom and Dollops caught up with him, and the boy's eager hand plucked at his sleeve.

"Guv'ner, Gawd love yer — Gawd love yer, sir; you're a man, you are!" he said with a sort of sob in his voice. "I'm glad you chucked it. It was breakin' my heart to think that I'd have to call you 'Sire' all the rest of my days, sir — like as if you was a bloomin' horse!"

THE END